The Last Hangman

Peter Nutty

authorHOUSE®

AuthorHouse™
1663 Liberty Drive
Bloomington, IN 47403
www.authorhouse.com
Phone: 1-800-839-8640

© 2012 Peter Nutty. All rights reserved.

No part of this book may be reproduced, stored in a retrieval system, or transmitted by any means without the written permission of the author.

First published by AuthorHouse   01/20/2012

ISBN: 978-1-4567-8626-7 (sc)
ISBN: 978-1-4567-8628-1 (hc)

Printed in the United States of America

Any people depicted in stock imagery provided by Thinkstock are models, and such images are being used for illustrative purposes only.
Certain stock imagery © Thinkstock.

This book is printed on acid-free paper.

Because of the dynamic nature of the Internet, any web addresses or links contained in this book may have changed since publication and may no longer be valid. The views expressed in this work are solely those of the author and do not necessarily reflect the views of the publisher, and the publisher hereby disclaims any responsibility for them.

For my mother Nancy, my father Len, and my wife Claire,
I love you all very much.

Pete

Prologue

THE GROUP OF SIX MEN laughed as they jostled for position, drunk. It was important to be at the front and so at least four of them, those with muscle, had their arms spread in a desperate attempt to elbow the other two to the back. Any second the shutter would act with lightning speed to capture the moment. In the background, two bodies hung limp from the rafters of a wooden, disused, railway bridge. Two locals would not return home that summer evening; a Negro mother and her son. Their clothes were now bloodied rags following a beating and several failed escapes. A rope had been cut in two and used to bind their hands tight behind their backs. Another was fashioned into a noose, two in fact, which were now taught around their neck, their heads hung pathetically downwards. The boy was covered in blood. A pool of the stuff stained the muddy track under him as it dripped to the floor. His tongue was hanging out of one side of his mouth and his eyes bulged open, a deathly stare aimed directly to the ground. His mother seemed more at peace, eyes closed, dangling from the end of a rope. *Click*.

'One more!' shouted the cameraman, wavering on his feet, making sure the occasion wasn't going to be lost due to some malfunction of film or camera or, more likely, his state of mind. More jostling occurs and two of the men fall forward into the dirt and start rolling in laughter. A second, *click*, could be heard and signaled the end of the scrum. At least three of the group was partly out of the frame at the time of the second take, but nobody cared. The hastily arranged photo shoot had finished. Within seconds they were gone, hotfooting quickly like wildcats. They drove aimlessly, two cars speeding in opposite directions, going anywhere just to get the hell out of there. The adrenaline finally eased and they ended up together once again down a dirt track heading towards, Jericho, Texas. The sound of their drunken hollering slowly disappeared in a distant cloud of dust.

About an hour later, three white men allegedly attacked Jim Anderson, a 29 year old, partially disabled, black man before chaining his ankles to the rear bumper of a rusting seventies Chevrolet pickup truck. They drove along more than two miles of road before the mutilated and headless corpse was found somewhere along a hill leading to Church Street gas station and Eagle Creek Nature Reserve, located just outside the small town. This clearly racist attack prompted one black congresswoman to complain of, *a firestorm of hate across this country.* Many racial atrocities were still being seen in the United States and countless other countries worldwide. Racial hatred, harassment, and discrimination were still being manifested with a vengeance.

Chapter 1

Thirty Years Later

THERE WERE TIMES WHEN JOHN Arnold simply had to pinch himself. It was only a small occasion, but one he'd remember for a long time. These special moments seemed to be happening more often too, he noticed as he plucked a bottle of Bollinger's from an ice bucket close by. The big man smiled as he poured another glass of champagne, his third. Alone, and relaxed for a while, these were good times. Lounging on a sun bed and protected from the fierce, midday heat by a parasol made of palm leaves, the Texan wondered how things had a knack of working out in his favour. That he was the CEO of a major oil and gas exploration company helped. There was very little in terms of everyday needs that didn't come his way, but there were other, more important, things he'd gotten simply by luck, or so it seemed. Like the stock he'd invested in almost three months ago, using some spare cash he didn't want his wife to know about. The small minerals company had massively over performed, not quite as predicted, and now the stock had tripled in that short time. How did that happen? He'd only speculated on the share price having read somewhere in the FT that the stock was ripe for growth over a much longer period, but how accurate was all that stuff? Now, in a fraction of the time mentioned, he was almost half a million dollars richer, if he chose to sell, of course. Pure luck, perhaps. Or was he a shrewd investor after all? Arnold smiled. Pure luck, he reasoned.

The oilman took another sip, savoring both the chilled taste of the champagne and the warm hospitality of the Middle East; one complimented the other. It was his first time in Dubai and he was taken aback by all the wealth and the luxury that now surrounded him. From where he lay, in complete comfort, he watched the clear, warm Gulf waters lick the white, sandy beach, mesmerized by the frothed-up waves trickling in quickly one after another. He noticed more than one ultra-smart waiter scurrying over the hot sands with ice buckets and cold drinks for others like him, wealthy people. Whatever he wanted, he could have. The Madinat, Mina A'Salam, one of a handful of plush, Jumeirah Beach hotels, chosen and paid for by somebody he didn't know just yet, was shear luxury. The place warranted a seven star rating. Looking at the vast extent of gold leaf used on the ceilings, and the playing fields of marble on the walls and floors in the lobby, not to mention the ultra-slick service, it was easy to see why.

He had a suite, which was in fact a four-bedroom villa he found out much to his surprise. It was positioned overlooking the beach. Inside was shear, unadulterated luxury. The bathroom, a small establishment in its own right, was tastefully tiled in different kinds of Mosaic, complete with gold plated taps and fittings. A solid marble bath took pride of place in the centre of the room. Designer bathrobes, shampoos, and other lotions and creams, were conveniently placed close by and also beside each of three sinks. Egyptian cotton swathed the lush-filled duvets that covered a gigantic bed, and was the reason he'd overslept that morning. The pillows were bigger than his front door at home in Texas, and his front door was larger than most! The hotel even provided a personal butler such was the opulence of the place!

John Arnold hadn't relaxed in this way for years. It was previously unthinkable to spend so much precious time in such a reckless way, given his position. But things were changing, and in any case, the last week had brought good results. Attending the World Petroleum Congress, held close to his hotel over the last four days, had paid dividends. Once again, he'd gotten lucky. He'd normally shy away from these kinds of gatherings, but this one was different. Dubai, now in the doldrums with their overly adventurous property and leisure-lifestyle ideals backfiring, were in lots of trouble following the crash of the world property markets. The Middle East financial hub was in a mess; their investment pipeline had become blocked on the back of all the troubles. It had pulled a vacuum even, practically overnight. Whilst that was rather unfortunate for the ruling, Al-Rashid family, they kept loyal to the master plan knowing that soon, their luck was about to change. Amazingly, that change of luck would also rub off on John Arnold, he'd just found out.

Following secret seismic surveys in new locations never before explored in the Gulf of Arabia, the once, oil-rich Emirate was about to get another invitation to be a major player in the worlds energy markets. With new reserves of oil and gas finds estimated to last another thirty years, according to privileged and confidential reports from the survey, their financial woes would soon be over. The declaration would indeed be spectacular news when it eventually breaks.

The Dubai idea was brilliant, and still is. But it needed financial support, a lot of support. Now, with property developments coming to an abrupt halt and people leaving in their hoards, the Emirate was at a make-or-break crossroad. Russian, Indian and Chinese investors were in a quandary over whether or not to keep pumping the cash into such lavish, spectacular developments, the likes of which were now floundering. Even the locals were in limbo when it came to investing in the countries real-estate; and by doing so stay loyal to the ruler, Sheik, Ahmed Bin Kalid Al-Rashid. The ruling family realized the dream was crumbling. It was as if the developers had used cheap concrete for the financial footings and now nobody knew how to prop it up. If it wasn't for their rich neighbor, Abu Dhabi, who would only patch things up for so long, Dubai would have been in complete financial ruin! The trouble over the past five years or so was dwindling reserves of oil and gas, whereas in the past it wasn't. In years gone by they'd had plenty of it and invested well, or so they thought. But these were extraordinary times. Dubai, along with everybody else, was struggling against the financial headwinds building strongly from the west. They were in deep trouble, the extent to which was unknown. And probably never would be.

Soon though, with the latest find, the good old days would return. Once again Dubai would have oil and gas, and money to boot, stacks of all three. The dream would continue. It might even be finished if there was an end to it all! But to keep the energy dollars rolling in they needed partnerships. Oil and gas companies that had the knowledge, experience, and resources to retrieve the vast amounts of reserves that lay waiting to be extracted from under the seabed of the Arabian Gulf, the very same water John Arnold now contemplated as he watched the waves lapping at the golden sands in front of him.

But any exploration and extraction of hydrocarbons wasn't an easy thing to do in these regions. The vast amount of riches lay in very shallow reservoirs, rather like a coal seam only a meter or so thick, as one of the high ranking energy ministers had described it during the many debates he participated in. The oil and gas would indeed be difficult to get out of the ground without the *know-how*. That was how an Emirati Sheik had quietly put it to him during a conversation prior to an unexpected, and hastily arranged, fringe meeting with His Excellency, Sheik, Al-Rashid, which was held in strict privacy. John Arnold, pleasantly stunned by what he'd been told, was sworn to secrecy, naturally.

Horizontal and directional drilling technology was the only way to get at the oil, and even these methods would have to be greatly advanced by modern standards. From that perspective, there were few companies in the oil and gas world that could do it. So the Emiratis would only court partnerships with experienced companies with the right skills, the right people, the right technology, and the right track record. They needed companies like his, Advanced Strategic Energy Incorporated.

During the past fifteen years, and under the leadership of John Arnold, they'd become a major player in these affairs. Where exploration was concerned, ASEI had strived hard to further develop cutting edge technology and were now considered the leaders in that field. By the time three dimensional modeling of oil reservoirs potential had becoming fashionable with the other majors, a very modern approach at the time, ASEI had moved on. They thought to present data in that form was pretty mundane, inaccurate, and somewhat dated. To that end, ASEI geologists and physicists had worked closely together to long surpass three dimensional modeling. By analyzing seismic data in other ways, and using high powered computers that handled complex formulas and algorithms with high-speed, they presented the results using mind-blowing, state-of-the-art, holistic models that practically allowed you to navigate, step-by-step, through the reservoir as if walking through a cavern or cave. The pinnacle was the ability to slice up and dissect, with pin-point accuracy, the entire rock formation. Complex geography, including the fractures or faults that occurred under the seabed, could be sectioned and opened like a book to show what lay hidden for millions of years; the shallow, porous rock that contained the oil.

They no longer referred to, *estimated oil reserves*; they knew exactly what they had. When you looked at their models, it was easy to see why. In the oil business, ASEI dealt with only the facts. That kind of stuff quickly got the attention of the government-owned oil companies in the Middle East, particularly the Emirate of Dubai. To them it seemed that ASEI had not only gone racing ahead and embraced this technology with some considerable love-affair, they'd practically stamped their authority on it and soon made it a trademark specialty of their own, especially when compared to more traditional methods.

When John Arnold set aside five million dollars to undertake the technical development over seven years ago, he'd struck lucky once again judging by the outcome of recent results. In combination with the late uptake of their competitors to invest in the same way, they were miles ahead of the others! In comparison with today's need for advancement in geology, a complex enough science of its own, and the increasing demand to retrieve the dwindling and difficult to retrieve energy resources, John Arnold had almost, single-handedly, demoted their competitors back to the days when the best technology the industry had to offer was the nodding donkey!

However, whilst the advances in geology continued, that science alone was not enough. ASEI had no option but to develop horizontal, and revolutionary, directional drilling technology at the same time; how else could the oil production tubing get correctly positioned in these thin and complex reservoirs? With outside assistance from the drilling companies, they did this with the same passion as they'd embraced the advances made in their approach to unraveling the secrets that lay beneath the earth's crust. But, it was a work in progress and took longer than expected. When the time came to use the new method of drilling, expectations were not that high. Nevertheless, they had to take a chance; they couldn't sit back and wait forever. The oil was out there and they needed it. The first gamble occurred in the British sector of the North Sea where they used their new tools with some anxiety. Fortunately for them, it paid off with large amounts of oil recovered from difficult reservoirs previously considered non-profitable.

With increased confidence, the technology was then taken further afield, off the coast of Nigeria. That was the biggest gamble of John Arnold's career, and also that of ASEI, since the investment was far more than they, or any other exploration company, could afford to lose. Had it not gone to plan, ASEI would have been history, much to the delight of their competitors. On the contrary, it was exactly the opposite, but for significantly different reasons! Nevertheless, on the worldwide scale of things, their oil reserves were now massive in comparison to other similar-sized companies. With the addition of the new Dubai find and the right shared-production agreements and partnerships, those reserves would soon be mind-blowing!

So ASEI had a good track record and soon, it would be even better. It wasn't all plain sailing though; nothing ever was where ASEI were concerned, hence the terms *advanced* and *strategic*. Perhaps somewhere in the name the word, *lucky*, should have been included! The company only ever got involved with difficult to get energies, whatever shape or form they came. That's where the highest risk and rewards ratio could be found. In this particular case, it was oil, in deep waters, in hostile conditions, in shallow reservoirs, and in Nigeria, which up until recently, lacked most of the infrastructure to support such large operations. But, on John Arnold's direct wishes, they invested heavily. It seemed to the board, and others who'd already had bad experience in the region, that they went into this latest project simply on the say-so of their CEO; it was a whim! The board didn't have a say in it, they'd realized when talking about it in private afterwards.

Then, to add to the downside of the deal, and rather astonishingly having being leant on by the hard-fisted government, part of the Nigerian deal was to position a refinery in the region to process the heavy crude oils. This happened much later on in the project and John Arnold, despite all the legal wrangling, which counted for very little where the Nigerian government was concerned, eventually had no option but to agree. It was either that or pack up and go home. The board thought he was mad, their competitors thought he was mad, the industry thought he was mad. Refining wasn't their business, they knew nothing about it!

Then, even more amazingly, halfway through the project and with almost three billion dollars spent, the Nigerian government once again leant unfairly on ASEI, this time insisting on a chemical plant to be positioned alongside the refinery to process the heavier, tar-like oils into lubricants amongst other things. John Arnold was up in arms and the reality of doing business in Nigeria hit home! Months of additional legal sparring from armies of lawyers representing ASEI followed. They were now threatening all sorts of compensation. The mountains of legal claims were backed up by complex penalty clauses, which were being issued on a daily basis it seemed after the initial contract was once again contravened. These were met with similar counter-claims from the Nigerians, especially the one threatening to cancel the whole thing, regardless of what it said in the contract. After months of this, ASEI reluctantly agreed and things advanced. Again, they had little choice and were in too deep to pull out. But, knowing they were beaten, they did at least manage to negotiate the build of a more complex facility; a vinyl-chloride, vinyl-acetate and an isopropanol unit was included in the deal. These massively expensive chemicals would soon be in demand, due mostly to the expected appetite for manufacturing composite and plastic goods in India and China, argued John Arnold with good foresight.

Again, by pure luck, ASEI fortunes changed in this particular episode. Not only did the offshore, oil exploration and production part of their operation go exceedingly well, the onshore, downstream part of the business also proved to be very lucrative; this was the exact opposite to earlier fears expressed by the board. After somewhat of a poor start due to the refinery equipment malfunctioning very early on, they were now making lots of cash down there, a lot of this from the refinery. But, more amazingly, the chemicals side of the business was making more cash than they could ever have imagined! Another stroke of luck and, despite protests from most of the board to rather wisely stay clear of the region, many of whom also strongly disagreed to buy-in to the refining and chemicals business too, their investment was now paying off in a big way, making John Arnold somewhat of a magician in the eyes of some. As the oil gushed from the ground and through the downstream process plants, so the dollars gushed into the bank, lots of them. This prompted ASEI to rethink their portfolio strategy, which culminated in the company buying another five, run-down, refineries and two additional chemical plants. These facilities were scattered around Western Europe and the mid US. The addition of these also impressed the analysts in Wall Street; ASEI stock advanced handsomely, which only added to the success of their CEO, John Arnold.

And that's the reason he'd met the ruler, arguably one of the most powerful men in the Middle East, if not the world. He was certainly one of the richest. No doubt about it, ASEI had the experience, they had the right blend of talent, and they had the *know-how*, as it was so plainly put to him by the Sheik. So, by some considerable chance, that's exactly the same way he put it to, His Excellency!

Nevertheless, whilst all that was comforting, deep down, Arnold was secretly troubled by it all. He was a worried man. The constant flow of large sums of money required to bribe government officials to operate and gain the licenses in Nigeria was a criminal act, no matter what country you were dealing with. Bribery was bribery and it was a very serious offence, whichever way you looked at it. Only a handful of trusted members of the board knew about that, but for how long could he keep that up? Then, there were the local villagers, small tribe's intent on causing havoc. If they weren't arguing amongst themselves, they were arguing with the oil companies, only more so. One recent bout of chaos came about by them blowing up one of the inland gas pumping stations. That caused massive interruption to most of the operators in the region. Fortunately, ASEI were unaffected. The huge sum of money being paid out in bribes was their insurance against anything like that happening. Value for money then, or so Arnold believed. In any case, they were now settled in Nigeria, things were much quieter and the operation was good. In fact, uptime was very good and the cash flow even better, so why worry? The fact that the ASEI operation was also contributing greatly to a major environmental disaster in the process didn't occur to him!

The next challenge for him now would be to steer ASEI safely into the arms of His Excellency, and that was happening with considerable pace judging by the positive vibes being shown by the energy minister. He seemed desperate to forge some kind of relationship with ASEI, which caught the CEO unawares. Normally, it was almost impossible to get to discuss such things with these higher ranking officials early on in any oil and gas proposals. To meet the ruling family was unheard of! But, for reasons that were now obvious to Arnold, the national oil company would come knocking on the door of ASEI sometime very soon, presumably after being instructed to do so directly by the energy minister. With all that working out in his favor, John Arnold would continue to ride his luck, why shouldn't he?

His thoughts of an oil and gas marriage made in heaven were suddenly disturbed by a familiar voice. 'Don't forget to put sun screen on, honey.' It was Barbara, his wife of thirty years. To John the relationship seemed to have gone on much longer!

'I won't,' he replied, lifting his Oakley's and squinting at her. 'Champagne?' he offered, clutching the bottle from its icy surrounds and holding it up in the air.

'Nah, thought I'd traipse myself off to the spa. This heat is way too much for me,' she told her husband. Her loud, Texan drawl resonated across the beach. 'It's extremely hot, even in the shade,' she complained in the same vein. 'And there's no shade!' she finally moaned, even though she was completely covered from the sun by an umbrella, which had been hastily provided by the butler. The temperature was thirty nine degrees Celsius, cool by the regions standards. Ignoring his wife's habitual moaning, Arnold poured himself another glass of bubbly and then looked at his watch. Twelve thirty. Good timing, he thought. Barbara rarely left the spa in less than under two hours, plenty of time to enjoy other things that seemed to pop into his mind with alarming frequency these days.

'Okay, enjoy yourself,' he replied, practically ignoring all that had been said.

Barbara, now shielded under the same parasol as John, still wasn't happy. 'Why'd we have to come to the goddamn desert to relax?' she asked, looking at him as if he'd arranged this out of spite. 'You coulda gone to Arizona if you wanted to go to the desert!' she suggested to him, her tone full of venom. 'It's much closer to Texas, I coulda gone home and pottered around the house while you took your camel for a walk,' she continued, being sarcastic as ever. John Arnold was immune to all the bitching. *If only she'd moan like that in the bedroom*, things would be much more exciting, he thought to himself as he watched her waddle off to a waiting buggy close by, courtesy of the butler.

With Barbara out of the way, at least for a while, his thoughts quickly turned to Gaynor, his personal secretary. She was very bright, she was very clever, she was very young, and she was very close; she'd booked a room only three down from his, convenient for them both to catch up on the daily chores associated with running a billion dollar company. It was also very convenient for other things, the likes of which would have Barbara frothing at the mouth should she ever find out! He dialed her number, eased back into the lounger and waited anxiously for her to answer. When she finally picked up, John Arnold told her exactly what he wanted her to do; he gave her instructions of a special kind. Within ten minutes he was knocking on her door, pulse hammering away faster than a formula one racing car. She answered wearing stockings and suspenders and very little else, just as she was told to do.

John Arnold, you are one lucky son-of-a-bitch, he thought to himself as he entered the room.

* * *

The former soldiers went through the particulars of their planned attack for the third time. Attention to detail was important. They were meticulous, well trained, and rated highly by their peers in what they did.

Tonight, they would split up to form two, four-man teams, codenamed, *Eagle* and *Albatross*. Both assault teams would include an explosives expert. The remaining two, both higher-ranking soldiers and codenamed, *Condor*, would coordinate the assault from close by. They would remain on a ridge, armed with a Russian-made RPG-7 rocket-grenade launcher, to further stunt any counter-attacks or chases from the Nigerian military security forces patrolling the facility.

They were ready. *Operation Acid Rain* was imminent. Payday would follow exactly twenty-four hours later via an intermediary instructed to deposit an obscene amount of dollars into an offshore bank account after authentication of the attack being broadcast on the BBC World News bulletins.

* * *

Very soon, John Arnold's luck was about to run out. Whilst he was in the throes of sending Gaynor into orbit, over forty pounds of plastic explosive was being prepared to send their Nigerian operation in pretty much the same direction. Advanced Strategic Energy Incorporated wouldn't know what hit them!

Chapter 2

LACKLUSTER SEEMED TO BE A word that sprang to mind quite often these days. It wasn't all that late in the day but I had already begun to yawn as I peered, lifelessly through the tinted windows at the tall process towers and storage tanks of the oil refinery outside. With over five hundred thousand barrels of crude oil being processed every day the place was throbbing. Beyond that I could see the adjoining chemical plant in the distance. I longed for a change of scenery. Being lethargic was easy and motivation was becoming more difficult with each passing day. As usual, I was fed-up, bored, and it was warm. A large storm that had caused chaos earlier that morning had long passed and now it was rather pleasant with the sun high in the sky. Shouts of some description or other, which were fuelled by a soccer match between some of the workers on a longer than usual break, broke the normally tranquil surroundings. Anyway, it was purely academic, the noise outside was no louder than the steady drone of the air conditioning as it struggled to cope with the high temperature and humidity inside the office. My door was closed and the machine was set on *high* but still lacked efficiency. I set about reviewing the latest production data. Even at the best of times, concentration was difficult in this particular building, even for this mundane task. A commotion was brewing outside in the corridor. I had to take a look; I just couldn't help myself.

'It's like working with a bunch of schoolgirls!' shouted Rob Drew towards three, lackluster Nigerians stood expressionless in the corridor. They were waiting for the next instruction from the big man, which made him even more frustrated. 'And you don't help, Doug!' he moaned at me as he passed by.

'Ugh!' I grunted, unaware he was making conversation with me. 'What have I done?' I asked in self-defense.

'Bugger all. Absolutely naff all, that's what. Some bloody operations manager you turned out to be!' he blurted out loud, trying to get me to take more notice of the predicament he now found himself in. There was yet another leak on a pipeline within the boundary of the refinery that transported vinyl-chloride to the chemical plant very close by, no big deal. It happened all the time.

'Deputy, operations manager,' I reminded him, hardly bothered by all the fuss. Despite my protests, I was merely standing in for the main man, Tom Lewis, who was off work sick. 'Besides, you'll manage,' I told him, fed up with all the drama every time he had to fix a leak of this kind. The place was like a sieve at the best of times and no sooner this one was repaired there'd be another tomorrow, more even, the place was a liability! 'You need to chill out, Drew,' I added, with a hint of seniority. I then retreated back inside the inner sanctuary of my office and carried on studying the production figures, away from Drew and away from harm.

'Yahoo!' A shout came from further along the corridor. Rob was right; it *was* like being in school. Desmond Haynes, the senior operations walla had finally booked a seat on a British Airways flight home to New York via London and was now obviously pleased. He had already completed writing the emergency process shutdown procedures a week ago, but then found himself stuck. Any transport that could speed at an altitude of over thirty thousand feet was at a premium. Getting a flight out of the country was *doin is head in*, as he used to say, but now the op's guiding light was homeward bound. Rob Drew, the senior maintenance savvy, was faring less well in a job he hated and in a country he despised by the minute. Nigeria, especially Warri, had worn him down after three long years.

'If there's a leaking flange, go and bloody damn well fix it,' he ordered the three vacant-looking natives stood before him. Even under the most bizarre situations, Rob never swore, and at that bizarre moment his well-spoken accent seemed well out-of-place. The guy was under a lot of stress and it was beginning to show.

'We di tha las time, man!' argued one of the men, and all three agreed, they would rather stand their ground instead. Their facial expressions said it all; surely it was someone else's turn to fix the leak?

'We di tha las time!' he mocked out loud for all and sundry to hear. 'Forget it. I'll go hire an Orangutan, give him a wrench and he can fix the bloody leak!' came the distant reply as Rob despondently wandered down the corridor and disappeared back into his office. I sometimes wondered at Rob's lack of understanding in all of this. The scolded Nigerians just stood waiting for a nicer job to come their way, something different. A couple of years ago, prior to the arrival of a large oil refinery and chemical plant on their doorstep, they were busy *salespeople*, street hawking a variety of cheap and shoddy wares wherever they could. Rob's leak wouldn't perturb them in the least. Besides, the longer the leak went on the longer the locals had of reaping something back from the company. Depending on the fluid, there'd be any number of people filling pots and pans of all sorts by now, the plant security guards too, especially if they could use it for cooking!

My door opened and Des came into the office. The Jamaican-born American had two more days at the refinery and promised to be a nuisance before he left for home. I considered him to be a nuisance most of the time! Tuesday, he would get one of the guards, one that could drive, and head for Murtala Mohammed International airport, he gloated. The Jamaican was being a little too euphoric for my liking. He had already annoyed me earlier on. I had another three weeks to wait to complete my trip.

'Let's go see what Drew's up to,' I said, not wanting to hear another word.

'Let's not,' replied Des, suspicious of Rob's resources problem; he could find himself looking at a leaking flange if he wasn't careful.

'Unless you're going to fix the flange, go away,' we were warned. Rob Drew was busy punching numbers hard on the phone with one hand and holding open a worn-out, internal telephone directory with the other. The handset lay precariously perched on top of a bunch of shabby-looking paper folders, which were stacked a mile high and ready to topple. The handset and folders would be grabbed simultaneously with both hands the second Rob had a response, we reasoned. Des and I looked at each other. Rob had given us a warm welcome, as usual.

'Rob, we've come to let you know that Desmond leaves on Tuesday,' I informed him, a little uneasy knowing his body language earlier.

'Good,' he replied with genuine feeling and not taking any notice of us. His wholehearted sincerity dented Desmond's euphoria a little and the Jamaican turned to me looking as if he was about to sulk.

'Well, we'll have to send him on his way in good style, so how about a drink tonight?' I asked.

'No, piss off!' came the abrupt reply.

'No, piss up,' I corrected him with a big, teasing grin. Des did likewise; his pearly-white teeth lit up the room. The call was answered and our friend grabbed the hand-piece quickly, as predicted, whilst at the same time keeping his right hand on top of the folders to prevent the slippery stack from spilling to the floor. The later eventually happened and the event was met with disgust and more obscenities.

'Bollocks! Oh, err, not you, Bill. I've just scattered my in-tray over the floor,' he apologized down the phone to a stunned, Bill Loader. 'Load of crap anyway,' he muttered, still looking angrily in our direction. 'Alas, like I was saying earlier, Bill. I need a couple of guys as quick as you like. It's for that leak that everyone's avoiding like the plague. One of the control valves on the vinyl-chloride system is weeping, it's the flange connection,' he explained. Bill, the mechanical maintenance coordinator was also going to avoid the plague and told Rob to wait in the queue. Besides, Bill had more than his fair share of leaks to mend. There were leaking pipes everywhere along the pipe track leading from the refinery to the crude oil loading terminals further towards the coast, he went on to tell him. And that was only the start. Bill then ranted on about all the other problems he had to deal with, which were so bad he'd eventually left Rob feeling depressed.

'Why do you always have to ask me for help?' asked Bill, also fed up with our drama queen. Rob tried to hide his embarrassment from me and Des, both listening avidly to the conversation. He also realized he would have to wait, simple as that.

As was common in these parts, hydrocarbon leaks occurred on a daily basis due to some reason or another and, depending on the fluids, it was mostly a very dangerous situation. For example, oil leaks that sprung up outside the boundaries of the refinery were, oddly enough, seen as a bonus for thousands of families living in shear poverty close by. Most of the hydrocarbons were stolen by loosening the bolts on the flanges that connected the long pipes together. More spectacularly, if the pipe was fully welded, which meant there were no bolted flange connections, holes were drilled in the steel pipes by the locals so that they could collect fuel for cooking and heating and so on. The rule-of-thumb was simple; *if it could burn, they could use it and, therefore, it was valuable!* The only problem with that philosophy was that all hydrocarbons burned, especially petrol, so any pipe was a potential target. But, unfortunately for them, the lighter hydrocarbons like petrol also exploded!

Despite tight security and frequent patrols along the pipe tracks, we'd lost count of the number of times an explosion occurred, and it was almost always due to the locals trying to break into the pipeline containment. Rather astonishingly, smoking was the biggest contributor to these disasters! This prompted ASEI to embark on a series of free educational courses, which highlighted the dangers of breaking into pipeline containment. However, despite the increased knowledge sharing the statistics hardly changed. The number of incidents remained practically the same. The oil had a value and the locals, driven by poverty, were as greedy as the oil companies. Stale-mate!

Other than that, the heavy, tar-like liquid simply spewed into the rivers and swamps to kill off most forms of life. Even the drinking water was heavily polluted. It was an environmental disaster of massive proportions but nobody really cared, apart from the poor sods that had to put up with it day in, day out. Despite being told by me and countless others over time, the refinery and chemical owners, Advanced Strategic Energy Incorporated, continuously ignored our concerns and, simply put, did nothing at all about it!

With a larger than normal, Billy-goats-gruff, Rob slammed down the phone following his disastrous chat with Bill, got up from his chair and walked passed us without saying a word. He purposely bumped heavily into the three wise men, who were still loitering in the corridor. The sorry-looking, string-like figures were battered into the walls by two hundred and eighty pounds of muscle. They cursed in Pidgin English as he exited the building.

'That's that, then,' said Desmond. 'Tonight it is,' he added, confirming everyone's agreement! 'I'd better organize the beer.'

'Lovely, I'll look forward to it,' I replied, excited at the thought and with that decision taken we followed Rob's tracks down the corridor and onwards to our duties. Once back in the office, I was greeted by the sight of an old-aged man, a native from the nearby locality employed on *landscaping* duties, who'd prized open the taped-up window and was now trying to peddle an old and beat-up ironing board through the gap. Twenty Nairo's was a snip and I paid cash. It was too much of a bargain!

Later that evening, Rob had managed to get the resources he needed. A so-called *fitter*, one of the local tribesmen who had been trained earlier and shown how to use a spanner, was now charged with completing some routine maintenance on a faulty pneumatic actuator valve positioned on a liquid vinyl-chloride discharge line. The problematic piece of equipment was located beneath one of the eastside storage tanks. As soon as they could get the actuator valve to work correctly, the line would be isolated and a new gasket would be reinstated to deal with the leaking flange, which was now spewing small, and as yet harmless, amounts of vinyl-chloride onto the floor.

Drewy, as his mates called him, had gone through the procedure with the fitter three times and even spoke in Pidgin English so that there could be no misunderstanding. It was, without doubt, the best spoken Pidgin English you would ever hear. Not surprisingly, however, and in Rob's absence, the fitter accidentally unbolted the wrong end of the adapter. Drewy, the refinery mechanical mahatma, should have known better. Suddenly, the valve plug itself, including the flange, blew out due to the system pressure, resulting in a three-inch hole being openly exposed in the valve body. Now, much higher and dangerous volumes of vinyl-chloride immediately began to spill from the cone-shaped opening and spread around and under the storage tanks. It formed a massive white cloud, which continued to increase in size. The big man returned back to the scene and couldn't believe what had just happened; he was gone for less than a minute!

Needless to say, Drew was now in a flap. A major incident was lurking on the horizon. Nevertheless, and in the ensuing confusion, he would take his frustration out on the poor bugger he'd just instructed to work on the valve. With that decided Rob grabbed the native by the scruff of the neck and, in a temper, proceeded to physically kick him hard as he could up the backside! The poor sod genuinely believed that he should be punished for his mistake, and so he just bent over unashamedly and let him do it. The fitters mentally made Rob go even more ballistic and he kicked harder, whilst the receiver merely steadied himself for the incoming blows to his rear-end. It had all the ingredients of a Chinese endurance contest!

Meanwhile, the plant was still in normal operations mode and, therefore, the process was working to near full capacity. That meant several fully-laden vinyl-chloride rail cars were located within the area to supply raw materials to the process. Also, there were six articulated road-tankers nearby, full to the brim with the same stuff; a seventh had discharged its contents and was left empty. Along with the other chemicals, Vinyl-chloride is highly flammable. The entire place was a time bomb!

* * *

As dusk fell a small opening in the chain-linked fence lay open on the northeast side and *Eagle* was in position. The four-man team waited patiently for the first signal—two *clicks* on their *coms'* headset, which would tell them that *Albatross* were also on location. Two more *clicks* would then quickly follow and signal both teams were ready; another synchronized stage in the plan. Team-*Eagle* was well hidden with an optimum observation point directly beside their target. They watched in amazement as Rob Drew continued kicking the rather unlucky worker. Things were going in their favor. They didn't know what had gone wrong but they did know the gas cloud would distract prying eyes stumbling upon their clandestine activities. In a matter of minutes the explosives would be in place and detonated.

* * *

'Do you know what I want?' asked Desmond. 'What I really crave, man,' he continued, as we sat talking and drinking large volumes of beer in the camp bar.

'I've no idea,' I replied, waiting in anticipation for something stupid to come from his mouth.

'A really nice sports car,' he informed me, eyeing an imaginary Ferrari in his pie-in-the-sky mind.

I laughed, spurting a mouthful of beer in the process.

'Something funny?' asked my Jamaican friend.

'No, not at all,' I replied, still giggling to myself. I could just imagine it. Knowing Desmond the way I did, he'd be dressed as some kind of pimp, furry dice and velvet garb to boot, cruising around the streets of his home town, New York, head bashing back and for to the sound of Eminem! The more I thought about it, the more I giggled. I sensed Desmond was ready to pounce on me.

'Hey man! Wha you on bro? Wha kind o shit you bin smoking, Doug?' he asked double-quick and sounding really rasta all of a sudden. That set me off again, but before anything else was said, all hell broke loose.

It was practically pitch-dark outside when the general alarm sounded. This was also the signal for Rob to finish his one-sided kicking competition. No sooner had the remote-control panels come alive with red, flashing warning lights the operators immediately shut down the process and began venting down the reactors. Those precautions would make no difference at the end of the night!

Des and I, along with Bill Loader and a handful of other expats, were well on with the party when we heard the wailing siren.

'That's it, the balls in the river. We'll nae get another drink now!' said Jock Stanley, appalled at the thought of having to finish the session prematurely. For the next fifteen minutes or so the air was filled with Scottish obscenities whilst Jock and a few of his hardened drinking pals swallowed the remaining beers before responding to the alarm at all. The rest of us sobered up in an instant and quickly made our way to the plant to see what was going on; after all, it was the general alarm and I was the acting operations manager!

'Gonna use your emergency procedures quicker than you think, Des,' Floyd Barns chuckled, but dreaded the thought of using anything that Desmond had recommended in such an emergency. Desmond was not amused.

'They'll work, smart-ass,' replied my deputy, sternly.

'Well, we'll soon find out, wont we?' More laughter followed.

'Give it a break. It's not that serious,' I said, with calming effect. 'And you two stop quibbling and grow up,' I told them and directed a serious glare at the two schoolboys following me out of the bar. We quickly made our way towards the refinery about half a mile away.

As all this was going on the escaping vinyl-chloride gas cloud was soon measured to well over fifty meters in diameter. It continued spreading across the plant. The refinery fire team, eventually called over by Desmond to deal with the incident the moment he got there, tried to control the release by directing a water monitor at the valve to form a temporary ice-plug from the freezing reaction that occurred, but this was blown out several times.

In the intervening time, and aided by the increasing commotion, the lead *Albatross* soldier settled himself behind a small building close to the utilities plant and sighted his dated, AK-47. He slowly pivoted to bring the night-sight around to at least a full half-circle to scan the area. He made sure they were covert before pressing his intercom button located on the lapel of his flak jacket—two quick *clicks*. Likewise, *Eagle* acknowledged the cue immediately. Five minutes later, and with the Semtex firmly in place, another two *clicks* from the team leader gave everybody two minutes to make good their escape. Another fifteen minutes after that, more delayed explosions would follow.

By now I was on the scene trying to get Rob's attention. The leak wasn't that big a deal. We could block in the pipeline by using a couple of valves located further upstream I wanted to tell him, but was distracted from saying anything when I saw two men dressed in black clothing running at speed from the opposite storage tank area behind us. They seemed to be carrying something or other. It looked like a rifle of some description? It was odd to say the least. I called out to the blacked-out figures but it was in vain, no sooner had I seen them they were gone. I imagined I was seeing things in the heat of the moment and so thought no more of it. Instead, I turned around and carried on helping with the emergency, dismissing the mysterious figures from my mind completely.

The noise from the exploding tank behind us was deafening. The metal split open like a sardine can and ignited the gaseous, hydrocarbon contents causing a massive flame that travelled through the plant towards us at lightning speed. Upon seeing this, my heart missed a beat and my stomach churned. Along with several others, I hit the deck with an almighty *thump* as the fireball came our way. We shouted to the rest to get down. Not realizing, four operators who were watching the events from a distance were badly burned the moment they turned around only to see the flames engulf them; they were alerted to the high-pitched noise coming from the fireball. The firefighters were more fortunate since they were well protected with full-face visors and fire retardant tunics. The flames eventually reached Drew's gas cloud coming from the other direction, near the storage tanks closest to us, and caused a smaller explosion. Soon, a flaming torch was set-up from the contents of the pressurized discharge pipe, which was now constantly being fed by the leaking vinyl-chloride.

Three more workers were knocked off their feet and left flabbergasted from explosions courtesy of *Albatross*. A combination of vinyl-chloride and air explosions, along with five pounds of Semtex, demolished a small hydrogen plant and several utility buildings in the process. The situation was getting worse by the minute. It was at this time that I decided to move out and shouted a signal to evacuate people from the area. Nobody argued and we withdrew in haste.

Then, in a very short time, a safety valve opened on one of the feedstock tanks due to the intense heat radiated from the flames; the same ones that had ignited the contents of the discharge pipe. The noise from the releasing gas caused the many onlookers, local villagers who were minute's earlier busy pinching fuel from a similar leak close to the boundary fence, to cheer as if it was some kind of fireworks display. It was a sad sight for those who could appreciate the dangers that surrounded us. Several minutes later, the villagers got what they wanted. It was another perfectly timed explosion and one the oil thieves would remember for the rest of their lives, at least those who survived it would! There was an almighty, *bang*, louder than any cracking of thunder, which deafened everybody when *Eagle*-target two exploded. It was another one of the storage tanks and resulted in a massive *bleve* and fireball. Four firefighters, called back to the scene to spray water on the tanks, which were by now becoming red-hot from the flames, were vaporized in front of our very eyes. They didn't stand a chance as we watched their bodies vanish into thin air leaving behind a small flame that barely outlined them having been there at all. This also disappeared very quickly. You could hear the screams and cries of the oil thieves as they watched in shear disbelief before turning and running away, many were ablaze, covered in burning chemicals. They were panic-stricken and left a variety of oil-laden vessels behind; pots, pans, buckets, bottles, all of which smashed or rattled along the ground following their desperate attempt to flee the area.

The last explosion damaged all but two of the remaining storage tanks, but it didn't matter. Team *Eagle* ensured the rest would follow the same fate, eventually. They exploded in the same fashion as the previous two tanks. This they did, in turn and almost within seconds of each other. I was tucked away, unnerved, but for the time being protected by the wall of a brick analyzer house. Rob Drew had also taken refuge alongside me when *Albatross* reconfirmed their presence on the northeast side. Yet three more *bleve's* materialized from the exploding tanks and vaporized the surrounding environment. It was as if a nuclear warhead had been detonated about four hundred yards from us. Another several onlookers, and other passers-by, were severely burned from the radiation. Rob was struck dumb at what was happening. He looked older than his thirty-five years. The situation was out of control. I saw people screaming, some were burning alive, most were hysterical, and now they were running in all directions. I sensed Drew was no longer with it and I felt the same. There was nobody in control. Nobody giving instructions; nobody wanted to, it was every man for himself.

As I looked around for some form of help we seemed to be surrounded by a bombsite. I must confess that I was absolutely scared senseless and getting even more panic-stricken by the second. Massive orange flames licked at us before sporadically disappearing into dense, thick black smoke, which bellowed in all directions. Our surroundings were being totally eclipsed with each fireball. My body shivered uncontrollably and my heart felt as if it was going to explode along with the tanks. I wanted to run for my life along with everybody else but I dare not move. Not yet anyway. For some strange reason I just knew there were more explosions to come. *Eagles'* onslaught had subsided but *Albatross* had used a delayed detonating mechanism with finesse and now these explosions wreaked their relentless power; it was awesome!

I continued watching as one of the first bullet tanks exploded. The large vessel separated into two sections as a result of the force, about two thirds of its length hit one of the two water stock tanks that fed a large portion of the fire-fighting equipment. The force from that impact sent the thin-walled vessel flying for over one hundred yards, narrowly missing our sanctuary, before the tank section demolished the pump house. This time it completely took out the one and only remaining, fixed fire-fighting resource. That damage was followed by the demolition of the corner of the boiler house as yet another heavy-metal shell from another exploding tank was propelled through the air. This part of the tank finally ended up about five hundred yards outside the boundary fence, in a field. The impact on the boiler house ruptured a six-inch natural gas main that fed the fired-heaters used on the plant. To add to the already unreal situation, the gas started to escape from the pipe with a vengeance. Another part of the last but one bullet tank to explode travelled north over the warehouse, then demolished a flammable store before ending up in another field; the sixty-two ton section having travelled over six hundred and fifty yards.

The bullet tank closest to the railway line failed in a slightly different manner. The main shell plates just peeled open like an orange and the two dished-end caps were then propelled at tremendous speed through part of the polymerization unit. It was completely wrecked. Various pipelines opened up and some of the manholes leaked to form fires around the remaining tanks. They continued to burn for several days, we later learned. My stomach was turned inside out, it was in a spin. There was no saliva left in my mouth. I desperately feared a heart attack when I eventually came from behind the wall that had protected Drew and me. We were amidst, what could only be described as a war zone. There were burnt bodies everywhere, some were still alight. Several of the injured screamed out for help. My heart continued to pound. I could feel my chest caving in, painfully, desperately wanting more oxygen. The adrenaline was pumping but I couldn't sustain the energy. I felt weak on my legs and realized I was a feeble figure of my normal self. My nerves just couldn't take it.

The damage caused that day would eventually be calculated to approximately five hundred and sixty million dollars, mostly attributed to the chemical plant. The damage caused to the local community and surrounding environment was incalculable. Lost revenue would be measured in billions in whatever currency was used. Thick, black smoke bellowed from the fires that were fed by the various burning chemicals and crude oil for days. This caused *acid rain* to settle over millions of acres of rain forest that covered most of the Niger Delta; the result of the chemical reaction with the atmosphere. Thousands of huts and, as yet, incalculable numbers of trees, rivers and farmland were damaged nearby. The shock waves from the force of the blast could be felt over thirty miles away. Parts of the plant equipment burned with such severity and ferocity that it required the locals to mobilize the military. For once, they were in agreement. There were eighty reported deaths and seventy-two severe injuries, most of them burns. *Operation Acid Rain* was headlines with all the major news networks, including the BBC World Services. The damage could easily have been more but for Desmond who had played his part with extreme courage.

Chapter 3

Advanced Strategic Energy Inc. Headquarters—New York—USA

'I'M NOT PUTTING UP WITH this shit anymore. I want something done, now!' The phone went dead and Eamon Darcy was left mesmerized by the buzzing sound of a *dead* phone line resonating from a small, neat-looking loudspeaker placed on the table. He looked around the room at the others; all had been hastily summoned to the boardroom for the conference call, which had been arranged at lightning speed following the news. They kept their heads firmly fixed downwards, strenuously avoiding eye contact with the Senior Vice-President.

'The old man's none too pleased,' he muttered the obvious with a mishmash of facial expressions. He didn't need to say anything, the conference call had lasted over forty-five minutes and no explanations were needed to portray the mood of their top man, John Arnold, who was now on his way back from Dubai to sort out the mess. It was going to be a long night but the executive, eleven men and two women, made up from Presidents and Vice-Presidents, had to resolve a problem. And, as if his or her dilemma wasn't complex enough to disentangle, somebody would have to take the can for what had happened. The Nigerian part of their operations had attracted huge investment. They had taken a gamble going there in the first place and now there was no going back. The company had to deliver what they'd promised the shareholders. ASEI were in at the deep end.

Surely, somebody was to blame for allowing the goddamn plant to blow up? John Arnold had told them all. He wanted somebody's ass nailed high and very secure on the dismissal board by the morning, along with a typed press release giving the details of why it wasn't because of the companies incompetence in this business.

The scale of the incident, as far as they could tell in the interim period, was comparable with the many British Petroleum disasters that had occurred recently, such as the Alaskan oil pipeline failure, the explosion at their Texas City refinery, and of course the infamous Deep Water Horizon explosion in the Gulf of Mexico. All of those disasters, quite rightly, had the top brass in BP harshly criticized. Their company management strategy and individual management styles was sliced open and closely scrutinized using both the gross negligence and gross incompetence microscopes. It was no surprise then that every person in the room that night could imagine themselves sitting in front of congress trying to explain their way out of similar claims of gross incompetence, neglect and other nastier accusations, which were bound to follow. In the end, like all other oil disasters, it would probably boil down to greed! With those thoughts hidden on the agenda but foremost in everyone's mind, certain individuals were blamed almost at random and the meeting was mostly hostile; the blame culture increased with every passing hour. In the end, it was everybody's fault but nobody would admit to that!

* * *

'Beer, Jeremy?'

'Yeah, get me something to chase it down as well . . .' Jeremy Isaacs squinted along the optics neatly aligned high behind the bar, 'Bourbon . . . on the rocks,' he demanded. Eamon Darcy ordered the drinks, silently pointing out the bottle of Bourbon, two Budweiser's had already been shoved across the bar. The two men sat leaning forward on a couple of stools and, following the hostilities in the boardroom earlier on, hadn't quite gained back enough respect to face each other at that precise moment. It was past two in the morning. The board had resolved nothing. There was nobody to blame, just yet; everybody had a concrete alibi it seemed. *I told you so,* was mentioned several times and supporting memo's and e-mails would be hastily retrieved overnight to prove it. So far, John Arnold was holding the can but that wouldn't last and nobody had the balls to come out and say that, at least not yet anyway.

'Now what do we do?' Darcy asked, still looking straight ahead. He sipped half the contents from the bottled beer as soon as it arrived. Trying to protect your own patch was thirsty work.

'We gotta talk to the natives. Give em some money. Loads of the stuff, it's the only thing these bastards understand,' said Isaacs, coming up with an overly-simple solution all too quickly. Rather surprisingly, he'd taken a somewhat cavalier attitude to the problem. He didn't seem too perturbed by recent events, which Eamon found rather disturbing given the gravity of the situation.

'C'mon, Jeremy, how'd the hell will we get away with that, for Christ's sake?'

'Easy, go get some additional funds from somewhere. We've been dishing out cash to certain government officials for years. Or have you forgotten?'

'And then what, smart-ass?' he replied. Darcy hadn't forgotten. He knew what the numbers amounted to, he knew who got paid and how. He knew it was wholly illegal, and he knew Isaacs was the mastermind behind it all. The contempt for each other was laid bare as the two men continued to avoid each other. Isaacs gave a smug grin and then laughed mildly to himself. He studied the label on his bottle of Bud for a while before answering.

'Go over there and give em the cash. Let em smell it before stuffing it down their greedy, cash-thirsty throats. They'll stop what they're doing,' he said. 'Trust me.' The word, *trust*, registered immediately with Darcy, it was ironic to say the least! He ignored the remark.

'What about the Old Man?'

'John? Don't worry about him. Don't tell him . . . or the board for that matter. Just do it.'

'Don't tell the CEO . . . or the board . . . mm . . . yeah, right . . . sounds like a real good idea! Sounds like good advice. Why didn't I think of that? Shouldn't be too difficult to pull that off,' mocked Eamon. On top of the earlier euphoria in the boardroom, the big Irishman had finally had enough. He raised himself of his stool, placed a hand on Isaacs shoulder and leaned in closer to his colleague so that his mouth was only inches away from his ear. He tightened his grip, hard, before talking slowly, menacingly and with some underlying anger. 'You're a goddamn, crazy son-of-a-bitch, Isaacs, do you know that?' he whispered, angrily, his strong Irish accent penetrating Isaacs conscience. Isaacs squirmed but remained motionless. Eamon, eager for some kind of response, a reason to take it further even, eventually eased his grip a little upon noticing the room quickly emptying. The drunks had focused on the quick build-up to trouble and were now discretely edging themselves to a safe haven, behind the pool tables positioned further across the room. As drunk as they were, they could sense the build-up to a brawl three bars away. Eamon watched them, half-laughed in amazement, and then half-sighed in disgust for acting in the way he did and immediately dismissed any ideas he might have had on Isaacs.

'Yeah, well this crazy son-of-a-bitch is gonna save your sorry ass,' replied Isaacs, still resisting the need to look at the Irishman directly. Eamon slowly eased away. Isaacs, the smaller of the two, tried to shrug off the incident by remaining still but had little option other than to rub his shoulder the minute Eamon let go his vice-like grip; it was painful.

'Oh gee, thanks! I didn't know it was my ass we were debating in there tonight?' replied the big man, concerned at where this might end.

'You're gonna be the one left holding the baby, man. Besides, you're the one he wants, Eamon. You gotta be smart.'

'Me! Where'd you get that from?'

'I'm family, remember?' he smirked; being married to the CEO's daughter give you certain privileges and nobody knew that better than Isaacs! Eamon tried to ignore him, but Isaacs *was* family and for that reason, he *would* probably know the undertones coming from John Arnold, even at this early stage. Feeling a little disheveled, Darcy sat back on the stool and began throwing other ideas around in his head.

'You're serious, aren't you?' Eamon frowned, worried that an alternative approach hadn't readily sprung to mind.

'You'd better believe it. My father-in-law wants blood. Anybody's blood I bet. He's just had a multi-billion dollar business blow up in his face, not to mention all those poor bastards who were torched alive, just how many we still don't know yet! The Nigerian's are going crazy! And Congress is probably putting together an investigating committee as we speak. Put the lost production losses on top of that and he's gotta lot of explaining to do. He needs an out. If you don't set somebody up, it's your ass that'll be spread all across the FT sometime soon, nothing surer. He's probably setting the wheels in motion as we speak. Call it a safety net if you like. The Street will want answers, Eamon.' Jeremy Isaacs, who hadn't quite reached the seniority of his drinking colleague just yet, but was a VP nevertheless, downed the bourbon in one and ordered another two, one each.

Eamon Darcy was deep in thought. A million horrible things bolted through his mixed up mind at that precise moment. Just how much did Isaacs know? Would his father-in-law divulge such things? He doubted it, but could he take a chance? Would John Arnold make him the scapegoat? They had good history together; they were friends, weren't they?

'Okay, suppose there's an out,' he finally succumbed to say. 'You've obviously got something worked out, as if I should be surprised! What're you thinking?'

'Like I said, it's simple, man. We can't just make a deposit or wire transfer for obvious reasons, so we need to get somebody to go over there and pay em the greenbacks in cash.'

'Like who?'

'Richard Hammond.'

'Richard? Why should we use him for goodness sake?'

'He wants to go further doesn't he? You know he'll do anything to get up to the top floor with us,' said Jeremy. He refrained from telling him it had originally been Hammond's idea in the first place. The facts were he'd long ago tried to get Isaacs to agree to such a notion, even before this recent calamity had struck. The initial proposal was for slightly different reasons then; it was to close out other clandestine, non-oil-related deals that would have been to their mutual benefit. It wasn't designed to stop the locals blowing the place to bits! Now, all of a sudden, with dead bodies piling up, miles of polluted rivers and steel shrapnel littering half the Delta, it wasn't such a bad idea perhaps, and instead of pushing on with the details that he'd already discussed with Hammond the moment they'd heard the bad news from Nigeria, he paused and simply allowed the more senior man to mull things over.

Isaacs was taking a gamble with Darcy. How convincing could he be? John Arnold, his father-in-law, would slaughter anyone to iron out the mess in Nigeria. He knew that much. Slaughter anyone other than Eamon that is. He liked Eamon Darcy, immensely, but the Irishman wouldn't know that. Instead, and under the circumstances, he would put too much trust in Jeremy Isaacs, who in turn would put too much trust in Richard Hammond, and that would be catastrophic for both of them, they'd later find out.

Eamon sipped his beer, he was deep in thought. He knew Richard Hammond, knew him only too well. Like them, he too had worked for the oil company for a long time. They'd all joined around the same time and all had helped each other along the way. Some were helped more than others, of course. It was just a matter of the degree of friendship between all three individuals. Hammond was desperate to join them at board level and so could be manipulated with ease. There were unspoken reasons not to doubt it. Dodgy dealings involving all three of them in the past ensured he would agree. They both knew that. But he was a little unstable, crazy even. Both Darcy and Isaacs had witnessed that a long time ago. That's why he wasn't a Vice-President, he was too unreliable. Worse, he was too unpredictable!

'How much?'

'I dunno . . . half a million, more maybe?'

'Will that be enough? I mean, it seems too simple!'

'Sure it's simple, it has to be. They've got nothing,' he went on to say. 'There's absolutely nothing out there for them other than bribery or poverty. One's a pain in the ass, the other gets them at least a little bit of what's on offer in life's little box of luxuries. Why'd you think they get these crazy, fucked-up military men to blow these facilities up?'

'Ugh? I still don't get it. Who says the military blew it up?'

'A retired Colonel called *Pops* last night,' he replied, referring to his father-in-law's nickname in the Isaacs household. 'He's an ex soldier, he's some kinda of hired military man, a mercenary or something like that. Anyway, he's making some really good cash from all the sympathizers down there. You know the game. The bastards who pulled off this little stunt were paid big bucks by the locals to send that plant into orbit.'

'Where'd the money come from, I thought you said the locals were poverty-stricken?'

'They are, but there's plenty of influences from other country's hell bent on giving us Americans a hard time around the world. I wouldn't put it past Iran, or even Russia being behind this one. They are known to have strong dealings with the tribal elders; they would love to get involved with all the rich-pickings down there. The Iranians would only be too pleased to pay a small army to cause such massive disruption! Yeah, the Iranians or some other screwed-up country that has a grudge against America probably funded the whole thing. God knows, I bet there's a string of other nations out there willing to do the same. The villagers, or in this case, the elders would only encourage it. They've had enough according to soldier boy. We've polluted half the fucking Niger Delta and they've had a gut full of it, as if you don't know!' said Isaacs. Darcy nodded, he knew and he always felt guilty about what they were doing. The entire board knew what was happening, but the alternative would cost too much money. They'd never get the same high returns if they had to have a cleaner, leak-free operation! If they could stop the locals tapping into the pipelines almost at random it would help!

'We gotta get in amongst the tribal leaders, the elders, and start paying em off instead of the Iranians, or whoever it is that's funding all this. Trust me,' added Isaacs, not in the least concerned about the environmental disaster they'd caused in Nigeria, they'd take care of it one day. *Until then the villagers would have to manage,* he would say when asked about it.

There was that word again, *trust*! 'We'd need reassurances,' said the big man, not remotely sure where to place his trust. He was still worried and even less enthusiastic now after knowing the place was deliberately targeted. Nevertheless, he was listening, which meant he was willing to take a chance.

He knew Eamon had reluctantly taken the bait so Jeremy smiled and took another sip of Bud.

'That'll be taken care of. Now, drink up,' he ordered with a light slap to Eamon's side and looking him in the eye for the first time that night, 'I'll talk to Richard in the morning,' he said confidently. 'Meanwhile, you've gotta think what you're gonna tell *Pops*!' Jeremy clicked his fingers and a disgruntled barman shrugged his shoulders at the rude gesture. Nevertheless, in no time at all two more tops were flipped off a couple more beers and two more shots were slid in front of them. Eamon loosened his necktie and drank, uncomfortably.

'Yeah, right, what do I tell *Pops*?' he mumbled to nobody. Eamon frowned and looked around the bar as he downed his beer. The drunks had returned from their refuge. The problem was solved, perhaps. He just needed to convince the CEO, or perhaps he might not even mention it, as Isaacs had so brilliantly suggested to him earlier!

Eamon then swigged the Bourbon. Another swig drained the glass and was the prompt to leave for home, he was tired and getting tipsy. He'd need to have all his wits about him tomorrow. He got up to leave, patted Isaacs on the back as he rocked unsteadily on his feet and then made his way to the door.

'Why the fuck had Arnold lumber us with a coupla shitty process plants?' he muttered, slurring his words and kicking out at the furniture as he went along. 'Nobody wanted them in the first fucking place!' he moaned as he stumbled out of the door.

Back in the Niger Delta About Two Months Later

The distant drone of a marine engine gradually broke the silence of the still, pitch-black night as the medium-sized fishing craft carefully motored upstream of one of the many sinuous waterways that snaked through the Niger Delta. Oron Ogaji, an ex-Nigerian army officer of ten years, leaned closer against a fallen mangrove tree, stilled himself, and waited and listened as her bow cut steadily through the flat, calm water. Occasionally, voices could be heard downstream of where he lay hidden, the muffled sound carried upstream by what little wind there might have been. Words were not yet decipherable. It was obvious to Ogaji, and to anybody else who may have been lurking deep in these lush mangrove swamps on this darkest of nights, that they were those of the occupants of the boat. Probably course directions to the helmsman from villagers placed on the bow; locals, well equipped with the knowledge required to help navigate these spaghetti-shaped, murky waterways.

The fact that they had managed to get this far without being stopped and searched by the *Naval Special Security Task Force* was in itself a milestone. *Operation Acid Rain* had had a massive impact. A state of emergency was in place and the Nigerian military authorities had deployed an intense number of gunboats to patrol and police the Delta in addition to setting up checkpoints along all the main roads throughout the region. There had been many confrontations between the local villagers and the military along this stretch of river recently. Stories of boats being damaged during the outbursts of violence that followed a *search* were rife, their crews almost always beaten by the hard-handed soldiers, and there were even reports of whole crews going missing under mysterious circumstances. Ogaji waited patiently, heart beating fast. There would be violence in these parts tonight.

His friend and partner, Mundab, was hidden on the opposite riverbank, positioned in thick vegetation not twenty yards from the landing rendezvous. The two men had been staked out along this stretch of water for more than seventy hours waiting for this precise moment. They would be well paid for the night's work but there was more in it for Mundab. It was a personal thing, a vendetta. He had seen close members of his family killed by government forces, their bloodied talents paid for by the international oil companies. And now it was payback time. Ogaji hoped that his colleague too would be experiencing the same sensational rush of adrenaline that now pumped through his veins as they lay waiting patiently to strike. He could hardly wait.

Soon the boat finally became partly visible in the dark. Her bow and starboard side was silhouetted against the many shades of black that outlined the contour of vegetation that grew on the riverbanks, differentiating the lush growth from the dark brown of the polluted river and swamps alike. He could hardly have ignored the dull light that penetrated weakly through the dirt-stained glass of the wheelhouse, which further identified the blackened outline of her compact looks. His intelligence briefings, though mildly simplistic and hardly that intelligent, were accurate enough and for once his patience had paid off. He would soon be rewarded, no doubt about it. Without any movement whatsoever he stared at the craft from where he was secretly positioned, half-leaning, half-standing, half-peering but wholly concealed; tightly tucked away behind the large limb of a fallen mango tree chosen for that very reason. Ogaji waited and watched. Mundab would do the same. To the east, the weather was deteriorating and somewhere up in the heavenly darkness, puffed-up shadows were starting to build with a vengeance. The heavy-laden rain clouds now appeared much darker against the black overcast sky. Within minutes it would be lashing down.

For the umpteenth time he went through the routine. Mundab would make the first move but he would need to be double sure of his target. Three hand grenades tossed into the wheelhouse and the forward deck would be quickly followed by a long burst of machinegun fire that would spray the entire boat. Its wooden superstructure would offer little protection for those onboard. Once Mundab had spent his ammunition, it would be the signal for Ogaji to do likewise, from the opposite bank, attacking the other side of the boat. Any refugees would have their backs to him. That would wipe out the remaining crew taking shelter from Mundabs' onslaught. It would be totally unexpected. They would receive gunfire from both sides at closely timed intervals. If they cocked up and it was a military vessel, a gunboat for instance, then they would take out a few soldiers but would almost certainly get killed such was the military superiority and enormous firepower that would inevitably be used against them. They could not run and take sanctuary in these parts of the Delta. The rivers were swollen and they would surely perish in the surrounding growth. There was no hiding place.

Suddenly he heard voices coming from the boat. The language used was almost certainly broken English for what little he could hear. Pidgin English probably, he reasoned. More muffled sounds came his way, another language, Yoruba or Ibo perhaps? That little gang could be from either the Southwest or Southeast. Although he was up to his ankles in mud he was comfortable, secure in the knowledge that he was being hidden by the dense growth and well positioned along a small peninsular where the river narrowed to a fork beyond. If Mundab kept good timing as planned,

Ogaji could complete his follow-up attack from where he was. His hideout was found by pure luck and he was pleased with the break. The hideaway would not have been made possible if it were not for the height of the swollen rivers, which substantially increased the water level. The rainy season ensured that most rivers were in flood. Tributaries and mangrove swamps seemed to exist as one great expanse of water on times, which greatly hindered navigation and access to the smaller villages. The rain would soon start to pelt down. It would further help conceal his location and so, under the circumstances, his lair seemed adequate. Surely, nobody would see him from here!

The boat had edged higher up the river now, towards where Mundab lay in hiding. It was now a matter of timing. What would Mundab be thinking? The diesel engine knocked in rhythm as her exhaust spluttered and choked low in the water. The boat slowly inched forward. The normally ill-trained crew used for this type of work was behaving too; they had kept relatively quiet. Even so, they were audible to a small degree. They were too quiet for his liking though and much to his increasing impatience he decided to take a closer look. The night-vision goggles were taken from inside his rucksack, the lenses cleaned before he zeroed in on his quarry.

'Thank God,' he whispered to himself. He could plainly see the crew scurrying around the boat. It was then that he made out the object floating in the water; something was bobbing slightly on the surface, just in front of the starboard bow. One of the crew had spotted it too and was pointing in the same direction as the boat was now being slowly maneuvered, towards Mundabs' lair. He watched carefully as another member of the crew partly-secured the floater to a noose, the thin wire was attached to a wooden pole and was now being pulled tight against the strain. A boat hook was also being deployed. The long, wooden shaft was extended into the water by a third member of the crew who tried to turn the floating object inwards, towards the side of the vessel. The large mass was being dragged unceremoniously into the boat. Ogaji sensed a problem.

'Nothing can go wrong, not tonight, please, God!' whispered Ogaji looking to the sky in prayer. Dark clouds once again stirred, bundled together and rolled overhead as if to acknowledge his concern. Then the heavens opened and the rain lashed down in buckets. He was as near to one of the richest reserves in rain forest plant species and animal life as one could get. Yet, apart from disturbing the wildlife, Mother Nature was the last thing on his mind!

Chapter 4

SMALL DROPLETS OF RAINWATER QUICKLY turned into large pellets and began to splash onto the deck and windows of the *Mista Delta* as she made her way upstream. The wooden vessel was benign of the dark surroundings or the circumstances she was asked to perform her task. Apart from the helmsman, a young Nigerian who went by the name of Binman, and Phillip Laxrois, a hired mercenary who were both standing, the rest of her sweaty, human cargo remained seated next to one another, helpless in the confines of the wheelhouse. There were three in all, two Nigerian businessmen from Lagos and one American; an impostor, supposedly from the political wing of the newly formed, Environmental Rights Action Group. Their feet seemed to be riveted to the deck in trepidation of what lay ahead. They knew very little about the people they were asked to meet. Apart from the fact they were tribal leaders, so-called, elders, they were somewhat clueless. Contrary to brief reports in New York, these people were better organized than they were given credit for. They were responsible for causing massive disruption against a number of oil companies in the region. Most of these so-called *disruptions* involved serious violence and they had built up quite a reputation. They were hardened criminals who'd all committed murder at least one time or another. And if that wasn't bad enough news for the oilers, they had strong links with Iran!

But for now, that did not matter. By some means the delegates had been reassured they would come to no harm. Everyone could be bribed and, after all, that was what *they* had come to do. Money talked in these parts and so for that reason they were deemed safe so long as they coughed up their dollars. Payment would have to be in abundance. The three-man *delegation* had an objective but if they were honest to themselves, it was ill conceived, dangerous and simply stupid. They did not really know what to expect. If they had a choice at that moment in time, which of course they didn't, or if they had any sense, which was equally doubtful, they would offload their cash to Laxrois and ask him to turn the boat around and go back to where they came. At least they would be safe.

Having been further east earlier in the bright, sunny light of day they were now heading south in the gloomy, dark of night. A make-shift map, penned on an old water-proof canvas, placed them ten kilometers north of Warri, a highly populated fishing village well placed in the Delta for trading. They had long since turned off from the main artery of the river Niger, itself a great expanse of slow flowing water, effortlessly spreading out to touch the low lying land that formed this great Delta as she did so. Now the ageing craft navigated an unnamed tributary with some difficulty, which was made more treacherous by the floodwaters, especially at night. But they managed somehow and were now nearing their destination.

Phillip Laxrois stood quietly smoking a cigarette. He was sweating along with everybody else on board. There was no air conditioning, the boat was too old and on top of that the inside of the entire wheelhouse leaked and was now soaking wet from the torrent of rain that now lashed down on her.

'How long?' the American asked anxiously, breaking the gloomy silence in the process.

Laxrois shrugged his shoulders. 'Coupla minutes maybe, coupla hours . . . who knows?' He spoke adequate English for a Frenchman but the accent was still deep and in any prolonged conversation some words would be difficult to pick out.

'We kinda thought you might?' Hammond told him. The sarcastic reply was met with the contempt it deserved.

'Might?' he questioned.

'Might know when we get there,' replied the American, now busily consumed watching the rainwater mingle with his sweat as he spoke.

'You seem anxious to get there, mister.'

'You could say that,' he replied, swiping at a pool of water collecting around his feet.

'Well, you're nearly there now,' come the reply. 'Isn't that what you wanted?'

'Yes, just damn pissed off with the thought of having to be here at all!' The underlying animosity was clear from the tone of his voice. The trip so far had been extremely tense between both men. The Nigerians looked to the floor. They didn't want to get involved in the ensuing conflict.

'Ugh,' shrugged Laxrois and spat on the floor before taking another deep drag on his cigarette. 'Take a look,' he ordered and threw his head in the direction of the left window. 'Take a good look my American friend,' he continued as smoke exhaled from his lungs and filled the rancid space. The American knew it was pitch dark so remained uninterested, he kept watching as a small lake developed on the deck around him. 'You pay me to take you to where you want to go, Mr. big fucking American, so . . . I'll take you there. If you think you can do it by yourself, then be my guest, go do it. I'll help you off the boat,' he sneered, taking another drag, taunting his passenger. 'If not . . . fine, you stay here. Now just shut the fuck up, hey!' There was no retaliation. Both men just about managed to hold their composure. It would be sorted out at another time. Until then, Hammond ignored him, looking towards Binman instead. The young helmsmen sensed he was being watched and turned his head around.

'Wa you lookin at, man? You shood be kind an all!' he mouthed, following the lead provided by Laxrois. He wasn't taking too kindly to being scrutinized in this way, either. Laxrois smirked at the rebuke. Hammond merely shrugged his shoulders and looked to the floor; under other circumstances he'd give the boy a bloody good hiding!

In the meantime, the boat continued to inch forward as the humidity once again shut in the warm night air. It was becoming unbearable inside the cramped vessel. After days of travelling in these torrid conditions the stale smell of sweat was thick. It leached from their shirts, the sticky-like cloth material gluing itself to their bare flesh underneath, the sweat glands remained constantly open, secreting, continuously trying to cool them just as nature intended. Diesel fumes had added to their discomfort too, and the reason two of them had become nauseated earlier in the trip. The sick had been washed away with two buckets of polluted river water. Outside it was slightly better. The rain helped reduce the humidity. They would get soaked through to the skin if they ventured on deck but for the time being they were sheltered, well partly sheltered! Not surprisingly, they felt a little safer in the confines of the leaking and dilapidated wheelhouse. They never complained about the weather, they had other things on their mind.

Except for the movement of those on board, only the rhythmic knock of the diesel engine could be felt as the small fishing boat slowly and silently edged through the calm waters. The *Mista Delta* pressed on. Her fishing days were long over but her engines had supposedly been overhauled by the locals to ensure she would be reliable and worthy of a very important passage deep into the mangrove swamps of the Niger Delta. Unlike other, deeper parts of the river, there were no currents to worry about along this particular stretch of water. They had taken a course well off the main channel, which was now located some fifty or so kilometers to the east. The *Mista* was merely cutting her way through a shallow tributary, a long section that connected a mangrove swamp that edged the Cross River National Park. She was being pushed deep inside a vast landscape carved out from two former Forest Reserves of Bashi-Okwango and Oban. They had to be careful with their navigation and more careful with the traffic. These waters were frequently used to reach many of the remote villages in nearby Cross River State. The presence of other boats would make it difficult.

Then, suddenly and without warning, the crew began to go into frenzy. Even above the noise of the rain lashing against the wheelhouse timbers the commotion outside was increasing and languages of all descriptions filled the air. The crew had seen something or other in the water and had become alarmed!

'Qu'est-ce que c'est?'—*What is it?* The Frenchman's accent seemed even deeper and he spoke fast, demanding to know what was going on. He ordered Binman to move aside. Again he spoke in French but anyone could have understood what he wanted by the tone of his voice and the actions he made. Puzzled by the commotion on deck, and struggling to look through the window due to the enormous size of the wheel, Binman failed to hear the command. He should have been more aware of his surroundings. Without hesitation, the tall European grabbed the unsuspecting crewman on the shoulders with both arms, turned him around, and practically threw him forcefully backwards through the wheelhouse. The Nigerian, a black boy of about twenty two, his body bare apart from *Adidas* three-quarter length shorts, which hung loosely from his skinny waist, was sent soaring over an insecure table. He ended up sprawled against the bulkhead and the deck. He had hit over several cups, a few small plates, and a half-full bag of sugar before finally breaking one of the legs off the table as he came crashing down on the boards. Splinters pierced his skin and blood began to drip and then mingle with the sweat from his glistening body. He had paid a severe penalty for his inquisitive actions. The others stood rooted to the spot and merely looked on. Phillip Laxrois cared not in the least about the boy. Instead, he wiped the condensation from inside the window before pressing his nose against the glass to peer out and see the half-naked and harried bodies of several of the crew running from the foredeck to the starboard side of the boat. Their bare torso's were wet and glistened; shorts hung loose around their waists and stuck to their thighs, the result of being soaked from the rain. His rowdy crew had seen something in the water.

The Frenchman quickly left the safety of the wheelhouse, allowing the boy to groan in agony as soon as he was gone. Nobody cared. A villager and former member of the local Ijaw tribe, the young boy had not bargained on this. That was ill discipline. Surely he was needed free of injury, but if that's the way it was, fine. Part reason for his silence was the fact that he'd not yet been paid, but he would, eventually. The price was right and that's all that mattered. That's why he was there in the first place. He didn't mind what he had to do. Money was hard to come by and having grown up in the poverty-stricken villages that littered the Delta he could take a beating. He did not know if the risk was worth it since he never considered being caught. The risk was such that it was better that he didn't consider the consequences. Along with the rest of the crew, the boy had long since revolted against his own kind, the Ijaw. He still believed in *The Movement*, believed in their fight for fairness, the right to be heard but that did not pay and, therefore, like many others he had sold his soul for extra money, *extra Nairo's,* frequently working underhandedly against his comrades and sometimes fellow villagers. To be caught would mean instant death.

'Silencieux!'—'*Quite!*' he hollered in a strained voice directed toward the troubled crew and they immediately did as they were told. Several of the skinny, dirty-looking Ijaw turncoats actually stopped what they were doing altogether. Laxrois was fearless and they feared him, literally, every man on board. He had a reputation as long as the River Niger itself and was not a man to be messed with. He had seen brutality, violence and many deaths to last a lifetime. The very nature of his trade ensured that. Depending on the price his employer was willing to pay depended upon the degree of violence, brutality, and deaths he was willing to inflict. The French mercenary cared not a hoot for his victims, only that they held a monetary value to him and sometimes they were worth a lot of money. They were priceless. Laxrois was amazed at the value placed on even the lowest of lives. Yes, it had been a good partnership in Nigeria. Plenty of low life, plenty of willing clients, and the commission was good, very good.

'Fucking imbeciles!' he muttered to himself in English and further scolded those in front of him. By the time they'd dragged the floating object alongside he was there, standing and waiting. Once again, several of the Nigerian crew was pushed aside so that the big man could take a look at what was being hauled up from the water. No sooner had the snared prize reached the lower part of the boats gunwales it was apparent that the *floater* was in fact a body. That alone had little effect on those who were by now manhandling the bloated corpse. They were hardened men, most had seen death many times but as the stiff, water-saturated body rolled over during the scramble to get it onboard, the face came into view. There was a sudden gasp from the onlookers! Those of the crew who had a physical hold on it also shrieked in shock at roughly the same time.

The face and head had been split open and the rancid flesh now gaped wide. The wound had swollen from a combination of the impact of a machete and the effects of being in the water. There was evidence too that predators, in the form of marine life, had also eaten parts of the head, face and upper body judging by the soft pulpy parts that were visible. Tissue hung off, torn from the sharp teeth of larger fish. The smell that accompanied this awful sight was just as penetrating. The putrid stench filled the air choking many, if not everyone on deck. The whole thing was incredible and the *monster-like* corpse was discarded in an instance, hitting the water with a splash. It bobbed just below the surface momentarily before floating on its way. The sound of someone being sick set off a chain reaction amongst the crew and pretty soon all but two were throwing up. There was an epidemic. Whoever it was in the water had met the ugliest of deaths and could even have been inflicted by the military police such was their ruthlessness against those who resisted their authority. Naturally, Laxrois was unaffected by what he saw. He had a fair idea of what had happened to these sorrowful remains of a human being.

The *floater* had been in the water for about thirty-six hours. Like many in these parts, he was a mercenary but lacked the experience to go it alone. His work came from others; something that he thought would change with time. He was obviously ambitious but this time his work had failed him. Unbeknown to Laxrois at that precise moment in time, he had actually met the *floater* no more than two weeks earlier. He had persuaded the ex-Nigerian military man to meet with local tribesmen to broker another deal involving the sale of stolen arms. As it turned out, the man negated on the promise he made to Laxrois shortly before the arranged meeting took place. The Frenchman later learned from his sources that the man had taken up the offer of a better-paid job. He couldn't keep his mouth shut about it during the heavy drinking bouts he succumbed to in the seedy bars of Lagos. Far too often the word got out of what he

The Last Hangman

was up to. The latest on the street was that he was lined up to murder a delegation of so-called businessmen who were to meet several Ijaw close to an unnamed location downstream of Warri. No sooner had the loudmouth taken up his position along the riverbank, ready to lay in wait for his prey, the betrayed tribesmen had caught him, taken a machete to his head and hacked him to death in front of other would-be traitors. It was to be Mundabs' last well-paid job. Fortunately for Ogaji, they did not know he had an accomplice and so he still remained covert unaware of what had happened to his friend. He hadn't realized yet that he'd been working alone for the last thirty-six hours!

Laxrois was disgusted at the way his men behaved. They had no stomach. He spun on his heels and returned to the wheelhouse, spitefully kicking one of the crew bent over in sickness, bile dripped from his mouth. He would take the helm personally. He had done so many times and thought nothing of it. Steering the boat he surged the vessel forward towards a pontoon located some fifty yards to the left. As the boat swung around he noticed a slight movement along the right-hand side of the riverbank. It was the smallest of motions that had caught his attention through the corner of his eye. It came from the centre of a small clearing, sheltered from the river and seemingly well hidden. Even in the dark and through the mass of raindrops, he spotted a dark shadow that momentarily changed in contrast against the well-formed rushes that protected a point where the river narrowed. That slight glimpse was enough to tell him that something or someone was there. He would keep a watch out tonight, who knows what could happen. Meanwhile, on deck, the smell of vile sickness replaced the previously repulsive smell of the rancid corpse.

* * *

Whatever it was, Ogaji realized it was probably nothing, dead dog or some other luckless mammal, who knows? Nobody on board cared. No sooner had the *floater* been dragged onboard it was gone, immediately let go to drop back into the water. Whatever they had snared was unimportant. They had let it go and turned away. Ogaji had seen that for himself. Yes, probably a rancid dog or goat judging by the size, bloated with gases after being so long in the water, nothing to worry about. He tried to relax a little but couldn't. He was naturally becoming too anxious. Something was about to happen. Any minute now he told himself and tensed in anticipation. Another few yards would create the perfect opportunity to launch their attack and so he watched as the boat swung around with an increased roar of her engines towards where Mundab should have been. All too quickly the boat reached its intended mooring without incident, her crew jumping over the side with ropes ready to secure her to a wooden landing. Silence followed as *Mistas'* powerful, six-liter diesel engine was cut in an instant. Where was the gunfire? What was Mundab doing? Had he fallen asleep? Mundab had lost his nerve, Ogaji was convinced. He could not believe his friend had not opened fire. He had the perfect chance!

Once alongside there was no more fussing on board the *Mista Delta* thereafter. Ogaji was confused and breathed hard as he wiped his brow. He turned and lay with his back against the thick base of the rushes that protected him from being seen. Tonight was a disaster and he hadn't a clue why?

'Fuck Mundab! He'd kill the little bastard himself when he saw him,' he muttered. Ogaji's blood boiled as he considered his dilemma. How could he make his escape? They were relying on nobody being around. The inflatable rib was their previous means of getting from there. They had planned to speed downriver the minute daylight broke. Soon after that they could be anywhere in hiding. That route was now out of the question, the rib was tied up too close to the *Mista*. Ogaji calmed himself with difficulty. He could lay low for several more hours yet. Dawn would soon come and time was of the essence. He would wait and see what transpired and then somehow make a run for it. He hoped Mundab would get caught and be tortured or get shot or preferably both. He would take no part in his escape plan. Unbeknown to Ogaji, Mundab had suffered a far more terrible ordeal. Not for the first time that night, deadly poisonous snakes, the kind that slithered in and around the riverbank and mingled amongst the rushes looking for prey, were never far from his thoughts.

Chapter 5

THE AGEING BOAT WAS NOW motionless but secure alongside her wooden river mooring. Her engines had lasted. Some distance away, Resident Dowoonda, Rilwanu Iteimor and Dele Olowoyo, three Ijaw tribesmen, waited patiently but cautiously, hid inside a rather large and camouflaged tent erected in a small clearing located two kilometers inland from where the *Mista* was moored. A Red Cross emblazoned across all four sides of the canvas was a reminder of the way things were, a remnant of even worse times in these bloodied regions. Twenty or so heavily armed men were positioned around the immediate periphery of the clearing. They too sat patient, expressionless, waiting for the American to arrive. Several more were hidden some way back. All were alert and in a state of readiness, even though they considered themselves safe from the prying eyes of the local authorities. The military security forces and patrolling riverboats were wreaking havoc of some kind or other in the area. Also, and of equal importance, they were a safe distance from their own kind, local Ijaw villagers who would surely want to know what it was that was so important it needed a tent? But had they stumbled on the tent and seen its occupants they would not have bothered to ask!

The facts were that oil and politics are poles apart in this, one of Africa's largest oil producing countries. The riches from millions of barrels of exported and refined crude oil should have, at the very least, ensured that disease and hunger were a thing of the past. With poverty as bad as it's ever been, worse even, anger and resentment ran deep throughout a region that was already too familiar with the effects of political corruption, famine and disease, pain and suffering, tribal warfare and too much bloodshed. And all this amongst the putrid, oil-saturated and polluted environment they now constantly fought hard to save.

The men inside the tent had good reason to remain hidden. All three were reputed lead-members of the Ijaw Youth Movement and wanted desperately by the Nigerian Government for, amongst other things, murder, organizing violent protests and demonstrations, and all sorts of civil disobedience against the many oil companies that were resident in the region. All of which, they argued, were only interested in reaping the enormous wealth from their oil and, even worse, seemed hell bent on polluting the rich and beautiful Niger Delta. In their eyes, the oil companies gave practically nothing in return and since an over corrupt government deliberately ignores their pleas for dialogue the protests have simply become more violent. Recent attempts by the authorities to repress the Delta insurgency only added to make matters worse. Although expensive to fund, one recent particular spate of bloodied violence, *Operation Acid Rain*, was a huge success in their eyes, but it came with a premium; there were over one hundred and fifty lives lost. It resulted in about twenty oil pumping stations shutting down for fear of becoming the next target. This caused product levels to drop by over a third.

Operation Climate Change was another massive bout of violent disorder carried out earlier in the year and again, had been very successful. The resulting effect on the oil companies was measured as gigantic with even more losses in oil production than ever before. The knock-on effect for the government was also disastrous with much needed revenue, estimated at billions of dollars, lost due to the disruption. In the aftermath, the Ijaw tribal community, rightly or wrongly gave the organizers who led the violent disobedience, Dowoonda, Iteimor, and Olowoyo, the recognition they deserved by making them leaders of the Youth Movement. Under calmer times they would be a leaderless tribal community, unlike the tiny neighboring Ogoni tribe which first started the protests in the Delta. The Ijaw had no recognized leaders, spiritual or otherwise, they seemed not to need any. They did, however, have one thing in common with the Ogoni tribe's people. They all felt the same inside about the way they were being treated and now there was a feeling of absolute hatred against the oil companies and collaborating government alike. It was no wonder then that all three men are wanted and they trusted nobody.

* * *

The American, Richard Hammond—alias *Sean Carter*, was amongst the last of the crew to leave the boat. Straddling *Mistas'* gunwale he leapt the last foot or so and landed heavily on the wooden deck of the less than sturdy pontoon, its sun-baked and less flexible wood loudly creaking from the sudden impact. The weathered timbers hardly flexed with every subsequent movement. Looking around he realized that the only thing that resembled civilization was in fact the *Mista*, an old fishing boat, and even she looked a mess in these awkward surroundings. The wheelhouse could be compared to a shed that had been patched in a number of places with differently colored wooden planks. It had seen better days. The structure had taken a number of hits from poorly misjudged off-loading of fish, the heavy cargo supposedly swung alongside in baskets from her short mast and intended to be landed on the quay. Through lack of timing and brain power the synchronization had broken down on numerous occasions. The large baskets of fish had scored direct hits against the frail cabin many times over the years according to the repairs.

Beyond the confines of the boat he looked at his surroundings. It only confirmed what a god-forsaken country he was in. Should he become lost he would surely stay lost he thought to himself, naval patrol boats or not. They were in a clearing alongside one of the rivers that snaked off a larger river downstream. Across the calm water he saw many mangrove trees that edged towards, from what little he knew to be a swamp, the entire surroundings being edged by dense growth and the start of some kind of rain forest. To his left, and where he could see the flustered crew members quickly walking, sometimes stumbling as they maintained the pace behind Laxrois (who had naturally taken the lead), was different forms of sparsely populated vegetation, which gave way to dense forest some fifty yards further.

It had stopped raining sometime in the night. The sun, still low in the sky, was hazy. The bright morning light would be slow to materialize but that would change. Soon, ultra-violet rays would break through the thin blanket of morning mist that covered the lush vegetation and the temperature would rise, and the humidity, and the discomfort. It would rise from the east, so they would be heading north he presumed judging by the location of the dull, orange-like ball and the direction of passage taken by the crew. But even that brief attempt at global positioning was futile. In a few seconds the sun would disappear, hidden by the dense forest that would accommodate and shelter their planned meeting with the lead members of the Ijaw. Navigation then, was almost impossible and not for the first time on this trip the American felt lonely, vulnerable and afraid but there could be no going back. He had to complete what he had come to do. With that in mind he quickly caught up with the rest of the crew and fellow passengers, the two Nigerian businessmen, who had not said a single word and who were still unaware of what was to come. For that reason alone they were slightly more relaxed than *Carter*.

Orders could be heard from the direction they headed. Laxrois was in a foul mood, confronting anybody who didn't appear to be pulling their weight. They knew all about their guide, or at least they should have known and should have been afraid. The three non-warriors had sampled their first taste of his immense impatience. They had witnessed the strength and brutality of the former Legionnaire in those few seconds it took to inflict damage on Binman last night but nobody moved to stop it. The Nigerian businessmen wanted to but knew they dared not help the youngster, who had now been left alone on the boat in agony. They tried to talk to him earlier that morning, to see if he was okay, but Binman was frail and very weak. When he finally managed to slowly pick himself up, tears welled in his large, white but bloodshot eyes. His fall had been broken in part by the table but he still crashed down heavily on the hard decking and was now lying motionless in some considerable pain from several bruised or broken ribs. His arm was clearly cut and bleeding. The deep wound was open and the pink-colored flesh was sharp in contrast against his black skin. He remained quite in a makeshift bunk. His bloodied, bottom lip quivered and his body slouched. The youngster was shaking with pain. The Nigerians would try to help when it was safe to do so. The American would stand his ground. He showed not even the slightest sign of remorse. Nobody else on board showed any pity for the injured black boy and he in turn never expected any. His fellow Nigerians, however, wanted to help but they couldn't, they daren't. The two remained helpless when others were around and for that reason, they felt cowardly.

Within an hour or so of entering the forest, and without warning, Ijaw tribe's men surrounded them. Both startled and frightened for their lives, most backpacks carried by the crew were dropped on the spot. Simultaneously, their rifles and sub-machine guns were raised in readiness. What followed in those prevailing seconds was total mayhem, a standoff by both sides. Heavily armed men stood shouting nervously and gibbering loudly at each other and in all fashions of language. It seemed no side was prepared to stand down or drop their arms and the confusion continued. The noise became louder with each increased threat. *Sean*, along with the Nigerian businessmen, had fallen to the ground the instant they were ambushed. You would have almost thought they were dead. Hearts pounded, teeth clenched, and faces grimaced as they gripped the damp earth for cover. The three civilians pressed themselves deep into the damp, muddy ground in a vain attempt to vanish.

Not surprisingly, it was Laxrois who made the first move. He had expected the ambushed greeting from the Ijaw and was rather surprised it had not been earlier, alongside the mooring where they were significantly more vulnerable. That's what he would have done. Achieve the maximum effect. Shouting loud enough for his own crew to hear above the mayhem, he ordered his men to lower their weapons at once. This they did but with much hesitation. They were still twitching right up to the point where their leader also ordered the Ijaw to stop their shouting and threatening behavior. The Frenchman was conscious of the fact that the confrontation was merely a show of strength. The Ijaw were merely flexing their muscle, but he was equally conscious of the fact that his trigger-happy crew would retaliate. They were mostly wanted criminals, many of them hardened murderers and many more were former Ijaw tribesmen; now exiled due to their betrayal of the Youth Movement. They would not want to be recognized, or even worse, caught. Both the crew of the *Mista* and the Ijaw were ill disciplined. If that weren't the case they would not have caused such a stir. Laxrois, therefore, sensed the consequences of such a standoff. It could alert the patrolling armed forces. Nevertheless, it was a gamble that he had to take. The Ijaw would not allow anyone into their territory without them seemingly being threatened or taken hostage, as was the case recently when two Armstrong Oil company helicopter pilots were taken hostage as they landed spare parts at one of their remote oil pumping stations. Armstrong Oil was held to ransom by the Ijaw. The ransom demand was simple enough, leave the country or the pilots would remain hostages indefinitely. The situation was resolved by a compromise, a combination of money and a promise of dialogue with both Armstrong and the government, the later still allegedly being awaited by the Ijaw.

Ordering his men to pick up their belongings before dragging the three, *dead* and trembling civilians off the ground and to their feet, Laxrois, along with everyone else in tow, started to walk towards the direction where one of the lead tribesmen pointed with an oversized machete. All three of the city dwellers looked disheveled and sad, their faces and clothing muddied from the forests decomposing foliage. Embarrassed by their actions, they followed as instructed. In a shorter time than expected they were almost at the arranged rendezvous. What appeared to be miles of dark, dense forest undergrowth with creepers trailing from every branch above suddenly turned into a long, grassy clearing with much shorter grass further on. The early morning sun had risen higher in the sky and now blazed down on each of them in turn as they exited the jungle-like surroundings. The damp, cool of the forest had been quite comfortable for them, apart from the insect bites, but now they were experiencing the same effect when one leaves an air-conditioned building or car. It was the familiar sensation of dripping sweat as the heat and humidity quickly closed in around each one of them. They would, however, be ever thankful for the variety of bush hats shading their eyes and protecting them from the worst the sun had to offer.

The point Ijaw had soon taken them well into the clearing now and for the first time they were in full view of the tent that was pitched on the much shorter grass. The large, red crosses were visible for all to see and similar to those field hospital tents used by the military. Laxrois stopped and half-held up his right arm. His men stopped immediately in anticipation, nervous fingers twitched on triggers, some readied themselves for what might come, others were not quite sure what to do. They felt uncomfortable with their rifles and pistols lowered considering the threat they were confronted with. Should their weapons be needed ready to fire they would definitely be second to the Ijaw. For all their outlawed and past criminal activities they looked sheepish, timidly looking at each other for a lead as to what to do next. The Ijaw had already stopped and were now busy surrounding them, rifles pointed, machetes and spears poised ready for the first sign of attack. The situation was as tense as it had been since the first confrontation. The older of the Ijaw, the lead tribesman and the same one that had led the way from the woods, was now talking in Pidgin English to the others. They in turn seemed to be pointing at the men they now surrounded. Had they identified one or two traitors?

There was some kind of dissent amongst them, they were not happy with the situation. There followed a short burst of angry exchanges between several of the Ijaw and that was enough to convince Laxrois to act. He was not about to allow the situation to deteriorate further. Clearly, all was not well amongst them and for the first time he sensed that this could have been a trap. Had he been double-crossed? He wouldn't wait to find out. Smartly pointing to the tent the Frenchman promptly made his way toward it. His bold action took the Ijaw by surprise. They stopped their disagreement and watched as Laxrois continued towards the tent, pushing two of the younger natives out of the way without as much as a second glance as to what the others might do or say. He didn't give a shit about the consequences now. He steadied his automatic weapon, which was slung loosely and ready around his left shoulder, before stopping at the entrance to the tent. He looked back to check his rear-guard before speaking.

'Resident, are you in there?' he called out. In an instance there was a low-key reply. He was in there. Laxrois gave a less than trusting look over his shoulder and slowly entered the darkened tent.

Chapter 6

He guessed there would be at least three of them and he was right, it was a lucky guess. The men were stood, waiting in anticipation for him as he entered the hot, sweaty confines of the tent.

'Resident, it's good to see you again,' he lied, speaking in broken English. Laxrois greeted Dowoonda like a long lost brother and held out his right hand in a sign of friendship. None of the three Nigerians said a word, they remained speechless. There would be no shaking of hands. Instead, they touched and fidgeted with their weapons. Hand pistols were tucked into their waists and concealed by loose fitting shirts; the hammers cocked ready to be drawn and used in an instant. Laxrois, smiling at the rebuff, spat on the floor near to where they stood and then stared at each and every one of them in turn. He could not allow them the satisfaction of rebuking him. That prompted a reaction.

'No, contrary to what you think, Laxrois, it is not good to see you. It is never good to see a mercenary! Where are the others?' Dowoonda spoke without hiding his underlying disgust and forlorn dislike of Laxrois. He knew the mercenary wasn't sincere in his greeting and there was no need to act as if they were friends. He knew what the foreigner did and why he was meeting with them. There would be no formalities. Resident Dowoonda was in no mood to make small talk with the Frenchman. He detested him but suffered him for reasons only known to him and the other two leaders alongside him.

'Hey, relax,' said Laxrois, and half-raised his arms to ease the tension. 'Let's not get too uptight here!' he pleaded in a heavy French accent. Laxrois was no fool and had sensed the hostile tone of Dowoonda's voice. He would humor him as best he could. He looked at the others for reassurance but their expressions give nothing away. He'd recognized Rilwanu Iteimor the instant he walked into the tent. They had dealings in the past. The large muscular man was stood a little further back and to the right of

Dowoonda. He did not know the third person, Dele Olowoyo, but whilst he was no threat to a man of Laxrois' caliber, he did not want to provoke any of them, not just yet anyway.

The fact that he knew two of three men was no coincidence. They had talked many times in the past, mainly through intermediaries to get to where they were at this moment in time. It would be their last meet. That there were only three was a bonus. He would think through and plan his every move from here on in. He knew what he had to do. It was just a case of timing. The final outcome was something of a foregone conclusion. His mind had already been made up about that. The obvious tension and distrust that existed between them had convinced him of what he suspected would be required of him. This particular partnership had gone way beyond its sell-by date. Pity, it wasn't in the agreement. It didn't have to be this way, he thought. Anyway, he made new agreements and changed old agreements all the time. And if he needed any more convincing, he did not, luck was on his side. There could have been more of them inside the tent, causing him a little more discomfort in dealing with what was to come. He should have asked for names perhaps.

They kept their distance and steadied themselves. Laxrois' false niceties would make little difference. The Ijaw had placed many demands on Advanced Strategic Energies Inc, who had secretly arranged this meeting and now two of them were being met. The first of these were talks with a prominent Human Rights Activist who was willing to promote and support their cause in New York and London in such a way that would have maximum impact from what they did or did not do. They wanted governments around the world up in arms at what was going on in their region. Secondly, they demanded five hundred thousand dollars, which would be distributed equally between them. It was the carrot to overcome any *difficulties* and, not surprisingly in this poverty stricken region, also removed any further obstacles that seemed to constantly get put in place and used as yet another reason not to meet.

Still smiling to maintain his hard, disconcerting image, Laxrois continued to appease Dowoonda before telling him that the three men waiting to meet with them were not used to being in circumstances such as these. The tribesmen outside would have to pull back further into the forest before any talks took place.

'Why do you ask this?' Iteimor asked bluntly, approaching Laxrois as he spoke. His black, plump and pimpled face was covered in sweat, the whites of his reddened eyes were glaring, menacingly; his distrust was evident. 'Why should these men be afraid? Are we not friends?' he continued to ask, arrogantly.

'Indeed we are. Every one of us but your men, young and brave as I know they surely are,' said Laxrois, hesitating. 'They are showing too much aggression. Tell them to back off a little. It will help. I can assure you. My people feel threatened. We do not want any needless bloodshed.' Laxrois became very sentimental but for all his role-play, sensed an ever-increasing aggression that was being shown by the two Ijaw who had spoke so far. He now felt very uncomfortable and in his mind assured himself that he would react sooner rather than later if the situation did not improve. Dowoonda, who seemed to be the decision-maker without consulting the other two, shouted to the elder of the tribesmen waiting outside.

'Andab!'

The tall, thin native, the same one that had conducted affairs ever since the *ambush*, came quickly running into the tent whereupon Dowoonda spat out another couple of disgruntled words that were in a language that nobody other than the Ijaw could understand. From any discerning onlooker he appeared to be angry. It was Andab who then continued shouting instructions to the circle of heavily armed tribesmen, who slowly started to lower their weapons and retreat a few yards further back towards the edge of the forest. The relieved look from the crew of the *Mista* was obvious. The tension had been building up both inside and outside the tent. But now, with the Ijaw seemingly accepting their presence, the meeting proper could take place. Laxrois signaled to the three waiting men and they were beckoned inside the tent.

The two Nigerian businessmen were introduced as Ardelle Gist and his colleague Brandt Allto, two senior executives of Delta Oilfield Supplies, a company that did exactly that if the Ijaw allowed them to. They were the biggest suppliers to the many oil companies in the region. For the second time in that short period they'd been there, there were no handshakes at the time of asking and the Nigerian's felt embarrassed having been left standing with outstretched arms. It was not a good start.

'Gentlemen, what these people do is of no of importance to you but you will know they are connected to the oil companies in some way.' The Ijaw leaders said nothing as Laxrois spoke. Instead they frowned at the men stood nervously and cringing before them. Whilst they would accept the agreed bribery, nothing else would change by the presence of these two men. They despised the likes of Gist and Allto. Soon though, they would be relieved of their money and be murdered. Unaware of their fate, Laxrois continued the introductions.

'And this is *Sean Carter*. Sean is from the Human Rights Activist group based in New York.' The environmental stance was a ploy, although Laxrois was not told this. But he knew. As always, he made it his business to know. The American would almost certainly be connected to one of the many oil companies with interests in the region. Laxrois knew that much without having to even ask anyone. No in-depth research required. They all were. Not surprisingly, Laxrois didn't give an elephant's backside where the American came from, or what he did. The Frenchman knew the plan and that's all that mattered. The alias used by the American was merely the bait. The importance, however, was placed on using the connection with the Environmental Rights Action Group as his business. The two Nigerian businessmen were legitimate enough, they were unsuspecting accomplices and perfect for executing the plan. Between them they have attracted a meeting with those responsible for interfering in oil company affairs and a *deal* would be worked out, so to speak.

Upon hearing his introduction the American walked nervously towards the centre of the tent to meet the men he had travelled over fifteen thousand miles to see. The three leaders walked toward him too, arms spread wide, ready to embrace the one man they believed would help them. Grinning widely, they spoke first in Nigerian and then in English as they seemed to greet *Carter* in a combined series of soft and heavy-handed slaps all around his chest, arms and back. It was far too mystifying and prolonged for the liking of both Laxrois and Carter, who had by now became less nervous as he steadied himself against the barrage of slaps to his body. This time there were handshakes and they were rigorous and warming. Almost too false to be true, thought Laxrois!

'Mr. Carter,' said Dowoonda, again leading the conversation. 'We are pleased that you are here. My people are at your disposal to do whatever you think fit for our cause.'

'I've been trying to get here for some months now,' said Carter, speaking for the first time. His New Jersey accent was noticeably broad and over emphasized by the tense atmosphere inside the tent. 'You're difficult people to get hold of, you know that?' he said with a nervous smile. Laxrois looked on, the initial greeting was friendly and that was a good start. The Ijaw believed the man before them was there to help. He hoped the American wouldn't start to say the wrong things. They're outlaws and the wrong dialogue would raise suspicion. *Don't say the wrong thing for Christ's sake*!

The charade would have to continue while Laxrois worked out what to do about the heavily armed Ijaw outside. They still stood waiting in readiness but, thankfully, much further outside the periphery of the tent.

'Do not worry, Mr. Carter, we can always be contacted and always with the knowledge that we are safe, as you can see,' said Iteimor gesturing to the small army outside. The overweight man looked directly at him as he spoke, eyes bloodshot, nostrils rising in anticipation, he sensed something was about to happen. He then lifted his garb to display an array of weapons that lay slung and concealed around his loosely clothed body. The incredibly ugly Ijaw leader was grinning following the display, openly taunting them. He was menacing, looking adversely at his prey trapped inside the tent. Brandt, Ardelle and *Sean* merely looked back with the anticipated look of city dwellers that had never in all of their lives been a part of such an extraordinary encounter. Laxrois wasn't interested in their bravado. Instead, he fondled the Minimi machine gun, which was hung not quite pointed at his target but cocked and ready for action, nevertheless.

'We have the money,' it was Brandt Allto who managed to mumble something and quickly gestured towards a briefcase he held in the hope it would ease the contempt shown towards them, not to mention the obvious brutality that was building up inside the tent. He wanted to get the hell out of there.

'So you have. Open it!' ordered Olowoyo, the one Ijaw who had said nothing at all so far. The big man watched wide-eyed as the two men fumbled to open the briefcase, nervously but quite quickly nevertheless. The earlier furor shown to Carter a moment ago had disappeared as all attention focused on the money now being displayed with the urgency and efficiency of two men wanting to get the hell out of that tent as quick as they could.

'Count it!'

Olowoyo's voice was raised and the demand prompted the two Nigerians to empty the contents of the briefcase onto the muddy floor. With their hands visibly shaking, the two men started counting the bundles of hundred dollar bills before embarrassingly realizing that each was counting over the other; one counted faster than the other who counted louder! They stopped after losing themselves in the count and coyly looked up at the men standing before them. Their nerves would not hold out much longer. In the end they merely held up a stack of hundred dollar bills that were neatly bundled into quantities of five thousand and referred to the rest as being a multiple of what they had just shown them. The tribesmen quickly reckoned the amounts in their minds and accepted the amount to be half a million dollars, or close to that amount anyway. When he'd finished the mental math, Olowoyo continued to question the two men with even more vigor whilst Iteimor, in the meantime, edged himself slowly around towards the back of them. The two men remained kneeling, still frozen to the ground from their ordeal and even more afraid now that one of the Ijaw was behind them and out of sight. What was he doing?

'Where did this money come from?' Olowoyo demanded. He seemed disgusted and gave a dirty smirk that masked his true anger.

'It's from a private bank account, err . . . held by the company,' Ardelle sputtered in poor English. 'Put aside for the benefit of helping causes such as yours,' he hastily added. Ardelle, noticeably frightened, was now cowering even more. He felt he had too. He could not bring himself to say the truth; he did not want to further offend these men stood before him. He just did not know what to say. Every man inside the tent knew what the bank account was for. But that wasn't their purpose. They wanted Ardelle to tell them. They wanted him or Brandt to say the words themselves so that they would insult them. It would give them at least some kind of reason for what was to come. They knew exactly what the money was for and what it was meant to do. It was a fund for bribing the leaders of the Ijaw Youth Movement to stop their violent, or for that matter, non-violent protests against them. In the eyes of the oil companies, Brandt and Ardelle would have been heroes if they could broker a deal, or a bribe to be more accurate. Enough money would be required to get the Ijaw to refrain from their violent protests. To volunteer to take this trip into the very heart of the Niger Delta and meet with these people seemed a small risk to take compared to the multi-million dollar contracts their company would receive if they succeeded. They had grossly underestimated the feelings amongst the Ijaw. Even the vast amount of money laid out before them was a mistake. It would be welcome of course, but the source was wrong. It was from the oil companies and the Ijaw considered this was their money in the first place.

Laxrois realized what was coming and would remain calm. It may even be to his advantage, he reasoned and apart from slowly inching his right hand towards the trigger of the Minimi still swung low around his lower body and secured by a belt around his waist, he would do absolutely nothing. He would watch the fate of the two pitiful Nigerian's who were by now acting out their last few seconds of life. Sean Carter looked too at what was unfolding in front of him. His stomach turned and he was becoming nauseated. Any minute now he would feint from a combination of the intense humidity, heat and what was about to happen.

'And what is our cause?' asked Dowoonda, and with that simple question posed at them, both Gist and Allto realized what was happening. They actually had a nervous breakdown. The sweat poured from their foreheads. They were becoming disorientated and amazed with the speed of how the deteriorating situation had developed. Stunned speechless, they remained kneeling before the rugged and hatred face of Dowoonda. They profusely wiped their worried brows with dirt stained neckerchiefs that normally hung from inside their shirt pockets. Almost simultaneously they began to weep as fiction turned into reality for they indeed knew what was to come. Their most worrying fears were being realized. Gist tried to stumble to his feet in a vain attempt for mercy and a damp patch clearly appeared around the crotch of his trousers. They looked pathetic.

'What . . .,' stuttered Gist as he returned to a crouched position, he was too weak in the knees to stand. 'What do you mean? We have brought you money. Look!' he cried, pointing to the wads of cash on the dirty floor, the tears streaming from his eyes. It was a moving, last desperate plea from a man about to have his throat cut from behind. As he pronounced those last words he wouldn't know that a blade was flashing towards him. Blood oozed from a gaping wound in his neck where Iteimor's razor-sharp knife had cut across his throat with lightning speed. Allto's fate was the same. Being too slow to react upon seeing blood gush from his colleague's throat, the Nigerian practically let it happen. He never stood a chance. The startled men clutched at their throats and felt the gaping holes and blood that spewed between their fingers before they fell over. They lay wide-eyed and curled up on the ground with gargling sounds coming from the oxygen that hissed from their deflating lungs. The escaping air mingled with the blood from the open wounds and bubbled over the fleshy tissue. A wide gash could be seen on their badly shaven throats, pieces of tissue hung loosely from their necks. The increasing pool of blood was deepening with every dying spurt of escaping liquid and the muddied floor of the tent began to turn dark red. In an instant they were dead.

'*Operation Acid Rain* is only the beginning my friends,' boasted Iteimor, smiling at the money before them and not in the least perturbed by the mutilated bodies on the floor. Carter could not believe what had just unfolded before him. He looked towards Laxrois for reassurance that he himself would not be harmed in the same barbaric way. He need not have worried. Iteimor, who had by now wiped his knife clean on the clothes of the bloodied and dead men, gave the reassurance he so desperately needed.

'Do not be afraid, Mr. Carter. Take a look,' he said, opening his arms to display their bloodied work. 'These treacherous leeches, they are the scourges of our people. Scum! They are not like you or us. These people are greedy. They believe we would sell our people for money, forget the cause for a few thousand dollars.' The real Richard Hammond couldn't believe the mess he was in. He thought his time was surely up as Iteimor continued. 'That is what the oil companies and the government believe we would do,' he added. As he spoke he slowly turned his attention to Laxrois, once again his eyes menacingly transfixed on the Frenchman, who'd not flinched in the slightest at what had just happened. They knew he was no better. A mercenary who, every now and then, mingled amongst them, murdered for them, coordinated meetings and secret rendezvous' with whatever government official sought to remedy the appalling situation and yet, he cared not in the least about any of them. He was interested only in the large amounts of money he received for doing it. But they would not bring any harm to Laxrois as long as their campaign for justice continued. He was their only connection to the outside world and, as always, he delivered.

'Yes it is true, we will take their bribes. To a small extent the money will help relieve the pain and suffering of our people,' explained Iteimor who continued speaking without taking his eyes from Laxrois. 'But the price we pay is huge, Mr. Carter. The trash that you see before you deserve everything they got. They are naive thinking they could come here and give us money to stop our protests,' he declared. Carter gulped. If only they knew, he was no better! Iteimor carried on reeling off their grouses. 'They underestimate our feeling of hatred towards them. Cutting their throats was far too humane. They deserved a much slower and painful death. Like so many of our people suffer, Mr. Carter, living in poverty, disease ridden and helpless amongst all the pollution. Their bodies will end up where they came from. A reminder to the oil companies that we are no longer interested in their blood money. We want justice and fair play for our people.' His English was better than the others. He had at some time been well educated and he got his point across well. Carter felt guilty. He wished he'd never come. He was stunned and as speechless as Allto and Gist had been prior to being murdered.

Iteimor neared the two men on the floor and started to grind the right heel of his ragged and torn boot into the bloodied face of Allto, even though he was dead. It was obvious that the men he now shared a tent with had seen this type of barbarism many times before. Nobody but Carter was effected by the gruesome murders of the two oil workers. Talk about the Nigerians being naive! He now realized he must have been stark raving mad to do this. Even though Jeremy Isaacs sowed the seed to Darcy, it was really his, Richard Hammond's idea! The others must have thought him crazy and because of what had occurred right in front of his very eyes, he knew why!

But now he faced a massive dilemma. Was he as safe as they made out? Has that bastard Laxrois entered into a greater conspiracy with the Ijaw than he was led to believe? Would he double-cross him? How the fuck is Laxrois going to kill these people? He had promised he would. It was a deal. Share the money, two hundred and fifty grand each but they had to eliminate the source of the attacks made against ASEI, which he now realized was proving more difficult than Laxrois made it out to be!

It all seemed pie-in-in-the-sky at the moment. He was fighting for his life and they were trapped. Jesus! He had just witnessed the most horrific murders and they were completed without fuss and right in front of him. Are they thirsty for more blood? What's Laxrois thinking? He has to do something. Inside he was pleading with him. *Murder them for Christ sake!* He was willing the mercenary on. *Murder them. Go on. Go on!* That's what Carter was paying him to do. What else is going to happen next? How the fuck do we get out of this? Christ! Carter couldn't hold back, his whole body twitched and he just pissed himself.

The Ijaw leaders had by now become more active. According to the small talk amongst them there were things to do. Carter's mind was spiraling out of control and his heart pounded. There was no chance of any outside help. His employers knew only a fraction of this; he didn't tell them the entire plan, especially not about cutting a deal to share the money, that's for sure. Oh, how they would enjoy his predicament at this moment in time. How had he been so stupid? He kept telling himself this over and over. He had no idea that events would turn out like this. And so quick! Two murdered in an instant and now he stood face-to-face with the most ruthless of men, surrounded by bloodthirsty animals itching to flex their brutality towards him and the rest of their crew perhaps. All of these things were being spun around inside the muddled mind of Sean Carter and yet, more importantly, he knew he still faced the most mammoth task of all. For his own personal survival, and to a lesser extent to cover his tracks, how the fuck was he going to murder Laxrois? Carter once again became nauseated. Eyes wide and streaming and his stomach cramped in pain, he bent over and was sick, partly over the muddy, blood-filled floor and partly over the dead bodies of Gist and Allto. What the fuck was happening to him?

Olowoyo, Iteimor, and Dowoonda stopped what they were doing and looked on. They were pleased with what he had done. They thought he had purposely emptied his stomach over the two dead men and for that alone his actions were met with approval. Laxrois, however, pretended to look away. Whilst Carter's weakness disgusted him he realized it would open an opportunity for him to act. Constantly aware of where each man stood in the room he waited until he sensed they were at least within five or perhaps six feet of each other. At that moment, Iteimor and Dowoonda were busy foraging the dead bodies for more goodies, wallets, identification, credit cards and whatever else they could use for their campaign. Olowoyo had started to collect the money, placing the neat bundles of dollar bills in a woolen sack brought along for that reason; a briefcase would attract too much attention! Soon all three men were preoccupied with the same task. They concentrated on what they were doing. Their greed would prove to be the biggest mistake of their lives. In a minute all hell was going to break loose.

Carter was still keeled over, sick, phlegm and bile dripped from his mouth. Olowoyo had to be by the other two before Laxrois would make his move. He felt the adrenaline pumping the blood as it rushed into his veins, filling every muscle in his body as the build-up began. The sensation was electrifying. He knew just how Iteimor had felt the moment he'd decided what he was about to do. The urge for restraint was unbearable and it was all he could do to stop himself twitching with excitement. At that moment in time it was a feeling better than sex. Soon he was going to climax, getting off on what he was about to do but he had to decide before he lost it completely.

'Let us go, quickly! We are done here.' It was Olowoyo who urged the others to flee. 'Mr. Carter, you must come with us, c'mon get up,' he ordered. 'We have plenty to talk about,' he said. The money was gathered safely in the woolen sacks and now it was time for them to go elsewhere. Where they would go Laxrois had no idea but the opportunity was about to be lost. Carter was going to be a bloody problem as usual. He was positioned between the mercenary and the three men that were about to be spread over every square inch of the canvas tent behind them. Olowoyo was still too far away for Laxrois to deal with all three at once, nevertheless, it wasn't going to get any better than the present time and with his mind made up he made his move.

With lightning speed he spun on the spot and, with his right leg, kicked Carter in the side of the head sending him tumbling into the two blood-drenched corpses on the floor. At the same time he brought the lightweight Minimi around to point at his targets. The three Ijaw, instantly alerted by the limp body of Carter crashing to the ground, acted almost as quickly and spontaneously lifted their small pistols and started to aim at Laxrois. Unfortunately, unlike Laxrois, they were ill-trained in armed combat of this kind and would fire their weapons before the barrel aligned with their target. It was all too late as the Frenchman squeezed his index finger on the trigger, keeping it pressed firmly down as the bullets started spraying the left side of the tent at first before coming around and spraying Iteimor and Dowoonda full in the upper chest and face. Pieces of flesh were ripped off as the bullets tore into the clothing and skin. Blood spewed from their bullet-riddled bodies. Olowoyo, covered in blood from the two men being massacred in front of him, managed to fire off a couple of rounds in the direction of Laxrois, but the Frenchman had now gone to ground and rolled over to the right hand side of the tent. Another long blast from the automatic and once again the Ijaw man was sent flying backwards, this time actually through the thin canvas of the tent as flesh and blood splattered the shredded cloth. What followed was total carnage.

Outside, just as the crew were adjusting to getting somewhat more at ease after the partial withdrawal of the Ijaw tribesmen, the gunfire was instant and deafening as shots were fired indiscriminately by all concerned. It was retaliation from the noise of gunfire inside the tent. The crew dived for cover in the longer grass and returned fire at the tribesmen, who were by now well hidden in the forest fringes and more focused on their targets. Cries of agony filled the split second vacuum that formed from even the slightest lull of gunfire.

Carter, lying motionless and dazed on the floor was awakened by the ear-splitting noise of automatic, machinegun fire. The brutal kick from Laxrois was merely meant to get him from out of the line of fire but it was delivered with such ferocity that a three-inch gash was oozing blood from his left cheek. Part of the cheekbone was exposed. His head was thumping and the American was barely conscious. Through glazed eyes he could see the large frame of Laxrois as he started to rip open one side of the tent and make ready his escape. He could taste the blood of the murdered Nigerians, which covered his face and upper body. He had no strength remaining and he was too numbed to be afraid. Still in shock he once again looked up at the only moving object inside the tent. It was Laxrois, still frantically slashing at the tent with a knife and edging back as he slowly peered out at the carnage going on outside. He had hold of two woolen sacks. He had the money. As he struggled to gain consciousness, Carter fumbled the ground and to his muted surprise found the handgun that had belonged to Olowoyo! It had been thrown forward as a volley of bullets struck him. In and out of consciousness for only seconds, he feebly held it in his hands, pointed the barrel at Laxrois and fired. The last thing he saw as he lost complete consciousness was the big man falling backwards from a single gunshot to his back.

Chapter 7

Two Years Later—New York—USA

If the consequences surrounding these events were not so dire it could have been a scene from a family comedy show. The floorboards creaked as a middle-aged man carefully crept across the wooden landing that led from the bedroom to the stairs of the building. The other occupants of the house were sound asleep and the harder he tried not to disturb them, the louder the noise seemed to echo from the loose boards.

'Shit!' he cursed under his breath, trying desperately to maintain the night peace. The crack-like sound of another timber was just loud enough to break the silence and get the attention of the family pet, a black Labrador that was by now awake with pricked ears, waiting in anticipation like a coiled spring. Any minute now, he thought, knowing what was coming but trying his damnedest to ensure it didn't. The man held a silent prayer as he took another step towards the stairs. A louder creak followed the downward pressure of his foot, which was enough to send an affirmative signal to the dog. By means of that precise indicator the animal sat upright before taking off at a racing pace towards the direction of the stairs. The dog picked up even more speed along the hall approaching the bottom of the risers.

Upon seeing his master for the first time that morning the Labrador flew, running up the stairs with such ferocity that he missed every other third step and reached the top of the landing in under a couple of seconds. With his tongue at the ready and tail wagging, the dog pounced up to greet his owner and proceeded to lick him to death. Desmond Haynes compared it to being bowled over by something rolling down a hill, only this time he was bowled over by something rolling up a hill, his beloved Labrador. It was as if the dog had been sentenced to death and the only way to get a pardon was to pour as much affection onto the occupants of that house as was physically possible. The animal did just that, every time, every morning, and to every one of them. It did not in the least matter to the mutt that it was still dark outside, but it mattered to everyone else! Needless to say he was not man's best friend at that moment in time. All hell broke loose.

'Desmond!' a woman's voice could be heard coming from the bedroom.

'Go to sleep, it's only the dog!' he whispered back, still reeling from the impact. Her response was typical and loud.

'Bullshit! You get yor big, black ass back in this bed. This instant, y'ear me?' she wasn't a woman to be messed with judging by the tone of her voice. Her black, Louisiana drawl emphasized the slang and the feeling.

'Go to sleep woman, the dog must've been disturbed by something outside,' he lied, pondering her remark about his big ass. She had a cheek!

A light went on and a hefty-looking black woman appeared from the bedroom tying a chord around her dressing gown as she made her way towards the fracas. The small landing was filled with her large frame the instant she came out of the room. Once again the dog went into action. Same routine, leaping up at her from almost four feet away and eager to show his affection to yet another unsuspecting occupant of the house. It's at times such as these that a dog needs to understand what is going on in life. The second he got to within arms reach of the woman, and whilst he was still in full flight, she quickly caught the unsuspecting mutt by the scruff of the neck and just held him there, suspending him in mid flight. The dog just wriggled like hell. Neither human being flinched at this strange and outrageous treatment of the dog. The animal just hung there for several seconds before she let go her grip, which allowed the dog to scurry off back down the stairs trying to come to terms with what had just happened. They carried on the conversation.

'Look, honey,' she said, a look of desperation spread across her worried face but her tone now much softer. 'Come back to bed. This is doin you no good. It's four-thirty in the morning. C'mon, come back to bed an I'll make some coffee,' she said, clipping her words. 'We can talk som. It'll do you good, there's no rush an besides, I'm n'all that tired. We can play 'round a little. Naw what am saying? That'll work won't it, honey?' she said, pretending to be overly shy, tantalizing even. She then started to loosen her dressing gown to reveal what she considered to be some chic, sexy night attire. Being well over two hundred and fifty pounds, it wasn't a pretty sight. She teased him anyway, pulling down a strap and exposing her large breasts, one of which had already been half-hanging out through the low-cut side of her nightdress anyway. She knew Desmond liked her breasts and would normally be quick to react. But not today, he had other things on his mind. That wasn't going to work she soon realized, her emotions dropping to the floor. Instead, he instantly became uncharacteristically shy and turned away, smirking with embarrassment at the sight. She always did that, he thought, but she meant well. His wife, Suzanne, was a good woman and sex she told him took a man's mind off whatever it was that troubled him. She was right of course, but it was the way she went about it. Even at the slightest sign of him being troubled she got her breasts out and put them on display, cupping them in her hands simply to turn him on, or so she said. The only trouble was she did it in such a way that he half expected to see next week's State Lottery numbers tattooed on the nipples. He wished they were.

'Its okay, Sissy,' he replied almost reassuringly and using her nickname. 'You go back to sleep. I'll take Guinness for a stroll as soon as it's light.' The black Labrador flinched and stood nervously to attention, he was safer downstairs.

'Desmond, I'm worried, honey,' she confessed. Her old friends, trouble and anxiety, were never far away these days, it was permanently stamped across her face and it showed. She covered herself and walked towards him. There were tears in her eyes, he noticed. It had been another sleepless night for the middle-aged black man and there'd been tears too. There was no denying the sagging flesh that hung below his eyes. Trying to keep his worries to himself was becoming more and more difficult. Nevertheless, he did so with grace. He held out his arms to comfort his wife.

'There's no need to worry, Suzanne. We'll be fine, just fine. You wait and see.' Desmond put his arms around her as he spoke. He was tender and his words seemed comforting enough, at least for the time being, but she sensed the hollowness in his voice. Desmond, she thought, it will not be fine. She knew in her heart of hearts it would not be fine and now she was suffering and, even worse, her man was suffering. Carefully and delicately he began to rub his large hands across her back. He could feel the sobbing motion as he continued to soothe her, sensing the tears rolling down her cheeks.

'What'll we do, Desmond? What'll happen? What's there for us? The children, God bless them. The house an all. I'm so afraid, honey,' she whispered in between sobs.

'Don't cry, Sissy, it'll sort itself out, we'll sort it out. These things have a way of sorting themselves out, you'll see.' He continued comforting her for a few minutes longer before slowly walking her back into the bedroom and insisting she tried to get some more sleep.

At the first sign of light and with Suzanne once again feigning a sound sleep upstairs with the kids, Desmond Haynes put on his waxed *Barber* jacket and *Hunter* wellington boots from the outhouse and proceeded to walk outside with Guinness. His beloved dog was on a lead and livelier than ever. They looked the part. It was raining as he strolled down the short drive of the detached house. Beyond the gates and to the south, the well-lit road was coming alive as the *Apple* slowly awoke, even at that ridiculous hour! The traffic would increase by the minute, early commuters desperate to get to work and beat the rush. If he turned right he could get into Manhattan in fifteen to twenty minutes by car without too much fuss. To the left and towards the Hudson River, the road he walked was connected to a deserted street that led to some waste ground where Guinness would be allowed off the lead; playtime for an hour, at least. Desmond would watch the dog go about his ritual routine, chasing pigeons, seeking out small birds in long grass, smelling a couple of wrecked cars, cocking his leg and squatting wherever he felt like. All the while Desmond would think of nothing else other than his current predicament. It was a strange sensation. It came over him all too regular. An ever-present feeling of loneliness seemed to surround him wherever he went. It was following him with a vengeance. Even Clove Lakes Park, a beautiful area of Staten Island where he and Suzanne chose to live with the kids forevermore all those years ago, looked different this morning. He'd felt more of a stranger each time he walked from his home. Each day was slow, and each day was taking its toll.

'*Just passing by on a brief visit*,' he muttered, feeling sorry for himself. He no longer saw his surroundings as beautiful any more, or as anything come to think of it. His once cherished feeling for the place was deadened long ago. *I do not belong here*, he began thinking all too frequently. Stopping for a moment longer than Guinness was prepared to wait, he looked at the *For Sale* sign nailed to a stake that was hammered into the near side of the lawn, closest to the road. The reality hit home. The Lab' also seemed to sense something and no longer continued hopping and jostling in his usual, playful manner. Instead, the canine began chewing and pulling at the lead around his neck, unaware of his masters anguish, the sadness and worry he constantly tried to fight. It was no good. His determination too was diminishing. The fight was feeble and seemed to no avail. Events in Nigeria came flashing back all too frequently and that alone had caused him to go almost insane and now, on top of all that, he had other problems.

Nearer home he kept looking at the real estate sign in the front of the house, which was beginning to lean from the ongoing battering of wind and rain. It was dilapidating slowly but surely from the elements and it would only be a matter of time before it too fell apart altogether. It just about summed up Desmond's predicament at that moment in time. He was losing his will to continue and for that reason, he was losing his battle. The past weeks and months had been the most stressful of his life. Yet, no more than eighteen months earlier he was gainfully employed in a good job, well paid with excellent prospects of promotion. But for now all that had gone in one foul sweep. He had been dismissed. Fired through no fault of his own, or so he believed. He felt betrayed, deceived. The feeling of being brutally cut from the right to work was humbling. That it happened in the prime of his life made him bitter and he was worried sick. The feeling had not left him since that day almost eighteen months ago. He thought of Suzanne, the kids; Clive and Vivian. Not for the first time he cried as Guinness pulled him on his way, the tears mingling with the raindrops that landed on his face as he walked. Then Nigeria came flooding back again as it so often did. Images of burning and dead bodies flashed in front of him. The panic-attacks started and he was afraid, he was desperate.

Guinness, as usual, was first through the door shaking his entire body back and forth in double time, ridding his black, shorthaired coat of the moisture that had slowly gathered from the light, morning drizzle. Desmond, much the better after his walk, quickly followed with an old towel in hand and grabbed the dog but not before the floor, a small sideboard, several coats, and the inside walls of the utility room were speckled with brown stains where Guinness had shaken himself dry.

'Son-of-a-bitch, stupid mutt does that every time!' moaned Desmond. 'Goddamn dog does it on purpose, I'm sure!'

'It's no use talking to him like that, Pop,' a young voice shouted out from the adjoining kitchen. It was fatal and enough to send Guinness into action; another familiar voice! Off he darted before Desmond could say another word. Clive, the eldest son, was sitting down at the breakfast table and leaning over ready in preparation for the welcome he was about to get.

'Whoa, Guinness, steady on there!' The young boy grabbed the pet around the neck and grappled with him, friendly. The youngster began rubbing his pal all over in the most affectionate way. The dog responded by trying his hardest to bite at him but as the whole family knew only too well, there was little danger of any damage being done from the dog's soft bite. Clive just laughed at the dog's feeble attempts.

'Hi ya good buddy,' he said. The dog had soon rolled over on to his back and spread his hind legs akimbo. With eyes closed, a clenched like look on his face and his tongue hanging out he just laid there, unashamed whilst the youngster continued to play and tickle his belly. 'Hey, Pop! You know you're wasting your time talking to Guinness like that,' the young boy shouted across the room towards his father, who was struggling to get his wellington boots off.

'Say wha?' replied Desmond, his Jamaican accent clipping the words short in pretty much similar fashion to Suzanne.

'Shouting at Guinness like that, it's not going to get you anywhere. He can't understand what you're saying, so why say it?'

'Ugh,' replied his father, wellington boots flying through the outhouse. That's all he needed. All of a sudden there was an animal psychiatrist in the family. 'Oh yeah, says who?'

'I do, there's no way he can tell what you're saying, Pops. He's a dog, remember?'

'Well, how about he gets to learn just a few sentences. Like,—there's no goddamn walk tomorrow!—Uh? Or, here's a good one,—there's no dog food left!—That'll bring his English up to speed. What'd ya think?' he teased. 'Perhaps he'll understand the next time he decides to decorate the outhouse with his big hairy ass that I ain't joking no more!' Clive laughed at his father's sense of humor, especially when he swore mildly. His father always had something funny to say and most often than not he swore, but not around Sissy, she'd have something to say about that for sure.

'You wouldn't do that!' said his son in mild disbelief. He'd noticed his father's wry smile in a flash, just before he turned away after saying it. The boys had no idea what had happened to their dad. He hadn't been to work for some time. Suzanne had told them that Pops, as they called him, was taking some time out. There were no questions from their children. If that's what mamma said, then that's what Pops was doing.

Peter Nutty

'So, what do you say to a dog that just decides to do whatever he wants, young man?' asked Desmond continuing the play.

'Well . . . all the dog hears is, well . . . gobbledygook. You know, just a load of garbled sounds coming from your mouth. You might as well be a Martian for all he cares. Then, all of a sudden you expect him to know and understand every word you say. Gee dad, it took us nearly five years before we could talk proper and . . . . even longer to understand grownups and . . . . well . . . we still don't understand you!' said the kid and laughed.

'You mean you can talk, but . . . can't understand what I say? Well . . . well . . . my . . . my! At the ripe old age of twelve. Wow, I never!' his father just walked past, expressionless, jokingly shaking his head in amazement. Clive just stared back, watching him as he left the room. The young boy was bewildered. Meanwhile, the morning post was being scrutinized and arranged in some form of order by Suzanne, which hardly ever stayed that way. Letters went missing almost at random in their house.

'There's a letter from N'Orleans, honey. Looks like it's from that law dude, Hey! Cock!' she shouted out. 'Bouts time too. They's bin messin us black folk about 'nough,' she said and quickly handed him the letter before returning to the kitchen where she'd been preparing breakfast earlier. Guinness immediately rolled back over and stood to attention at the sight of her. He was suspicious of the person that had stopped him in mid-air a few hours previously. If the dog could have swore he would have. Instead, he paused a while, making sure nothing else was going to happen to him before rubbing his nose back into Clive's lap for more attention.

The combined smell of strong coffee along with bacon and eggs drifted from the kitchen and filled every downstairs room in the house. Desmond sniffed the trail towards the general direction of the kitchen, towards the sizzling food whilst looking at the letter in unison. It was addressed to him personally. He seemed to weigh the contents as if he could have decided its value before opening the white, plain envelope. The bundles of documents contained inside were pulled out and again examined carefully in his hand. There was a neatly typed cover letter and several other bits and pieces, which were half-pulled out as well; they were stapled to the covering letter.

'It's not, Hey! Cock!' said Desmond angrily as he read the correspondence before him. 'It's, Heycock, Sissy! Heycock!' repeated Desmond, correcting her in frustration. 'Dumb son of a black bitch!' he shouted across to Suzanne in mild disgust. He frequently called her by her nickname and he frequently shook his head in annoyance. Sissy knew exactly what she'd said, and she meant it. She didn't know what exactly it was Lawyer's did, but she did know they were not trusted and because of that they were disliked by most black folk for one reason or another and so that was good enough for her. She neither trusted, nor liked them either!

The letter heading at the top left-hand side of the first page read, *'Lance Heycock & Associates, S.C. Law Office.'* Their trades were described by lettering on the right-hand side, where the words, *'Attorneys and Counselors,'* was typed in green, bold, italics and edged in a fine black outline for full effect. The regional address, zip code and contact telephone numbers followed this.

'Pretty fancy, must get paid too much,' Desmond muttered as he continued to follow his nose, which brought him straight into the kitchen. He sat down holding a pair of large spectacles ready to read the letter, which he now had placed before him on the kitchen table. The contents of the first page briefly informed their client that an informal meeting was needed to address the case proper. The preliminaries would be dealt with. Following that, statements would have to be sought from witnesses willing to testify in Court, *should it go that far.* Desmond nearly spat on the kitchen table. He disapproved of the wording used. *If,* was not an option in his mind, *when,* would be more appropriate. There were other trivial matters, which was all jargon to him. Then, a long paragraph related to pre-trial discovery was explained; this would follow pending the strength of their case. If they were successful, another shake of the head, the hearing proper for his pending lawsuit, Haynes versus Advanced Strategic Energy Inc., would be planned to be heard in the New Orleans Parish, Civil Court, sometime in June. There was no mention of whether or not this would be allowed by the court mind you. The lawsuit, which had to be filed with the County Court well before then, would be for—*Wrongful dismissal and racial discrimination.* They would contest that ASEI had contravened, again he didn't understand the jargon—Article VII of the Civil Rights Act of 1964, and then the appropriate sections that were violated followed. It would most likely last for approximately four days, said Lance Heycock, his would-be appointed attorney.

Desmond then read the much smaller print, especially since it described the payment method. Heycock & Associates would be paid by, *charging lien.* This entitled the company, after suing somebody on a client's behalf, the right to be paid twenty percent of the proceeds from the lawsuit, if there are any, before their client, Desmond, received those proceeds. Desmond frowned but it was the best thing under the circumstances. He had no money to put up front. There were further instructions for him to contact Heycock's secretary at his office in Port Arthur, Texas. They needed to make arrangements. He would be required to go to the Texan's office sometime in May where he would help plan the lawsuit and identify any witnesses that could testify to his claims. This also included pre-trial activities where settlement efforts could be discussed, but Desmond ignored that section completely. In Lance Heycock's experience, both parties settled almost all of the civil lawsuits of this kind out-of-court, amicably, but this wasn't mentioned in the letter.

There would be no out-of-court settlement. Desmond had made his mind up. There just wouldn't be enough money on the table. A whole bunch of other documents were attached to the attorney's letter. Explanations of the legal jargon that technically outlined the case, the proceedings and customs to use when in Court, especially those relating to, *His Honor*, Judge, Roland Hastings. Also, a template was attached to allow him to enter a list of names to be summoned, for one reason or another, during any preliminary hearing. Finally, there were a couple of small brochures giving directions to get to the Law Offices in Port Arthur and also the courthouse in New Orleans. A list of hotels, etc., that may help him upon arriving in both places was attached. Desmond was once again impressed and said so but as usual in the Haynes' residence, nobody was listening.

Amongst the names he would list in the contents of the witness register would be me, his trusted friend, Doug Archer. I'd previously offered to appear as a character witness. Desmond smiled, got up from the table and walked over to where Sissy was frying all kinds of fatty bacon, sausage and eggs; good heart attack stuff. He discretely pinched her buttocks.

'I'm going to phone Doug a little later on. He'll need to know what's happening,' he told her.

'Oh, leave that man alone. He don't need no dumb black man phonin im up all this time!'

'Just making sure he's still okay to help me out. You know me, Sissy,' said Desmond defending his black ass! At that moment, Vivian, the younger son came into the room and saw what his father had just done to his mother. The youngster, not slow to miss an opportunity, did the same and pinched his momma's buttock upon Desmond's departure. He gave the impression that his father was still doing it.

The Last Hangman

'Ooh!' she purred. 'Later, honey, later. When dem boys have gon outa play,' responded Sissy in the only way she knew how, with excitement and passion. Both Clive and Vivien began to laugh as their mother turned and realized just who it was that had pinched her buttocks.

'Hey! whas' goin on ere? Whas' appenin? You boys bin playin me up for days. You gon get yor ass whipped. Now git out ma kitchen.' With that said the boys fled as fast as they could, laughing hysterically along the way at their mothers' reaction. Desmond looked on as they sped past with Sissy hot in pursuit. 'Dem boys gonna get they asses whipped, Desmond! I swear! You hear me? They's gonna get em whipped one o these days!' Desmond just continued looking at her with a stupid looking frown, wondering what the hell had just gone wrong in the thirty seconds since he had just left the kitchen!

At precisely six-thirty that afternoon Desmond picked up the phone and dialed the international number for England, followed by the area code for Dorset, and then the six digit number that would try to connect him to my home address.

'Hello!' It was my wife, Julie who answered the phone. Desmond briefly greeted her and enquired about her well-being and of the children? Julie informed him that they were fine. I was not at home she quickly explained. Then she blabbered on moaning about how I was, *the husband she didn't have*!

'I was still at the oil refinery. Surprise! Surprise!' she chirped with a high-pitched tone and nearly going into song. Julie was being sarcastic and Desmond sensed it. He wondered if she had in fact been drinking such was the woman's silly attitude. He made his mind up that she had. He knew Julie from old. There was no love lost between her and me. It was only a matter of time before we split up or made up. Either way, Desmond didn't care. He quickly told her he would phone me at work and apologized for disturbing her. She said it was no problem. She'd been disturbed most of her life, she had to be after being married to me all these years she told him abruptly! Upon hearing the way she was talking, Desmond was convinced that she had been drinking, but on the contrary, she was totally sober and before Desmond tried to end the call she asked him if he could pass on a message, if he managed to get hold of me that is; something she could never quite manage to do by all accounts! Desmond naturally agreed and waited for the message. Julie spoke to Desmond in a clipped voice that seemed rather calm considering the context of the message.

'Could you tell, Doug that his dinner is in the bin and that she is not prepared to skivvy and cook and wait around in the house for him all day under the false pretence of him coming home. When he gets home, *no!*' she quickly corrected herself. *If,* he gets home, *she* would be out with one of her many boyfriends!' she told him and then said *goodbye*, quickly putting the phone down before he had chance to reply.

'She's kinda mad I guess,' he muttered to nobody and put the phone receiver down before slowly walking back into the lounge.

'Sissy,' he shouted out. 'You ain't the only one who's having a bad day, honey!' Then Desmond did something he'd not done in months. He laughed at what Julie had said and now it was Suzanne's turn to look on in disbelief. It had been a long time since she'd seen her husband laugh and it gave her hope.

'Knowing my pal, he *wouldn't give a shit,* as those black folks say,' said Desmond still smiling and Suzanne agreed. She knew me only too well.

* * *

There were plans to be made and both of us would have a lot of work to do. It had been almost eighteen months since his departure from ASEI. That time had not been properly utilized and Desmond conceded that most of it had been wasted. He could have been searching for former dissatisfied employees willing to testify against his old company—former colleagues, those who had a genuine and sincere grievance of some kind or other against the oil giant. If it was discriminatory, then so much the better, said Lance following his first telephone conversation to discuss the pending lawsuit. There was no way of telling what type of reaction he would get. Some of the former employees he knew but most he did not. The response to-date was mixed. He hadn't a clue how to go about getting prospective witnesses. He thought that would be Lance's job. And it would be eventually, but that would just take even longer—Lance had told him that, genuinely. *Just make the call and get a feel for their willingness to testify,* he had instructed Desmond in a rather motivating way. He would need help though and hoped it was coming in the form of, *Yours Truly.* Yes, we would soon be busy, very busy indeed.

* * *

He knew it from memory and calmly re-dialed the international number that would get me at work. The digits clicked away in the earpiece of the receiver as the call was being connected. At the same time, Desmond looked in the drawer located underneath the small, wooden table that housed the telephone. He wanted something to write on. He took out a small writing pad to make notes of our conversation. He knew I was likely to make suggestions and he had learned by now to take notes. *I'd be my usual pedantic self.* As he turned the pages he was left momentarily saddened. The name, *Brandt Allto*, numbed him a little. It was scribbled along the middle of the page of a small writing pad and a question mark was heavily penned alongside. The note had brought back memories for Desmond. Just then he was reminded of another close friend that he'd almost become to forget. Allto was somebody he'd worked closely with in Nigeria. He'd drowned during a fishing trip somewhere in the Niger Delta. Desmond refused to believe it for some time until in the end he had to accept it. His denial was attributed to shock; ASEI had told him that. It was a natural way for a human being to react, they said. He underwent mild counseling at the time but, nevertheless, Desmond thought otherwise. Allto, a senior accounts manager with one of the contract companies providing all sorts of parts that were required to maintain their Nigerian operation, simply hated the water. He had defiantly refused to travel to several offshore or swamp-based facilities whenever Desmond had asked him to. Strange then that he died from drowning, he thought. Had he been kidnapped? Or even worse, murdered! *No way Des*, he reasoned and laughed at his stupidity. Who would remotely want to murder Allto, a charming man with absolutely no political motives or enemies whatsoever?

Desmond dismissed the idea and reprimanded himself at the time for allowing his mind to run away with itself. Anyway, he had enquired vigorously within ASEI and also the Nigerian government with whom Allto had dealings with constantly. He finally gave up when, following a request made by Desmond to the American Ambassador in Nigeria to follow-up on Allto's death, a senior executive with ASEI forcefully told him to refrain from asking any further, embarrassing questions. It was not unusual for ASEI to reward several of their sub-contractors and government officials alike for their *services*. Desmond knew that certain *rewards* were given to high-ranking government officials in return for lucrative oil contract awards. He had no problem with that and had even been part of many organized trips to accompany those officials on those very expensive occasions. But now, he was interfering and putting their relationship in jeopardy, said the high ranking official and Desmond reluctantly agreed with him. With that, he let it lie and involuntarily believed the cause of Allto's death was that of drowning. Besides, he was preoccupied with defending allegations of gross negligence that had cropped up not long after Allto's death. Whilst he had the inclination to enquire further, he was more concerned about his own welfare and that of keeping his job. The phone began to ring in Desmond's ear. He ripped off the note, screwed it up and threw it in the bin under the table. Allto was history.

Chapter 8

DORSET, ENGLAND IS A BEAUTIFUL part of the British Isles with lovely country villages littered along a coastline boasting miles and miles of superb, crystal-clear water that lapped sandy beaches. It is a haven for tourists, retirees and the elderly and, therefore, very popular throughout the year. It would be the last place you would expect to see an oil refinery. It was late in the afternoon when I closed my bloodshot eyes, put my head in my hands and slowly dragged them down over my face as if trying to pull the skin to below my chin. Even after all this time the events in Nigeria were never far from my thoughts. The nightmares were getting few and far between but the memories of all those burnt and dead bodies following the explosions would never leave me. I still saw people crying out for help!

I yawned before opening my watery eyes and continued to look at the pile of paperwork neatly placed to one side of a wooden desk that hadn't seen polish in years. The desk itself was pinched from a retired general manager and must have looked pucker at one time. The rest of the room was slightly bare of furniture or fittings. A map of the world occupied one wall and a number of oddly, color-coded year-planner charts, which were out of date, decorated another. It was Sunday and I had promised Julie, my wife of twenty years, that I would only spend a couple of hours in the office. I would be home for lunch around one-o-clock. I'm well used to working unsociable hours but it was something that I was now beginning to regret more and more as I got older.

When I was appointed to the position of operations manager at the age of forty-five I was overwhelmed by such an important and prestigious post and although the responsibility was daunting, I considered it a challenge; it was the biggest refinery in Europe. Now, after only a year in the job I think of other far more important things in life. Right now it's the kids. I had not seen them in months, my teenage son and daughter. At the last time of asking they were doing very well in University. I think? I was beginning to miss them immensely as time goes on though and, at this precise moment, I am overcome with guilt. As the guilt inside me turned to frustration and then slowly turned into a feeling of emptiness, they somehow mean everything.

Working overseas coupled with longer hours with each passing year had taken its toll. I have become a visitor in what could once only have been described as a very caring, family home. There was plenty of love and we all listened and shared in everyone's triumphs and disappointments, and we shared each other's problems. As my workload became heavier, the longer hours became even longer and the stress built-up. I merely switched off more and more until, in the end, it was all I could do to speak or give even the slightest acknowledgement to those at home. Nobody had problems except me. Stupid! It wasn't that I didn't love them either. I did, very much, but that's how it is for thousands of families under similar circumstances of my kind. After a while they refrained from telling me the trivial things and then hardly told me anything at all. Before any of us knew it we had drifted apart, living separate lives. The children did whatever they did, I did too much of whatever I did as usual, and neither one of us ever knew what the others were doing. My marriage had suffered almost the same fate. There were times when I missed my wife too but not anymore. Those days had long gone. A dysfunctional family I think to myself, although it wasn't all bad; at least these thoughts kept me from mulling over events in Nigeria.

Coming to my senses before the subsequent and more traumatic soul-searching began in earnest, I heard a noise. That short period of self-pity was nipped in the bud by a familiar voice.

'Hey, Doug, how're you doing?' I recognize the voice and quickly re-engaged in the business that lay stacked and idle on my desk, keen not to be seen daydreaming. Some aspects of my career were based on bluff but I don't believe anyone knew that yet! I intended to keep it that way.

'Frank, you frightened the life out of me! I'm fine, how are you?' I ask. If it weren't for bad luck I'd have no luck at all, especially considering the underlying tones that were sure to surface when the general manager decides to put in a weekend appearance!

'You know me, Doug.' he answered and flexed his body the way unfit, old-aged fitness freaks do in the belief that you'll be convinced they're in good nick for their age.

'And how is Linda?' I ask, ignoring his floor routine but not forgetting his *charming* wife. I was playing the ultra-polite managers rule; the unwritten one!

'Sends her love, Doug,' he lied. 'You and Julie should come around and visit us more often. She thinks you're getting a bit of a miserable old git in your old age!' he joked, playing the same game. He probably meant it though. I wished I could have responded likewise. I needed another two job grades to talk in that manner.

'Linda's right. I am a miserable old bugger, Frank.' I admitted, just to please him. 'What brings you in here?' I ask with a smile and waited for the real reason for him coming in this Sunday morning. It wasn't long in coming either, he must have had a golf tee booked.

'I just happened to hear about the fuss being made over the *pond*, Doug.'

'Oh, what fuss is that, Frank?' I replied, deciding to play dull.

'C'mon Doug, cut the crap. None of this *don't know what you're on about*, stuff! We're friends, remember? I haven't got time for bullshit. I had a call from New York yesterday, so why not tell me what the hell is going on?' he answered back, looking straight at me. He was right. I was just in protective mode. Not for the first time in our relationship, Frank was being sincere. He was as genuine a guy you could wish to meet, but he was a company man through and through and could be a ruthless old bastard when he needed to be and for that reason, I always edged on the safe side. Who could tell what his mood was?

'I suppose it's the *Desmond thing*, right?' I replied, coming clean.

'Yeah, the *Desmond thing*,' he confirmed.

'I just think the company is screwing him, Frank. You know the guy, his pedigree. Look what he's done for us,' I offer, referring to nothing in particular.

'Doug, there is no way on earth you're going to give evidence against this company. I will not allow you to do that,' he said sternly. When Frank said that it caught me off guard, how on earth did he know my intentions? Only Desmond and Lance Heycock, the attorney, knew of my pending help!'

'It's not *against* the company, Frank. It's *for* Desmond,' I corrected him.

'Don't play with words, Doug,' Frank warned me. 'It's the same thing. You know what I'm saying.'

'It's *not* the same thing, Frank,' I contested. 'If you think that giving evidence for Desmond relates to sledging the company, you're wrong,' I argued. The conversation had got off to the worst possible start.

'Now, listen to me, Doug,' said the GM, edging closer, 'I'm here to ask you as a friend,' he went on to add with the same sincerity. 'Don't say a word, and don't even get involved. It'd be a damn crazy thing to do.'

'C'mon, Frank. You're overreacting. I'm not going to say *anything* about the company,' I reiterated, feeling uncomfortable by being seated during the heated conversation. I couldn't argue properly sat on my backside so promptly stood up and started to pace the room before continuing. Frank didn't budge an inch at this. 'It'll just be about Desmond, a character reference for goodness sake!' I continued in vain and still a bit off guard that he knew I was getting involved at all. 'What's the big deal?' I asked him, frustrated at what was unfolding in front of me. 'He's a true friend, Frank. We should give him a break.'

'Friend?' he quickly argued. 'What's the big deal? Doug, I'm your goddamn friend *and* I'm the big deal all in one. Listen to me. Watch my lips for Christ sake! Don't go down that road, Doug. I'm telling you. You're on thin ice my friend.'

'Oh we're still friends are we?' I argued mildly, wondering just how strong the relationship was. 'What about my other friends, Frank? What about the guy we just shafted, can you answer that?' Frank ignored me and walked to the window. He looked despairingly out of the dirty glass to the huge refinery outside and slowly shook his head, then sighed; it was because of my stubbornness, I presumed.

'It'd be suicidal for your career, young man,' he then warned me quietly. 'Why else would a VP phone me late in the evening to enquire about this, Doug? It's gotta be bad news,' he told me with all the confidence of somebody who was right. Anyway, it was too predictable I decided; a career stopping cannonball was being fired across my bows. 'You won't be going any further, Doug!' he repeated, putting it rather bluntly. Frank was giving me ample notice but as usual, I wasn't listening.

'Well, perhaps I don't want to go any further,' I confessed sheepishly.

'Oh, that's a new one on me. When did you decide that?'

'C'mon Frank. Leave it. I'm tired and a little frustrated by all this. And besides, talk is cheap right now.' It was not going to be my day. Frank had decided against leaving it and went on the attack.

'Too goddamn right talk is cheap. Who was there for you when you wanted out of Nigeria, Doug?'

'That's not fair, Frank. We got badly screwed up out there, Desmond too, if you cared to remember?' I reminded him, thankful I'd thought about something good to say about Desmond. It was a bad move.

'Remember? Remember? I can tell you what I *do* remember, Doug. I remember the goddamn place was blown to fucking bits!' he retorted, now angrier than I'd ever seen him before. 'And don't think for one minute that anybody's forgotten what you and Desmond were doing there when the place went into orbit either!'

'If you're trying to say something, Frank, why not go ahead and say it,' I shouted directly at him. Well, he was trying to say something and all too quickly he did. The innuendoes were soon turned into accusations.

'Oh, perhaps you *had* forgotten, how convenient! Two senior guys, *one of them in charge*,' he emphasized before continuing. 'Getting drunk in the bar while the place was blown up isn't exactly what ASEI would call professional, Doug! Now, ask me again what I remember?' he said accusingly and staring me out at the same time.

'What's that supposed to mean, Frank? I was merely standing in for Tom,' I reminded him, overly defensive now. 'It didn't matter who was in charge, you know we had no control over what went on,' I replied angrily but also realizing for the first time that ASEI had quietly held Desmond and me partly responsible for the events in Nigeria, although nothing was ever mentioned in the debrief following our return. It was a massive blow.

'You know what I mean, don't act stupid with me a second time, Doug.'

'Go screw yourself!' I replied. My vocabulary shocked me but made little impact on Frank.

'I'm not asking you anymore, Doug. I'm telling you. Leave it alone. Desmond will sort it out by himself. He's tough enough. Don't leave me without options, Doug.'

'Are you threatening me? Cos if you are you damn well picked the wrong person to fight, Frank,' I told him. I was livid and under the circumstance I probably over-reacted. I hadn't shaped up to the GM before and found myself in a new territory. He started it and by God I was about to finish it. It felt good, I think!

'Yes, I am threatening you,' he told me straight and all too simplistic. 'Then, when I've finished threatening you, those all-important *eggheads* in New York will threaten you even more! They'll put you through the mill and if it gets that far you're going to be history, Doug. Understand?' he asked, not in the slightest way looking for an answer. 'And while we're at it, don't forget who you're fucking talking to!' he added, red-faced. I wasn't bothered about the threats from him or anybody else but the fact that he flexed his authority in all of this made me see red too.

'Oh my, we're back on official status are we? I was wondering when you'd turn back into the general fucking manager again?' I mouthed back at him. 'I had a friend here a minute ago. Where'd he go, Frank?' I subconsciously tried to pinch myself. What was I saying? I was a crazy bastard. He's the general manager I was reminding myself. Anybody sitting ringside would also remind me of that fact too, and also that Frank, in his own peculiar way, was still indeed a good friend, but again I wasn't listening. The GM closed in on me. His face was still red and he was pissed off. Apart from carrying the can for Nigeria it was also obvious that New York were not happy with the situation. I was an idiot. That much I could tell. It was Frank's brief to make them happy. I had undermined his authority and pretty soon, assuming I didn't get involved, I would have another position in the company. If I did get involved, God knows? I didn't care.

'Take this as an informal warning, Doug,' said Frank finally trying to compose himself; after all he was the manager of one of the biggest businesses in Europe and nobody should argue with him because of it he must have reasoned.

'I'll put it in my diary, Frank.' I replied sarcastically and having the last word. With that he left. My career with the company was over. Losing it when I was working overtime just about summed me up and it was a bitter pill to swallow. I had done nothing wrong of course; just a bad day at the office. For the next ten minutes I pondered the situation. How on earth did the company know what we'd planned? And why would a Vice-President of the company intervene in this way? Just how aggrieved was I?

I had no sooner calmed down when there was a knock on the open door; the GM failed to do that polite activity earlier I suddenly realized. Pete Harries was one of the senior operators and had heard the commotion.

'It's good to see you, mate,' he said. I wasn't sure if he was being sincere or not so I put up a guard. I was immediately convinced that Pete's presence was an excuse to get an exclusive on what had just occurred. But then again I was probably over-sensitive after Frank's appearance. The reality was that Pete was a friend of sorts and it was good to see him. I would tell him about sparring with Frank if he asked. I couldn't care less if anyone else knew.

'Pete!'

'Don't be so surprised, Doug,' he replied.

'Sorry mate, bad timing,' I said, still pumped up.

'No need to apologize, mate. I heard the fracas. I was next door rummaging around for some sugar,' he told me. How convenient, I thought! 'I couldn't help but listen to what's happening with Des. Bad luck,' he then said, picking up on the argument he'd overheard.

'Bad luck my backside. He was stitched up!' I told him, still extremely annoyed at Frank and less annoyed about the treatment of my friend. Pete was not in the slightest bothered about the tone of my last remark but laughed at my good humor anyway. He knew what I was referring to. He'd heard the entire bust up. It was difficult to explain why Desmond had been dismissed by the company for gross negligence or something like that; the wording on the dismissal was vague considering what, where and the how of the matter, and not even Desmond was clear as to why he'd been given the bullet! Pete, in the meantime, now prized for the detail. He couldn't tell the others without the detail!

'So, what did he do that was so bad, Doug?'

'Don't really know. It's strange. One minute he's the hero, the next he's on the scrap heap.'

'Have you talked to him lately?'

'Yeah, he's down, Pete. He's taking out a lawsuit, *unfair dismissal, racial discrimination*, that kind of stuff.'

'No, I didn't know that. Good for him, I hope he screws these bastards.' I sensed another aggrieved employee.

'I'm going over there to help. I really don't know what I can do?' I told him being honest. 'Character witness is the talk, but that's better than doing nothing.'

'And the company knows about that, right?'

'Nope, well . . . yeah, they do now!' I corrected myself. 'But I don't care. I'm going to help Des in any way I can, Pete. It's the right thing to do.'

'Was that what the fight was over?' asked Pete, knowing the answer. At that precise moment I'd have felt guilty if I hadn't told him!

'Yeah, that's what I and Frank were arguing about, Pete. You have a scoop my friend.'

'Well . . . good for you then. I'll tell it in your favor, Doug,' he said, itching to carry the news forward to others in the refinery.

'Oh, thanks,' I replied not sure if I was being sarcastic or even grateful.

'Okay, okay, only trying to make light of it all,' he teased. 'But in all sincerity though, be careful, Doug,' advised my friend being more serious. Pete knew the score. To get involved in company, personnel affairs at my level meant trouble. ASEI had dismissed Desmond Haynes, fairly or otherwise, and that was that. Nobody, least of all me, should question their judgment or challenge their principles. They had an unwritten code of conduct and stick to it. What a load of nonsense!

'I'll be fine. The company can go and take a hike. They'd do me favor if they got rid of me too!' I declared. Pete got the message. He felt the same way and we both smiled. It was good to see him following Frank's little escapade. We hadn't seen each other in ages and we work at the same place. Another long lost friend!

'Want a cup of coffee, Pete?' I asked holding up the kettle and smiling to confirm all's well. Pete grinned back but it was short lived. He too was under a cloud of uncertainty. Last month, the refinery operations were such that the required feed, naphtha, used at a chemical plant for manufacturing ethylene, a costly product at the time, was restricted. This resulted in approximate losses of over fifteen million dollars. Needless to say, Frank was not impressed and the executive management in New York was even less impressed. The production cock-up would be managed though, one-way or another. The numbers would be crunched at corporate headquarters. By the time the bean counters played around with them there would be no recorded losses. Nobody on the outside would know. Somebody would be held accountable. It had already begun. An internal enquiry was into its third week. Three people had been suspended. It hadn't reached Pete's level yet, but it would.

'No thanks, I really haven't got that much time, mate,' he replied, and made to go but I called him back.

'Hey, Pete, heard anything about Nigeria lately?' I asked, fishing for some feedback.

'Like what?'

'Like, who was responsible?'

'We all make mistakes, Doug. None of us are perfect, mate. Wrong place at the wrong time, see you around,' and with that said, Pete made a hasty retreat. I returned a small wave. He had confirmed what Frank had said. The word was out about Des and me. The company propaganda machine had already started; it didn't matter that we were innocent. Fuck, they had a nerve. This was going to be ugly. I carried on where I had left off the best I could, delving into a mass of paper but Pete's words were mincing me inside and if I was honest, I was frightened.

Today I was working on one of those commercial issues that could have been handled by a senior accountant within the company, or so I thought. The explosions in Nigeria had caused millions of dollars worth of damage and the repair costs had to be accounted for. Who best to assist than somebody who was there at the time? Because of the fatalities and the cause of the explosion it made world headlines, led by the BBC World Services of course—unbeknown to me *Condor*, *Albatross* and *Eagle* got their just reward. As could be appreciated, it was total mayhem in those first days and weeks following the incident. The Nigerian's had little idea what to do and the infrastructure needed to handle such a major task just wasn't there. The British and US government assisted as much as they could but there was little they could do. The engineering companies, however, came in their hoards. Hundreds of workers from all nationalities arrived in Warri with the right skills to complete the rebuild of the plant. Many were Indians seeking a change from their own poverty-stricken surroundings. The local economy had never had it so good. And, as any experienced accountant or insurance company employee involved with major disasters of this kind will testify to, controlling purchase orders and payment of customers for undefined work that involves large amounts of money can prove to be agonizingly difficult. The logistics became a nightmare, made especially more difficult by our geographic location. The company insurers knew this and sent their own team of safety experts to assess the damage, surveyors and assessors who had the right experience and knowledge that was now required to make the refinery safe following the explosion.

In addition, the insurers sent many additional accountants, assistants and clerks, who were needed to help the already over-stretched refinery financial department. They would scrutinize and fully justify, determine, account for, and meet any payments made relating to essential safety work in the period immediately following the fires. In addition to this, they would endorse payments for subsequent engineering works that were required during the rebuild of the damaged refinery. The largest part of this task was undertaken here in Dorset where we had the right resources for the job. ASEI employees' worldwide also assisted us. They considered it a jolly! The plant owners and the insurers could appreciate the situation was becoming more chaotic by the hour, but there were obviously very many important safety-related tasks that needed to be performed with speed. Many invoices were paid immediately, without question and in good faith at the time so that those companies could be reimbursed for the good and valued work they performed for a battered oil company that were by now, very desperate for their help. Between them, the Oil Company and their insurers agreed that all payments made then, and for repairs required in the immediate future, would be contested at a later date.

Well, we had finally reached that later date. More to the point, I had reached that date long ago in fact, sometime during the last few months. As one of the company representatives for ASEI, I was partly responsible to ensure their interests in the whole affair. Along with the chief accountant, I'd spent a few months with the company insurers in Lagos and London. Both were making claims and counter-claims and contesting payments of every kind. By now I could spot a ledger at five thousand yards. Smell it even. My recompense was nearing. We were close to the end and down to the last twenty contested invoices. Payments made on several of these were to the same company, JG Engineering, to a total value of five hundred and sixty-three thousand dollars and was now simply being verified. I thought that these particular invoices would be the easiest to tackle before I went home. The payment was for safety access work during that initial period when the refinery was still unsafe. There were schedules of rates for personnel employed and a few extra demands for equipment hire costs, etc. Nothing over complicated. Few details were given about the work, however, and there were even fewer details about the company—it was as if they didn't exist.

A signature from the responsible person authorizing the work order was clearly made by another expatriate, Tom Watson, a trustworthy employee of twenty years foreign service and an experienced engineer. His delegations of authority extended beyond the amount shown on each respective invoice and so the company considered him responsible enough to make these types of authorizations using his own judgment. ASEI and their insurers had scrutinized over a hundred such work orders authorized by Tom with no complaint. I knew him well, he was one of the nice guys; *like me*, I mused. Nevertheless, I was obliged to follow the enquiry through and, therefore, sent a message asking for the details via e-mail; my knowledge of computers peaked with e-mail. I had tried surfing the web but stopped at, www.computersarecrap.com. Tom, like me, was now safely

The Last Hangman

back in Dorset and would receive the request the following morning in order to resolve issues surrounding the payment. Waste of bloody time, I thought as I posted the message. Thinking that my work for that day was over, my screen instantly flashed back an auto reply, which jumped out of the screen at me.

Tom Watson was away on company business and would not be back in the office until March 23rd.

'Two weeks!' I cursed at the screen then immediately looked for another contact on the invoices I now gripped in frustration. Cheryl Davies was the company accounting assistant responsible for the payment. I immediately sent her the same message.—*Could she inform me of the details regarding the company to whom payment for five-hundred and twenty-five thousand dollars was made a little over eighteen months ago? Thanks—Doug Archer.*—I quoted the invoice number and promptly posted the message. Strangely enough, I felt like a bully. At that moment the phone rang and I hesitate before daring to answer it. Is it Julie, I ask myself cautiously? After all, it's late and I had broken the promise of an early return home . . . again. I can tell by the tone of the ring it's an outside line. Perhaps it's Frank ringing to apologize! No such luck. That bastard will bury me from here on in.

'Hello,' I answered, braced ready for any event; a verbal battering from my wife or the unexpected apology.

'Doug, is that you?' I recognize the voice and sigh in relief. It was our hero.

'Des, great to hear you, man.' There's a pause before I get an acknowledgement.

'Hey, Doug, how you doin, man?' he asked.

'I'm fine,' I replied. 'Hang up, Des. I'll call you back,' I tell him and he put the phone down as instructed. The company can pay the phone bill for the next few minutes. It might be the last of their worries if we have our way. The return call was answered within one ringing tone.

'It's good to hear you again, Des. How're you keeping?'

'Likewise, Doug, I'm fine,' he informed me. 'Hope you're doin' okay too, man?' Without waiting for an answer Desmond quickly brought me up to speed. He'd received a letter from Heycock, he told me. The preliminary meeting with his lawyer was to be arranged sooner than expected, but longer than anyone could have remotely imagined nine months ago! *Could I still help?*

'That's no problem. Of course I can.' My response was instant following events of the last couple of hours. How could I refuse? 'I'll be there, it'll be good to see you and Suzanne again, Des. How is everybody?'

'Like I said, we're fine, just waiting on things. I want all this to happen, get it over with, man. It's been a long time coming, Doug.'

'Yeah, sure, I know. Don't go worrying yourself too much. We'll do our best. Have you talked to your attorney since receiving the letter?'

'Not yet. First thing tomorrow morning,' he promised. 'He says he's itching to file the lawsuit. Wants me, err . . . us to go over some things. I've mentioned that you're willing to play a part.'

'Okay. Say when and I'll be there.'

'I was thinking of next week, say Monday, if that's okay with you?'

'Fine, I could do with a break from this place,' I replied being honest.

'The company will find out that you're a player though, Doug.'

'Forget it, Des. I know what I'm letting myself in for.' I didn't tell him about Frank, or that they already knew. Word travels fast though and everybody in the refinery would know by Monday anyway. I was convinced.

'I asked the lawyer not to mention it, but . . . well . . . he said he had no choice. That's the proper thing to do and anyway, all witnesses must be revealed for some pre-trial discovery bullshit or something like that. It's the law,' confirmed my learned friend. With that revelation I stopped wondering how Frank came to know the game plan as Desmond continued talking down the phone. 'I'm a bit worried, Doug. Don't want you getting into trouble for me! You know what their capable of and the depths they'll go to.' Desmond *was* worried but it was too late for that. I already knew the depths we were going to.

'Like I always say, *shit happens*, my man!' I said, trying to sound like a black-American. Des says nothing; he hasn't noticed my poor accent. 'I couldn't give a damn, Des. They burned you up, pal,' I continue in the same tone. I don't know why though, the accents crap and this is too serious. There's another long pause and I sense that Desmond is trying hard to keep his emotions to himself.

'Des!' I said, down the phone . . . no response. 'Are you still there?' I then asked.

'Yeah, I'm here, hanging on in there.'

'Okay, good. I want you, Suzanne and the kids to know that I'm not scared of anyone in ASEI. They can't do anything to me, this is England remember? We do things different over here,' I pretended, knowing they'd do exactly the same thing. 'You're going to win this lawsuit, just wait and see,' I told him without any confidence whatsoever. Desmond thanked me again and the next few minutes were taken up with small talk. I finished by telling him I'd let him know my travel details before hanging up. Des insisted that I only do what I'm asked to do at the hearing; if there was one. He still had to submit a case yet!

Not for the first time that day, I rubbed my tired eyes with sweaty hands. I feel sickened at the treatment of Des. I also concede that it's unlikely my friend will win his lawsuit. I base my thoughts on two substantial facts. The first, Desmond has little money, none in fact; he's relying heavily on winning this lawsuit against the might of a major player. Secondly, unbeknown to Des, I talked to his attorney, Heycock, late last year and he agreed that very few lawsuits of this kind ever get anywhere; too many accusations and counter-accusations. The company usually had a personal record of their ex-employees, they were usually doctored and all read bad. There would be too much confusion and unsubstantiated evidence, hearsay most of it with very few facts presented at all. The lawyer had said that convincingly. He doubted it would ever go to trial but he wouldn't say that to Desmond. Why make things worse. Nobody should be able to do what ASEI did to him and get away with it. I decide there and then, I have some limited savings and would forward a payment to Des first thing tomorrow morning. That should help fund him part of the way towards getting closer to the American justice system. More importantly, ASEI should surely be taught a lesson, but how?

It was over two hours later than planned and four hours later than the time I had told Julie I would be home for lunch when I finally left the refinery. As I drove from the office, the rear view mirror was filled with the slender, tall shapes of the process towers that became smaller with time and distance. Eventually, they slowly diminished. I continued to drive from the plant and began to anticipate the arguments that were bound to follow. There were other options. I'd thought more and more of just moving on recently but hadn't had the time to sort things out, but I would get there eventually. But for now, I was resigned to simply going home to Julie whom, over the years, I had slowly but surely begun to despise.

* * *

At 7.30 the following morning, Cheryl Davies, an attractive and carefree young girl walked merrily into her office and sat down. Her smile was the result of having earlier flirted briefly with the security guard manning the reception desk that morning. The middle-aged man couldn't help but smile at her. With a glint in his eye he informed her that she looked particularly attractive that morning and, still smiling, thanked her for brightening up his day. She thanked him in return, winking as she said it. It gave him a feeling of desire. Comfortably sat at her desk she sipped a cup of cappuccino dispensed earlier from a machine in the main corridor of the building. It wasn't long before she'd turned on her PC. Opening her e-mail for the first time, she was surprised to find an *urgent* message from a member of the senior management. The message sent yesterday afternoon by me was addressed to her and labeled, *confidential*. She clicked onto the icon and eagerly read its contents. Strangely enough, and for no apparent reason, tears started to well in her eyes. The contents had shocked the young girl and soon she began to cry profusely.

Chapter 9

The money I sent to Desmond was appreciated with several more phone calls from Suzanne. Desmond was either too proud or too choked to thank me. Three hundred dollars was spent quickly to buy a plane ticket so that he could travel to Texas and more was set aside for accommodation. The rest I hoped would be spent on Suzanne and the kids.

When the time finally came to go to Texas the day turned out to be very long for Desmond. The trip from New York to Houston was tiring and the connecting American Eagle flight to Port Arthur was uneventful, apart from a loud-mouthed drunk who slobbered and slouched until he tipped his gin and tonic over the front of his shirt. The latter prompted him to inform a flight attendant that he could fly the tin-bucket of a plane better than the idiot who was currently doing so could; Desmond agreed!

Now, barely one hour after landing, Desmond waited in the comfortable office of his new lawyer, Lance Heycock. A polite enquiry from Gloria Reynolds, his secretary, had resulted in a mug of hot, black coffee being placed on a low-level table in front of where he sat. The last week had been a long wait but now at least something was happening, which made things a little more worthwhile. They had arranged to meet at two thirty. His attorney was nowhere to be seen. Desmond paced around the room, he was soon very impatient.

The lawyer's office was typical but Desmond wouldn't know that; it was his first visit to such an establishment. The walls were tastefully decorated and fine, leather furniture was neatly placed around the room in no particular style. As if keeping with tradition, a solid-teak writing desk that housed only a computer and a brass adjustable reading lamp was strategically placed directly opposite the door. Large prints of sailing boats competing in one race or another hung at various locations on the walls. The camera had caught the awkward-looking vessels cutting their way through rough, offshore seas; they were spectacular. The lighting was arranged in such a way that it enhanced the images. The yachts and foaming seas came to life. The prints seemed real and gave one a sense of being on board. Spray and foam covered the boats as their bows splashed down hard on the water that swelled underneath them and their foredecks were awash. The crews worked frantically to trim the sails as the yacht hulls planed to one side. They were battling with the raging sea and Desmond was part of it. They looked stunning, he thought. How he would have loved to be on one of those yachts right now.

Behind the desk, professional and educational degrees, certificates and awards from various law schools were displayed on the wall for all to see and no doubt, was an attempt to remove any disbelief as to Lance Heycock's capabilities as a lawyer. The left-hand side of the room was bright and very scenic. Floor to ceiling windows gave an impressive view of a nearby and well-manicured golf course. He neared to a table on the left wall and picked up an old, black and white photograph. It showed a bunch of young men posing side-by-side, it was taken during what seemed to be a fishing trip. They must have been good times, he thought. Fishing rods were slung in every direction. There wasn't a fish in sight but they were happy. One of the gang had obviously shoved his way to the front and now stood tall and proud while the others tried to remove him. The camera had caught the haphazard pose. They were in good spirits judging by the enormous grin across their faces. Sporting memorabilia filled in every other available space, which at least kept Desmond amused for some time longer than his patience would normally allow. The whole room gave a sense of power.

'Sorry to keep you waiting, Mr. Haynes,' said Lance Heycock, breezing through the door and into the office with a flurry. The rounded, overweight man extended a hand in friendship as the door closed behind him with a dull *clump*. There were no apologies for being late.

'It's good to meet you finally, have a good trip?' he asked, not giving a damn either way. His other hand flicked his long, grey hair back over his head. Desmond, a little startled at first, jumped to his feet and shook his attorney's hand without saying a word. He quickly recognized Lance as the brawn that had edged his way to the front of the fishing photo; even after all these years his features were unmistakable.

'Now, let me see,' continued Lance, not bothered that he hadn't received a reply. He was quickly seated behind his desk and in no time at all mid-way through half-leafing or half-reading a compilation of documents contained within a blue paper file. 'You seem to have a case, Mr. Haynes. Not much to substantiate the evidence though,' he reminded his client, looking down at him through half-rimmed spectacles, the kind old lawyers wear. 'Anyway, if what you say is true, and there's no reason to believe otherwise,' he added quickly, cautiously. 'We'll nail these suckers, right?' said the attorney and then he mildly punched the air in front of him. Desmond hadn't said a word yet. He sensed Lance to be a light-hearted chap on the outside and right now, he held a big, friendly-looking grin that emphasized his wrinkled brow and double chin. It was exactly like the grin in the photo, only older looking. He was also a fighter by the sound of it, thought Desmond, which didn't overly surprise him really. He wasn't sure what to expect of his newly appointed lawman but whilst the first impression was somewhat cavalier, it was welcome, nevertheless.

'Yeah, we got a good case alright,' replied Desmond sounding faint-hearted. The Jamaican was tired and Lance was quick to notice the lackluster reply.

'Okay, let's cut the crap here and just get on with the details. I see here that I've...' Lance then hesitated upon seeing the details. 'Err...we...err, others employed in our company,' he clumsily clarified, slowly realizing that this was the first time he'd set eyes on the file. '*We've,*' he emphasized. 'Penned a few requests and settlement figures here to cover lost wages, mental anguish and attorney's fees,' he added, looking at Desmond for some sort of approval. He mentioned his fees last and seemed embarrassed asking for the payment. 'Here, take a look,' and without further ado, Lance leaned over the table and handed Desmond a letter-sized legal pad with a couple of bullet points outlining what he'd just said. The settlement fee was accounted for on the following page and, combining the three sums, amounted to a little over three hundred thousand dollars.

'No doubt you're tired after such a long trip, Mr. Haynes,' he then said, watching Desmond quickly scanning the headlines. 'You can take a look at these notes in your hotel room if you wish,' he gestured for good measure. 'The figures are all neatly summed up on the back, as you can see. You can add a little on if you so wish,' he then offered rather apologetically and raised his glasses as if asking Desmond to commit a crime. 'But I must warn you, we would probably expect to settle for less,' said Lance being realistic, more honest, more professional. 'Two-hundred and fifty, sixty thou' maybe, but that's a good deal, trust me.' Lance was straight to the point and very convincing. Desmond had the impression of being bulldozed into making a decision based on the two sheets of paper he held in front of him. His loss of earnings was calculated at one hundred and fifty thousand. Mental anguish was a pitiful ninety thousand dollars, pittance. The settlement would cost Desmond twenty percent if they won. A lot of money for one letter! There would be no payment if they lost the lawsuit. Lance wasn't expecting too much. 'If you're happy with those figures we can fax them to Briggs right now if you want to?' he said, speculating. Lance gave an inquisitive stare towards Desmond following his request and now the overweight man seemed impatient. His client looked straight back at him with raised eyebrows. He was somewhat surprised to say the least!

'Who in the hell is, Briggs?' snapped Desmond, placing the pad face down on his lap whilst looking hard at his attorney. No, he wasn't going to trust him.

'Oh, he's the attorney for Cranton and Associates. Same old story I'm afraid,' said Lance feigning an apology. 'One of the largest law firms in New York!' he announced. 'And yep, you guessed it, commissioned by Advanced Strategic Energy to fight the case. Briggs' is one of their brightest stars, a senior with the company and not yet thirty. The enemy!' he whispered, jokingly. Lance then suddenly realized that Desmond hardly knew any details at all about the legal aspects of the lawsuit, especially the appointment of Cranton's superstar, John Briggs, brought in to defend the accusations made by Desmond. He realized he should have kept him up-to-date with what had just been arranged, however, he'd done nothing except inform him of possible pre-trial dates, which he knew hadn't even been discussed. There would be no trial of course. All of a sudden, Lance became acutely embarrassed. The fat lawyer hadn't really prepared anything other than the settlement details that now lay face down on Desmond's lap in the hope that his client would be shrewd enough to accept the money and return home to his family almost immediately the offer was accepted. Desmond stood and threw the legal pad back on to Lance's desk. There was nothing on the desk to disturb.

'I ain't bothered with this shit, man!' His Caribbean accent was full. He hadn't even bothered to look at the full settlement fee on page two. Lance's jaw dropped. He knew that he had misjudged the situation and tried to apologize for the second time in as many minutes.

'I understand how you feel, Mr. Haynes. But the fact is those guys do these kinds of lawsuits for a living, every day of their lives. They know their stuff,' confessed the attorney who looked over sympathetically at

Desmond. His expression and tone of voice said it all. Desmond had no chance.

'So, we ain't got a chance, ugh?' said Desmond, overly despondent. He pushed back from his seat. 'Is that what you're telling me, Mr. Heycock? Because if it is I'm damned if I'm going to accept it,' he told him with conviction.

'They *never*, I repeat *never* go to court for these kind of civil lawsuits, believe me. They won't budge on this one,' said Lance quickly, once again strongly reminding him of what he was up against. 'They're willing to settle this one without any fuss, no legal fees, nothing. They'll make sure you're financially rewarded, Mr. Haynes,' he said persuasively. The Texan knew the out-of-court settlement was their best option. Their only option perhaps, but he found it difficult to tell some of his unsuspecting clients that. The outcome usually favored the side with the biggest artillery and in this instance, Cranton & Associates had an army that could blow his three man law outfit to pieces. In any case, an out-of-court settlement offer was purely academic. He had definitely misjudged Desmond Haynes who fired back at him in double-quick time.

'That's bullshit, man! A nigger boy from New York has been fired for no substantiated reason whatsoever and already you're on their side for a couple of dollars more than three hundred grand? That's chicken shit! My salary was ninety-five, gross, last year. You can shove your offer where the sun doesn't shine, Mr. Almighty, wheeling, dealing, lawyer man. What's the matter with you? You think I'm crazy or something? You afraid?' he asked, searching. Desmond confronted Lance with a vengeance he never knew he had but the Texan showed no emotion whatsoever as the barrage of scorn against him continued.

'I am not about to lie down and let some grubby team of lawyers' trample all over me. I don't care if Advanced Strategic Energy got the President of the United fucking States defending them. I'm going to fight this, so help me God. If you, Mr. Heycock, haven't got the guts to stand up and fight for me, then I'll get somebody else who has the balls big enough to take these people on.'

With that said, Desmond turned and proceeded to walk towards the door. He momentarily stopped before actually going through it and looked back to face Heycock; he thought it would be the last time he ever set eyes on him. 'You could have told me what you were planning over the phone, said it in the letter you sent me or something, man. There was no need to drag me all the way down here to tell me you intend to argue for an out-of-court-settlement. You're full of shit, man. All I ask is for a wrongdoing to be put right, justice. That's what all Americans are entitled to, isn't it?' Desmond's emotions were flowing and Heycock just held his head down, ashamed at what was happening in front of him. 'The law is there to protect us from the worst society has to offer us, Mr. Heycock. But I guess the law just ain't enough some times,' he said, dejected. The sadness was portrayed throughout his entire, fragile body as he summed up his feelings. 'We also need protecting from people like you. Good day, Mr. Heycock.' With that, the dejected black man began to walk out of the open door.

'Mr. Haynes, hold on!' Lance rushed from behind his desk and quickly grabbed hold of his client by the arm. They were both stood in the open doorway. Desmond looked him in the eye before slowly turning his glare towards his arm, to where Lance held him in a vice-like grip. The attorney was flustered and looked in all directions. He had to say something that would defuse the situation that had developed, and quick. He was anxious to speak and he was going to of course, much to the reluctance of Desmond, who tried to break the hold on his arm and continue his exit out of the room. No way, Lance held his client firmly and began speaking with even more passion than Desmond could ever have imagined.

'Please . . . listen to what I've got to say. You won't find a better lawyer in the whole of the US than the one standing before you now. And . . .,' he hesitated, returning Desmond's scathing look, eyes penetrating straight back at him. 'I apologize for what I tried to do in there. It was wrong. I realize that now, believe me,' he argued, his sentiments briefly touching Desmond's feelings but his guard was still intact; his emotional shutters were up. For his part, Lance knew he had let down a client, albeit a non-fee paying customer but nevertheless a valued customer. Sure, he could have made quick bucks out of the settlement arrangement. That was easy money. What he was asked to do right now was take the route that paid the hard way. Make it pay in the Courtroom, which he normally tried to avoid like the plague. With his mind made up, and not for the first time in his life, Lance Heycock shook his head and proceeded to take the first steps towards earning money the hard way. The first obstacle he had to overcome, however, was stood in front of him. He would have to go for broke if he wanted his client back.

'So, if you want to talk about the courtroom, let's talk. Yeah, let's do just that. Let me tell you what it's like out there in front of a jury, the Judge, the defense council and the press. You ever experienced that, Mr.

Haynes?' Lance was right in close now. Desmond could smell his spearminted breath. 'No, you have not. As emotional as you are right now, you have not. Can you imagine what it's like when some, super-smart lawyer tears you apart on the witness stand? They make fools of people like you and me, and I'm an experienced campaigner! The whole case can be won or lost on that stand, Haynes, because . . . everyone is watching . . . everyone is watching, Haynes . . . watching your every move, every word, the slightest hiccup, a momentarily lapse of concentration, every inch of the way. Have you got the balls, Haynes?' he then asked. Heycock had spun it around and Desmond just stood and listened, his eyes transfixed on Lance Heycock's sweaty face as he listened to the script being unraveled from Lance's mouth. He was taking in everything the lawyer was saying.

'I've got the balls, Mr. Haynes, I've definitely got the balls and don't you ever underestimate that!' There was no way Lance was going to take Desmond's remarks of being afraid laying down and now he was seething. 'Making a wrong judgment about the way we should handle this lawsuit is one thing, mister, but saying I'm afraid is another, pal.' It was time to put the record straight with his *former* client and Lance was giving him both barrels. 'I can tell you now, there's no way you can take these bastards on without me. Do you hear me?' This was a different man, thought Desmond. 'I've fought more racial harassment lawsuit than you've had shits, son! And you accuse me of being afraid? Well, let me tell you, you son-of-a-bitch, Lance Heycock is afraid of nobody. Not you, not Advanced Strategic Energy, not Cranton and their fucking harem of legal misfits, not Brigg's, not any fucking one! Understand?' he shouted at him, red-faced.

If it wasn't for Desmond's strong willpower to see this through, despite his condemnation of his attorney, it would have ended there and then. But Lance had changed that. He was now very mad, very mad indeed and in those few melodramatic moments that Desmond declared this case was going to the courtroom, with or without him, the real Lance Heycock had put him straight. It had triggered off the most amazing reactions from both men. It had been a long time since Desmond had been answered to in such an irate way. It had a humbling effect. The two men stood quite for a few seconds before Lance, his face red as a beetroot and sweaty, broke the ice.

'No pain, no gain, right?' he finished in a quieter, more friendly and sincere manner.

'Yeah, right,' replied Desmond, feeling as if he'd been assaulted, and he had verbally. He turned and walked out of the office as Lance quickly followed and shouted at him through the closing door.

'I'll phone you at your hotel, Mr. Haynes. First thing in the morning,' he quickly shouted after him. Desmond stopped in the corridor, turned and looked back at Lance stood waiting in anticipation outside his office door. 'We . . . err . . . need to discuss the lawsuit, Mr. Haynes,' he added feebly.

'It's Desmond, Mr. Heycock. Just call me Desmond . . ., *son!*' he replied, half-smiling after getting the last word in, he was too old for Lance to call him *son* and Desmond felt better for saying it. Although it was a small stand it eased the situation. He continued to walk along the corridor and past Gloria who'd witnessed the entire confrontation. Lance nodded and shouted at him once again.

'Okay, Desmond. Oh, and by the way, it's Lance, *son!*'

'Okay, Lance, *son*, see you in the morning.'

'You betcha!'

Christ, he'd been in the courtroom a thousand times, he thought, now back safe inside his office. He'd argued racial discrimination of all sorts in courtrooms of every kind, but this was different. How could he argue the case? The fact that there was little to go on was neither here nor there, he just couldn't do it, and definitely not against Cranton and his cronies. They'd paste him for sure but that didn't really bother him. There were other reasons for not contesting this one. What in the hell had he done to take this on? No, more to the point, why didn't he just let Desmond go? It would be better that way. Lance was frightened. Yeah, this was definitely different. The chances of Desmond asking him to defend this particular lawsuit were a billion to one, yet it had happened. He'd unwittingly accepted the work and now he was frightened by what he had to do! Lance walked over to his *trophy desk* and looked at the fishing photograph and cursed. He was at the front as always during those carefree, youthful days. He was stronger than the rest of his friends; he'd be at the front of any photograph! He picked it up, paced quickly across the room and placed it, face-down, safely inside one of his desk drawers out of sight.

Chapter 10

I HADN'T QUITE GOT TUNED INTO the conversation before Desmond started to tell me all about it. His lawyer had tried to coax him into an out-of-court settlement but according to Des, his reaction to the arrangement had the Harvard lawyer reeling on the ropes.

'He accused me of cowardice, man. That was his downfall though. That big lawyer dude was desperate, man,' he told me. 'He was on his knees begging me to forgive him in the end, Doug,' he added.

'Mm, good for you, shoulda dumped the old fool,' I replied without feeling. Make no mistake about it. Desmond had ripped Lance Heycock to shreds. He failed to inform me of Heycock's counter-attack. Of how he humbled my hard-nosed friend by talk of what it's like in the courtroom, the bloodthirsty lawyers like John Briggs, of power crazy Judges, and indecisive or corrupt juries. And it happened right in the doorway of his office, for all to see! Desmond's only argument against my advice to drop him and find another lawyer was that he thought, with my help, we should manage. We had enough damning evidence, he told me confidently, much to my utter amazement. I knew what he'd said was all bullshit! We had very little supporting evidence, nothing in fact.

I put down the phone, removed my shoes and lay sprawled on the bed. The Marriott was comfortable as usual. The call to Desmond was to have been a quick one. I merely wanted to inform him that I was staying in Houston that night instead of Port Arthur as planned. It had gone on for over thirty minutes! I had to go I told him. I was simply knackered, but he couldn't understand that simple truth. I hung up on him but not before I'd arranged to meet the following morning at his hotel, a Red Roof Inn, near the Port Arthur commuter airport. From there we would meet once again with Lance Heycock and plan a way forward. I had two weeks to help. As I lay on the bed I wondered in all honesty what on earth I could do. Now and again a car horn would sound outside and disturb my thoughts, but other than that, it was quite. The Galleria was closed and that was a good thing, I could relax, there was hardly any noise to disturb me.

It wasn't long before my thoughts trailed back to home. They usually did in hotel rooms, alone. I thought of Julie, but why her? Did I still love her? If I was honest about it, I couldn't say that I didn't. I worshipped the ground she walked on once upon a time. We had our usual squabble prior to my departure though. She didn't care to ask where I was going and I preferred not to tell her. For sure, for most of our married life we were very much in love, especially during our courtship and even more so in those early years of marriage. After giving birth, twice within eighteen months, Julie was quite naturally besotted by the two beautiful children we both now adored. They meant everything to us both, but seemingly more so to Julie so she said on more than one occasion, as if I hadn't noticed. She'd previously told me that she felt more secure with a family. So, the next sixteen years or so was devoted to the task in hand. All her time was spent with the children and it was as if I didn't exist. I was more than pleased for her and the children, less pleased for myself, naturally. That was the reason for working away from home so often, I supposed. Nevertheless, after speaking to countless other fathers they all seemed to be in the same boat and I accepted the fact that I was now second best. It was not too long before I got used to the idea of just supporting my family financially with the odd trip to the playground now and then, or a trip to the beach.

On the face of it, we appeared to be one very happy family. I quite enjoyed the freedom Julie gave me to pursue my career, but as the years went by the children grew up and sooner than we realized, they no longer wanted to spend their time with their mother. They had friends and pastimes that did not include her. She was merely a taxi service, taking them to wherever and whenever they needed to go. For her part, Julie got accustomed to having coffee mornings with several of her wealthy friends. We even moved house at her request, to a little village so that she could meet more influential women in the same situation as she now found herself in. It didn't work out as well as she would have liked. In fact, it didn't work out at all. Most of her neighbors hated her. They had seen her develop into someone she was not. Heirs and graces appeared within a short period of moving into the neighborhood. She began to buy expensive items of designer clothing. Even worse, she became boastful about it.

The coffee mornings soon became few and far between. When her friends considered her false and undesirable, she began to gossip about their social affairs, ending up enemies with most of them. They slowly and inevitably chose to ignore her altogether. Finally, having learned the hard way, she got the message and stopped the gossiping, but it was too late. Instead, she turned her attention to me, accusing me of ignoring her. *Neglect after all these years looking after me and our two children*, she had said. It came as no surprise to me. I had bought my wife everything and anything. Even significantly increasing the mortgage so that we could move house to be where she wanted to be. Julie repaid my kindness by becoming fat and boring. She constantly embarrassed me and when I told her so, she became bitter towards me. She was spiteful whenever she got the chance. In self-protection, I became immune to her constant source of hatred and merely switched off in her company.

Not before too long, the thoughts of a broken marriage were replaced by events in Nigeria. Screams and pathetic cries for help filled the room, large explosions pounded my mind and large fireballs lit up the room. This carried on for hours until finally, I drifted off. When would it all end?

The sky was overcast but it was warm as we drove past the bayous. It wouldn't be long before we were there and, as usual, Desmond was straight at it in no time at all.

'Don't take any shit off this lawyer dude, man,' said my friend, sober and unprovoked, as we drove to his lawyer's office. My head thumped from the previous night and now I just played along with it.

'Thanks, Des.'

'No, really man, he just tries to act the hard legal bruiser, but he ain't nothin. Not after I put him right, man. He nearly shit in his pants!' he said looking at me.

'You must be some, hard, son-of-a-bitch, Des,' I told him.

'I can be a nasty piece of shit, Doug,' he quipped. 'You don't know me for real, man.'

'Is that right?'

'Yep, I could have been a black belt, bro.'

'Could have?' I questioned. Desmond avoided my cross-questioning like the plague and changed tack.

'I remember a fight I was in, way back some,' he reminisced all too readily. 'Chicago. I was coming out of the *Nike* store when two dudes tried to mug me, man. Sorriest thing they ever tried to do. Ole Desmond just spun, made a few textbook moves and dropped them right there and then, man. Both of em, they were on the pavement out cold. Passers-by were stunned. Nobody tries to pinch Desmond Haynes sneakers without suffering. Know where I'm coming from, Doug?' he said looking straight faced at me.

I laughed. 'You really did that?' I asked. There could be no doubt. Desmond was filling me with bullshit, yet again.

He was nervous and it showed. 'Yep,' he bluffed, less convincingly. The poor guy hadn't stopped talking since I picked him up from his hotel room that morning. There were no greetings, just a barrage of abuse that questioned my hotel reservation arrangements and timekeeping. I could see the sweat begin to form on his leathery, black, forehead. He wore thick, large rimmed glasses that seemed to cover most of his face, which gave him the appearance of looking stupid. And usually he was.

'Did I tell you about the time I laid out three guys in a bar once?' I blurted out, baiting him for more of the same.

'Don't give me any of that shit, man,' he laughed out loud. *'You ain't laid anybody out*, unless your friends with an undertaker!'

'It's true, man!' I teased him with my ever poor Caribbean accent.

'Doug, if I had an elephant, you'd have a box to keep it in!'

* * *

After the briefest of introductions and handshakes that squeezed the life out of each other, we were now assembled around a large conference table in a meeting room inside the two-storey law building of Lance Heycock. It was Desmond's second visit to the establishment. There were three others whom we had just met. The grey-haired attorney had introduced them as his associates and they were already briefed as to what type of case they would be presenting—a civil lawsuit with little or no evidence! Chuck Graham and Anthony Christianson were introduced as two associate attorneys and were sat to my right. On the other side of the table, alongside Desmond, was the company paralegal, Dillwyn Davies, who greeted us with *the* most vigorous of handshakes that had, along with his dress sense, given a first impression of him being, *thick as a brick*, as Desmond had so bluntly told me later on.

We wasted no time at all in getting started. Buckets of coffee were consumed as Desmond gave the most detailed account of his employment with Advanced Strategic Energy Inc. Those around the table took notes. If it was convincing enough it would be polished slightly and amount to his testimony, that of a model employee. If it was flawed in any way—they usually were, then the team would just have to polish that much harder, said Lance rather unconvincingly.

Desmond began quietly. He seemed relaxed as he informed them about how he came to work for the company after many years as a contractor. Then his duties and responsibilities at the time of his dismissal were explained and a job description of some kind, recited from memory by Desmond, seemed to support what he said. Next, we listened as our friend proudly told us of his achievements, of which there were many. Finally, he described his general wellbeing within the company, his feelings, his ambitions, his career aspects, the high points and the low points. Chuck, Ant and Lance questioned parts of his account of things and constantly interrupted him. How were things between him and the company—before and after Nigeria? Was it the same relationship throughout every aspect of his career? Who thought you was a good employee? Who didn't like you? Who did? How many black employees did you know personally at Advanced Strategic Energy? Are they still there? Are they happy? The questions were relentless. He talked of his times in the Middle East, Nigeria, and the North Sea and also of Dorset, England where, along with Nigeria, he'd spent many happy months working with me. So far, he'd worked for one of the finest companies you could ever wish to work for.

'It's difficult to say anything bad about Advanced Strategic Energy,' said Desmond, catching everybody by surprise, but he was right. ASEI were a good employer and looked after their employees well, usually. Trying to disguise their astonishment following Desmond's generous appraisal of ASEI, the lawmen continued their interrogation, questioning him for names and positions of colleagues and associates that he worked for, worked with, and worked against. The questions just never stopped. Finally, it was Ant who got to the bottom line; there weren't any more questions they could have asked by my reckoning.

'So, where does that leave us?' he asked. Des took his cue and informed his listeners and interrogators alike of where that left us, so to speak.

'I was dismissed for gross negligence,' he said rather humbly. 'It was indirectly related to something that I'd been personally responsible for although, obviously, I didn't think so,' he added, feeling a little dejected. Lance shuffled through a host of papers in front of him whilst Desmond continued to talk us through the final days of his employment. 'I hadn't long returned to work following the Nigeria incident. You know about that, right? The explosion and all that ugly stuff!' said Desmond looking directly at the lawmen. Everybody nodded. Neither I nor Des had mentioned this as far as I knew so I naturally assumed they'd gleaned it from the news networks; the entire incident seemed to fill a lot of gaps in the media at the time. 'Anyway, a valve on a crude oil process unit owned by the company in California had been incorrectly operated during a period of high demand and caused an emergency shutdown of the process. This came about due to two significant facts.' Desmond stood and paced the room as he spoke; he looked and acted like a lawyer all of a sudden. 'One, the permit that granted a workman to complete essential maintenance of a similar valve was identified incorrectly. The workman realized this but took it on himself to close another valve that he believed to be the right one,' he went on. 'This caused a loss of pressure and the process was shut down with production losses estimated in the hundreds of thousands of dollars—as usual,' he muttered, sarcastically. 'Secondly, the operating instructions for the system was poor and somewhat dated compared to modern operating instructions, where the instructions are more understandable. The plant is really old; why ASEI bought it is anyone's guess!' Again, another sarcastic remark uttered in despair more than anything else. 'Anyway, one thing led to another and they over-pressurized the system.'

'What happened then?' asked Dillwyn getting bored.

'Oh, they just blew the heat exchanger apart, that's all,' replied Desmond as if it happened every day.

'And . . . ?' probed Dil, hardly struck by what he'd heard so far.

'There was a fucking big, *bang!*' Des shouted out loud and startled us all at the same time. 'And they blamed me for it,' he added, getting to the crux of the matter. 'They said the shutdown procedures were incorrect and that's why I was roasted.'

'How come?' asked Chuck, confused.

Desmond frowned at such a stupid question. 'They said I was responsible for ensuring the shutdown procedures were in place and up-to-date.'

'And they weren't, I guess,' speculated Dillwyn knowing the answer.

Desmond turned to look at him before he spoke. 'Nope,' he said quickly, trying to keep calm. 'They weren't cos I knew nothing about them, simple as that.'

'If you knew nothing at all about the system, seems kinda strange to me to give you the bullet?' argued Chuck with good reason.

'Well, maybe that's why we're here!' Desmond responded, slowly mouthing the words, keeping his emotions in check.

'Either you knew or you didn't,' said Chuck not letting him off the hook. He was not in the least bothered by Desmond's body language. 'Did you know the system or not?' he asked forcefully.

'No, I knew nothing about this particular system. I've never even seen the plant. I haven't even been to California!' he emphasized, shrugging his shoulders to support his statement. 'So from that perspective, I knew practically nothing at all. But according to them I should have known this particular system. It's called, *being held accountable*,' Des told us despondently.

'Accountable, how could he be accountable?' I asked nobody in particular. 'He was based over a thousand miles away,' I said to them all.

'Doesn't matter, depends on what your job description was at the time and what you're asked to do,' confirmed Ant. 'Roles and responsibilities and all that good stuff.'

'With modern communications he could've been a million miles away and still been responsible if that's what he was asked to do,' commented Chuck.

'Or that's what it says in his job description,' interrupted Ant getting back to the piece of paper in question.

'Ant's right, legally. It all depends on what your job responsibilities were,' said Lance and then continued to deflate the situation. 'And let's not forget the scope of work. If he *was* the operations engineer for that process equipment design, and for arguments sake let's assume he was, then he was accountable, as the company had so plainly put it.' Lance blunted our enthusiasm. I stood and joined Des by the window and all four lawyers adjusted their chairs to look at us.

'Okay, where's your job description, Des?' asked Ant, despite Desmond's recital earlier on.

'Ugh? I . . . err . . . don't know,' replied Desmond, embarrassed all of a sudden.

'No problem. We'll just ask Advanced Strategic Energy to provide a copy,' I said, trying to get on with things. Lance looked to the ceiling in despair before fiddling amongst a pile of papers and eventually producing the required paperwork. Desmond had sent it over twelve months ago!

'I see,' I said, looking at a shamefaced Desmond. The job description said exactly what we didn't want it to say, but not in so many words. I continued with my argument.

'There's nothing concrete here though, is there?' I held the limp document up in the air. No response.

'It seems like an arguable case from that,' suggested Ant. 'Besides, there's more damning stuff than that.'

'Like what?' I asked leaving the rest of the lawyer's looking vacant in our direction.

'Like a multitude of sins committed against the company that contravened the personnel rules and regulations for starters. Your friend there practically drove a bus through them in the course of his career,' Ant told us, holding up a copy of his personal records sent over from ASEI some time ago when they'd first looked at the lawsuit. I grabbed the few sheets and took a quick glance.

'So, what's the big deal?' I argued, squinting at the three page report. 'We all do that from time to time,' I told them wondering what in hell Desmond had been up to.

'But you haven't been dismissed for gross negligence, *have you*?' said Lance, quickly taking the papers from me and throwing them on the table. 'Advanced Strategic Energy is on solid ground. *Gross negligence* is proven in their minds and it's going to be difficult for any opposing legal team to prove anything to the contrary,' he said in plain English. We just listened, stunned at the admission. Ant broke the ice and was first to look at both the job description and Desmond's personal records before passing them around the room. Gloria was asked by Ant to make a copy for each of us, including any other documents produced at the end of the day.

'Okay, what is it that makes one of the largest oil companies in the world dismiss a senior engineer for no reason whatsoever?' asked Ant ignoring the reasons presented so far for Desmond's demise. We all looked at him in amazement. Was he thick?

'The crime doesn't fit the punishment,' he argued telling us nothing new. 'We're clueless apart from a poor job description, a few misdemeanors committed against some ill-devised company rules and regulations, and a poky letter of dismissal that we haven't even seen yet! These poky papers are probably meaningless,' he said, rolling his copy up in a ball before throwing it in a bin placed over ten yards away from him. It was a long shot and the paper ball went straight in the centre. All net! We were mightily impressed at his skill! Lance shook his head in bewilderment then slowly rose from his seat and joined us at the window. Three down three to go. He looked out of the window as he spoke.

'Those poky bits of paper formally state the facts, Ant,' Lance said pointing towards the ruffled paper now safely in the bin. 'It's exactly the way Desmond has presented it. Are you blind?' He returned to the table and from the same pile of documents produced the letter of dismissal and there was a scrum by the lawyers to see who would scrutinize it first. Apart from learning that the letter was approved and signed in part by Messrs Jeremy Isaacs, the VP for Human Resources, and somebody by the name of Richard Hammond, whom Desmond or I had ever heard of, there were no further details to be had and the letter completed the rounds without comment. We half expected Ant to slam-dunk it in the same bin.

'There's got to be more?' enthused Ant not letting it go. The paralegal, Dillwyn, agreed with Ant. Lance conceded slightly and progressed with the questions out of frustration.

'Okay, what was happening at the time of your dismissal? What were you doing? Did you upset anybody? Think back, did anything unusual happen?' The questions once again came firing back in. For that reason, Dil had produced a flip chart and made bullet points of the questions that were now peppering Desmond from all angles. The large-sized, white sheet of paper was quickly filled with red ink. Step-by-step, Desmond went into detail regarding each and every question. Even after another hour or so, the cross-examination continued, this time there were further questions asked by the team—the counsel for the prosecution. Nothing unusual came from nearly three hours of questioning. Names were put into frames for further background research. Nobody had been tasked to action anything just yet though. The usual petty arguments were scrutinized as time went on but in all reality, they were harmless and, therefore, meaningless to what we were trying to prove.

One flick of light was offered when a subordinate challenged the need for a series of essential over-pressure relieving safety valves on one particular gas compression unit. A sacking offence in the safety conscious world of the oil industry surely, I thought. We soon learned that this was resolved in Desmond's favor and very much to his credit, which eliminated the question from the chart. Another was a rollicking from a senior VP, Jeremy Isaacs, the same Human Resources guy that had signed the bullet form. He was annoyed at Desmond for constantly querying the death of his Nigerian friend, Brandt Allto. He had drowned during a fishing trip up the river Niger. That's all there had been to it. Desmond's refusal of this simple explanation culminated with him asking the United States Ambassador in Nigeria to investigate further his friends misfortune—there were too many facts that did not add up, he argued. Lance scrubbed the incident off the board quickly but not before several outbursts of poor intellect followed.

'Up where?' shouted Dillwyn. The lanky, ginger-headed paralegal had slowly nodded off at the later stages of the conversation and, when prodded by Ant, had awoken with a jerk. He had missed most of what was said but had managed to catch the tail end.

'The river Eiger!' exclaimed Chuck. He had obviously got his rivers mixed up with his mountains—geography was obviously not his best subject.

'Won't catch me up there,' said Dil. 'Probably got murdered by a yeti. The stupid sod,' he joked, again poorly mixing up the Himalayas with the Bernese Alps in Switzerland. Chuck looked back at him, puzzled. Lance gave a pitiful smile as usual. His associates had embarrassed him too many times for him to be too upset about what came out of their mouths. He just accepted it now. Dil liked to *smoke*, and so it was generally accepted that he was constantly geographically further from most parts of the planet anyway, never mind the Eiger or the Niger! Nobody took what he said seriously, apart from Desmond, who just shook his head in dismay. So, there we were, astounded by their lack of legal brilliance one-minute and then further swallowed in total inaptitude the next. It just got worse.

'What did the Ambassador say?' asked the ever-alert Ant, probing some more.

'Leave it, Ant,' ordered Lance, overly-agitated by the question. Ant grunted his disapproval.

'Nothing, no reply,' offered Desmond ignoring Lance's advice. 'Just dried up, man.'

'Didn't you pursue his cause of death, dear?' asked Gloria, who appeared from nowhere and was now busy clearing away the many cups that were piling up to one side on the table.

'C'mon. Let's get back to where we want to be.' Lance was getting really frustrated with it all. He said we were wasting time and I kind of agreed with him.

'No way, I was too busy fighting for my job with Advanced Energy by that time. I'll pursue it one day though,' promised Desmond, frowning at his attorney.

'Good for you dear, good for you,' replied Gloria as she walked off with a tray full of cups.

After Desmond terminally answered several more searching questions for possible leads, the day was finally through. We were tired but still full of resolve judging by everyone's upbeat commitment to help Des fight his case. They knew he was a good man with many good traits. Those had come out loud and clear during his account of his demise with Advanced Strategic Energy; his supposed testimony, I assumed at the time. It was Dil who hit home with what was needed. The lanky man gave a rallying call to each and every one of us. We should meet early the next day and give it all we had, he reminded us. Don't be too despondent. We had only just scratched the surface, he insisted and we fully agreed. It was just after six-thirty in the evening when we adjourned. Desmond found a local bar nearby and we settled for a couple of beers.

There was something odd about today. We both knew that but said nothing. We had a couple more beers and tried not to mention it.

Chapter 11

BY THE TIME DESMOND AND I had arrived in the conference room the following morning, Chuck and Ant—*The Blues Brothers*—we'd noticed a remarkable resemblance, had completed at least two hours work looking at previous lawsuits. Lance too was already busy planning the strategy for the next few days. There were about seventy bundles of neatly-typed transcripts, each about two inches thick and bound by red ribbon, placed at one end of the rectangular table. The three men sat opposite writing notes on legal pads placed before them.

'What's all this?' asked Desmond playfully slapping the tops of the unevenly balanced bundles of bound papers.

'Hey, look who's just turned up!' It was Chuck who had the first words to say that morning.

'That's our homework, son,' said Ant, annoying Desmond with the *son* bit. He wasn't bothering to acknowledge Desmond in any other manner we'd noticed. 'Previous case histories related to racial discrimination,' he went on. 'We've trawled the vaults of the New Orleans Justice department, son.' He made sure we knew they'd been at it since very early that morning, just as we should have been doing, which annoyed Desmond even more. Soon though, the bundles would be evenly shared between him and his colleagues, who in turn would then be vigorously engrossed in learning the minutest of details in each and every case. There could be something of use they could use in their claim for unfair dismissal and other race-related issues.

'Coffee?' asked Gloria who was also on the case.

'Thanks. Better make his extra strong,' I told her pointing towards Desmond. 'We had a few beers last night, celebrating our first day here,' I added, and with that playful remark Gloria scurried off quickly to the percolator. Desmond just grunted.

'You won't be celebrating nothing if you don't get your sleeves rolled up, get your head into gear and give those damned names to Dil. We gotta get some witnesses here.' Ant was in no mood for any banter. It was obvious. Since our agreement to go for broke he was the one that seemed most up for it. There would be no delay in submitting our lawsuit. Chuck, as usual, just grimaced, shook his head back and gave another penguin-like chuckle that made Gloria smile out of pity but had Ant frothing at the mouth in an instant.

'Why do you do that? You're like a buffoon!' snorted his colleague. Both Desmond and I frowned at Chuck before looking towards Lance, who merely shrugged his shoulders. The top lawyer pointed a rotating finger towards his head as if making out that Chuck was mad and quickly continued taking notes from an open law book placed in front of him. Ant just looked away as Chuck nonchalantly held his silly-looking grin.

'Now, now Anthony,' interrupted Gloria, who seemed to have had a calming effect on Ant. He, in turn, gave a suppressed *grunt* whenever she returned a cheeky smile back to Chuck, whom she constantly admitted, she liked very much. He was getting on in life. Sixty maybe, she thought. Chuck's usual task was matrimonial affairs. Divorce lawyers earned good money for putting two people through hell. I made a mental note to like him, just in case I needed him. Gloria must have as well. She thought he was adorable, cuddly, a good attorney and as always at that moment in time they needed him. I walked over to where she'd placed a notepad and took my seat.

'Okay guys, where we going?'

'It's like Chuck said,' piped up Lance. 'We've got what we wanted from the archives. It'll take us some time to review case histories of this kind. There's a whole bunch of civil lawsuits brought against one company or another, most of them *class action* suits.'

'What's that?' asked Desmond still the worse for wear.

'It's where several people file a suit against an employer for a wrongdoing. Usually, they've all got the same grievance. From their perspective it's better to go in mob handed. Safety in numbers, and besides, it cuts down on the paperwork, costs and all that,' replied Ant, thankfully now more relaxed. Desmond nodded. The phrase was familiar to him all of a sudden. He'd heard the term used at Advanced Strategic Energy before.

'Welcome back,' said Lance sarcastically, as if Desmond had been away for days. 'That's just the type of information we require. The more details we get from ill-doings, or lawsuits filed against Advanced Energy, the better,' he declared, which surprised nobody.

'What about discrimination?' Desmond chipped in. 'Those poor bastards that have been bullied because they're black, man!' I sensed my friend's frustration.

'That's what we aim to find out!' Lance replied with a frown. 'What do you think we're doing here?'

'Sorry, got carried away,' said the black man looking sheepishly.

Out of shear frustration, and to get things moving, Ant then called out to Dillwyn. No reply, 'Dillwyn!' Ant shouted louder down the corridor towards an office where the paralegal had scurried off earlier. He was busy surfing the net.

'Yoh, somebody calls me!' Dillwyn Davies had a Welsh accent that could not have been any deeper or any more Welsh. He had the finesse of a trawler man and the looks of an underweight refugee, clothes and all.

'Desmond's going to give you some names and addresses, aren't you, Des?' said Ant looking persuasively at Des as he spoke. The black man agreed. That's why he'd come in the first place, he thought.

'Right we are then, no sweat. Come this way,' said Dil, who just threw out his left hand and gestured towards his office. 'I'm down here on the right. They've put me in the archives out of the way, see,' he told Desmond pointing to a little cubby hole. His Welsh accent was a treat and everybody warmed to it. Dillwyn was a law unto himself. He was rude, comical and very, very funny on times, a real valley boy for sure. He had absolutely no manners whatsoever and didn't really see the need for any. His ginger hair was constantly in a mess; it hadn't been combed since the last court appearance some six weeks previous. He smoked pot and was usually in a world of his own. Every now and then he would contact the mother ship and return to planet earth, so to speak. The door closed behind the two men and we heard Dil bringing Desmond up to speed with the latest technology the world had to offer. Desmond braced himself for what might come his way for the next hour or so.

With coffee in hand and Dil quietly making a search of any persons unjustly done against from names that Desmond would have to recollect, I sat and listened to Lance make out the basis for the lawsuit. With his paralegal tied up for the present time, Chuck was asked to take notes. Ant, not one to be left out, arranged a flip chart alongside us but not too close to the table. He sat next to the blank paper armed with a felt-tipped pen and announced his readiness to write down the bullet points.

The Last Hangman

Once again they came thick and fast. The blank sheets were soon filled with heavy black scribbles; Kenner v Jones, Jaspin v Muller & Co, Maggot et al v Crane Brothers, all racial lawsuits and so the list grew. Another clean sheet quickly followed. Pre-trial discovery—when and where? The law—The United States Constitution, Nineteen Eighty One, and Article eight was mentioned and something from that was the course of address. Then there were the intended courtroom players—Lance, Ant, Chuck, and Dil? Documents and policies required from Advanced Strategic Energy—employment handbook, racial and diversity policies etc were quickly added to the list. Prospective witnesses, who could Desmond convince to testify? Prospective jury members an all black jury would be nice! And so on. All of these matters needed to be addressed by one or more members of the team. Accompanying each and every point in red felt-tipped pen were the initials of the sponsor. They would be charged with the follow-up actions in order to make further progress in the case.

Meanwhile, Desmond had supplied a host of names to Dillwyn, who'd continued surfing the net for contact details. There were the good guys and the bad guys. Those Desmond held responsible for his dismissal and those he thought had gone the same way as he had done.

The only person we'd ask to question from ASEI would be the person who sanctioned Desmond's dismissal, Richard Hammond. He'd know the details and was our only real thread to explain the facts for sure; we hoped he'd cock-up under questioning, although Lance thought otherwise. These guys were smart, he told us. That's why Isaacs wasn't asked to testify, Lance told us, unless Briggs asked him to that is? The whole affair had taken most of the morning. According to our legal team, the case histories weren't providing much. So far, we were building up the lawsuit based on one guy screwing up, which was hardly likely given his position in the company!

Chapter 12

'You're a lucky son-of-a-bitch, John,' said Eamon Darcy, discretely reminding him of other, more sinister, outcomes. John Arnold acknowledged what he already knew by handing the Irishman one of his finest, Cuban cigars. Smiling, he gently nudged his friend in the ribs, topped up his glass with red wine poured from a vintage bottle of Chatenauf-de-pap, before raising his glass to propose a personal toast, directed only toward Eamon.

'To even better times to come,' he said with a big grin across his face, savoring another fine moment, this time with a lifelong friend; his best friend.

Not for the first time in John Arnold's company, Eamon was in awe. 'To even better times,' he repeated, reassuringly, shamelessly believing it and, not for the first time, overindulging in such a grand occasion. Eamon had nothing but total admiration for his CEO. They were attending the launch of the Republican nomination for the Presidential elections. Jason Arnold, heavily funded by his brother, John, was going head to head with the incumbent, George Wade, the later faltering on promises made through no fault of his own. World finances were in a mess, unemployment was rocketing, borrowing was practically non-existent, taxes were not being paid, and neither he, nor any other world leader had a grip on the situation; it was out of control for the time being!

Jason Arnold, by default, could almost have a free run to the White House such was the financial chaos, spiraling unemployment figures, and misunderstanding of the American public; and for that matter, the rest of the world.

From nowhere, an immaculately dressed waiter produced a *Zippo* lighter and both men started to suck hard on their, *Partagas*, cigars, the smoke partially blinding the poor boy. Unfazed, he stood his ground, meticulous and steady and making damned sure the tobacco would stay alight. Once the tobacco burnt red hot and the ash glowed he made his exit, leaving the men to enjoy their smoke. They were over the Nigeria incident, thank goodness. The fallout from that could have gone either way, nevertheless, lady luck was still on John Arnold's side. ASEI had rebuilt the refinery, had rebuilt the chemicals plant, had rebuilt their relationship with the Government, and more importantly, had rebuilt investor confidence. ASEI shares had rebounded from an all time low and now the two men reveled in the good times once again, which were *about to get even better* once Jason reached the White House!

Not only had they gambled most of their personal wealth on buying ASEI stock at a knocked-down price of fifteen dollars, they'd gambled on funding Jason to run for President at the same time, the later in order to get access to lucrative deep sea exploration rights in the Gulf of Mexico. With the stock currently trading at forty dollars and Jason Arnold almost guaranteed being sworn in as the forty fifth President of the United States of America, both gambles were paying off it seemed. How lucky was that? Or was it a shrewd investment? Arnold smiled, just lucky he reasoned. Wall Street, and any other financial law enforcement agency, would refer to it as, *insider dealing*!

As the night went, it turned out to be a great success. Jason made sure to plug his brother, John on several occasions. He also mentioned Eamon by name and he never forgot to put the ASEI brand up on the pedestal either. It was great publicity, not only for the company but also for John and Eamon who were now busy sucking hard on the large Cuban's. Yes, they were popular and, judging by the applause showered in their direction, well liked. They too would become powerful men soon and everybody in that room knew it. The two men always enjoyed the company of Senators, they enjoyed the limelight just as they enjoyed each other's company, and it was obvious. Ever since they were in school together, ever since they went to college together, ever since they worked at ASEI together, there was a strong bond between these men. So, when John Arnold got rewarded, he made sure his first lieutenant shared in his success, albeit rather shady on times Eamon thought, but only to himself.

Whilst the night was still young—there were other parties and other speeches to be delivered by Jason, who was now engrossed on the *thank you* trail, something he'd promised his armies of supporters once he'd secured the nomination—the occasion was brought to an abrupt halt by the sudden presence of John Arnold's son-in-law, Jeremy Isaacs. Deep down, Arnold despised him. He tolerated him only for the sake of his daughter, Beth, whom he'd do anything for. Whilst his son-in-law was a senior VP of the company, something Beth had insisted *daddy should take care of* early in the marriage, he had a knack of either sticking his nose in matters that didn't concern him, or opening his big mouth at the wrong times; at least John Arnold saw it that way!

He also knew Jeremy played on the back of his high-ranking position within the company. It was the father-son relationship and family affiliation to the all-powerful, CEO thing. He made sure everybody knew he was the son-in-law of John Arnold; it made him seem impregnable when it came to flexing his muscle, which was ludicrous on times. When it came to friendship it was even more ludicrous, he ruled the roost, none of his friends had a say in matters and if they did Isaacs decided it was mostly unimportant or he simply dismissed the facts. Needless to say, he had few friends; the few he had were either hangers on or yes-men, they were all losers. But the bullying never stopped there. Isaacs used the same tactics within the company and being the VP for Human Resources—where else was he going to fit in at that level?—He'd made some pretty bad and nonproductive decisions, which not only infuriated the workforce, it infuriated the hell out of John Arnold!

'Hey, Pops!' he said, loud enough for everybody to hear. 'Fancy seeing you here!' he added sarcastically and slurring his words. Isaacs was in a slap-happy mood, his eyes were red and he struggled to keep his balance. Both Eamon and John made their excuses and left immediately without saying a word. Not for the first time, the big man was seething inside. Sooner or later, John Arnold would address his son-in-laws antics once and for all!

To take his mind of things, and since Barbara wasn't expecting him home anytime soon, he had Charlie, his *trusted chauffer*, drop him off at Gaynor's, rented apartment. He'd given her the heads up on the way home. Once there he was able to relax a little. Stockings, suspenders, high-heel shoes and a whip, his favorite combination, had a calming effect on him, especially the way Gaynor performed with them! Meanwhile, Charlie, a handsome forty-something Austrian, waited patiently in the limousine. Whilst his passenger was enjoying the privileges of being a CEO, he enjoyed the privilege of being a chauffeur. It gave him sufficient time to text one of his many lovers. When Barbara Arnold picked up on hers, she couldn't wait for Charlie to drive over and *park-up*, so to speak. She knew all about Gaynor, Charlie kept her well-informed on that front.

Although Charlie's fees were a bit extortionate she thought from time-to-time, he was a good man and he was good between the sheets too, and that was worth every penny! So, while John was getting his backside whipped on the east-side of town, Charlie was getting his whipped on the west-side of town. With both men hard at it, but all four reaching for the stars, it was Barbara who touched them first. She had the biggest climax. She was ecstatic. The Austrian pushed buttons she never knew existed. Her husband could never do that and never would, even if they were married for another thirty years. Charlie sure knew how to drive and his parking was inch-perfect, he was pure heaven!

When they were finished, Barbara reflected on the situation. She reveled in her role as the CEOs wife, it provided her certain privileges she'd realized, but these were constantly being stretched; for example, she was now on the same footing as her husband when it came to having sex with their employees! And, like her husband, she'd stashed a lot of cash out of site for rainy days, which she knew would come; it was inevitable knowing her husband and given their lifestyle!

By the time John Arnold stepped out from Gaynor's apartment, his buttocks still raw, Charlie was waiting, a big smile across his face. When he got home, Barbara too had a smile across her face.

A happy wife is a happy life, he whispered to her in bed, just before getting on top of her to start what Charlie had already finished. Barbara smiled and just let it happen, she'd be asleep before the end anyway, happy in the knowledge that one of his employees had beat him to it!

* * *

The next day was as busy as ever. For the first time I had a feeling that we might be getting somewhere. Between us, we'd managed to drag up at least two similar cases of *unfair dismissal*, both related to the oil industry and both under similar circumstances that Desmond now found himself in. Like the rest, I worked hard to find more of the same, proven cases that we could relate to in our lawsuit.

'You're lucky to have such a fine friend, young man,' said Gloria startling me; she'd sneaked into the room unnoticed. I was sat alone in Ant's small office browsing through some of the *Case Lawsuits* stacked high, neatly placed on a chair in the corner.

'Oh! Sorry Gloria. I was in my own little world then. Yes, Desmond is indeed a friend, but don't tell *him* that. I'd hate for him to know!'

Peter Nutty

'Oh Doug, don't be such a rascal. It's not that bad . . . is it?'

'No, not at all, it's just something we've got going,' I replied with feeling.

'Men!' she said, then gently shook her head and handed me a cup of Earl Grey. I thanked her and sipped the weak tea, which was delicious. 'Tell me about the explosions, dear?' she then asked straight out of the blue. Again, I wondered how much they knew. Neither Desmond nor I had gone into any real detail. Anyway, it was in the public domain so what did I care!

'There's not much to tell really, just plenty of loud bangs and fireballs everywhere, that's all,' I said casually, not wanting to go any further.

'It must have been a horrible ordeal!' she said. I remained silent. I really didn't want to discuss it but Gloria had a way of opening you up. 'I can tell you're being coy and modest, Douglas. Come on, out with it,' she ordered. Gloria had been the first person ever to call me by my full name since school. It was rather nice.

'You get over it.' I replied and instead of answering her questions, returned to Case File # 2347689—Jarvis V. Walton—1964.

'And Desmond . . . is he over it?' she then asked not bothered that I'd turned away. Gloria wasn't taking no for an answer so I stopped what I was doing.

'I don't think Des will ever get over it,' I replied still holding the file open. 'It's made his predicament harder to accept, that's for sure.' Gloria pulled up a chair and plonked herself alongside me. She was old-aged but felt warm. I'd noticed the same feeling even from a distance. I imagined she would have made someone extremely happy as a wife.

'Go on,' she prompted. I had little choice but to tell her, so I closed the law file shut and turned to face her.

'Well, it kinda started like this. One minute we were drinking and laughing, it was Desmond's leaving bash!' I explained. 'The next, the shutters came crashing down on the bar. We thought we'd offended *Digger*, the landlord. Then, before we could have a go at *Digger* for putting a premature end to the beers, we heard the sound of the alarm.' I said, looking dejected—she knew we liked to drink beer.

'Des was out of the place in a flash upon hearing the sirens. He was one of the first people to notice a vapor cloud coming from the vicinity of the storage tanks. It was caused from a leaking valve,' I told her. 'Instead of going to the chemical plant like he should have, he immediately alerted the fire department in the adjoining refinery and actually travelled with them to the scene—the firemen could easily have got lost!' I added without meaning to be sarcastic. Gloria gave a wry smile. I then described how I saw the blackened figures running from the storage tanks and she edged closer. Then I told her of the explosions that followed without going into too much detail, but Gloria was adamant, she wanted the gory bits as well.

'Were the explosions that bad?' she asked again, as if in doubt.

'They were *that* bad,' I confirmed. 'Des and I remained well out of range of the *bleve's* though.'

'*Bleve's*, what are they, dear?' She wondered at such a peculiar word.

'Extremely hot fireballs, they're nasty,' I squirmed. Gloria sighed, put a hand on my leg and rubbed my thigh in a motherly kind of way. I continued with Desmond's story. 'It wasn't until the natural gas main had fractured that he was really noticed at all. The escaping content hissed out with some velocity and was obviously forming an invisible vapor cloud. Up to that point, we knew there were several dead workers and many more injuries. The firemen were unable to contain the fires that had now started to burn out of control, since they had no water—their resources cut off during the explosions,' I reminded her.

'Goodness!' she said. I had her attention of course and now proceeded to narrate the detail in more spectacular fashion.

'At that time the situation had changed dramatically. The latest gas escape, given the time, would ignite with a much bigger explosion than the previous ones put together,' I told her making it a little more dramatic than it really was. A squeeze of the leg accompanied the narrative. 'As I kneeled over to attend some of the injured workers, I watched as Desmond quickly got behind the wheel of an empty road-tanker, which was parked at the loading facility with its rubber tires alight. He brought the tanker around to where he thought the furthest part of the vapor had dispersed to and tried to reverse the tanker into the source of the gas cloud. He was shouting and cursing—he couldn't see where he was going. I realized what Des was trying to do . . .'

'Ignite the gas cloud before it became too large,' she interrupted taking me by surprise. I didn't think of Gloria as being technical.

'Mm . . . mm,' I nodded and carried on. 'Forgetting what I was doing, I ran over and shouted instructions at him through the broken windscreen of the tanker cab. I could see the sweat running down his face; his eyes were popping out from their sockets. The man at the wheel was unrecognizable.' Gloria was being taken in by it all judging by her grip on my leg.

'Desmond must have been frightened for his life!'

'Who wouldn't be?'

'Go on, Doug,' she urged.

'He acknowledged my hand signals and just about heard me shouting the distance he still had to go to reach his destination. The next few seconds could only be compared to being in a slow motion movie. We both looked at each other for a split second, the two of us alone and realizing what was to come, we somehow smiled. Still frightened, we kept up our smile as the lorry backed slowly into the gas cloud. Why we smiled? We'll never know; nerves probably. When I was sure that he was on the right course I immediately felt the tension go away from my body. I held no fear by now and, instead of running like I should have done, just calmly put my hand up, partly covering one side of my face whilst still looking at the tanker reversing back. Desmond too just covered his head, nodding gently as he continued with what had to be done. Within seconds the flaming tires ignited the escaping gas with an almighty *Oomph*, like the sound of a large gun-barrel exploding to propel its projectile.' The grip tightened further and I could feel her nails digging into my flesh.

'The tanker was uplifted along with another section of the boiler house and several other small bits of equipment. I remember being catapulted through the air, once again feeling my stomach churning over and I was visibly sick as I caught the sight of the lorry being lifted in the air. I could see Desmond's face as the fifteen ton truck was flipped over. He had one hand gripping the wheel of the lorry, the other was held out in a vain attempt to protect him in some way—he no longer thought of covering his head. He was open-armed and unashamedly searching for protection. His face was clenched, braced ready for the impact, which was bound to follow and he screamed in anticipation as he waited for the pain to kick-in. When the dust had settled, and with the gas main alight but now safely burning under control—I managed to get up and, still confused, with my heart, chest, and head pounding once more, I ran to the stricken tanker to search for Desmond.'

'Was he badly hurt?'

'Yeah, but we didn't know just how bad. He was well and truly trapped, unconscious and bleeding inside the upturned tanker. It was one job the fire team could manage, however, and they immediately proceeded to use their heavy cutting equipment to cut him free from the wreckage. It was several hours before he was finally rescued and taken to hospital, a hero. It was later calculated that another couple of minutes and the explosion from the increasing gas that escaped from the ruptured main would have almost certainly extended into the refinery where several sphere-type, propane and butane storage tanks were located. The failure of these would have been unthinkable.'

'Oh my, poor love,' she muttered. A tear welled in her eye.

'Don't cry for Desmond, Gloria,' I told her. 'He doesn't deserve it.'

'Douglas!' she scolded.

'Only joking, what he did that day the company should have been forever grateful? Anyway, as if his courage during the incident wasn't spectacular enough, the manner in which the company treated him later in the US certainly was,' I told her, and Gloria agreed.

'You're not kidding, either,' said Gloria. We heard footsteps in the corridor. It was Ant coming to reclaim his office. 'But there's more to it than that, Doug,' she then quickly said, quietly, only for me to hear.

'Ugh, what do you mean?'

'Just be careful, Douglas,' said Gloria clearly giving me a warning of some kind. Just then, Ant entered the small room and immediately apologized for disturbing us. 'Oh, it's okay, Anthony, I'm just leaving,' she told him, clearing away my empty cup.

'Gloria, what do you mean?' I asked again and not bothered that Ant was listening.

'I'll leave you to work it all out, dear,' she whispered. 'Just be careful.' She winked and without further explanation she left the room. She seemed ill-at-ease all of a sudden. I also noticed that Gloria had smiled uncomfortably at Ant when she left, as if she'd been caught saying something she shouldn't have said. My head began to wonder what it all meant, if it meant anything at all. But then I also noticed Ant giving a derisory look in Gloria's direction as she made her way out of the room!

Chapter 13

Later that afternoon, when we were sat eating a late lunch or perhaps it was an early dinner judging by the lashings of food served up by Tasty Bell, one of the local sandwich sellers, Lance dropped the first bombshell. He'd talked to Judge, Roland Hastings, who happened to be presiding in New Orleans. They had a mutual understanding in these matters. If there has been an injustice, Lance would have to file a lawsuit pretty damn quick. Lance had only known about the case for just under eighteen months! His Honor would need to review the preliminary details within two weeks—May, twenty-first. Any later than that, the lawsuit would find itself on the shelf. The Judge would be out of town. Following that hearing, if he decided there was a case to answer, the earliest trial date would be the end of June. Not too long to wait then, said the Judge. Lance then reminded us of the facts. To-date, we had nothing to substantiate what Desmond was contesting. Nothing, was indeed a very substantial fact, apart from possible witnesses that may, or may not have suffered the same racial abuse that their client had suffered during their employment with Advanced Strategic Energy?

Fact, our case was weak and we were on thin ice. The two previous Case Lawsuits we'd dug up earlier were not that good after all, said Lance after scrolling through the details and deciphering all the jargon for the benefit of Desmond and me.

Fact, a settlement arrangement was his best option but Desmond had refused to co-operate on these grounds.

Fact, the Judge would practically insist on a settlement after reviewing the lawsuit!

Fact, disregarding the fact that we had only two weeks to prepare and present a case for His Honor to review, we had barely four weeks to prepare for any pre-trial discovery hearing, that's if, His Honor granted such a hearing. That, in the Judge's opinion, just wasn't enough time.

Fact, Cranton & Associates had assigned one of their brightest lawyers to contend any allegations of racial discrimination and/or unfair dismissal made against their client, Advanced Strategic Energy Inc. John Brigg's was the best with an ever-increasing list of courtroom battle honors beginning to stack high in his curriculum vitae. Lance confessed that he had bargained on an out-of-court settlement and had taken the liberty of discussing the details with Brigg's. *Bastard*, thought Desmond flinching in his seat.

'You kept that quite,' he muttered loud enough for us to hear his disgust. The old campaigner ignored him. To his credit, Lance blamed himself for underestimating Desmond's resolve in wanting justice against his former employer. Desmond had insisted on getting Advanced Strategic Energy in a court of law to justify his unwarranted dismissal, he said in his defense. Lance did not show any emotion for his wrongdoings, if there were any. He stood proud, intact. That was that, he had said then continued with some additional words of warning.

'Gentlemen, we have agreed that we are willing and able to fight this case,' he began. *Are you sure, I thought?* I kept my sarcastic views to myself whilst Lance continued to speak. 'We haven't filed the case, yet! But we will,' he added enthusiastically. 'Once that is done, we have to substantiate it. If we win, then fine. We will be able to press for punitive damages that will ensure our efforts are not in vain.' He hadn't convinced anybody of this, incidentally. I don't think he wanted to either. 'If we lose, we get nothing and like the rest of you, I will find myself looking for another job to pay the costs that could be charged against us.'

Crikey! For the first time in all of the times we've talked about Desmond getting his due justice, here we are deliberating what the circumstances are if we actually lost the case. It hit home to me. Perhaps I should phone Frank and apologize. Lance had wired up the alarm-bells in readiness, just in case. He knew we were up against it. If we wanted out, then now was the time to speak up—a second warning shot had been fired across my bows. Not once had I considered the consequences should we lose. And if we did lose, then lose we would, in a huge way, big time. Des had very little to lose, obviously. Lance had everything to lose, naturally. Especially so since he only got paid a percentage of any awards made to Desmond. The associates would probably be protected by some sort of complicated insurance policy—the lawyers would probably have written the small print themselves! And then me, I had a lot at stake too. My job would be the biggest asset. I would be stripped of that, no doubt about it. Not straight away, but in time. A matter of weeks probably, depending upon how clever their human resources people were at fabricating a convincing reason for instant dismissal. Pretty damn clever I guessed judging how swift and efficient they had dealt with Des. The Nigerian propaganda material came flooding back and it sent shivers up my spine.

'Bugger em.'

The Welsh accent echoed around the table but surprised nobody other than Des and me. It was the die-hard, and Bolshevik, voice of Dillwyn. His resolve was much better than ours was for sure. He smoked all kinds of bad stuff and besides, he had nothing to lose either. It was just the response they had expected from Dil. If we were up against the American Fifth Fleet and looking certain death in the face, Dil would have responded in the same manner.

'Thanks Dil,' said Lance sarcastically, his face screwed up in mock amazement. Chuck began yet another bout of giggling. Dillwyn momentarily forgot himself and acknowledged his friend's good humor, he also laughed. They both chuckled and that sparked condemnation from Ant.

'You want to know something, Lance?' he said, turning to face his employer. 'Sometimes I despair! I really do. We should sue these two sons-of-a-bitch for pretending to be professionals?' The New Yorker was annoyed with his two colleagues and his reaction was to be over-sympathetic with himself, then with Lance, and then with the overall situation. In a strange way, Ant's frustration had come across in a humorous kind of way, but even his feeling of hopelessness was nothing compared to what happened next. Dil stood up, clenched his face, clenched his backside, and clenched every other part of his body that might have been slightly loose and broke wind.

'Sorry about that boy's, couldn't help it,' he told us, seriously straight-faced. 'It just slipped out!' Even I thought about giggling along with Chuck at the sound of Dillwyn's backside giving off some gas. But it was the way he apologized that did me. His accent I think. Ant was amazed. The poor man thought he was working with idiots, and he was. No wonder he was constantly challenging his sanity.

'It might have been something I smoked,' added Dillwyn in a vain attempt to defend his actions. That was enough. It was too much. The genuinely, sorrowful look on Dillwyn's face was a picture. He just stood there waiting for something else to happen, while in the meantime the rest of us looked on in utter disbelief. Lance let it be known that he sincerely hoped that nothing else was waiting to come out from inside his paralegal.

'Are you quite done?' he asked fed up with it all.

'I think so, Lance. Sorry,' replied Dillwyn for the umpteenth time.

'You been eating peelings, Dil?' enquired Chuck who then fell about laughing. In the end we could not contain ourselves. Dil had broken the ice in the crudest of fashions and we all smiled. Then we all giggled, and then it turned into laughter. Even Ant laughed with us after realizing the funny side of what had just happened—which was disgusting and not funny at all under any other circumstances. So there we were. A room full of grown men, all intellectuals to some degree or other, and faced with a massive mountain to climb, sat around a table laughing at the crudeness of a *professional* member of our team. We had to present one of the biggest civil lawsuits we would ever get involved in, against one of the largest companies in America and we were falling about the table laughing at somebody farting in public. It couldn't get any worse!

* * *

I laughed and laughed and then laughed some more at what Desmond had just told me but now I was tiring. We had *managed* to find a bar—*Kamps*, and after several beers my friend had talked me to death. How he manages to tell the story's he does was beyond me. Unfortunately for me and everybody else there, he had many more stories to tell.

'Picture this, Doug,' says Desmond loud enough for two or three other people in the nearby booth to also have the privilege of imagining what he was about to picture. 'About eight or nine of us are sitting around a coffee table on some oil platform in the North Sea, man,' he began to say. 'Seventy foot waves outside, hundred miles an hour winds battering the shit out of us an' all, and we're inside telling our *most embarrassing* stories,' he says. Desmond tells us this as if it's a crime. 'Well, one thing leads to another and we're right on it, man.'

'On what, Des?' I ask leaning over the table, a bottle swaying in my left hand. A waitress interrupted him by picking up our empties. Desmond continued the minute she left.

'The . . . the . . . err . . . the most embarrassing . . .' stuttered Desmond, struggling to speak. The words sometimes got stuck he informed his audience in a drunken stupor. 'The most embarrassing stories, man, and bro have I got one for you,' he finally managed to blurt out. It was as if he'd just remembered to put his mouth in gear.

'Well, go ahead, tell the story before I nod off,' I urged.

'Trevor Jones, r-e-a-l religious,' he then said with a spooky look and emphasizing the fact slowly. 'He's at home with God, bro. Don't warm to none of the nonsense we were talking about. Anyway, we all had a story to tell, Doug,' he said to me and the others, swaying as he talked now. Desmond usually had more stupid stories to tell than most of the others so we just let him continue. 'Soon we were in hysterics at some of the things these guys were getting up to, man,' he said, wide-eyed. I could see Desmond becoming excited at what he was about to tell us. He would have to rush because I wasn't going to be in the land of the living soon, I was going to be asleep in the chair if he didn't hurry up.

'Then it's Trevor's turn, right? So I turn and ask him what his most embarrassing story is? Just like that,' said Desmond with a click of his fingers. 'Real big mistake, man, I shoulda known. Big Trev lowered the newspaper he was reading and gave us the most scathing look you ever saw. I knew then that I should've asked,' he muttered to the floor, still slurring and meaning to say, *should not have asked*. 'But, I already did,' he informed us looking dejected but proud. 'And by now the others, the rest of em you know, the ones sat with us,' he said, explaining the seating arrangements that fateful night the best he could. 'Well the others, well, they just kinda looked in the opposite direction. All of a sudden, they didn't want anything to do with it!' he moaned in disgust. Desmond was drunk and enjoyed the hoard of people who had now assembled around the table to hear his story. 'Well, Trevor, well . . . he just looked me straight in the eyes and asked if I really wanted to know? If I really, really, wanted to know?' repeated Desmond. 'Do you know what I mean, man? He was one angry son-of-a-bitch and I thought he was gonna kick my ass! Anyway, he comes right out with it and tells us that his momma caught him masturbating. Well, man. You coulda cut the air with a knife. We all felt kinda stupid cos the big man, Trevor, was raving mad. He was going nuts inside cos he felt all embarrassed an all.' His audience looked on expressionless, not sure if they'd heard him right. *Did he say masturbation?* asked one confused woman to her husband who had the presence of mind to ignore her.

'So, no big deal, what happened then?' asked another one of the girls who'd taken a serious interest all of a sudden.

'I tried to reassure him, young lady,' he said to the girl and everybody looked in her direction. 'Like you said, I told him that it was no big deal, lots of guys get caught pulling their pudding by their momma,' he told her, giggling, as if it was an everyday event in his house! The guys laughed and

The Last Hangman

there were a few blushes and even a few chuckles from the females in the audience. 'And then, guess what?' asked Desmond to everybody present.

'What?' enquired an impatient guy listening in the next booth.

'Trevor stands up, frothing at the mouth and shouts out. *No big deal! No big deal! It was for me*, he shouted aloud. *I was fifty seven at the time!* Ha . . . ! Ha . . . ! Get it, Doug. Fifty-seven, the guy got caught by his mamma at the age of fifty-seven. Ha . . . !' Desmond was now rolling around the table in uncontrolled laughter. The onlookers too had laughed at his story. I had fallen asleep upon hearing the punch line but Desmond just carried on amusing his newly found friends. The bar had become alive. Tomorrow was going to be another long day in the Port Arthur office of Heycock & Associates. It would be even longer for Desmond.

* * *

The reality of a, *Summary Judgment*, was something that could possibly be requested by the defense council prior to any trial. And that's exactly what would happen we soon found out after Lance had discussed the issues with Judge, Hastings. This notion alone ensured that the afternoon was made well use of. We had to make a genuine issue for the trial to proceed and continued to do just that. The last thing we needed was insufficient evidence—although that's what we had. I had made more than thirteen phone calls to friends, colleagues and associates at Advanced Strategic Energy. Most of these were requests regarding the possible route directories and retrieval methods of working agreements relating to terms and conditions of employment, racial harassment policies, and anything else that might resemble the same. I made the request by pretending to be in the throes of endorsing a punishment of an employee working for me in England. I wanted to be absolutely correct and go by the book in what I intended to do, I told them under false pretences. I could not give details of those involved or of what they'd done, other than the fact that I was considering dismissal proceedings due to racial harassment. Nobody suspected my motives for the request.

After several small but friendly conversations to pick up on the latest gossip in the company, I was soon furnished with what I needed. The access route directories were scribbled down in my best computer hand writing—jargon.com. I promptly logged on to a computer and with Dil guiding me through the Internet, dialed up my computer terminal via my external log-on details. We both searched the company Intranet database to see what we could find. The whole examination, retrieval and printout time was just under two hour's total and produced thirteen documents in all. The documents were controlled by the human resources department. They related mostly to gross misconduct and negligence and had been recently updated it seemed. Still, there were no policies relating to racial harassment, or anything remotely relating to that in nature. At least this small part of our task yielded a result, our first break.

'Are you sure?' asked Lance.

'Yes, we're as sure as we can be. We've opened their policies up like a tin of sardines. No racial discrimination policies, we were certain.' Dillwyn agreed with a nod. The company policies relating to gross negligence and gross misconduct were there though we warned him. They were pretty much black and white. Desmond was guilty, no doubt about it judging by his terms of employment, said lance after scrutinizing the documents with a fine tooth comb.

The Forty Second, United States Constitution—Title 42, The Public Health and Welfare—Chapter 21, Civil Rights—Section 1981, Equal rights under the law and, Section 1981a, Damages in cases of intentional discrimination in employment, is a mouthful. They described the laws related to racial discrimination and the heavily detailed documents were now laid open on the large conference table. Lance and Ant were once again busy referencing paragraphs from it. The lawsuit would be based on Article VII of the Civil Rights Act of 1964 and also cite section 1981 and 1981a, and those highlighted paragraphs from it. Meanwhile, Desmond and Dillwyn continued their research into whom and why other distressed employees had left the company. Along with those he'd already contacted prior to meeting his legal councilors, Desmond was remembering the names of people he'd not seen in years. They had, in one way or another, been subjected to racial harassment, or just plain bullying, or both. Some left due to racial hatred even. For some time we listened to them complain about anything so long as they were aggrieved about it. Dil had considered sending them an e-mail to let them know what they intended to do, but trust and confidentiality was of the utmost importance. After discussing it with Lance, he thought better of it. Advanced Strategic Energy could easily access and examine the contents of e-mail, just as they themselves were doing at that very moment. Things were speeding up but the lawsuit was still taking ages to prepare and shape into some kind of presentation. It may have to be more compact with less supporting evidence to be quicker but it would have to be right. No, ifs, buts, or maybes, it just had to be right.

* * *

Jeremy Isaacs wasn't all that perturbed by recent events, just damn frustrated. The call from the company's lawyers, Cranton & Associates, was made out of courtesy more than anything else. One of their senior legal guys who went by the name of, Dinger, had given him the heads up on a pending racial discrimination lawsuit, which was now in the process of being filed by a former employee, Desmond Haynes. It was destined for the New Orleans Parish. Surprise! Surprise!

Isaacs remembered only too well all the fuss surrounding Haynes dismissal some time ago; he couldn't remember the exact time but he did recall it was messy and none too pleasing for his liking. The other stuff, like unfair dismissal, Dinger hadn't bothered to tell him, it was unimportant he thought compared to the racist allegation. But he did mention that another employee from England, Doug Archer, despite previously being persuaded to keep his nose out, was still going to give evidence if it went to court, which Dinger doubted very much. Nevertheless, if Isaacs could put a little pressure on things in England, it would help wrap up things without too much fuss. The English guy obviously wasn't listening and if he didn't get the massage pretty soon, it would only cause a stir in their topsy-turvy, spaghetti-wrangled way of doing business.

Feeling inconvenienced by the way he had to deal with these trivial goings-on at his level, he made the call to Frank, who was at home and enjoying his favorite tipple, a cold Martini, shaken and not stirred, whilst playing bridge. It was the second such call from Isaacs. The first was charming, this one was the opposite. This time he ordered Frank to be less persuasive and more direct with what was being asked of him. He damned well better make sure Archer was going to keep his snout out of this matter, he'd told him rather abruptly. When he put the phone down, Frank hadn't the desire to play bridge anymore. Unlike his Martini, he was both shaken and stirred!

* * *

That night, we chose a different bar to celebrate another milestone in my working career. A fax from Frank, obviously bandied around and read by the hotel staff before being politely and confidentially sealed in an envelope, was waiting for me at the lobby reception. Due to reorganization at the refinery I was no longer operations manager. I would be told of my pending position upon reporting back to the plant. In effect, I was being constructively dismissed. The fax was hand-written and sent from his home address, which said a lot about the haste with which it was dispatched! I needed a lawyer but not once did I think of Lance Heycock & Associates! It worried me not in the least. After eight bottles of Bud, I'd decided that I'd knee Frank full in the crotch at the first opportunity—Desmond agreed with the idea. He paid for two more beers before leaving me on a stool by the bar; he had to phone Suzanne and the kids. Meanwhile, it was obvious that the ASEI propaganda machine was still silently turning and slowly mincing us up. I felt even more alone, vulnerable and saddened with each bottle of beer.

Chapter 14

AFTER SEVERAL IFS, BUTS, AND maybes—because it just wasn't right, Lance had no option but to tweak the contents as he continued to outline the lawsuit to the Judge. John Brigg's, JB to his fellow entourage sitting alongside, was up on his elbows, half-leaning over the table listening to what was being said. He constantly intervened, like good lawyers were meant to. Only part of our case had been presented to the Judge so far and he couldn't wait to rubbish it. And rubbish it he would, but he would have to wait a little while longer for the privilege. We were sat comfortably inside the private Chambers of Judge, Roland Hastings, pondering our ill-prepared lawsuit, our masterpiece, which according to Lance was evidently crap!

We were at our first hurdle, a pre-trial meeting with the Judge; in my limited knowledge of the law I took this to be the, *Summary Judgment*, part of affairs. We had to prove we had a case and so far we could not even prove Lance had a license to practice law never mind racial discrimination, judging by the smirk on JB's face. Everything we had to do at a later date in order to get a verdict in Desmond's favor would prove to be an even bigger hurdle.

Lance had put our cards on the table, we didn't have much of a hand but part of the lawsuit cited, *racial discrimination*, and that meant a hell of a lot in these parts. New Orleans supported human rights and equality was always high on any agenda, from the government to the military, from large department stores to the classroom, from the sports ground to the steel mills and now it had spread right through to the very roots of society.

Most black folks knew what *article seven* was all about. So, in my opinion, I was right to think that at least one State in America had solved their racist problem. Wrong. For all that had been done to rid the wrongdoings of discrimination, racism was still a huge problem in

Louisiana, and elsewhere in the States. His Honor could ill-afford any mistakes on this one.

In its entirety, the lawsuit alleged that Advanced Strategic Energy Inc supervision and managers created a work environment hostile to black employees and made racial derogatory and demeaning remarks. On top of that they were discriminated against in every way, including pay and bonuses. The plaintiff, Desmond Haynes, had been wrongfully dismissed because he was black and not through *gross negligence*, as would be argued by the defense council. In addition, we accused the company of keeping blacks in low-level positions by neglecting to give them proper training or promotion. The last allegation was Dillwyn's idea. It would be hard to convince the Judge that this did not occur even if that statement was wrong. He had influenced us all to agree and we did, apart from Lance who'd fiercely objected but finally relented when he took another scathing look from Desmond.

'It's hardly a strong case, counselor. You haven't entirely convinced me. What about a settlement?' said His Honor, straight off the bat! Judge, Roland Hastings knew the reply. He had asked Lance that same question during the telephone conversation they held to arrange the meeting. He would formally ask the question anyway so that it would be recorded. He was well on track and going by the book.

'I'm sorry, Your Honor,' said Briggs quickly, he'd seen his chance and decided to take it. He butted in before Lance could say anything. 'Advanced Strategic Energy Incorporated denies these allegations. However, ASEI are a caring company. They recognize the contributions made to the company by Mr. Haynes prior to his dismissal, but the fact is he is now a *former* aggrieved employee. That makes a big difference in lawsuits of this kind since we all know that in such circumstances, allegations are made very much without substance and the plaintiff is likely to drag any unsubstantiated allegation into the courtroom. It's designed to distract from the truth and maximize publicity, Your Honor.'

'I know what it's meant to do, counselor!' snapped the Judge quickly. JB turned to his colleagues for support but they merely sat still, scribbling down some detail or other and pretended not to hear the Judge's comments. They were being courteous and were well trained not to make eye contact under these circumstances!

Briggs' carried on regardless; he'd soon have the Judge eating out of his hand. 'My client would like it known, for the records, that we do not hold against him the fact that he is, err . . . excuse me, was,' JB smiled and corrected himself. 'Very much an aggrieved employee, he has an axe to grind if you ask me. Whilst my client does not admit to any wrongdoings, I wish to inform you that an out-of-court-settlement is within my remit.'

'Well, Mr. Heycock, what are we waiting for?' The Judge was on the case. It would be wrapped up nicely if he could put a little pressure on.

'Your Honor, my client does not agree to any kind of settlement. Mr. Haynes merely wants fair play. I ask you kindly that we go for trial by jury.' That was it. Lance hadn't bothered to dip his toe in. He'd simply dived in head first from the top board. Now, it was all down to His Honor, who would have been crazy to grant a trial at that moment in time. Lance waited to see how cold the water was. The Judge thought for a moment longer than anticipated, which made things rather chilly. He wouldn't grant a trial now, would he? It was too soon and they had practically nothing to go on, and in any case, he would surely tease him for a while longer assumed Lance.

'Your Honor,' he began calmly. Not bothered to wait, JB was up before the Judge deliberated too long. It was a bad sign when somebody in authority rubbed his or her chin in any law establishment, worse in a Judge's chambers. It usually meant they were about to make a wrong decision and JB recognized it straight away. He had more than enough ammo left yet, plenty to put the case to bed early and he'd long decided to use it. Why take a gamble? JB stood with both hands resting on the table before him. His parasites prepared to scribble the details. 'Advanced Strategic Energy has a zero-tolerance policy for any discriminatory practices anywhere in the work place. We can prove that beyond any reasonable doubt. No jury is going to agree with these allegations,' he said with conviction. He was sincere and probably right. I for one would have believed him if I didn't know about the non-existent racial harmony policies or whatever it is they called them these days.

Briggs then half-turned to face Lance before continuing. 'My client has always worked hard to make sure its hiring and promotional practices are fair and equitable for all employees. It's a mistake to think you can roll them over with these unfounded scraps of hearsay. Take the money,' he offered with a tactful dose of reality. That appeal to Lance was a good move, sensible enough and anyone other than Desmond would have accepted a cash payoff there and then. The Judge bore down on Desmond and the frowned look was a give-away. *Ask how much and then accept it, you dull, son-of-a-bitch*, was written all over his reddened face.

'What's on the table councilor?' asked the Judge without removing his gaze from Desmond.

'Very little, Your Honor,' said Briggs with a sorrowful look on his face that hid a gleaning smirk deep inside.

'What will you accept, councilor?' he asked Lance, still keeping his stare firmly fixed on Desmond who had by now started to smile back at the larger than life figure sat on the desk ahead of him. While that was going on, each lawyer knew exactly which councilor the Judged referred to. Now they played a game of chess. It was bravado time between Lance and JB. The Judge would be ref.

'Nothing, Your Honor, like I said . . . '

'There's something on the table, councilor,' said the Judge cutting Lance off. 'Think about it. What are the goddamn figures?' He spoke without turning his head. His question was aimed specifically at any one of the two lawmen but he looked only at Desmond, who was really annoying him with that silly grin on his face. When His Honor asked a question he wanted a straight answer. Any one of them could reply as far as he was concerned.

'Two hundred thousand,' Briggs said aloud before Lance could conjure up a larger, more ridiculous amount. JB was first off the blocks again. I wouldn't have been surprised if the sum had surprised two or three people passing by in the corridor. It was said loud enough for them to hear. Lance stood up and responded almost immediately. There was nothing else for it.

'We're not taking the money,' he replied firmly. 'Their *so-called* policy regarding zero tolerance against racial discriminatory practices in the work place doesn't exist. My client will not accept any settlement other than a courtroom verdict, Your Honor.' Without acknowledgement, but with the seed of doubt sown, Hastings once again read the details included in the lawsuit neatly typed in front of him. The others did the same! Nothing had changed since they last read it.

'This lawsuit does not seek specific damages, councilor,' he said to Lance, but it was a reminder to all of us. 'The bottom line is a bit much though, don't you think?' He lowered his glasses further down his nose and looked at us all—Lance, Ant, and Chuck, Desmond and me. He frowned at the sorrowful sight before him.

'Perhaps it's a typo,' said Briggs sarcastically. Everyone ignored him save for a few giggles from his paralegal. Lance looked at Desmond and then at me. Was there a slight sign of embarrassment? He then turned to look at the Blues Brothers, who'd stayed neutral by looking directly down at the table. We had warned him of being too greedy. Briggs should keep his mouth shut and Lance should have listened to us, I wanted to say but couldn't. He turned to face the Judge.

'We estimate it would take that sum to cover lost wages, mental anguish, and attorney's fees and so on. In addition, we would seek twenty million dollars in punitive damages, Your Honor,' he said all too confidently. He ignored Briggs altogether and sat down without adding to or referring to whatever else was contained in the lawsuit. Briggs just looked at the table, shaking his head in amazement. As far as Lance was concerned, the words were in plain English. There could be no mistaking what the words meant or what the math was. The Judge was not amused. Earlier he was trying to force our hand. He wanted a settlement. The money was there, take it, he encouraged us with all the body language of a lap dancer. We stood firm and the Judge looked angry, probably by the fact that Desmond had out-stared him. His anger would multiply after the ensuing chaos that would follow his decision. It seemed as though we were playing a game of poker. Lance had thrown the last card on the table on behalf of the plaintiff. The rest of us held our cards close to our chest. So did the Judge, so did Briggs. The Judge hardly flinched at the huge amount, which surprised me. It was quite natural apparently to go for a massive amount of money. It raised the profile of the case and showed we meant business.

'Twenty million . . . mm!' the Judge pondered what had been recited by Lance. He imagined the amount. It must be difficult for any Judge to consider such unimaginable amounts of money. It was ridiculous.

'Tsch!' Briggs spat and grunted his disapproval to the others sat beside him upon hearing such a vile figure for the second time. Lance was expressionless. Desmond was relieved that His Honor had removed his glare and now the black Jamaican just sat expressionless, looking embarrassed from what he'd done.

'A jury, ugh . . . it'll be a tough one!' he muttered to himself. The Judge was right. It would be hard convincing any jury of Desmond's demise. 'Are you up for it, Haynes?' asked the Judge. He took Desmond by surprise.

'Yes sir. I'm up for it,' Desmond replied, excited.

'Young man, may I remind you that when you are in my presence you address me as, Your Honor, got it?' Lance looked away in embarrassment, how many times had he briefed Desmond about the Judge's hatred at not being called by his correct title?

'Sorry, Your Honor. Won't happen again,' he replied quickly. Desmond had learned a lesson and felt foolish once again; he had given himself a black eye. *Young man*, he then thought. Shit, he was over fifty-years of age! He looked at me as though it was a lost cause. So far, so bad, I thought. In his heart Desmond was already beaten.

The Judge had made his point. He'd also made his mind up. Despite Desmond's despondency, I sensed the decision was coming our way. Briggs could see the dollar signs amassing on his monthly salary and waited for the announcement—he was in a win-win situation. He knew what the Judge was thinking. He half-expected it considering the nature of the lawsuit. Safety case, preparing for a trial like this, the deposition, time spent in Court, bonuses for a verdict in his clients' favor. It would be a big payday for them and they would make a lot of money—including the Judge.

'Very well, you've got it,' announced the Judge from nowhere. 'When can you start deposition?' he asked.

'Anytime, Your Honor.' JB was first again, right on the ball.

'Anytime suits us, Your Honor,' replied Lance looking woefully across the table towards Briggs. Time was not a problem, he had no other clients.

'At Cranton's one week from today. The trial will be heard here, four weeks from today, any problems? Fine,' the Judge didn't wait a second for any to be raised. 'Good day, gentlemen.' A court deputy held the door open. Of course there weren't any problems! Holding the deposition at the offices of the defense council was no problem! His Honor walked to a bookcase and scanned a shelf that was head high. I doubted he was looking for any book in particular. We gathered our belongings in a sloppy fashion and scrambled through the door without another word being spoken.

'Nice one JB.' Those patronizing words were muttered by a paralegal working for Briggs as we walked through the corridor. He was sat next to him throughout the fifteen minutes it had taken us to convince the Judge we had a case, or an argument of some kind more like. He wore an Italian designer suit that matched his immaculately combed black hair and walked along with a continuous smirk that barely wrinkled his sun-tanned face. I hadn't seen him before and I already hated him.

'Rich pickings,' murmured another to his senior attorney as they walked in close proximity to us. It was loud enough for us all to hear. Briggs acknowledged him with a wink. Advanced Strategic Energy wouldn't be happy with the preliminaries, but it was expected. Another result destined to go in the bag he must have thought. Old JB was already done with our case and would probably assign a lesser-experienced lawyer to deal with the formalities. He was off to report back to Cranton and onward to drink champagne somewhere. Ant gave him the bird behind his back.

* * *

Still partly wet from my shower, I sat uncomfortably on the edge of the bed drinking, Bud Light and listening to the ringing tone down the receiver. I thought about Frank's fax, which had been crumpled up and tossed in the bin. Now I was sober it frightened the shit out of me even more. CNN Evening News was on the box but the volume was muted. A Martin Luther King look-alike was pointing his finger in an attempt to get across some point or other. It would be room service tonight; Desmond could go get drunk alone. I couldn't keep up with him and besides, I still had work to progress from England, operations manager or not. The phone was answered just as I'd taken a sip from the bottle. A little surprised that I'd had an answer so quickly, I slurped down the beer and straightened up from my slouched position on the bed.

'Hello!'

The line crackled slightly and the voice on the other end seemed distant but polite and there was no mistaking it belonged to a young female.

'Cheryl, is that you?'

'Yes, who's speaking please?'

'Hi Cheryl, its Doug Archer,' I said politely. I assumed she knew who I was and only needed a brief introduction before quickly apologizing about the quality of the phone line—it crackled like hell. I went on to explain my whereabouts and my reason for phoning. There was complete silence at the other end of the line.

The phone call had been short lived. Cheryl was abrupt and gave very little detail; I would have to sort it out upon my return to England. After a couple of hours alone in my room, I went into my usual indecision mode and met Desmond in the bar, drunk to way gone midnight and then returned to the room after leaving Des arguing with a couple of rednecks downstairs. We'd decided to go to New York first thing in the morning in preparation for pre-discovery something or other, as Lance had tried to explain to me. I tried to sleep in but it was all in vane, Nigeria came flooding back as it inevitably did, and all too frequently on times.

Chapter 15

THE CURTAINS SWAYED AND ROLLED gently from a light breeze that penetrated a gap in the partially open doors that led from the wooden deck outside and into the bedroom. Every now and then a gust of wind whipped the curtains open, enough to allow the rising sun to light up the lifeless and darkened room. Four half-full glasses of spirits of one kind or another were placed precariously at the side of each bedside table—two were heavily caked with lipstick. The remains of a white powdery substance lay scattered across a glass plate placed on a cabinet to one side of the room. There was no doubting the fact that whoever had got undressed the night before was either in a rush or a struggle had occurred. Items of clothing had been thrown off aimlessly and now lay strewn around the room.

Thankful that the torments and nightmares that he now suffered had finished, at least for another night, the male occupant calmly pulled back the sheets and got to his feet, looked briefly at the female companion lying partly exposed, naked in his bed before swiftly making for the bathroom. He stood in the dark for a couple of seconds looking into a mirror, hesitating, not wanting to see any reflection or image that might connect himself to reality of any kind, to anywhere or anyone. The man splashed his face with cold water several times before he reached out and, with one *click* of a pull chord, lit up a strip-light above the mirror. It showed the wet, feint and worried face of somebody who had not slept in days or even weeks. Even in the bright light that reflected off the mirror he seemed to be still in the dark. The person staring at his reflection was no longer in control, he needed help. The last two years had been all about endurance. Survival in a business that strived for the spoils and riches, for ever-increasing technology and innovation that had to be balanced with an everlasting and desperate need to decrease resources and manpower—cutting costs was routine and *downsizing* was now the buzz word. Call it what you like, it all meant the same. He was in an industry that relied heavily upon its reserves, its responsibility to shareholders and return on investment. It was about oil, an ever-decreasing commodity that has been, and still was being exploited by the world. The crown jewels of modern day energy were constantly being fought for somewhere in the world and protected against somewhere else. The riches that are provided by this black gold could be cruel to the industry that makes it shine though. Its very existence manipulated by the dollar. When the price is good, all's well and the shareholders are quick to be told. The other way and the oil industries are ruthless and without pity to its beneficiaries, as the man in the mirror knew only too well.

Opening a cupboard door and from inside a small, gold-plated pill-box he picked out two tablets and placed both in his mouth at once, swallowed hard on a glass of water before slowly opening his eyes. Within minutes, Richard Hammond was wired! He gently rubbed a scar on the left-hand side of his cheek, as if inspecting it, and smiled before applying some make-up to hide the outline of the deep-purple tissue. It was his *Nigeria Medal* he told anybody who cared to ask. The drugs were kicking in, he could feel his body slowly transforming, there would be no more worries for a couple of hours at least by which time he knew he would have to replenish the narcotic. The good times these days were short lived and getting shorter by the day judging by the increasing dosage of stimulants he know heavily relied upon.

The drive from his hometown in Oakland to Manhattan that morning was better than most days. It would take at least a couple of hours and so he settled comfortably in the leather seat of the company, S class Mercedes and watched as the beautiful scenery around Ramapo Valley disappeared behind him. It gave way to the thriving, and sometimes not so thriving, industrial towns that now supplied the Big Apple well over a hundred miles away. His thoughts that morning though never strayed too far from work—the events of the last twelve hours were a million miles away. In his mind he'd soon started to piece together his intended business for the day, but for some reason or other he struggled to think straight. It wasn't the drugs. They were working for him, so how could he explain it? Something or someone was troubling him. It would not be too long before he found out.

Chapter 16

Advanced Strategic Energy Inc, corporate headquarters occupied the top eight floors of a fourteen-storey building that overlooked Central Park, they were only a couple of blocks or so from Cranton & Associates. The location was smart. Compared to other world oil companies they were being measured as a mid-sized player, but with strong growth they'd soon be a threat to all the rest if they weren't already. Whilst their offices hardly competed with many of the same sized companies that based themselves in Manhattan, they were still recognized as one of the elite, corporate New Yorkers. There were many other oil majors that would have loved to be located across from Central Park. Advanced Strategic Energy Inc was there and the others were not. All in all, ASEI were comfortable and more importantly, successful, very successful with interests, partnerships and alliances that were the envy of companies throughout the world.

Almost an hour before Richard Hammond would arrive at his place of work, another car slowed to a screechy halt in the basement parking lot used only by executives of the company. The *reserved* sign was totally ignored as a tall, rugged-looking man got out of the car clutching a briefcase he'd grabbed from the passenger seat. He stood for a moment, looked around and patted the lapel of his jacket, lightly. He needed to feel the browning pistol that was concealed, tucked away under his jacket and securely holstered around his left shoulder and upper chest. On top of this, he wore a heavily waxed *drizza-bone* raincoat to conceal the weapon further. The thick lining and waterproofed raincoat would also protect him from the morning frost. A young black man was walking nearby and spoke as he passed.

'Good morning, how are you today, sir?' he enquired. The courteous remarks were ignored. Instead, the heavily dressed man started to walk swiftly to the elevator without even the slightest glance at the passer-by striding in the opposite direction. He had a host of conversations going on in his mind and the young man was not taking part in any of them.

A stairway led from the basement to the ground floor proper. He knew this would also take him to the reception area. That was the route he'd planned to take and so, having climbed the concrete stairs for only one level, he continued his journey, navigating his way through the building meticulously and talking to nobody. He passed no less than three armed guards on the way to an elevator located to the right of the lobby and within sight of the main reception desk. Coming in from the executive parking lot was a confidence trick he'd mastered many times; it usually meant nobody would challenge his being there and it had worked. He calmly entered the lift at the same time as several others. Soon enough, the ring of a bell informed the occupants that they'd reached the thirteenth floor. The next floor of the building, the highest of the eight floors owned by Advanced Strategic Energy Inc, naturally accommodated the top brass—several Senior Presidents, Vice-Presidents and CEO of the company, all of whom formed the Executive Board of Directors.

He slowly shuffled along with the rest and made his exit out of the lift. Two people remained inside as the elevator doors closed behind him he noticed; they were involved in executive matters. The group he mingled with quickly made their way down a short corridor. He followed, listening to the customary early morning chat, which slowly filled the emptiness of the building. They soon entered a spacious, open-planned area. Not for the first time in situations like this a familiar sensation came over him and he twitched. The excitement was all too apparent. He'd missed it in the past couple of months though. It was a craving, and now that fantastic feeling was beginning to boil inside his entire body once again. If it continued the sensation that now engulfed him would eventually bring him to a climax; he couldn't control his urge to kill at the best of times. Patting his coat for the umpteenth time he felt the heavy metal under his jacket. He constantly needed reassurance that his weapon was still there as he made his way forward. He felt slightly exposed. In his mind he knew he dare not be recognized, not here anyway. There was only one man in the whole of America who could do that and he was not in the building yet, so he urged himself to maintain his discipline. It was imperative that he kept his anonymity for a while longer. He'd waited this long and he could be patient for some time yet.

Ignoring the small talk from those around him he continued with his vigilance but it was difficult. More people had exited another elevator and filled the room. The noise had increased and the sheer numbers had by now crowded his vision. To add to his frustration, the heat inside the building was uncomfortable making it even more difficult to concentrate. He loosened several buttons on his coat and tried to ignore the chatter, which was typical for most New Yorkers—a question answered by another question and usually revolved around last night's ball game, or one of the chat shows. He slowly ambled through a buzzing labyrinth of small cubicles that made up small work stations. The whole place had become alive now and he almost felt claustrophobic. The noise was unbearable to somebody who'd spent lifetime in the jungle. It intensified by the minute as phones started to ring and printers spewed out reams of paper and the talk got louder. The assailant maintained his guard, nevertheless, as even more people entered the building with something or other to say. He'd made his mind up to move further towards the outer part of the building. The offices were simply arranged and appeared exactly as described to him by the polite young lady who worked the reception desk well over a month ago.

Located around the entire periphery were glass-paneled offices used by more senior employees of the company, and these naturally had the views overlooking Central Park and beyond—Manhattan housed a host of landmarks that spread out to form New York and provided some pretty picturesque views. These offices could be made more private by closing horizontal blinds that hung from every glass panel. Furthermore, the interior walls were padded to allow for extra discretion and privacy, which allowed the occupier to work on more sensitive matters related to their business.

Richard Hammond was one such employee; he'd occupied one of these offices for the past three years. It was only a matter of minutes before the intruder had gained access following a conversation with a middle-aged black woman about the need to check out a faulty security system in that particular room. She politely informed him that it was his lucky day. She was in fact the secretary of the occupier and since her boss was not due for another hour or so, she saw no reason whatsoever why she shouldn't promptly let him in to undertake the repair. He thanked her in a poor accent and closed the door behind him.

* * *

Smartly dressed in an Italian, designer suit that resisted being creased from sitting in the car, Hammond continued cruising south along Highway

202. He had managed to ignore his troubles and continued fitting together the jigsaw of tasks that would form the day's events. ASEI stock had been up and down all week on Wall Street but the Dow was generally trending upwards. They needed to be on the same upward path. The morning was free and so he would use the time to catch up with analysts working on production and oil-price forecasts in Kazakhstan. New crude oil fields were constantly being explored in that region and just recently the oil reserves were being sucked from the ground with increasing rates. Production forecasts of six hundred and fifty thousand barrels a day were being realized and that figure would peak even higher, early in the year two thousand and twenty, he was told. Good and bad news. These latest breeds of oil were of a higher density and, therefore, had a thicker viscosity than conventional oils. For that reason they did not flow out of the ground so easily. They were difficult oils to retrieve from within the deep porous rock where they have laid dormant for millions of years.

There were also other problems. They were very corrosive in nature and production was constantly halted owing to the increased corrosion of the equipment being used. There was even more bad news when they eventually got the oil to the refinery. In the early days when little was known about their corrosive tendencies, several process units were seriously damaged with huge production losses incurred, nevertheless, with up to a dollar incentive off the price of less-corrosive crude oil, Hammond was not going to sit back and worry about the past. Part of his objective was to promote change at the refineries in order for them to at least manage some risk in processing more of these types of oil. He reasoned that if the oil refineries were not into stretching their risk management, which in turn would stretch their profit margins, then it would be pretty difficult to think of them surviving in the industry at all, and with that in mind he thought of other, less demanding things. The fact that engines weren't designed to run on unrefined crude oil never entered his mind!

Last night had been short-lived but it was a definite blast by his standards. His female companion for the night had long since been hauled out of bed and thrown out of the house with barely the rest of her belongings, half screaming in disbelief, half drugged from the same lethal cocktail of drink and drugs that fuelled the night's perversions. He didn't even try to remember her name such was his contempt for women he picked up from bars on the drive home, usually hookers he never paid. Like many males capable of operating at gutter level, Hammond knew only too well that sweet-nothings whispered in a willing ear—especially one that was already made willing by large quantities of alcohol that had saturated the brain—was like leading a dog to a lamp post. Nothing is surer in life, you just know the dog is going to cock his leg, wag his tail and go on his way. Sometimes though, they needed a little persuasion, rarely to get them into bed, but more often than not to get them out of there. They kind of act dumb in the hope that just maybe the nights sordid perversions were worth it, somewhere to stay longer term—they rarely had anybody or anything else in life.

After thirty minutes or so and with Kazakhstan well forgotten he steered the heavy Mercedes off onto Interstate 80, headed east for another seventy miles before changing direction back south along the New Jersey Turnpike and then east again on Highway 495. It was far from the ideal route but like everyone commuting to New York, there is no ideal route, they're all bad. The traffic was heavy but still moving as he drove into the Lincoln Tunnel. The whole trip usually lasted a couple of hours, something that Hammond needed increasingly more in order to allow him to get to grips with himself. Every day in the oil industry was different, and that environment had taught him some good lessons. He'd learned to be reactive to whatever came his way and, as he knew so well, self-protection was the name of the game.

Traffic chaos was now the order of the day as he slowly came into Manhattan. Moving at a snail's pace he passed the Empire State on his right-hand side before he took a left turn onto Park Avenue, which was followed by another left and then a quick right onto Fifth. Forty minutes after passing under the Hudson River, Richard Hammond arrived at his destination.

A copy of the New York Times was courteously placed on top of a leather-inlayed desk along with the Wall Street Journal, Financial Times, and several Oil journals he hardly bothered to read. The mail had yet to be opened by Moira, his secretary of two years, but she would ensure the more pressing and confidential issues would not be long in coming to his attention. Coffee was from a percolator located on a small bookcase under the window and allowed the recipient to admire the view across Central Park and beyond. The streets were alive now, buzzing with people and traffic, mostly yellow cabs intermingled with the odd horse and carriage that frequent that part of Manhattan. Hammond placed his briefcase on the desk, took off his jacket and looked immediately at the *WSJ*. There were several reports informing the reader of oil production and export reductions being made by Saudi Arabia, Venezuela and Mexico. It was the second time this year that similar cuts had been made in a bid to raise oil prices. The report went on to say that these three major oil exporters had agreed to make the cuts, some four hundred and fifty thousand barrels a day, in order to seek reductions by others of the OPEC countries who were meeting later in June of the same year. Hammond guessed that this amounted to approximately a little above a half of one percent of the world demand for oil—about seventy five million barrels per day were being produced. He didn't believe these latest reductions would make any difference to the market. He should have paid more attention. Instead, he turned to the sports page of the *NYT*. He'd let the analysts that worked for him take care of it. That's what they're paid for.

'Yankees were crap again, Mr. Hammond.' Elmo the porter, mailman and general gofer made the remark as he passed the partially open door. It was just loud enough for Hammond to hear and nobody else.

'Yeah, yeah, tell it to the turkeys in Vegas, not to us here in New York, right!' he replied, referring to the owners. Elmo, a black American with ancestry going way back to somewhere in North Africa, said nothing at first and just continued grinning. He didn't know what Hammond's reply was meant to infer.

'*Vegas?*' he asked himself. 'What in hell is he on, did he hear me right? We're in New York, shit!' he muttered. 'I thought he knew something about the game. These guys are something ain't they?' he asked nobody. 'I've got more between my legs than he's got between his ears!' Elmo continued on his journey still mumbling as a crunched up piece of paper hit him on the back of the head, it was thrown by one of the junior clerks who had by now taken refuge behind any one of four screens to his right-hand side. He carried on pushing the mail trolley through the open offices bereft from reality and totally unaware that anybody would want to remotely make fun of him.

Meanwhile, Richard Hammond sat back and looked around the room. He'd become more relaxed, the drugs had delivered the optimum effect. He then reflected on the situation, it was a fine appointment, he knew that. Why should he beat himself up all the time? Hammond pondered his current predicament. Perhaps it was time to change his ways, why not? He had an excellent job; even if it went no further he could be comfortable with it, if he tried. He was an executive manager and his only responsibility was to the Board Director for European Business Development, Glen Harvey Jr. What the hell. He would change. The drugs were working and so at that moment in time he decided he would change his ways. Harvey would be pleased too, he smiled to himself. They never saw eye to eye and if he mellowed that would be welcome, it would even stop Harvey from feeling insecure every second of the day; Hammond believed that he should have had Harvey's job and Harvey in return thought the same.

'Could have done it, no problem at all,' he bragged to himself, sure that nobody could hear. 'Glen Harvey,' he said quietly to himself. He was jealous but compared to Hammond, Harvey was class. He had steered ASEI towards many good deals and that was quickly noticed by John Arnold, who'd fast-tracked him through the ranks. But his track record of late was flawed with silly statements and stupidities and, unfortunately for him, the board knew it and so did the CEO. One of Harvey's prime objectives was to develop the companies' interests in the emerging third world countries, especially upstream, onshore activities and, through strategic planning from forecast oil reserves, continue to liaise and help develop the downstream processing sector. That objective was a spin drier since it seemed to Harvey to be a catch-all. Whatever it was, it was hell of a challenge. For his sins, he was also further challenged to meet the demands of ever-increasing, environmentally friendly fuel markets, something that was recognized as being another tall order in the topsy-turvy world of the oil industry. Harvey once said that he compared his task to one speech made famous by President Kennedy. The former President informed the world that, *America would land a man on the moon within the decade, he didn't know how they were going to do it, only that they were going to do it*, or words to that effect. What Harvey found difficult to come to terms with was the fact that he didn't have the resources or the power of the President of the United States to fulfill his promise, especially with oil prices spiraling out of control in the wrong direction. He was failing in his objective and constantly regretted making the comparison. Amongst his peers he was considered a liability and, like the others, Hammond knew it all too well. But what could he do he constantly bitched. Glen Harvey, meanwhile, was off work suffering from stress!

Chapter 17

I WAS KNACKERED. THE NIGHT HAD been a sleepless affair as predicted and I felt tired and awkward. Thirty minutes in the shower had improved my condition but I was still buzzing from the beer and a little confused after talking to her yesterday. By the time I'd put the phone down, a self-composed picture of Cheryl Davies, a girl I'd never met, was lodged deeply in my mind and it troubled me. When she eventually spoke, the young girl confirmed that she had received my e-mail. There was a host of accounting documents that supported the many payments made following the explosion, she hastily added as if I shouldn't be questioning anything that went on in the accounts department at that time. That much I knew, I answered her back using a strong tone but later regretted it. The files for this particular account would be made available upon my return, she informed me confidently and then quickly put the phone down before I could say another word. I somehow sensed she was very nervous though, I'd had a canny knack of getting these things right. I thanked her but not before a continuous buzzing tone rang out from the earpiece that signaled the premature end of the conversation.

Dismissing that conversation for the time-being, I dressed and met an irate Desmond in the lobby. Desmond was hiding something. He'd upset somebody, probably the redneck he was drinking with last night. I was convinced and looked for signs of bruising whilst Des looked uneasy in the opposite direction. There was silence as we made our way to the airport, which was unusual for Desmond. It only confirmed my suspicions that he'd lost an argument to a bunch of scallywags with a combined IQ of four or five! We'd arranged to stay at Desmond's place during the deposition and commute to Cranton's daily. It made sense at the time but now, I wasn't too sure that it was a wise move?

* * *

As usual, the e-mail for Richard Hammond that same morning showed most of the headline mail, heavily typed in bold lettering, indications of new and unread mail sent late last night or even earlier that morning. They were mostly from several of the offshore platform installation managers based in Russia, Kazakhstan and Africa. This was a vital part of the morning such was the communications network and his need to know. Hammond was used to a heavy payload through the Microsoft system, in fact he preferred it, easier to reply, but more importantly for him it was easier to file those all-important messages for later retrieval. He referred to the more sensitive of these as, *evidence for the defense.*

'Morning, Mr. Hammond, I trust you had a pleasant journey this morning?' Moira knocked the door briefly and had quickly entered the room with a blue plastic folder containing the morning mail, which by now had been opened and put into some form of priority to the best of her knowledge. She was clued into the world of Richard Hammond, well versed in what his objectives were and the way he worked to achieve them; shoddy and careless, so the priority of importance was not that precise. Without waiting for a reply—she never usually had one anyway—she immediately continued to talk in haste. Something was bothering her.

'I think you should know that, Mr. Darcy and Mr. Isaacs were in your office last night,' she then said, the words coming out all too quickly. Hammond stopped reading the paper that instant and looked at Moira in surprise. He'd been visibly shaken and his eyes contested what she'd just said.

'What did you say?' he asked her quickly. His response was immediate and said in disbelief.

'Mr. Darcy and Mr. Isaacs, they were in your office last night,' repeated his secretary with the same speed.

'All right, all right, I heard that bit,' he ranted at her. 'Well, what did they want, woman? Did they tell you what they were after?' Hammond had become aggressive now. 'Did they say anything?' he repeated, impatiently. His mind immediately began to search for their motive as he waited for her to reply. He smelt trouble and did not have to think too hard for the reason why. There were so many bad things being brought to the fore; too many that needed to stay where they were in fact.

'A little after 7.30 last night, you had just gone,' she explained nervously. 'I asked if I could help but they ordered me to leave and go home for the night,' she told him. 'When I told them that you needed several important memos faxed to Europe they physically man-handled me out of the door!'

she added, feeling dejected. Moira's tone of voice lowered when she said this. She was annoyed at the treatment shown to her by two, supposedly respectful Vice-Presidents of the company.

'Nobody should treat me like that, especially not those two,' she muttered tearfully as she buried her face in her hands. Moira thought it was because, like many other employees of the company, she did not have the right color skin, it was black and that sometimes meant trouble when confronted with some of her white employers. But this time it was different, it wasn't about the color of her skin. Something was wrong, very wrong. She'd seen the way Hammond reacted to problems that occurred from time-to-time. Poor results from inaccurate forecasts made for some pretty ugly scenes, but this was special. Vice-Presidents never came down to thirteenth floor, never!

She'd also sensed Hammond's initial response, which confirmed her suspicion, something was wrong. Whatever it was, it was between Hammond and Messrs, Darcy and Isaacs. Was she about to have a new boss? She sincerely hoped so! Why would two VP's rummage through another senior employee's office, and in full view of his secretary? They were not being discrete that's for sure; they knew he would be told the first instance Moira saw him the very next morning.

'How long were they here, Moira?' asked Hammond, rather limply and knowing that it really didn't matter. What mattered was that they were there at all.

'Hell, Mr. Hammond! Are you listening to me?' Moira was getting visibly angrier and her eyes started to well and tears were about to stream. 'I was manhandled out of here like some kinda intruder. Those bastards, they ain't got any manners, Mr. Hammond. They're trash and I don't care if you know cos I ain't afraid anymore. I've had it, I've had enough, and enough is enough!' she screamed. Her mascara began to smudge as the tears ran down her cheeks. Moira fumbled for her handkerchief, it was a pitiful sight. Hammond got up from his desk and held her gently on the shoulders, as if to comfort her, but instead, edged her towards the open door. With great apathy and without even saying a word he slowly pushed her through it, into the arms of another, younger white female secretary who'd been passing and was alerted by the crying. If Moira hadn't had more than her fair share of indignity shown to her from the Vice-Presidents, Hammond ensured she just had.

He had no respect for Moira, how could he. It went against his doctrine; that of hating any other race that just happened to be anything but white.

The fact that Moira was very good at her job, the best he'd ever had in fact, never entered Hammond's mind. He never employed her for her secretarial skills, or any other skills she may have been able to provide the company. He suffered her, agonizing in the knowledge that if ever anyone pointed the racial finger at him, Richard Hammond, he could stand up and tell him or her that he had a black secretary and was proud of it. The premium was a little too high in terms of principle, but Hammond realized it was the best insurance policy he'd ever taken out. The door was slammed shut with some force as he quickly walked to the window and looked out over Central Park wondering what the hell his life had come to. Oh, how he wished he were home and out of the way!

That he chose to live so far away from Manhattan was not surprising, many workers would think nothing of it, besides he had the use of an apartment if he needed it. Times were that he did. Nowadays, the farther away from all of this the better, he reasoned. Less temptation, less to worry about and less intrusions into his seedy pleasures, of which there were many. The pills he'd taken earlier were working well and before Moira had informed him of Isaacs and Darcy, he was well focused on the planned events that lay ahead. He knew that it could be another tough one. *Shrink to grow* was another buzzword, it would soon replace *downsizing* and he knew exactly what it meant. Richard Hammond had no intentions to shrink, he'd worked too hard for that, completed too many good deals. A lot of them were rather shady, but what the hell. He did what he was asked to do. Shit happens and those on the top floor knew it better than most.

Nobody need remind him that people get hurt in business all the time. He was already hurting. No sir, he was not about to shrink. He would rather grow, and grow, and grow even more. Be where he should have been years ago, at the top, like the other VP's; Eamon Darcy, Glen Harvey and Jeremy Isaacs. Up at the same status and kicking ass, or so he thought. Hell, he had done enough favors to those above him. They owed him and they knew it, each and every one of them. They knew they could trust him and for his part he didn't give a damn. He had no scruples whatsoever and was ruthless with anyone in his way when it came to getting what he wanted, or what his superiors wanted to be more accurate. When there was some dirty laundry to be done, Hammond was their man, rewarded with the promises of better things to come. When the time was right of course, they would add. Well, the time was right. Right now, in fact. The events in Nigeria had never left him and he suffered because of it. He felt a wave of aggression bordering on hatred building up inside. That he was an embittered employee, there was no doubt. It had cost him two damn marriages and he'd even been left for dead for Christ sake!

He tried to calm himself, tried to control his temper. He needed to be patient, but for how much longer? He needed more pills. Isaacs and Darcy were menacing but they knew what he'd done for them, surely. Between them they'd resolved too many clandestine complications, some to the companies benefit but more so for their own. They wouldn't give in now. There was no point. His work of late was poor, but they wouldn't judge him by his recent performance. His achievements during his time with ASEI spoke volumes.

Eamon Darcy was a Senior Vice-President of the company and, partly due to his business acumen and partly due to his lifelong friendship with John Arnold, he deputized for the CEO. He was responsible for marketing and strategic planning and relied heavily upon his board colleague, Glen Harvey Jnr., who in turn relied heavily upon Richard Hammond. It was a strange relationship since each man could easily achieve what the other could, but that's how it was when you create jobs for friends! Darcy was no threat to him, reasoned Hammond. He had helped him to where he is now, the top. About four years ago, Darcy was struggling to make his mark on others within the Executive. At least he was until Richard Hammond initiated the dealings that allowed Darcy, and Advanced Strategic Energy, to strike it rich, albeit a short-lived success.

They tried to manipulate the market by buying more North Sea crude oil in one month than could physically be delivered. This resulted in other companies having to pay over three dollars a barrel more than they normally would have had for the same oil. The ordinary functioning of the market had been tampered with and the other majors were not at all pleased—undertones of illegal and monopolistic conduct began surfacing.

They'd contravened the Sherman Antitrust Act, one of the first parts of legislation passed by Congress to prohibit such things. Between them, Darcy and Hammond argued their innocence to a very concerned board of directors, stating that there had been grave factual misunderstandings by others in the market. Profits were raised and so the ASEI board believed them, of course publicly stating that that there was only a very fine line between creating an illegal monopoly and using experience to create a very clever trading position to legitimately enhance profits. The board stuck to this statement and stood their ground, strongly denying the charges at the time until nothing more was said. Darcy came through it unscathed and realized he owed Hammond, no problem.

There'd been too much laundry washed for Eamon to cause trouble. Perhaps it was payback time for his Nigerian dealings. No way, the presence of Isaacs really troubled him. What would a senior human resources VP want from him? Isaacs was not at all respected amongst the workforce, but Isaacs didn't care. He was secure in the knowledge that he had in fact married the daughter of the CEO of the company, Marie Bethan Arnold. Isaacs gloated on being married to Beth, as she liked to be called. Hammond hadn't been invited to the wedding, but as usual, everybody employed with the company had a graphic account of the day's events. The grandeur of the occasion, carpets of flowers, buckets of champagne, members of congress, the police commissioner and the mayor of New York, the usual players.

Chapter 18

There was nothing immediate he could do to resolve the problem, nothing he could do but wait and find out what it was that was so important that they needed to physically remove his secretary from his office. He looked around the room for clues. There was nothing out of place, pictures hung square and ornaments that were placed around several bookcases seemed untouched. His desk drawers, whilst locked, showed no signs of forced entry, nothing unusual. In fact, he realized just how tidy his office looked. He did not possess a safe or anything of that nature. Whilst his work was sensitive it was not that sensitive. Perhaps they simply needed the latest forecasts?

'Shit! They could have got that from Moira,' he cursed out loud. His disquiet was soon enhanced when, at the top of the e-mail list of new messages, he saw a classified message from *Jeremy Isaacs.—*Title*—Meeting*. It was circulated to three more people, Dwight York, the Human Resources Team Leader and Isaacs second in command, Gerald Sinclair, another senior executive employed in a similar role as Hammond but working the Gulf Coast operations, and Eamon Darcy. A red exclamation mark flagged alongside the message indicated that it was sent on an *Urgent* basis. Nothing else on the title gave any further clues as to what the meeting was about.

'Little shit,' he mouthed out loud. The message content merely requested his presence at a meeting, along with the three other recipients, to be held in Isaacs' office at ten-o-clock that morning. It was politely and electronically signed, *Jeremy Isaacs*. Hammond ignored all other e-mail messages and, instead, answered the phone that rung at that precise moment. It was the secretary who'd comforted Moira no more than ten minutes earlier. She informed him that Moira had gone ballistic, swearing and throwing files all over the place and, furthermore, she'd gone home. He in turn informed her that he was genuinely sorry to hear that and went on to say that earlier that morning she confided to him that she felt unwell after arguing with her boyfriend before coming to work. He thought that it was the probable cause of her outrageous behavior. She acknowledged his concern and further informed him that she would take care of any pressing matters that he needed and promptly gave her name and office extension number. Hammond thanked her and put down the phone.

He failed to tell her that he didn't give a toss if she jumped out of the thirteenth floor window, in fact he would encourage her next time!

The secretary failed to say that Moira had in fact instructed her to tell him, *to shove his job up his ass! She, Moira Mathias, had had enough of being abused, ridiculed, and above all else, had a gut full of working for a company that treated her like a second class citizen. The management showed no respect whatsoever to their black employees and damn it, they were due some*, and with that she grabbed her coat and was off.

Nobody could reason with her as she stormed out of the building. Most onlookers felt genuinely sympathetic towards her. The black people certainly did, but some younger employees, the white ones, cheered and laughed at the outburst, visibly encouraging her, spurring her on with racial comments in an attempt to fuel her anger.

Get her to bite, man, they whispered to each other so that she would act in an even more outrageous manner. Cries of, *dumb bitch*, and, *way to go, black girl*, could be heard from not too far away. These were her work colleagues, she thought. At that moment in time she was down. A handful of genuine sympathizers tried to comfort her, they were mostly black but the others, the white folks tried to ensure she was going to stay down; they enjoyed the morning fracas and even encouraged it. It made a good start to the morning as far as they were concerned.

'If you can't stand the heat, you're better off out of the kitchen,' said Elmo who piped up with these latest words of wisdom as Moira passed him, being half-helped and half-escorted out of the building. Even he, Elmo, was not perturbed in the least at the treatment now being shown to Moira. Not once did he give a second thought to the predicament she was now facing. He suffered it all the time. He could handle it though and that made him different from the rest. He considered himself a good employee, never complained even though he took his fair share of stick.

'Moira should toughen up a little, Rich,' said Elmo unsympathetically to one of the guards who greeted his remarks with the contempt they deserved.

'Shut the fuck up you asshole, or I'll shut you the fuck up!' he replied angrily. He had every reason to sympathize with Moira. The color of his skin was the same as hers. All in all it was a shameful scene to say the least.

For the next thirty minutes or so, Hammond frantically made a number of *search* requests using an Oracle database that housed the world crude oil production figures, the data openly available from an external source well versed in providing statistics of this kind. They'd amassed this information over a long time. ASEI merely minced them around using a Weibull statistical model to provide an estimate of what was *probably* likely to happen to the costs of crude oil when compared to the estimated supply-and-demand requirements around the world. The entire process was based on probability, the statisticians loved it but the oil companies loathed it. It ignored wars, environmental disasters and other less dramatic world events, like the reductions being made by OPEC at that very moment, for example! Hammond knew that, that's why the company employed him. Along with Harvey, they'd need to turn the statistical stuff into some form of reality, something useful. Now, he didn't have time for all that, his mind was clouded and he couldn't think straight. Panic set-in. Nevertheless, he knew he needed to be prepared. He did not have the time to get any of the analysts to provide the latest batch of forecasts, besides they would simply do what he was doing anyway.

The ASEI strategic, or long-term business plan, is based on a number of things, such as capital expenditure and investments on new ventures, operating costs, and other text book values. But the biggest factor that influenced the strategy, and also dictated the direction of where the company was heading, was the use of forecasts that tried to predict the price of a barrel of nominated crude oil. In this instance, Hammond used the data from the Brent oilfield; the Gulf Coast analysis used West Texas Intermediate as the benchmark. Capital expenditure for investments is dependent upon, amongst other things, the crude oil forecasts over a period of time, oil reserves, and most importantly, returns on investment. God only knew how those oil prices were going to trend. The Board of Directors always implied they knew what the prices were doing, but they forgot to tell the industry analysts, because they didn't have a clue and Richard Hammond certainly didn't at that moment in time. At the best of times it's one of the great unknowns in the industry.

In the end, it all boils down to supply-and-demand, mostly at the gas stations—the only problem with that was nobody really knew who'd want what, and when? They just seemed to bluff each other, generally producing a series of trends that forecast whatever the accountants tell them to forecast. The whole workforce was suspicious of the accountants, whom they genuinely believed run the company and they did for the best part. It only takes a small diplomatic conflict in the Far, or Middle East, or for the major producers from OPEC to give the wrong signals to the rest of the world and it can send the price of oil through the roof. It's at these more prosperous times that the Board is a little more capable of running the show. On the other hand, during periods of over production with few military conflicts, the price of oil usually plummets. The later era was now occurring and establishing itself in such a way that Hammond, the Board, the analysts, the accountants, and even the bluffer's just didn't know what the price of oil was going to do. They couldn't force the price of oil up. There was little profit in peace these days and they couldn't start another Gulf war, or Vietnam, or even a civil war. If they could, they would and to hell with the ethics of it all, leave that to Congress, it was far more important to get a good return for the shareholders.

He quickly trended out the last several months' figures, enough data to familiarize himself with recent oil production and crude oil price changes. He realized how slack he'd been over the last couple of months. The trends seemed peculiar to him, nevertheless, there was no way he was going into the lion's den without even the smallest piece offering. He quickly printed off the tables he thought he might be questioned about and placed them neatly in his briefcase. Another rummage through the *WSJ* informed him of little more than he already knew. The situation in Saudi, Venezuela and Mexico dominated events. The last time OPEC and non-OPEC producers like Mexico made landmark oil export reduction agreements, the price of oil rose about twenty dollars a barrel, something he should have known but that information was too late for him to act upon now. He'd have to wing it! He felt a wave of anxiety sweeping through his body as he recalled being advised of this some time back. The forecasters had, for once, got it right but he chose to ignore the advice such was the poor and inaccurate performance of oil trends and forecasts of late.

A look in the mirror hanging on a wall opposite his desk told him to rearrange his neck tie, after which he replaced his jacket and neatly brushed down the sleeves to remove any fluff or loose cotton ends. After taking a long deep breath, Hammond walked swiftly out of the office towards the fourteenth floor.

'Damn!' he cursed soon after closing the door behind him, he should have taken a little something to calm the nerves, but by now he was well down the corridor and within sight of too many people. He spun around and quickly returned to the office, sat in his chair and fumbled with his keys to open a locked draw under the reproduction, antique table. It would not open quickly enough and he cursed again. When it did finally open, what he saw inside stopped him in his tracks.

'What the . . .' he stuttered, flabbergasted! His gaze suddenly turned to horror as the memories flooded back. Soon, it hit him like a sledgehammer. There, neatly placed inside was a bullet. The words, *Mista Delta*, were scribbled on a small card underneath. He panicked and looked around the room.

'Jesus, he's alive! He's actually been here!' Hammond rushed towards the door and opened it before scanning around the open plan floor. No one, nobody he recognized as the Frenchman anyway. All he saw was the clerks going about their daily work. There wasn't anybody who appeared out of place.

'No way, it can't be, he's dead, he's dead!' Hammond repeated to himself, but the card was real and it was there, inside his desk drawer, along with a bullet, probably a replica of the one he shot in Nigeria? His breakdown was almost complete when one of the guards confirmed that a man with a French accent had supposedly checked out the security system after Moira, his *former* secretary, had let him into the office earlier that morning. He described Phillip Laxrois better than Hammond could ever have done.

He was a nervous wreck now and tried hard to conceal his true emotions on the way to the elevator. Once inside and alone, he reached inside his jacket pocket and took out another two pills, which was six in all counting the previous two he'd taken in his office and the two before that, at home. He knew they would have the desired effect he so urgently required, but there was too little time for the pills to perform. He took them anyway. It could be a long meeting. He started shaking as he exited the elevator on the top floor and walked towards two guards seated a short distance from a security point located a little further on. The shaking continued; he half-expected Laxrois to jump out from behind one of the closed doors at any moment. One of the well-dressed guards beckoned him past the manned security point and further on down the corridor, towards an office with a teak door that bore the name of, *Jeremy Isaacs* neatly inscribed on a brass nameplate. The guard sensed that something was wrong, it was too obvious. The shaking increased and Hammond didn't know if it was because of Laxrois, who would almost certainly return at sometime, or the realization that this meeting was not about statistical oil forecasts. It was about him! Hammond never felt so exposed and vulnerable in all his life. He felt nauseated as the guard knocked the door.

Chapter 19

WE WAITED AT THE AIRPORT for only an hour before boarding the flight to New York. It was a pleasant day and my window seat gave me great views of the southern US and, hopefully, along the eastern seaboard if the weather remained fair. Desmond lay asleep as we cruised at thirty five thousand feet. I was instructed to wake him when the drinks trolley came by.

'Bar's open!' I said and prodded him in the ribs. He woke with a grunt. 'Two red wines, please,' I said to the attendant and she acknowledged my request by asking me for ten dollars. I fumbled around looking for the money as Desmond came to.

'Where are we?' he asked, a little groggy.

'In a plane,' I replied. Desmond looked at me stupid.

'I know we're in a plane yer jerk, but where are we?'

'I dunno, Beaumont?'

'Beaumont, we can't still be in Beaumont. We've been up for over thirty minutes!' he moaned. How he'd worked that out whilst sleeping was a mystery to me.

'Well, we're thirty minutes from Beaumont then,' I told him, amazed at how his body clock worked! 'You asked me to call you when the drinks came, remember?'

'I know . . . but that's if I was just nodding, not if I was fast asleep, stupid!'

'Oh, sorry, didn't know there was a difference,' I replied, hardly being apologetic. 'Besides, stop whining. Here, why not have a drink,' I said and handed him a glass of wine. We spent the next ten minutes sipping a red Shiraz, deep in thought.

'What'd you think'll happen, Des?'

'Ugh, what do you mean?'

'You know, Lance isn't exactly brain of Britain now, is he?' I remarked in earnest whilst looking out of the window at the vast landscape below.

'Yeah, I hear you. I kinda get the impression that the engines running but ain't nobody driving. I dunno, man. He's done this kinda thing before though. He'll get us through.'

'*Us?*'

'Yeah, *us*, you're in it just as much as me now, Doug.'

'Oh, right. I forgot, silly me of course it's, *us*.'

'It's frustrating though. Can't help thinking there's something else in all of this, Doug? Something keeps gnawing at me but I don't have a clue what it is.'

'Yeah, I get the same feeling. The dismissal is pathetic. There's a long line of people I'd hold responsible other than you for the problem in California. There's gotta be something else. In fact, I'm convinced there is, but what? We've covered all bases and I'm damned if I know.' I caught the hostess and charmed two more bottles of red off her and she charmed another ten dollars from me. Desmond emptied his into a small plastic cup and then leaned over me to peer through the window. I pushed him back into his seat.

'What is it about Lance?' he then asked again, mystified.

'We already discussed him, why'd you keep asking the same questions?'

'Cos, something's not right, that's why.'

'Yeah well . . . we don't really know for sure, but I agree. There's kinda something strange about the way he acts. We'll find out soon enough though. Stop worrying.'

'Stop worrying? If anybody else tells me to stop frigging worrying, I'm gonna smack em in the nuts. You get the bullet and then try not worrying!'

'Sorry pal. Just a saying, relax, have a drink. We'll be fine,' I told him unsure of the situation and quietly worrying about my own predicament.

'Why'd you think Lance was so eager for the settlement?' he then asked, pushing for more.

'Cos, it's how they do it, simple as that.'

'How'd you know how they do it?'

'Err . . . I just know . . . that's all.'

'You're full of shit, Doug.'

'Mm . . . like I said, have another drink.'

* * *

Jeremy Isaacs sat back, seemingly relaxed in a Captain's chair placed behind a beautiful and highly polished, teak writing desk. His glasses were raised and now rested on his forehead for the time being as he read from a single piece of paper that was plucked from a neat stack close by. The guard knocked the door and without waiting for a reply, entered the office.

'Mr. Hammond is here to see you as requested, Mr. Isaacs,' the security man informed him but had sensed the need to say as little as possible at that precise moment. On any other normal day he would have usually made one or two comments, just to say something in general out of courtesy more than anything else, but not today. It was not that normal a day and so he said no more than what he had to say.

'Thanks. Show him in,' Isaacs replied to the escort without lifting his head from pondering over the other loose-paged documents placed neatly on his desk. The man opened the door wider and stood to one side. Hammond walked confidently into the room. He'd felt a surge of adrenaline shoot through his veins all of a sudden. Without further conversation the guard left swiftly, closing the door behind him and returned to his post outside the fourteenth-floor elevator.

Hammond's mind was not quite on overdrive, but any time soon it was going to shift up a gear. He'd been in this particular office on numerous occasions, remembering very well each and every ornamental piece that graced the very expensive, and well-cared-for antique furniture positioned elegantly around the room. To find Isaacs sitting alone had taken him slightly aback and, seeing nobody else inside, thought he was early. He could feel the buzz beginning to kick-in; the tablets he'd taken earlier were beginning to take effect sooner than he thought. Overdrive was imminent and that sometimes meant trouble, he could become unpredictably aggressive.

'Good morning, Jeremy,' he said politely. Not getting a response he walked over to stand by the large windows overlooking Central Park. He ignored the views and waited patiently for some form of acknowledgment from Isaacs instead. After only a minute, standing was no good he realized. He soon became impatient and deliberately looked at his watch, sarcastically, as if to register his disgust at the others for being late. It was strange. Whilst the drugs made him feel more comfortable with the situation, Isaacs made him feel extremely uncomfortable and agitated.

'Take a seat,' said Isaacs registering Hammond's discomfort. He said this without lifting his head to acknowledge him even in the slightest way.

Again, that somehow unnerved Hammond who then simply shrugged his shoulders at the strange goings-on.

'Thanks,' he replied feebly and slouched himself in a leather chesterfield chair. Isaacs would deal with the subordinate in his own time. In the meantime, he simply continued to ignore him and, after a few short minutes the silence became almost deafening. As time went on Hammond just twitched and fidgeted in the two thousand dollar chair whilst the man behind the desk continued to study the documents laid out on the desk in front of him. It was a game of poker. After a further ten minutes or so, the frustration began to fester and boil over inside the impatient visitor. He tried to break the deadlock. Silence was not golden for Richard Hammond.

'Is this the way you welcome your fellow employees to a meeting, is it?' he asked. Hammond's tone of voice was audibly irate. 'Is it?' he asked again, demanding an answer as he slowly edged closer to Isaacs desk. Jeremy remained nonchalant, he considered himself superior, even masterly in his silence, preferring instead to concentrate on the details contained in the last of the documents. It was doubtful if he was reading any detail at all!

'What's your fucking problem, man? Answer me damn it! Where are Darcy and the others for Christ sake?' The deadlock eventually broke; Isaacs knew he'd taken this as far as he could.

'My problem, what's my goddam fucking problem?' Isaacs responded, looking at him quickly in the process. 'Well, I'll tell you what my problem is, Richard. You, you're my goddamn fucking problem!' he spurted out angrily whilst springing up from his seat like a cobra. He knew he'd taken this to the limit and retaliated with a vengeance, catching his foe off-guard.

'About time, thought you'd lost your lizard tongue there for a moment,' replied Hammond, surprised at the retort and, sensibly, he backed off quickly. He had not expected to be confronted in such a way. 'So, what's eating you up, man?' he asked, a little less offensive now.

'Desmond Haynes.'

'Desmond Haynes!' Hammond hollered in surprise. 'Haynes is history,' he said, as a matter of fact. 'We got rid of him eighteen months back. Don't tell me the nigger's applied for your job?' Hammond scoffed, laughing in his usual, pathetic manner.

'There's going to be a trial,' said Isaacs ignoring the idiocy.

'A trial, you mean in a court kind of trial! What the fuck for?'

'It's a racial discrimination lawsuit filed against the company.'

'Discrimination, how'd that come about?'

'Cos we screwed him,' he replied plainly. His reply was off the cuff and right first time.

'I know we screwed him, that's what we agreed, remember?'

'Yeah, I remember. What I can't remember is how we agreed to get rid of him in the way we did. It was to be concrete, no comeback, that's what I remember.'

'It was solid,' he replied defensively. 'He fucked up in California and he went on the grounds of negligence or something like that. I can't recall the exact detail but it was solid. Okay, we had to tweak a few things to make the lawyers happy but he's gone and we haven't heard from him since,' said Hammond, defending his ground.

'Haven't heard from him until now, that is,' replied Isaacs, despondently holding a single piece of paper in the air as if to prove the facts. Hammond didn't question the document; he accepted what Isaacs had said.

'How long have you known about it?'

'Long enough, at first we thought it would be nothing. We assumed Cranton and his boys could deal with it, you know . . . kinda pay him off, that kinda thing.'

'So, tell me you've done the right thing, man?'

'Yeah, that would be nice. It wasn't a problem then but . . .'

'But what,' asked Hammond wondering what was going to spring up next?

'Things have changed.'

'And now it's a big deal, ugh! Well, we got guys that can handle that. Give Dinger a call and tell him to get JB on the case.' The senior associate at Cranton was well versed in what was required. 'It's worked in the past,' added Hammond, but then realized Jeremy hadn't budged at the notion. 'What's the problem, Jeremy,' he asked. 'You running scared over some nigger boy all of a sudden? Dumb son-of-a-bitch deserved to go and you know it,' he scathed and now pointing his index finger straight at him. He knew Jeremy hated the blacks as much as he did, especially the well-paid *niggers* of the company, as they were so-called. The two men were lifelong members of the triple K. What did they care? They constantly abused their authority to fight the cause; justice had to be sought. And in their position of authority they had dished out the required justice. Yes, they were Klucker's, the both of them through and through. Dinger too, and boy had they dished out the justice between all three of them!

Ever since the day a young black boy stood up to defend his mother following Hammonds' drunken attempt to trip her up in a bar over thirty years ago, they'd been in the Klan. Their membership arose by accident, but they were destined to join, nevertheless.

It all started nearby to where they spent the weekend fishing, in a large expanse of wooded ground that closed in several, sizeable rivers. The location was remote but the waters were well stocked, courtesy of a poorly run trout farm located at one of the small, upstream lakes. Out in the clearing, alongside some bayous, there were a few small towns, nothing to shout about, but they all had a bar or two; and that's where it all started, in a bar. The young boy did no more than any sixteen-year son would have done. His momma, a cleaner at the joint, had been stopped in one of the bars after being taunted and then set upon by, what appeared to him, was a complete stranger. The young boy had only called in to pick her up following the end of her shift; his folk never frequented these kinds of places, besides they had better things to do. When he saw what had happened he was prepared to fight rather than see his mother sexually assaulted and humiliated by a drunkard for no reason whatsoever. But Hammond was embarrassed when the locals stopped him from getting involved further, they wasn't going to allow that to happen on their patch and told him to get out. When the boy left with his mother gratefully in tow, his friends ribbed him all afternoon and the following day. By the third day, Hammond had become absolutely enraged and turned into a man possessed, especially after drinking a bottle of Jack Daniels, his fourth in as many days.

It was fine justice then when they met on that fateful day. Mother and son were crossing the bridge and minding their own business when Richard Hammond got his just revenge. The others needed no encouragement either and soon joined in; they had consumed large amounts of beer and whisky, they were fuelled up for such a thing. The boy and his mother were beaten black and blue and then hung. The Klan was beckoning in them wild youthful days, and soon they donned the white hood and gown. They burnt crosses and played havoc amongst the blacks. They were extremely proud of what they'd done and other Klucker's would be forever grateful. They knew that much.

'No, as a matter of fact, I don't know it! I've been reading the details of the case here, and guess what?' Isaacs asked, holding up a few sheets

The Last Hangman

of paper before dropping them messily back onto his desk—the letter headings revealed confidential memos from Cranton & Associates. 'One of our own company employee's is willing to testify, God damn it!' said Isaacs in disbelief.

'Je-e-s-us,' said Hammond, drawing the word out and laughing in amazement. 'They're out of their mind!' he added, and then immediately tried to play the situation down. 'Who is this crazy bastard?' he asked, as if it were a game. 'Who in the hell is willing to do that?' he wondered.

'It's Doug Archer!'

'Archer! The guy from England, what in hell is he going to say?'

'He's going to give a character reference,' replied Isaacs as if the news was going to bring the entire company down. But in reality, whatever was going to be said was hardly dynamite. 'According to our people, he's the real deal. Long-standing company man with lots of credence,' he went on to say. Hammond continued to sneer after remembering the events in Nigeria. 'It'll start off with all the bullshit connected to Nigeria and the bravery awards no doubt, remember?'

'Remember! Oh I remember all right,' nodded Hammond, now smiling for all the wrong reasons. Dishing out awards to black people was a painful experience for their kind.

'We've already sent the shit flying towards Doug Archer's fan,' reported Isaacs. 'He's been made to step down as the operations manager with immediate effect. Pity the dumb bastard didn't get his balls burnt off in Nigeria!' he added spitefully and meaning it.

'Well, if he didn't then, that shit from England will certainly get em burnt now, and badly,' seethed Hammond in agreement and already planning his next move. 'They both will. Wanna leave it with me? I'll sort it.'

'Oh yeah, like the way you sorted out our problem in Nigeria, great stuff! All you had to do was hand over the cash and that was that. But no, you couldn't even get that right, could you? If you hadn't had such a thing about fucking mercenaries and other stupid deals that nobody other than you agreed to, we wouldn't be here now, would we? No fucking way! Enough is enough. I'll deal with the *nigger* lover first chance I get.'

'You can't get tied up with all this, let me handle it for Christ sake!' argued Hammond, sensing the situation was all down to him.

'What part of, *no fucking way*, doesn't your dumb-ass brain understand?' Isaacs rotated a finger in circles around his own head to make the point.

'Leave it, Jeremy! We both know why Haynes went, or shall I remind you?' he said, beginning to fight for survival and trying to stand his ground. He hated the fact that the human resources people always left the dirty work to those around them, as if they were whiter than white. They had the cheek to get off on their personal relations bullshit long after the event, which usually left a mess on everyone's shoes, except their own of course. Isaacs continued by adding more detail to the problem.

'I've been looking into his personal file; half the damn details are missing, as if I should be surprised! What'd you dumb bastards do? There's no mention of what he did in the North Sea, and the Nigeria file is as thin as a pancake! He was there for two years for heaven sake. He worked with the very men that you had slaughtered,' he emphasized slowly, as if talking to the dumbest chimp on earth. 'What were you thinking? That nobody would bother to ask? You're fucking spaced out, man.'

'Oh yeah, that's cheap coming from you! Who agreed for me to go to Nigeria in the first place anyway, ugh? Tell me that? You're the one that's spaced out. You're a fucking jerk, Jeremy!'

'Jerk my ass! I should never have listened to you. And what do we tell our legal guys this time? Come on . . . tell me what to say to Dinger now you've thrown half of Hayne's working record in the Atlantic fucking Ocean?' Isaacs was losing it and paced the room before spinning on his heels to confront Hammond once again. 'Hey, and that ain't all, guess who his attorney is?' he asked, finally spilling the real reason for his discomfort in all of this.

'I dunno, the Pope?'

'Nice one, smart ass. But you're close, very close. It's Lance, can you believe it? He wants his personal records for some pre-trial bullshit! Jesus, if this ever gets out. Christ!' Isaacs continued to pace the room before deciding to sit back at his desk; he felt more comfortable sitting, he reasoned.

'How the hell did Lance get involved in all of this?'

'God knows. And there's something else you should know, Richard. There's a good chance they'll want to get you on the stand. Since you were the mastermind behind the dismissal, and your names on the thanks-but-no-thanks letter, they'll probably want you to explain how we came to fire a totally innocent man!'

'What'd you mean, explain the dismissal?'

'I mean exactly that, explain why you signed off on some jumped up charges of gross negligence or whatever the fuck it was you bumped him off the payroll for?' Isaacs blurted out, knowing full well that it was

The Last Hangman

Hammond's signature that was alongside his on the letter that signaled the end of Desmond's employment with ASEI. 'They'll put you on the stand in a big, big courtroom, in front of a Judge, and a jury, and ask you dumb questions about the reasons why he had to go? Only thing is, we think you'll fucking screw up,' said Isaacs, rounding on him once again and preying it wasn't going to get that far.

'My, you're running scared, aren't you? My, oh my! I never thought I'd see the day. You've got to take a vacation, Jeremy,' said Hammond, giving yet another sarcastic grin as he spoke; giving evidence in a court of law wasn't even remotely on his mind.

'No Hammond, you're the one who's going to take a vacation, the further away the better. You've screwed this company once too often.'

'Oh yeah . . . like . . . where shall I go? Haiti, L.A, Singapore, that far enough away? Or how about that oil paradise, err . . . Nigeria! It'll be kinda nice, see old friends, perhaps we could do a little deal out there. The company can afford to send me on a short business trip now, can't it? Say, maybe two weeks. That'll be nice. Hey, I've got a great idea. Maybe I get to screw around a little with the accountants in England and bingo, there's the fare!'

Isaacs squirmed at the suggestion. The funding for their sordid Nigerian bribery came from Advanced Strategic Energy Ltd, not the global US Inc, set-up. The insurance claims following the explosion in Nigeria were mostly handled in England and ensured enough chaos in the accounts department to cream off the required amount to pay off the local tribes there, or so they thought. It wasn't as if they were screwing ASEI. No way, the insurers would pay for their dirty work and it worked, each and every time. But that's where they'd both come unstuck, Hammond had screwed it up! He always knew Richard was insane and this latest bought of obscenities only confirmed it even more. There was not one person in the whole of the company who would have volunteered to do what Hammond had tried to do in Nigeria. He'd fucked up big time, however, and was lucky to have narrowly escaped with his life. Just how he managed to do that was still a mystery to Isaacs. But, somehow, the people they engaged with to resolve the problem had been murdered and dozens more killed in the fracas that followed, just because Richard Hammond knew better. He never stuck to what was asked of him. Instead, Hammond employed the services of a mercenary of all things to murder the very people they were trying to befriend! Get rid of them and you get rid of the problem, he reasoned. That's how crazy he is. Isaacs loathed the man sat in front of him, but it wouldn't be for much longer, he knew that much.

'Go back inside your hole, Richard, where you belong. There are no deals, not any more. Those days are over. Come to think of it, your days are over too!' As those last words sunk in, Hammond froze and just stared at him in disbelief. The reality of what had just been said was like a stun gun that had been prodded throughout his whole body. Isaacs was equally as dumbstruck. How could he have allowed himself to give even the slightest hint of Hammond's fate? He was irate with himself and deeply annoyed at letting his guard down. He had divulged too much of the self initiated and well-deserved doom he knew was about to behold Hammond. Both men continued to stare at each other, waiting for the next move, before Isaacs picked up another document and continued reading, as if trying to pretend he hadn't said anything.

Hammond had had enough. He quickly rushed over to where Isaacs sat reading from the stupid discrimination lawsuit; it was a brief progress report. He bent over the desk and, gripping him by both shoulders, pulled his entire body close so that the smaller man had no alternative but to stop reading and look at him directly in the face. Jeremy tried to resist the assault but to little avail. His horn-rimmed glasses were dislodged from the bridge of his nose during the fracas but remained attached to one ear and now hung to one side of his face; he looked pathetic. Hammond let go one hand and quickly moved it to hold a vice-like grip of his tormentors' face; his cheeks were squeezed tightly together and his whole face contorted. In an instant, Hammond's irate facial expressions had reddened with anger and sweat began to run from his forehead as he bored in on his opponent. Isaacs, his face in agonizing pain from being held in the strong grip, tried to show no such emotion, not that it would show considering his predicament. He was remarkably non-perturbed by what had just happened and just calmed himself by remaining still. He mentally challenged the other mans every move, calling his bluff, smirking, goading him to go further. Hit him maybe in the privacy of his own office. Hammond had lost it and Isaacs hadn't even begun to say what he wanted to say yet.

Chapter 20

THE DEADLOCK WAS BROKEN BY a knock on the door and Hammond, now deranged, froze for a second before realizing the situation he now found himself in. Another knock followed, louder this time. Isaacs merely gave a distasteful and ridiculing stare. Both he and Hammond had full facial contact now. Slowly, Isaacs moved his eyes down, directly to look at Hammond's hands. To where they were holding an excited and wrench-like grip of his contorted face. He knew then that he didn't have to say another word before, what seemed like ages but was in fact no more than a couple of seconds, the situation would change. Hammond, also realizing the situation, slowly released his clutches and hesitantly turned away in silence, pretending instead to admire the scenery through the eastside window of the over-elaborately furnished room. He quickly reflected upon what had just taken place. He'd physically assaulted an executive of the company, no matter what the reason or that he felt he was provoked was no excuse, as would be proved later on, no doubt.

His head was pounding and his mind was in a gear higher than overdrive. He needed to control his emotions. Isaacs wouldn't be able to prove anything. He had no proof of the incident, just the psychological advantage of knowing what he'd done, or so he thought. That would work in his favor. If Isaacs didn't know it before, he did now. He knew the depths that Richard Hammond would go to when somebody screwed him around. Nevertheless, he also realized that in those several seconds of madness, he'd shown just how unstable he'd become. Deep inside, he was livid. Soon enough, the panic returned and a strange, demented feeling ran throughout his entire body once again.

After several knocks on the door, Eamon Darcy, and Dwight York, both suspecting that Jeremy was not in his office, decided in the meantime that they would wait inside anyway; like they usually did on these occasions.

As if they were doing something terribly wrong, they hesitantly opened the door and proceeded to enter. It was as if they had stumbled upon a crime. Both men instantly recognized that there had been some sort of fracas between the occupants just prior to their fumbled entry. Jeremy was replacing his spectacles and rubbing his reddened jaw when they entered; he looked ruffled.

Quickly composing himself, Richard Hammond turned around and greeted the new arrivals as if nothing had happened. Darcy said nothing, since he'd sensed something was wrong. Dwight on the other hand replied with a courteous, *hello*, and tried to make some small talk. *It had been a long time since they'd last met*, he'd said, but at least that trivial piece of information was enough to break the ice, Hammond replied with predicted accuracy, simply agreeing and confirming the fact. All four men realized that whatever was said during the next few moments was going to be a little superficial. They chatted about nothing in particular anyway, and soon enough the atmosphere was calmer.

When Jeremy had straightened himself out, he was soon seated behind a long, oval conference table to one side of the room. With the other three men also comfortably seated and waiting, Gerald Sinclair finally turned up. He entered the office through the open door and apologized for being late. He was full of the joys of spring, greeting everybody on first name terms as he went over to the percolator and poured himself a black coffee. Sinclair seemed well pleased; something or someone had stoked up his true feelings!

'Any takers?' asked Gerald, looking towards his colleagues and holding the pot up in the air as a gesture. There were no takers!

'Shall we begin?' asked Jeremy, immediately getting to his feet. They nodded in unison as he took several, letter-size sheets of paper that were stapled together from inside his briefcase and promptly handed them to each person around the table before sitting back down.

He looked inquisitively at Darcy before speaking. 'I believe, Eamon that you are going to go through the report for the benefit of the others?' he suggested. Eamon quickly acknowledged him by slowing nodding his head. Both Hammond and Sinclair quickly smelt a rat. The so-called report was not HR stuff but trends and figures from the forecasts they supplied. Why did Isaacs have them? What would he be doing with stuff like this? What was Darcy playing at?

'Yeah, no problem,' said Eamon speaking in his warm, Southern-Irish accent and keeping his cards close to his chest. He seemed to have a calming effect whenever he spoke. 'I'd be glad to do that,' he then added showing a smile to those sat around the table. It was obvious that the two men had collaborated earlier. The *meeting* had been staged and the others had sensed it the minute Isaacs opened his briefcase. They quickly studied the contents of the documents that were handed to them, which showed columns of data compiled from the last twelve monthly forecasts. There were also several graphs, trended and displayed for overall clarification of the year-end results. Both Sinclair and Hammond instantly recognized the material that Isaacs had given them; it was their respective departments that were responsible for compiling and issuing the reports for the executive management. To the untrained observer they were meaningless. Several sets of graphs showed similar trend lines that reduced in time, whilst others increased with time. It was not so obvious that some downward trends were good and some were bad. It was also the same for the upwardly trended statistical data.

'Why didn't you say we were going to discuss these figures,' complained Sinclair, his feelings changing somewhat upon realizing what was being discussed. 'I would have brought some additional data that affects some of this longer-term stuff!' The unsuspecting Gerald Sinclair was the first person to respond to the strange goings-on. 'These are too important to just review without some notice guys! I mean, the meeting should have been arranged in more time . . . with a proper agenda,' he protested whilst looking disdainfully back and forth between Darcy and Isaacs in what could only be described as, utter disbelief. Sinclair had the words *it's not fair*, scribbled across his worried face.

Hammond was already alert and naturally smelt a larger rat than the one he'd sniffed out minutes earlier. Whilst he half expected the meeting to be about the difficulty in obtaining good and accurate forecasts, the fact that Sinclair was now blowing hot and cold made him more uneasy than ever before. And since when were Human Resources interested in reviewing statistics of this kind, he kept asking himself? It wasn't his job! Not for the first time that morning, Hammond's mind worked hard. He quickly joined in and became united in Gerald's disapproval and took off at speed once again, it was obvious he was still high on causing trouble.

'What the hell's going on here?' he demanded to know. 'Jesus! You bastards are pissing me off!' It was obvious that his adrenaline was still at work, he was still pumped up and once again he mentally scolded himself for being so abrupt. When he knew he had to get a point over quickly he swore, sometimes rather rudely and any professionalism he tried to portray simply went out of the window, something that his superiors had despised in the past and would not tolerate in the future.

'Whoa! Just slow down a little here, Hammond,' replied Darcy quickly getting to his feet and holding a hand aloft in a calming motion. He was annoyed by Hammond's quick outburst. 'Just hold on a minute and let me briefly go over the facts,' he said, holding the report in the air. 'Then we'll discuss the reason why you've both been called to this meeting,' he told them. 'Understood?' he asked them both. They nodded, Eamon wasn't in the mood to listen to whatever arguments they'd put up for not going through the report anyway! Hammond registered what he'd said. There would be no awards for achievement. For whatever reasons they were there, it was because something bad had happened and it only involved him and Sinclair . . . no doubt about that. York was there as an observer and perhaps also help make up the strength in numbers. He wondered if the lanky, pathetic-looking man was involved as much as everybody else was in whatever conspiracy they'd schemed against them. Another *little shit* that worked the strings of the personnel department he thought inwardly and added him to his personal list of, *bastards*!

Darcy continued to give a brief account of the contents of the data that now lay loosely leafed and open in front of the five men. They huddled around the large conference table and took in the detail. Eamon never once hinted that there was the slightest problem with the forecasts during the last year. On the contrary, he was quite complimentary on times, which gave both business managers a sense of wellbeing. After deliberating for a while over the final page, he eventually wrapped up the first part of the act by quoting the summary of the document, the bit used for the executive directors of the company to quickly have an understanding of the facts without actually reading them. He then got up from his chair, dabbed his forehead with a handkerchief and poured himself a coffee without asking anyone else in the room. Sinclair and Hammond felt more at ease. It was a good account of their work and the fact that Darcy had acknowledged the difficulties in making the forecasts made them feel more at ease. Perhaps they'd got it wrong and large bonuses would come their way!

Before returning to his seat, Darcy veered over to where his briefcase lay closed on one end of the table. He carefully opened it and took out a letter-sized, brown manila envelope before snapping it shut again. The envelope was opened as soon as the big Irish man was sat back at the table. Another document attached to it contained several paragraphs of text that was highlighted in red pen. Whilst those present around the table could not read any of the wording, it was obviously heavily marked to draw the reader's attention to points of interest, or more to the point, those important sections of the document that the reader should be highly aware of. As if waiting in anticipation for the next volley of approvals, or congratulations even, the two men sat comfortably and eased themselves back into their chair. They looked towards Darcy in anticipation. Dwight, knowing what was about to come, merely stared nonchalantly down at the table, studying his reflection in the well-polished, wooden surface. Jeremy, like York, had remained silent throughout, looking accusingly and rather smug at the two men sat across the other side of the table. He also knew what was coming and could hardly wait!

'Gentlemen,' Darcy said, his tone of voice noticeably less calming now. 'I have in my possession a memo from our CEO. Yes,' he confirmed, looking towards the two business analysts in the unlikely event the pair hadn't registered the level of seniority he was referring to. 'John Arnold is one pretty pissed guy at this moment in time. It has been drafted and sent to me after the details of another analysis, undertaken and completed by a team of independent consultants that were hired by the executive board of directors, was sent to him earlier this week. Their findings prove that our business planning and strategic development group was seen to be ignorant of even the basic principles of world oil pricing and product margins trend analysis.' There was a stunned silence from the two men under the microscope as Eamon continued reading the contents to those around the table.

'These misgivings were to such an extent that the person, or persons, responsible for compiling the previous reports would be deemed incompetent by any other oil company.' They were dumbfounded at what had just been said. Their faces portrayed nothing but panic as Darcy placed the document on the table and then simply stared at the two men, who in turn looked back at him in sheer disbelief. 'That's you two fucking numbskulls!' he added, raising his voice. It was as if they had just been smashed in the face with a hammer; they were filled with terror. Isaacs continued his smug grin and, unashamedly, kept staring at both men, but more so at Hammond, whom he now despised more than ever.

'But, that's not . . .'

'Quite!' shouted Darcy. Sinclair had begun to offer an explanation, or it could have been an apology perhaps, or something of that nature, but Darcy gave him no chance and silenced him in an instant; the words hardly left his lips. Instead of listening to the bullshit that was sure to come, Darcy began to tear into his subordinates, aggressively and without remorse now.

He continued the reprimand in pretty much the same vein. 'Advanced Strategic Energy was seen as a laughing stock amongst their peers within the industry, a laughing stock,' he repeated. 'Gentlemen, you have made us look like fools,' he told them contemptuously, his face now red and frowning. Sinclair cowered to him before looking toward Hammond, who just ignored him. 'The company had placed enormous trust in you both, believed in giving you the responsibility to make decisions and judgments that not only affects the company's well-being for today, but also for the company's future and that of its workers, and more importantly its shareholders for months and years to come. They have paid you well, very well indeed, but you have let them down badly, gentlemen,' Darcy eased off as he let those last words sink in and then repeated the allegation. 'Very badly,' he reminded them, sending the message home loud and clear.

'Where was the forecast telling us that three more Persian Gulf producers were considering reducing oil production later this year? Did you not think for one minute that the Saudi's, the Mexican's and Venezuelans would be the only reductions?' Darcy looked at them in amazement. 'It was indicated at the six-nation Gulf Cooperation Council meeting for Christ sake! Are you blind? Oman and Brazil were two others also considering reductions, did you know that? If you did, where is it in your report? These are significant factors, gentlemen, not fiction. You both chose to ignore the very fundamentals of our business. The world is about to see as much as a three percent overall cut in world oil supplies and ASEI didn't know about it. Why were we the only company that didn't know? Because, gentlemen, we employ arseholes like you two to do our research!' Darcy had changed from giving a lecture and was now making it personal, he was becoming very angry. It became apparent to Isaacs that the big man had indeed, had his collar felt from the bigger man above him. The memo wouldn't have been sent in the post, he concluded. It had been delivered personally. Perhaps even Darcy wouldn't get out of this one, thought Hammond, strangely finding the notion rather amusing. After all, surely Darcy's the man responsible for this mess!

'Even the Dow Jones reported that the industry exporters will need to cut their output even further in a third round of cuts in order to start reducing inventories and move oil prices toward their goal of ninety dollars. In the meantime, oil prices are set to fall through the fucking floor and we're not in a position to do anything about it! You pair wouldn't know the price of a barrel of benchmarked crude oil if they sold it in the local whorehouse!' he shouted at them. Sinclair, along with Hammond, sat feeling quite inept and had little else to do other than look at each other coyly as more Irish scorn was heaped onto them.

'You failed to mention the proposed cuts being made by Iran and Iraq earlier this year never actually happened. Why?' Darcy wasn't looking for answers, he knew there wasn't any and without waiting, continued the verbal assault unabated. 'That resulted in some of our upstream, North Sea business planners predicting huge gains towards the second quarter. That was based on your humpty-dumpty forecast of seventy dollars a barrel. All very nice, I hear you say! What actually happens? Brent crude oil gets delivered at fifty nine dollars! Jesus! How the hell can you be so wrong? For crying out loud, the indicators were all there. According to this report we're going to get our ass bitten off using that forecast!' he told them, holding the report in the air as if to prove the point. Darcy wanted to go on and inform them that the global demand for oil was expected to grow by just one point seven percent compared with their last prediction of two point eight percent increase. Another complete and utter shambles, he wanted to say but didn't get the chance. Hammond had now quickly sprung to his feet. He'd decided to put a stop to proceedings. In his state of mind, he'd heard enough.

'What is all this crap?' he asked, having reached boiling point a few seconds earlier.

'Something bothering you, Hammond?' asked Isaacs, the HR man pouncing the moment Hammond opened his mouth. It was his turn now. He couldn't wait. Hammond, however, replied in his usual mode, he was totally wired up!

'Fuck you, and your rent boy there,' he replied, pointing to Dwight who'd instantly been startled at the accusation. The young, skinny-looking man jumped to attention upon hearing what Hammond had called him. Richard Hammond was on the back foot with nothing to lose now. He might as well go for the jugular. He knew what was coming and turned to face Eamon.

'So what are you trying to say, Eamon, what? What's the fucking point in prolonging the agony? Just fucking spit it out for Christ sake! That you want us out! You're gonna sack us! Is that it? Yeah, come on and fucking say it you fat, ugly Irish son-of-a-bitch!' he mouthed, holding his clenched fists up towards him, gesturing the need to fight. Whatever his fate might have been earlier to this action, Hammond had sealed another, more fateful one at that precise moment in time. He was doomed the moment he raised his fists. Sinclair meanwhile, remained seated, still gob smacked at what Darcy had just said. He was stunned by what he didn't know, by what he should have known and now, even more traumatized by the outburst being delivered by his colleague and opposite number, Richard Hammond. He couldn't believe what he was hearing. Hammond was now stood shouting obscenities and pointing a finger accusingly at everybody across the table!

'Is that why these two queers from personnel are here? They've probably been holding hands all morning, fucking smarting at the thought of firing us I bet.' Again, Dwight blushed; his gender had never been questioned in this way before. Isaacs, however, was a professional and said nothing. He knew the score, as always. Let him carry on, it was a dream come true. The obscenities came thick and fast, Hammond was pressing self-destruct. At that point, Darcy intervened; he had no choice but to try to calm things down. Even he was surprised by the way Hammond was reacting and he realized that he was becoming more and more crazy and aggressive with each second.

'Calm down, Hammond. That's enough now, do you hear me, that's enough,' he tried to say. Eamon spoke with authority, in a damage limitation kind of way now but his words fell on deaf ears.

'Forget it, Eamon,' shouted Hammond, who'd settle this by dishing out his own reprimands now. 'You're in the picture too if you remember!' he reminded him, pointing his finger in the Irishman's direction. Hammond was fed up with all the injustice shown to him ever since he'd taken up his position with ASEI; it was even more unjust when Darcy or Isaacs was involved in matters! Darcy shuddered at what had just been said. He went limp. Everyone but York and Sinclair knew what Hammond referred to. The picture showed all three of them, Hammond, Isaacs and Darcy. They stood, drunkenly posing underneath a wooden bridge in that small town in Texas. Behind them, two bodies hung limp and made a pitiful background. Meanwhile, Hammond was going berserk shouting anything that came into his head. He was high on a mixture of bad substances he'd abused his body with earlier on. Then, all of a sudden, when he'd finished mouthing off to the world, he decided to take his anger out on Isaacs; he'd show the *little bastard* once and for all he couldn't fuck him around.

Even Darcy's large stature wasn't enough to stop Hammond running over to the other side of the table to once again confront the HR man. Isaacs had mistakenly sat with a continuous smirk across his face and that was his undoing. He should have known better. It was the same that shameful day in Jericho; Hammond had gone berserk and couldn't get the rope out quick enough. He'd seen it then for the first time. Now, Hammond acted in the same manner and soon Isaacs had become alarmingly afraid for his life. Hammond was unpredictable, violent and extremely dangerous. Soon enough, Hammond was up and at him, approaching with speed as Isaacs stood up and quickly tried to edge backwards from his chair, raising his arms to protect himself from the obvious blow he was about to receive.

'Hold on, Hammond, you mad bastard,' Isaacs shouted as the crazed man come straight at him.

'Fuck you Isaacs . . . fuck the lot of you!' he cried before lunging at the small and petrified figure cowering in front of him. Two hard blows to the side of the face ensured the slightly built man fell to the ground with some force. The fact that he'd tried to protect himself from such a powerful and incensed man proved fruitless and he was knocked down in an instant from the first smash of the knuckle-clenched fist. He was sent flying and ended up unconscious from the second blow as another fist smashed into the side of his cheek, cracking the underlying bone into several pieces that fragmented and split open the skin. Darcy tried in vain to stop the inevitable happening before he too had become frightened of Hammond. Instead, he shouted into the open corridor for assistance. Dwight York, afraid for his life, quickly scurried well away from the fighting and discretely edged out of the office the moment Darcy opened the door.

Sinclair, who by now had come to his senses, had actually jumped on Hammond's back during the short time it took him to cover the short distance to get to his quarry but that too was in vain. He was thrown clear, sent crashing into a table that hosted several antique ornaments with some force and breaking all that was under him. Hammond wanted revenge and nobody, or anything, was going to stop him. He'd lost it.

As the guards came rushing in, two immediately went for Hammond, who'd become hysterical and was now madder than ever, swearing and still swinging out blindly at anybody within reach. They were not put off by this and soon overpowered him. The third guard kept his distance whilst pointing a gun in the direction of the assailant. Not before too long it was over. Richard Hammond was led out of the building in handcuffs and taken downstairs to the waiting NYPD to be charged and put in jail.

On reflection, both Darcy and Isaacs could have handled the situation better, they later reasoned. The friendship between them and Hammond had never stood the test of time; Hammond had made sure of that. The way he'd conducted himself ever since they'd given him a free leg up the company management ladder was nothing short of revolting. They should have gotten rid him well before now.

Meanwhile, a vase containing a bouquet of flowers had been conveniently positioned on a table to the far side of the room. Inside the floral arrangement, a concealed video camera had its lens pointing towards the fracas and captured the entire episode from start to finish. The early morning affray would make excellent viewing by others in the organization and, as if there would be any doubt, would almost certainly help in deciding Richard Hammond's fate with Advanced Strategic Energy Inc once and for all.

Chapter 21

THE TIME FLEW BY WITH Des, Suzanne and the kids. I've never had so much fun and, apart from the obvious touristy bits like Times Square, Rockefeller Centre, Central Park, and Grand Central Station, never knew Manhattan held so many other relatively unknown and interesting landmarks. But now it was back to business. The decision to depose at Cranton's was unusual but we realized it was a tradeoff. In Lance's opinion, Hastings had gone too far in favoring one side more than the other in arguing for the case to be heard at all, he was referring of course to the side that had very little evidence to support a civil lawsuit for racial discrimination! He had to redress the balance. They were a large international law firm with an office base in New York. They operated worldwide with small satellite facilities even in the remotest of countries, but in New York they were conveniently located three blocks down from one of their blue-ribbon clients—Advanced Strategic Energy Inc, and now we were there.

The room chosen for the arranged meeting was predictable enough. It was spacious with fine furniture paid for by over-expensive lawyers billing by the minute. Artificial plants hired by the hour adorned each corner and plenty of freestanding table lamps lit the room. The windows were purposely mirrored to reflect the inside of the room—to look outside would distract their work. It was a pity. The fantastic views of nearby Central Park were denied us as we sat opposite each other for the second time in as many weeks, give or take a few days.

So, for the next two days, we simply rolled our sleeves up and exchanged information, simple as that. Whatever they asked for, we give them, not that we had that much to offer. In return, Briggs and his entourage did the same. Our prospective witnesses turned up as promised and, starting with me, one by one John Briggs asked us simple questions. He was polite

Peter Nutty

and the discussions were straight forward, after all this was a deposition and not a trial, we were told. As the process progressed, there were a few technicalities creeping in we noticed and on times the questions seemed not to fit the argument. For the most part though, it was straightforward and fair. Dillwyn remained behind in Port Arthur and faxed us whatever we needed. The little we asked for, the Cranton team had it to hand, slick as ever. The only trouble was, Lance didn't ask for anybody to be questioned from ASEI. We'd rely heavily on the element of surprise, he argued. We went along with his argument. Little did we know there were other reasons for Lance saying that!

* * *

Back in Port Arthur, Desmond and I had had another blow out in Kamp's, the local bar frequented by a mixed-race of well-to-do people. In less than two days I'd have to return to England for one week to resolve some unfinished business with Frank whilst at the same time, Suzanne would join Desmond in Texas and end his flamboyant lifestyle. Bubba Kamp, the owner with whom we associated with as two regulars had become our friend in the space of days and was our reason for overdoing it. Bubba was all-important and it was imperative we drunk his beer and made him laugh—the lawsuit didn't seem to matter! One particular night, along with several other drunks, we slept for the night inside the alehouse without any problem—we'd had too much to drink to even remember where we were supposed to be staying. I was comfortably asleep on the bench inside the booth and Desmond on the pool table in the arms of an overweight black woman twenty years younger than he was. I was later informed they had wanted to get engaged and I was to be the best man!

A light mist that rose from the nearby bayou tempered the morning sun but had little effect on the humidity, which was already beginning to rise. Wednesday morning was as busy as any other day and people went about their business with purpose, including the lady whose sole desire it was to clean up the mess made the previous night at Kamp's. The bar came alive for the second time in as many hours when Moped—short for Molly Peddler, entered the joint. She laughed and hollered at the sight before her. Never in all her days cleaning at Kamp's had she witnessed the spectacle that was now displayed on the pool table towards the far corner of the bar. In front of her, sprawled across the green cloth in all here glory was Debby Shed; her nickname after most of the locals had put their *tools* in her. The bar's good-time girl was sound asleep with both her breasts hanging out, exposed for all to see. Her dress was also half removed revealing large and elasticized, white frilly knickers that were covered with beer that stained most of the front. Moped's amusement was completed upon seeing the sorriest looking, middle-aged black man you ever saw cuddled up to her. They seemed in love! He was half-undressed; his saggy-looking flesh also soaked in beer and his boxer shorts hardly covered his *tackle*. His head rested peacefully between his *fiancé's* breasts. God knows what happened last night but the end result was a picture and now Moped could not stop laughing. Slowly but surely the other drunken occupants awoke one by one from the sound of such high spirits before the inevitable happened.

'Wha! Hey, what's going down, man? Wha the . . . !' It was Desmond who had stirred first. His awakening was made more interesting by releasing his face from one of her soft, fleshy-breasts that had become sticky from the beer poured over them earlier. They had become partly glued to his cheeks as he slept. He was amazed at what greeted him and tried to get off that pool table as fast as he could, much to the disappointment of his companion who reached out to grab him. She cared not in the least that her breasts just hung out of her open dress. My head pounded but it didn't stop me from laughing along with the rest. Desmond never could resist a pair of forty fours and last night was no exception.

'Wait till Suzanne finds out,' I teased him as I managed to pull my leaded body up from the booth.

'Wha the ell you on about, man,' he snarled, spitting as he spoke. 'You won't do that to your ole buddy . . . . would you?' He examined me, sheepishly. I laughed some more but in no time at all we were gone, never to return to Kamp's. Never, so Desmond informed me time and time again.

* * *

Safely returned to England it was not long before I tracked down Cheryl. The date set for the lawsuit was two weeks away and operations manager or not I had work to complete, which was my excuse to make contact with her. I was dreading the confrontation with Frank but it would happen as soon as he knew I was back at the plant. I would be summoned.

As expected, she looked nervous as I entered the small confines of her office. I knew from previous conversations that something was wrong. I closed the door behind me and sat on the table in front of her. She looked every inch as pretty, just as I had imagined her to be. Cheryl knew why I was there. It was simple. All I needed was the minor details regarding the payment to JG Engineering. Nothing could be simpler. It was not that easy for Cheryl though and I suspected the worse. Money can be an evil thing. She got out the file and showed me the cost codes, approval for payment and what the engineering costs were for. Most of it was jargon to me. A signature authorizing the payment was indecipherable. Her hands shook as she handed over the file. They shook more when questioned about the company and their geographic location, bank details and contact names. The tears began to roll. There was no such company. I knew that, she knew that. Then, for some strange reason, I felt compelled to comfort her as she cried. The truth was not far away and so I just held her, feeling her petite body jerking against me with every sob. She felt warm against me and even with tears rolling down her rounded cheeks and onto pert lips, she looked beautiful. It had been a long time since I had held somebody with so much beauty. From that moment on I had two problems; the first was probably related to the girl I held in my arms. The other problem, the money one, Cheryl had yet to tell me about!

* * *

Frank Dawes was a miserable sod and I told him so. We just picked up from where we'd left our last conversation.

'Thanks for the fax anyway,' I told him, the sarcasm hardly noticeable amidst the anger.

'You knew the score, Doug. It didn't have to be like this.'

'I'm not really bothered, Frank. I respect your position,' I told him, meaning it.

'When's it all happening?'

'Couple of weeks, in New Orleans,' I replied. Frank didn't delve for any details; he'd probably already had the file sent to him anyway. 'Who's the new guy?' I then asked inquisitively, changing the conversation.

'The ops manager, oh . . . err . . . Pete Harries.' It knocked me a little. I couldn't blame the slimy bastard; I'd have taken the job under the same circumstances.

'That's nice,' I replied trying to keep calm about it all. 'And me?'

'I'm not sure what to do with you, Doug,' he replied, and understandably feeling uncomfortable with the situation. Frank began to pour two cups of coffee and looked uneasy at what to say next, it was obvious he didn't want this conversation.

'Oh, by the way, you never told me you were in discussions with the company lawyers, Frank. The fact that I'm now kind of in between jobs fits in just nicely with what they have in mind in New Orleans,' I told him with a lack of gratitude. Frank looked back at me as he poured the drinks.

'I did tell you, Doug, only you weren't listening,' he said with the same sarcasm I'd displayed to him earlier. He then walked over to me and handed me a cup. The coffee was made exactly the way I like it; weak, no sugar.

'C'mon, Frank. If I'm on my way just come out and say it. I'm not really that bothered, honest.'

'Oh, it's not that, Doug, well . . .' he hesitated, as if he needed time to think about what he was about to say, 'I mean, let's hope it doesn't come to that, hey!'

'Here we go. I'm not a mind reader, Frank. What's going on?' I sipped the coffee, it tasted awful!

'It's Nigeria, Doug. You don't honestly think that you can be part of a management team that disposes of their responsibilities just like that, do you?' Frank clicked his fingers when he said that.

'That's bullshit and you know it,' I replied.

'It's not bullshit to anybody else in the company, Doug. You were the operations manager, Haynes was your deputy. The top two ASEI personnel were there and you let the place blow to fucking bits, how can that be bullshit?' he asked, right on the money.

'I was deputizing, Frank,' I reminded him. 'Besides, the place went sky high because it was meant to. If we were operating the plant or not, the place was destined to go into orbit, it would have happened whatever we were doing and whoever was in charge. What could we do about it?'

'You could have ensured the place was guarded for one,' he replied.

'C'mon, give me a break, we had no control over that either,' I said, annoyed. Frank seemed to be scraping the bottom of the barrel for somebody to blame now. 'Perhaps it was the fucking Taliban on a training exercise,' I then suggested, such was my disinterest in the whole affair.

'And the leaks outside the fence?'

'It didn't make the slightest difference,' I contested for the umpteenth time and getting angrier by the second. 'Weren't you listening to what I've been saying? Besides, why wait until now to resurrect all this? We've been through the enquiry, it wasn't our fault,' I reminded him as if he'd forgotten for some strange reason.

'Wrong, Doug. It makes every difference. As long as that leak was spilling, all eyes were taken away from other things, like guarding the facility. *People were killed*, Doug.'

'Tell me something I don't already know.'

'The Nigerians want compensation from you too.'

'How can they blame me for that?'

'You should have fixed the goddamn leak.'

'C'mon Frank, you've been there,' I reminded him, so he'd be in no doubt as to what I was saying. 'The bloody place was like a sieve. There are leaks all over the place. It gives the locals the chance for some free fuel,' I said without sounding humorous. Frank never budged, despite knowing what I'd said was the truth; he'd seen it for himself during a three week stint just before the fireworks. I was in the shit and that was that.

'It's going all the way, Doug.'

'And all because I'm helping Desmond,' I hollered at him, shaking my head. 'It stinks, Frank,' I said getting to the point, and deep down Frank probably agreed.

'All I know, Doug, is that the company is not happy with the original enquiry,' he lied not committing himself either way. 'They want another go at it. They think that others, *including you, Doug*, are negligent,' he added with emphasis. This was all new to me but I knew how it was working now. ASEI were at it again and Frank was being manipulated from high up the corporate ladder; unbeknown to me, Jeremy Isaacs was the puppet master this time around!

'And if I give up on Desmond?' I asked, speculating.

'I'd guess they won't pursue the second enquiry too hard,' he replied. 'Might not even bother to pursue it at all, who knows?'

'And if I go ahead?'

'You know the answer to that, Doug.'

'Fine, let me know the date of the enquiry. I should be a seasoned lawyer by then, Frank,' I said, and got up to leave. I'd had enough of Frank's crap.

'Good, you gonna need all the courtroom practice you can get,' Frank shouted at me as I went through the door. My reply was simple and it was echoed through the corridor as I left his office.

'Bollocks!'

The next few days saw me complete most of my outstanding work and I even helped Pete settle into his new position. He was embarrassed by it all on the outside but deep inside he must have been doing cartwheels. It was a good move for him. My relationship with Julie deteriorated further the longer I was home. We argued at every opportunity, especially so because of spending my vacation time with Desmond. The marriage was dead in the water. To take my mind off everything that was piling up on me, I spent most of my workdays with Cheryl, trying to understand what exactly they did in the accounts department—it was a ploy! Most of our spare time was spent in one of the many pubs along the quay in Poole harbor where we slowly but surely got to know each other. The JG Engineering thing presented a huge problem but now, no matter what, Cheryl would no longer be responsible for the money. She told me how the ghost company was formed, how the money was paid and the person who authorized it, and it wasn't who I thought; Tom played no part in it and so I never bothered contacting him from then on in. This piece of information was well received by me; it just might give me some leverage in events leading up to the hastily rearranged enquiry Frank talked about.

But, more to the point, it was going to be useful in Desmond's lawsuit. It was obvious that a Senior Vice-President had created the ghost company and authorized the payments. It was the very same person who'd signed off on Desmond's dismissal. The payment to JG Engineering was theft on a large scale, but how to prove it was going to be difficult. He'd covered his tracks well and now Cheryl was left in the lurch. I wasn't a lawyer but surely we could implicate Isaacs in some way. He was not to be trusted, that was obvious but how could we get that out in the open. Or, even better, how could we get it out in a courtroom. I'd leave Lance sort that one out. In the meantime, I didn't know if it was good news or bad news!

That night, we had dinner at the Hotel du Vin and Bistro, a lovely converted mansion house located just off the quay. The ambience was perfect and with good food and wine, we fell in love with each other.

Sooner than I would have liked, I was needed back in New Orleans. The trial was imminent. After telling Cheryl of Desmond's predicament, she too became an aggrieved employee, practically overnight. Her whole attitude had changed towards her once *previously brilliant* employer. We said goodbye and arranged to meet very soon.

Chapter 22

NICK KNIGHT SAT BESIDE ME on one of the back rows of seats inside Section, 'A' of the Orleans Parish, Civil Court. The newly appointed and rookie journalist with the New York Times was restless and fidgeted. It was where he would be called upon to present the facts of a lawsuit to the nation. They would have to be pretty precise—only a few million people would be reading the paper.

'It's my first time inside a courtroom believe it or not,' he whispered to me.

'Oh yeah,' I replied, uninterested. 'How'd you end up here then?'

'Oh, it's a long story,' replied Nick and unfortunately for me he wasn't afraid to tell it. His path to the Section A Courtroom was made through associates working with the New Orleans district attorney's office he told me, still whispering in case he committed a crime. The papers legal editor, Joe Mayo, had called the First Assistant, Mary Lloyd. She was an old school friend of his wife. She had asked on his behalf for Nick to have official media representation on the case. Since there was very little interest—apart from the local press, Mary Lloyd arranged for Nick to be the official in-court media reporter. He would wear a badge, which guaranteed him entry each day regardless of the numbers.

'You won't need the badge, Nick!' I joked looking around the room at the numbers. He said nothing and had obviously missed the quip.

'My editor wants me to interview the litigants,' he then said, rather miffed at the request from his boss, Joe. 'I need your help, Doug.'

'Why's that?'

'I don't know these guys,' he confessed gesturing towards the Cranton camp. 'You need to introduce me.'

'I can't help you I'm afraid, Nick.' I told him flatly.

'Why not?' he replied, feeling rather spurned.

'Cos I don't know them either,' I said. 'Besides, newspaper reporters don't ask for introductions,' I added, ready to give the young man some worldly advice.

'Oh, is that right?' Nick asked this question as if I was being awkward all of a sudden.

'They simply shove a microphone in front of somebody's face and start firing away. Don't you watch the news?' Nick shook his head slightly, sighed and chose to ignore my advice altogether. Modern journalism had taken another, more friendly approach it seemed. At least the rooky journalist had thought so. Nick looked around the room as more people started to fill up the empty space. He would send his report via e-mail as soon as proceedings for the day were ended, with or without an interview.

At that precise moment, Nick's first mistake echoed around the room. Heads turned towards us as his mobile phone rang out and drowned out every other noise in the room. Nick grabbed at the small machine as if his life depended on it and tried to squeeze it silent. Without much luck he pressed hard on the green answer icon, ducked low between the rows of chairs and received the call. It was his editor, Joe Mayo, who was about to tell Nick the specifics of the interviews he needed.

'Nick, is that you?'

'What do you want?' he replied, angry. 'I'm in the courtroom damn it!' Joe couldn't care less if he was having tea with the queen of England. He was going to talk.

'Only interview those people who would have the greatest impact on any potential story, Nick.' Joe needn't have told him, Nick knew exactly what he had to do.

'Are you being serious? Stop treating me like I'm a teenager, Joe. I'm twenty-eight years of fucking age and I can handle this story without you telling me what to ask and who to ask questions to, surely! Do you think I'm stupid or something? What else do you think I'd do?' Nick raised his voice and the language being used turned a few heads. There was hardly anybody involved in the trial. Who, other than the litigants did Joe imagine he was going to interview? Nick wondered if he'd done the right thing accepting the job. Joe's voice could be heard screaming down the phone. It was not the response he wanted to hear from his rookie journalist.

'Nick, I'm telling you now, son. Don't ever try to give me crap over the phone like this, understand?'

'Joe?'

'Yeah,' he replied.

'Shut the fuck up for Christ sake!'

They continued with the full-blown argument inside the court for a short while longer. Nick was reddening all the while. He had recently been interviewed for a television host position and later as a reporter for a number of shows and cable networks including, *HBO Entertainment News,* and *Grandstand*, a syndicated game show produced by Major League Baseball Productions. He regretted failing the screen tests and the interviews went miserably wrong. But the spin-off had created some small success and helped him gain a reporter's job with the *NYT* for a limited period where he would have to prove himself, which was around about now.

Joe's voice was still transmitting around the court until Nick realized he had only one option left. He quickly closed down the cell. He would convince Joe some other time. To the editor, Nick was little known but, nevertheless, well suited to follow yet another racial discrimination lawsuit finally destined to go on for three, or perhaps even four days of litigation after several months of petty arguing by both teams of lawyers preparing the case. He knew that lawsuits of this kind would be the usual; uninteresting, *one* word against *another*, and each side counteracting the arguments presented to them in every way possible. He was not about to let an experienced reporter loose on this one, they were far too valuable. Besides, in America alone there were probably another two thousand cases of this kind going on right at that very moment. Black and ethnic minority American's with a racial grievance of some kind or other, some legitimate, others not so. But at least they would get a fair hearing!

Nick will be alright covering this one, thought Joe. Besides, Joe now knew what a determined young man Nick was. He would do it his way and nobody, not even Joe his boss, would change his mind. And so with that in mind Nick was dispatched, economy class all the way to New Orleans after proving to Joe that his initial introduction with Desmond Haynes and talks about the wrongdoings of Advanced Strategic Energy Inc. would be a worthy story.

There was a quite but consistent hubbub of conversation inside the court as we looked aimlessly around the old-fashioned room. Up ahead, we saw the plaintiff, Desmond, accompanied by Lance, Chuck, Ant, and Dil who were all plainly dressed and sat quietly waiting. The defense counsel, ably led by John Briggs who chose Armani to adorn his lean, athletic-looking body, looked every part the smartly dressed team of attorneys we knew they were. That team was crouched over tables and between chairs as they discussed the case from a mountain of legal documents piled high on one long desk before them. Every now and then the Court Officer would quite the group and the noise would die down only to increase some moments later as points of order were brought to the attention of their lead attorney. They were raring to go and their enthusiasm showed. Desmond, on the other hand, looked lost. He was sat quietly, non-perturbed by the legal jargon being quickly thrown around by the slick young lawmen assembled each side of this over elaborate chamber that housed the state judicial system. Another realm of American legitimacy was about to be tested.

The more he waited, the more uncomfortable Nick became I noticed. His boredom threshold was low and he was already fed up, that much I could tell.

'Relax, Nick,' I said. If it wasn't for the sympathy he felt towards Desmond he would have probably called time after the first few hours of his first day! The courtroom seats did not help our discomfort either, they were far too small, they were hard, and the row in front restricted legroom. They could be connected in such a way as to form a complete bench to seat more people during larger criminal trials if needed—it would've been even more cramped since these type of hearings usually drew enormous crowds of spectators. We dreaded the thought. Nick looked at his watch. Ten minutes to go.

'I wish I'd taken a job as a fruit salesman now, I feel like a sardine on this bench,' said the newspaperman, miffed by what he'd inadvertently volunteered to do.

'Then why become a reporter?' I asked without sympathy.

'It was by accident . . . after a heavy drinking session in one of the many New York bars I used to frequent looking for work following a couple of failed screen-tests,' he confided in me with a smirk. 'A friend told me that a move as a columnist in the *NYT* would improve my legal knowledge and experience of prosecuting related illegal acts of discrimination and there was no better place to learn than inside the courtrooms. A newspaper journalist reporting on such matters was the stepping stone I needed to watch and listen. But . . .' Nick looked around the room as if something had happened. 'I also need to get paid for doing it. Believe it or not, I actually volunteered to cover this story.' He needn't have bothered to convince me of that; his experience was such that he was destined to cover a cheap story and that's where New Orleans came in.

At that precise moment a guard walked quickly through an open door that led from the main hall and into the courtroom. He was holding a note and promptly handed it to John Briggs. The lawyer looked at it, quickly got up from his seat and immediately left the room. His posy looked on with mild amusement as their number one disappeared with the trial just about to begin!

The rest of us just sat and waited. There was no need to use the seats as benches this morning, the case being heard would interest no more than fifteen people and, although we didn't know at the time, would take no more than thirty minutes total. The register of lawsuits displayed for Section A, posted in the courtroom lobby, listed; 'Haynes vs. Advanced Strategic Energy Inc.' and in brackets the number, *three*; Court Docket No.3. There were further details relating to the title of the case and the court reference number, Case #C4060999. Due to several bail jumpers, ours was the first case to be heard that morning.

A ruffled stir from somewhere behind a door being opened to the right of the room signaled the arrival in court of the Administrative Law Judge for the Equal Rights Division of the Department of Workforce Development, who walked into *his* courtroom. The Court Officer, a middle-aged woman by the name of Wendy, who looked immaculately dressed in a grey skirt and matching blouse, immediately ordered the occupants to stand. They stood briefly until His Honor, Judge, Roland Hastings, took his seat. Wendy briefly rambled on about His Honor, and the case number and court docket number etc., etc. They sat down again and waited for the next instructions that would come from the Judge himself. Once he'd finished addressing matters of courtroom etiquette and taken the unusual steps of explaining to the jury some of the legal jargon they would hear he turned and spoke to the Court Officer.

'Miss Lloyd!'

'Yes, Your Honor.'

'Have counsel registered the complaint made by the plaintiff?'

'Yes, Your Honor, they have indeed, sir.' The Judge frowned at her address; it was her first day in *his* courtroom, she had a lot to learn.

'Have the defendants filed a written answer to the plaintiff's complaint?' he asked, knowing the answer.

'Yes, sir, they filed their response within the required time.' Another frown from the Judge as the preliminaries followed the required etiquette. A ruffled commotion echoed from the back of the court. Several of us turned around to see a much harassed John Briggs re-enter the room. The

Judge directed his questions to him the moment he'd made it back to his seat.

'What's your answer, counselor?'

John Briggs didn't quite stand up straight enough to address the answer for His Honors liking, due to being out of breath but, nevertheless, he quickly half-raised himself off his chair, leant one hand on the table in front of him and used the other to hold his tie in place as he replied.

'Advanced Strategic Energy Inc. denies the factual or legal basis for liability, Your Honor,' he managed to say, breathing hard.

'Very well,' replied the Judge wondering why Briggs was gasping for air. 'Miss Lloyd, please proceed to inform the court of the complaint made by the plaintiff.'

'Yes, sir,' she replied, and picked up a transcript in front of her, but before she could say anything the Judge cut her off.

'No, Miss Lloyd, I am a Judge, not a Knight of the Round Table!' Judge Hastings was not in a good mood and it was the third time she'd called him, *Sir*.

'Yes, *Your Honor*,' replied Mary Lloyd, blushing before starting to outline the complaint made by the plaintiff, Desmond Haynes. It was a lawsuit issued against ASEI for unlawful dismissal and racial discrimination. The defense counsel watched as their number one man plonked himself back on his seat. He was flustered. The three-man team led by the young black attorney from New York, tactically hired to defend many of the racial discrimination lawsuits brought against Advanced Strategic Energy Inc, sat silent. They had built quite a reputation. They would be hoping everything was okay.

Chapter 23

THE MOMENT THE TRIAL STARTED, Nick quickly realized why he should not have volunteered for this particular case after hearing the first plea from the defense counsel. No sooner had the Court Officer finished reading out loud the lawsuit brought against ASEI, lightly-detailed matters required to briefly outline the case for the benefit of the jury, the slick looking Briggs jumped to his feet and immediately informed the Judge that their council needed more time.

'Could His Honor grant an adjournment?' he asked politely. This was a shock to us and to the Judge. They had the case in the bag! But instead we listened as JB explained the reason why *they needed another couple of days reprieve to prepare and re-submit new evidence that would support their argument*, said JB, suspiciously. He swayed his right arm out towards the jury in an attempt to gesture something or other and continued to speak.

'Your Honor, my client is to argue that Mr. Haynes was dismissed for gross negligence and not for any racial motives. However, if these matters are to be argued then procedures and programs that were already in place to protect Advanced Strategic Energy employees against discrimination of this kind need clarification for the benefit and ease of understanding, especially for these good people.' He looked at the jury as he spoke, smiling, charming, and deceitful as ever. 'This is something, Your Honor . . .' he said, pausing for a moment. 'That is vitally important in order for a fair trial.' His voice and expression changed quickly to emphasize surprise at the unlikely thought of Hastings not considering granting any further time. He then continued with his over sympathetic gaze at the jury for several more seconds before slowly walking back to his seat. He sat down with a worried frown on his face. It was *bullshit*.

The Judge knew it was bullshit and for that reason he was confused. Lance was even more confused but he reacted accordingly, thank God.

He saw what Briggs had done to the jury. Why the deferment? Like the rest of us he hadn't a clue but he knew the game being played by Briggs was potentially damning. He was, nevertheless, quick to react to Briggs' theatrics. Lance obviously thought the charade deserved an ovation. He slowly rose to his feet, grimaced as if in pain, and stood for a moment in complete silence, showing complete disgust towards Briggs for his devious ways. Solemnly looking down his nose through half-rimmed spectacles, Lance glared towards the defense team for a few moments then at Judge Hastings—who had yet to give even the slightest indication of what he was thinking following Briggs' strange request—and then back towards Briggs. Heycock shook his head as he started to speak.

'More time! You need more time!' Lance appeared to look flabbergasted. 'Dear me,' he muttered as he coolly turned and looked at the jury for the first time whilst still continuing to address the Judge. 'With all due respect, Your Honor, counsel has had over eighteen months to prepare for this trial. And now they want more time?' Lance had by now turned his pathetic looks back towards Briggs and once again just shook his head slowly. Briggs, not perturbed in the slightest, just held his composure. Lance had the attention of the Judge. The other less experienced members of Briggs' team looked embarrassed. Lance tried to push home any advantage that may come his way. He held up his *brief*, pointing out that all evidence had been submitted very early on, pre-trial discovery had taken place without any concerns whatsoever, and that the legal arguments to support their case were well established.

'They would even be proven by, *Case Law*,' he lied and slammed the thin pile of neatly bound papers on the table. 'These briefs have already been FedEx'd to the defense council for scrutiny,' he told the Judge, forcefully. 'In return, we have received everything we need. Any further documents would be pointless, Your Honor. My learned friend is merely stumbling for time. Perhaps to prove something that does not exist?' He finished the last sentence with a flurry. There was little need to speak further; his expressions said it all. The few sentences he did speak lasted no more than thirty seconds or so and it excited everyone there. Nevertheless, this type of argument had been heard many times before. The Judge, who was sat upright, mulled over the situation and then leaned further back in his leather, reclining chair wondering what do say next. He rubbed his chin with his left hand—a bad sign!

Even though Lance had not said much in those briefest of moments, both Nick and I agreed that he'd scored handsomely against his opponent and at that point should have remained sat in his chair in order to allow His Honor to deliberate in his favor. But the adrenaline was still flowing. The temptation for Lance was too much and he felt compelled to say more, to further do something that would blast Briggs totally out of the water in those opening few minutes. And so, much to his regret, he did. In fact, his next unrehearsed comment blasted them both out of the water.

'Perhaps they still need time to implement their so-called, racial policy, if they have one?' he muttered, his doubts said loud enough for everybody there to hear. He tried to be as quite as possible of course, and in reality his words were barely audible but unfortunately the jury heard what he'd said. It was a cheap shot and Lance regretted saying it the second the words left his lips. Too cunning for his own good, he realized as the courtroom erupted with raised voices.

'Point of order, Your Honor, that's disgraceful!' Briggs was the first up on his feet as soon as he'd heard Lance utter those damning words. He knew the attorney was out of order and quickly seized his chance for reprisal. Another previously unknown member of the Cranton team, assistant attorney, Adam Chandler, was also quickly up on his feet, one hand on the table and the other pointing a finger at Lance, who'd by now quickly busied himself by burying his head in his briefcase as if looking for some document or other. Our friend was really looking for some form of physical escape, we decided. Needless to say, both counsels' were now standing and pointing accusing fingers and trying to shout aloud points of order to the Judge, who was definitely not amused.

At this point, Wendy, the Court Officer, was also standing and trying to maintain some kind of calm inside the room as well as acting as an intermediary between the Judge and the litigant's. Lance, usually calm and placid under such circumstances, had no alternative but to retaliate further. He ignored Wendy totally, opting instead to keep his glare on the Judge at the same time he held out a pointed finger at Briggs, arguing that Advanced Strategic Energy were guilty of discrimination to one of their employees and they knew it. Then, turning his head towards the jury in disbelief at what Briggs had tried to do just moments earlier, he continued to mock him directly for all to see. He informed them that, *they, the counsel for the defense, were just trying to prolong the trial in order to generate disinterest in the matter.* He opened his arms wide as he finished his sentence, collectively gesturing to the jury that Briggs had tried to undermine their entire resolve in the case.

Lance had taken a gamble, he knew that people only listened to what they wanted to hear and this jury was no different. Whatever Lance was saying, the words seemed to be about right and they were getting through. He'd won most of the jury over judging by the number of nodding heads. They were intelligent people and full of determination. No city lawyer was going to prove otherwise. Whilst the defense counsel was directing their frustration and accusations towards the Judge, Lance had directed his accusations in the direction of the jury so that they, not the Judge, could make-up their own mind. And he knew that scored points with the jury.

Amid the prevailing mayhem it appeared to be a class act, but not so in Judge Hastings opinion. He knew what Lance was up to and he'd heard what was said. At those last remarks, the Judge banged his gavel on the wooden pad that housed it. A loud *bang* rang out in an attempt to silence the mayhem caused by both parties. The Court Officer also tried once more to gain control, begging points of order as both counsels demanded the right to reply with accusations and counter accusations now being freely shouted loud enough for any juror in the opposite courtroom to hear! It was outrageous. It sometimes happened though, and God knows what the jury might or might not think. But, as good as it was, it was not about to happen again. Not today, nor any other day and certainly not in *his* courtroom.

The postponement was granted much to the annoyance of everyone concerned, but Hastings had made his decision based more in anger than on any reasonably argument. He simply didn't like the squabbling that broke out amongst the lawyers. Before adjourning the session the Judge reminded the court that he no longer intended to put up with these outbursts of bad behavior. The next person showing the slightest contempt would be cooling down in the county jail. He announced the adjournment, informed those present that they would re-assemble again in this very courtroom two days from now, *banged* his gavel once more to end the session and quickly left for his private chambers before anyone had the chance to stand during his exit.

After all the commotion had died down another hubbub of conversation followed the preceding lull. Nick and I waited at the back of the courtroom while Desmond talked briefly about the situation with Lance. His employment as Desmond's attorney was a tactical move—the same stunt pulled by Advanced Strategic Energy Inc. A black lawyer represents the company involved in a race discrimination lawsuit against them. How could they be racist? The defense team hired by Haynes consists of a white lawyer to be the lead representative for their black client? All good tit-for-tat stuff; absolutely essential from both sides point of view but usually a transparent and useless ploy with a sometimes over sympathetic jury. To his credit, however, Lances' credentials were already laid bare by others who knew him. We were told by another attorney defending a murder case in the next courtroom the same day that Lance was the right man for the job. He stood out from most of the legal profession involved in discrimination lawsuits such as this, said the murder man. He was one of the few attorneys' who genuinely believed in equal opportunity and fairness for all. Above all else, he was proud to stand up for equality, especially for his fellow black Americans, he told us sincerely. Why only last year he was part of the co-defense of a sixteen-year-old black youth remanded in custody for murdering a white lawyer in Jericho, Texas, he was proud to inform us.

New Orleans was no coincidence either. The southern state city was chosen ahead of New York to file the lawsuit—Lance had advised us of this and was another obvious and well trodden tactic employed to gain the sympathy vote from the mostly, black Americans—so many times themselves the victims of racial discrimination and hatred. This provided an enormous challenge for John Briggs, who had earlier petitioned for a change of venue, arguing that the location of the trial may have prejudiced one of the parties. When asked, *why* by the Judge they withdrew their claim, afraid of accusing any black juror of being biased towards the plaintiff—remarks that might later be misconstrued in court! And so they were afraid of being accused of racism, even though they would probably be right. To ensure a fair trial, JB knew it was paramount for a cross-section of white and black Americans to be on the jury because, if nobody else knew anything about being fair, the black community alone surely did. Even including murder! The black folk were, rightly or wrongly, seemingly always discriminated against. Always, and the legal profession knew it. The statistics would also support these facts.

Needless to say, Lance most often than not won many of his lawsuits either by out-of-court settlements or by default, something he neither condoned nor attributed to his ability as a lawyer. The jury was sometimes just as discriminating as the poor defenseless company that was being wrongfully tried in his opinion. It was just as hard a task for him to gain justice by means of a balanced and well-argued case for the defense as it was for his prosecution against them! He had apologized several times to fellow attorneys after such occasions and they in turn acknowledged Lances genuine sincerity.

So, as so many law people knew, there would not have been a fair trial but for the determination of John Briggs and the laborious procedure known as, *challenge for cause*. Each side could argue that a potential juror be rejected if it is revealed that for some reason he or she is unable or willing to set aside preconceptions and pay attention only to the evidence. This procedure had occurred and the outcome was in Briggs favor. Nine white and three black Americans were sworn in as the jury. Lance was always going to be the one with a fight on his hands. The lawsuit had little substantiated evidence. An out-of-court settlement had been rejected. The discovery process was miserable and now New Orleans had backfired on us. Why John Briggs asked for a postponement only he and the other lawyers from Cranton would know?

Chapter 24

We greeted a bemused Desmond and before anything else was said, Nick barged us aside and asked what was going on, why had Briggs asked for the adjournment? Desmond just shrugged his shoulders and Lance did the same whilst also wondering how a newspaper reporter of all things was on first name terms with his client! Desmond explained only after he'd been pulled to one side by Lance and rollicked for not telling him. He then ordered Desmond to introduce the reporter to the team; Lance, the Blues Brothers and last but not least of all, Dil, who had slowly followed behind after gathering the contents of his briefcase from a desk at the front of the court. They shook hands before Lance ushered us into a small room at the side of the hall.

'What was that all about?' asked Desmond.

'Beats me,' replied Lance.

'Well something's got up em,' said Dil, who was in a buoyant mood as expected.

'I bet it's the racial policies. But why say they need more explaining? That's just bullshit. They're hiding something,' said Ant throwing in his five cents worth.

'It was something connected to the note,' I said quickly. 'It's got to be. Did you see the way he left the courtroom? Something or someone had ruffled his feathers. It wasn't about the policies. They've haven't got any. Briggs wouldn't want to argue that. They're on their *gross misconduct* bullshit, remember? And don't forget, *it's us*,' I emphasized to the others. '*We're* the ones trying to highlight the racial policies, not them. No . . . Briggs didn't have time to think that one through,' I said, sounding like a lawyer. 'He panicked and said the wrong thing. Stalling for time probably, gentlemen . . . Mr. John Briggs has just shot himself in the foot one way or another,' I added, speculating to a high degree but everybody agreed. For the next few moments there were many more questions than answers thrown around and Nick jotted down a couple of reminders in a small notepad. He would discretely follow-up several of the more enticing suggestions later.

'Whatever it is, we'll know soon enough. C'mon, let's go. If anybody hears anything give me a call me,' said Lance who wasn't going to hang around, and before anything else was said all seven of us walked out of the marble-floored building into the bright morning sun. The breeze was still pleasant and very much welcomed. Nick suggested coffee at one of the riverside restaurants, it was close to our hotel and we could reflect on the morning's events. Desmond and I readily agreed and suggested a taxi to cover the two miles distance. Lance apologized and confessed that since the trial had been postponed it allowed him to catch up on some other matters of equal importance. Just what none of us had any idea! He said his farewell and started to walk towards the French Quarter. We watched as he pulled his trousers up high around his stomach whilst making a derogatory comment about the increasing size of his waistline as he did so. His white hair bounced on his head as he walked with some urgency towards his destination. I thought Lance seemed troubled by recent events.

The rest of the team also had matters of equal importance. The Blues Brothers wanted to go shopping and Dil would trawl the sex shops in the French Quarter, although he didn't actually tell us that. They were gone before me, Des, and Nick hailed a taxi. In next to no time at all we were speeding east down Canal and towards the Mississippi River. We soon came to a halt in front of the lobby of the hotel. Nick paid the fair for the relatively short ride and we walked the hundred yards towards the Riverside shopping mall. Coffee was ordered and we sat for a while admiring the barges and seagoing freighters that worked the Mississippi. The morning traffic was busy and the wide river looked splendid. She seemed to show off this particular morning. The sun glistened off her brown-colored water and her strong currents fought against all before her, relentlessly teasing the over-laden barges that tried to motor up-stream. She was wonderful and proud in all her glory.

'If this river could talk she could tell a few tales about racial discrimination,' said Desmond as a matter of fact.

'She surely would have seen most of it,' replied the reporter. 'The cotton fields upstream formed the worst slavery colonies around these parts,' he informed us. Then we just sat and watched without further conversation.

* * *

'What do you mean, Hammond's done a runner?' Briggs was holding the phone in a vice-like grip, unsure of what he'd been told earlier. The lawyer was trying his hardest to appear calm.

'Exactly that,' Vance Dinger told him. 'Like I said, there was a bust up a few days ago. The company fired him and he hasn't been seen since,' explained the senior associate trying not to sound too apologetic. He sensed his subordinate's frustration.

'Then we'll have to find him. He can't have vanished off the face of the earth? They'll want him on the stand, Vance.'

'I know that, but you can forget all about Hammond for now. He's not going to be put forward, Isaacs isn't too pleased at all about that happening.'

'What's he said?'

'Nothing, they're glad to see the back of him, less risk,' he added.

'It'll go against them, Vance. Hammond's got to take the stand and say exactly what we've instructed him to say. A no-show at this early stage is not good news.'

'I know, I know,' replied Dinger frustrated at being talked to in the manner Briggs was doing so at that precise moment. 'What'd you tell the Judge?' he asked, trying to keep calm.

'We needed more time to review our racial policies,' confessed Briggs all too humble.

'What? Are you fucking crazy, they got diddly shit in that respect! You know darn well that we're still trying to draft something for them to use. ASEI won't have them in time, no way.'

'Give me a break, Vance. I had barely two minutes notice. The Judge was already presiding when I took your call for Christ sake! What'd expect me to say?'

'Anything other than that, why didn't you just approach the bench and say Hammond was unavailable?'

'Cos I'm not all that convinced they'll actually ask him to stand, that's why.'

'Then what's your problem?' replied Dinger with steam coming out of his ears.

'Oh . . . nothing, Vance,' he sighed. The question had deflated him; he'd screwed up for once.

'I'll talk to Isaacs, see what his intentions are.' Dinger hung up without waiting for a reply. JB also slammed down the phone and walked stern faced from Mary Lloyd's office. He seriously considered Dinger to be a hindrance in his role at Cranton & Associates. Dinger was an associate, but knowing they way he worked, Briggs would rather they rename the company, Cranton & Impediments, that would be a more honest assessment of their abilities, he reasoned to nobody but himself.

* * *

We'd met Nick five nights earlier after he'd phoned Desmond from his office in New York informing him of his interest in the case. He mentioned that he was a lawyer and had taken a job as a reporter. He'd refrained from telling him he was fresh out of law school so that his inexperience wouldn't frighten my friend away, although he knew he would have to tell him sooner or later. Nick spoke further to say that he appreciated the fact that Desmond would not only be suspicious of him, but of any journalists keen to write even the briefest accounts of his plight, such was the public's need to know.

What is it that makes these trials what they are? It was the question he asked Joe Mayo. Could he write about it, please? He had received an affirmative from Joe only after Desmond's acceptance. It also ensured that Desmond would be paid by the NYT should the case become more appealing to the American public, but he had to get something good enough to go to print.

Even after the shortest of introductions to journalism Nick knew that, as in the legal profession, it was vital to get something on record and ready to print in case the trial threw out some surprises. They rarely did. Nevertheless, the newspapermen, along with their legal-eagle counterparts knew their stuff. Friendly intrusion usually got a more detailed account of the facts and that would suffice for the time being. They were ready and would just wait for any surprises to happen. A few lines in the early morning edition would, at the very least, give Nick a brief moment of glory—especially from seeing his name in bold print officially writing for the NYT. The column, however brief, would also ensure payment of the expenses claimed against the cost of the assignment. Nick had thought the phone call through and anticipated, even expected, Des to give some sort of lame excuse about not being able to make any sort of meeting or, even worse, that his attorney had advised him against talking to the press. He was right of course but, partly due to his genuine and noticeable sincerity and more to the point due to the reporter's lack of experience, Desmond agreed to meet with the kid from New York. Nick asked him to suggest a venue, he did not care where, a bar, restaurant, race track, anywhere that would make Desmond feel at ease. Nick premeditated this request. He reasoned that if Desmond Haynes made the choice of venue he would be more likely to turn up. This he did and true enough, two days previous to the hearing, Desmond honored his word and they met at Jimmy Buffet's Margaretville Café, located just outside the French Market.

That first meeting was different. It merely broke the ice. Now though, the two men began to discuss certain aspects of the lawsuit, the background and the comparisons with other companies he'd worked for throughout his distinguished and varied career. It bored the pants off me but I was happy to listen. Nick would need the background for his reports and occasionally I chipped in with some additional tidbits. Inevitably, the conversation turned to family life and that's where I left them to it and took a walk along the Mississippi.

Desmond had been married to Suzanne for thirty years, he told Nick. They were childhood sweethearts and had courted their friendship since junior school. They were engaged for seven years, from the age of sixteen. The marriage followed the announcement that Suzanne was three months pregnant. It was a simple affair made even simpler by the fact that neither they, nor their families, had sufficient money to pay for the wedding. Along with the immediate family, several friends gathered in a registry office to witness the blessing, which was followed by the most simple of receptions possible. Even that put a strain on the purse of Desmond since he paid for everything. He did not want to burden any family member for his *mistake*—his folks called it that. Desmond thought of it as the best thing that ever happened to them. No piece of paper legally informing the world of their marriage would make the slightest bit of difference to the way they felt about each other. They were madly in love and a family was on the way, September, ninety-two in fact. A baby boy named Brian came into the world very much amid the euphoria that surrounds such an occasion. He was weighed in at just over six pounds said Desmond, obviously aware that detail was important when talking about the new born. During this time he'd worked for an engineering company that specialized in high temperature piping systems.

With few qualifications upon starting, he finished six years later with a highly graded, engineering diploma and joined Welltechnic, one of several Texan oil exploration consultants hired to manage production platforms for major oil companies operating in the Gulf of Mexico. He was employed as an engineering consultant and had an office downtown, Houston. He worked hard and was respected amongst his fellow employees. Sure he had a bit of stick, mostly because of his color, but a lot because of his sense of humor. Desmond was not slow in sensing an occasion to spring a joke, or surprise his fellow colleagues to promote a bit of much needed hilarity, especially during more stressful moments. There was nothing too harsh about what was said. It didn't bother him at the time. After four successful years and several promotions within the company, Desmond was asked to manage a new construction project in the Middle East. Having got the backing from Suzanne and their ever-growing offspring, Brian, he packed his bags and left for the assignment working a three months on—one month off, rotation. The project was very successful with Desmond bringing it to a conclusion within time and, more importantly, within budget. Pay was excellent with further increases pending.

The Haynes' family standard of living began to improve very much indeed. Three years later and Desmond was once again headhunted to manage another project team, this time in the North Sea. British Petroleum were building several fixed platforms to be sited on the Forties field. They would be positioned one hundred and twenty miles north east of Aberdeen, Scotland. The requirement was for management experience of the hook-up team that would bring the platform jackets—the sub-sea structure that supported the topsides process equipment—from their fabrication yard in St Fergus via a barge and then connect them to the sea bed. The topside facilities; drill derricks, production vessels and piping, power generation and accommodation modules would then be positioned on top. Commissioning would last another year. Desmond had no previous offshore experience of hook-ups, but he understood the requirements from his days at Welltechnic. He listened and kept his mouth shut until such a time that he knew what was wanted of him. He soon understood the engineering aspects required, bringing the mammoth project to its conclusion with time to spare. He did this with admiration from the whole project team. He was not alone in doing so and such was his modesty, was quick to point this fact out whenever too much praise came his way.

His relationship with BP brought about a chance meeting with Raymond Floyd, a Business and Planning executive with a very good engineering background. Floyd was employed by Advanced Strategic Energy Inc. one of the largest upcoming intermediate oil companies in the world at the time. Both men attended a seminar on offshore production platforms, hook-up procedures and problems that could be expected. Floyd attended the seminar as a representative of ASEI. His brief was to advise the company of any potential pitfalls, including any financial implications that brought about the downfall of many other oil companies competing in this work. Floyd had heard the presentation given by Desmond and many technical conversations followed. He returned to the US and made two recommendations to the company. The first confirmed their strong feelings that it was well worth the risk to invest in mature assets soon to be offloaded in the North Sea. Secondly, if they were going to do so, they should try to employ one, Mr. Desmond Haynes, a black man with exceptional credentials who would be able to advise the company on matters relating to North Sea operations management.

It followed that the Advanced Strategic Energy Inc board took Floyds' advice, to the letter and Desmond was once again headhunted to the price of just over two hundred and eighty thousand dollars a year. A Company car, house purchase assistance and full relocation expenses formed an additional part of the package. He would be located in New York, the corporate headquarters of the company, with frequent travel to Aberdeen to oversee things from time to time. Desmond was justifiably overwhelmed at the offer, he accepted and the whole family celebrated his good fortune, his job security, the move to Manhattan, the increase in salary, everything.

Then there was the sad part of his life. Their only son, Brian, died in a car accident; a neighbor was driving at the time and their sadness at this news was indescribable. But, despite the tragedy they fought back and decided to have more children. One year later, Clive was born. A year later Vivien was born. They were a family again, but Brian never left their memories.

The next hour was spent narrating his experiences with Advanced Strategic Energy on other assignments throughout the world. He told of his time spent in the Middle East, China and Nigeria. His relationship with the many people he befriended, especially that of Brandt Allto, who'd mysteriously drowned on a fishing trip. The death of his friend had affected him badly, he confessed. His whole life story culminated in the telling of his heroics during the explosion and ensuing fires in Nigeria. After that, the company found him a position back in their New York engineering office writing operating procedures, something he'd got used to during his time in the refineries. He settled down to that with ease. He was finally at home with Suzanne and the kids he adored. Little did he know what was about to begin? Advanced Strategic Energy had sacked him for no apparent reason whatsoever, apart from some trumped up charge of incompetence and gross negligence, which was incredibly, easily proved.

When I returned they were drinking beer.

'Typical, you've got a drink problem, Des!' I tried to tell him but it had no effect.

'Another three beers, please,' shouted Nick across to the barman and then turned to me with a smile. 'You didn't tell me we were in the company of a hero, Doug.'

'Oh, he's mentioned it then,' I replied shaking my head from side to side.

'Just a few times, not too many though,' said Desmond chuckling as he quickly tried to play it down. Then I stood to attention in front of both men and spoke aloud.

'Desmond Haynes,' I said, pointing towards him. 'Had ensured in part that the only real casualties from the explosion were the companies' pride, its safety record with the Nigerian Government Regulating Authority was of little importance,' I quipped sarcastically. 'And . . . also . . . he saved their relations with the local community at large. He was regarded as a hero by both those present and absent in the Niger Delta for some time afterwards,' I said, and then held my bottled beer in the air before quickly adding. 'He's full of *shit*, but God Bless him anyway!'

'Hear, hear,' Nick endorsed my sentiments and started to down his beer.

'Doug, *you're* full of shit, man!' replied Desmond in his usual tenor before necking his beer too.

'Did he tell you about Suzanne, Nick?'

'Yes, why?' asked Nick inquisitively. He sensed something.

'Doug—'

'Now, now, Des, she's a lovely woman, Nick. You'd like her a lot.' My pre-amble had evoked a grunt from Desmond. He knew what was coming.

'Doug, don't you dare mention Kamp's,' whispered Desmond but it was too late, Desmond had dropped himself in it and I laughed. Nick must have wondered what the hell we were on about.

'Oh yeah, what happened in Kamp's?' asked our reporter friend. 'Will it make a good story?' he asked, wide-eyed. We both laughed. My lips were sealed—at least until Nick and I was alone.

That afternoon Nick sent the first of his reports to Joe Mayo. It was a couple of brief sentences that informed his boss that there was a fracas in a New Orleans courtroom earlier that morning. He thought no more of it other than to ask Joe a couple of questions at the end of his e-mail—*What was the judicial system coming to and were there other bust-ups throughout the courts of America? Should the NYT have a follow-up story?* Joe read the brief report and smiled.

Chapter 25

'Gerald, you okay honey?' asked Susan, she had to shout even though the room was quite.

'What? Oh, yeah, I'm fine sweetheart. Just listening to some music,' he answered back loudly before pulling one of the headphones of his I-Pod away from his ear so that he could adjust to the volume of his voice—and be ready for further questioning, as was usually the case.

'You've been ages listening to that thing,' she said affectionately, her New York accent not so broad as most. 'What's playing?'

'The March of the Slovak Slaves,' he replied, and then watched as she frowned. Gerald leaned forward. 'Puccini,' he whispered quickly before another question came his way.

'Oh, opera again!' she sighed and handed him a glass of red wine—Chilean, Cabernet Sauvignon, his favorite. Susan Sinclair was madly in love with her husband and there was nothing he could do to make her love him less or make things any different. Gerald felt the same way. They were not only husband and wife; they were lovers; friends; trusted allies and confided in everything to each other. It was not surprising then that she knew something was troubling him. He'd not eaten the lunch she prepared earlier, broccoli bake, and conversation was minimal, which told her he was keeping something from her. But for now she would not ask. Probably another shitty day at the office and he'd had plenty of those she'd reasoned earlier. Just how shitty the last few days had been, she'd no idea!

'What time is Jason coming home, Susan?' asked Gerald. Their twelve year-old son had been staying at his grandparent's house in Philadelphia for the week-end, about a two-to-three hour drive from their New Jersey home.

'I told you earlier, honey. Nine-thirty! Mom and Dad are staying over. Don't you listen to anything I say?' she said smiling and still resisting the temptation to delve into his problems.

'Sorry. I remember now,' he replied vacantly but still managed to return a sympathetic-looking smile back at her. All was well. Gerald placed the I-Pod on a table by the side of the large, striped-cloth armchair he was sprawled over before getting up and slowly walking out of the room. 'I'm going to take a shower,' he called out. 'I'll probably do a little work later on, honey,' he added and then promptly made his way upstairs. There was no reply from Susan. She hadn't heard him.

By the time she'd realized he was missing from the lounge the shower had been running for some time without any suggestion of anybody having used it. Steam slowly began to egress from inside the glass-paneled shower, through the bathroom and into an adjoining dressing room. It now formed a warm, moist cloud under the ceiling as Susan entered the empty room.

'Gerald? Gerald, honey!' she shouted, repeatedly calling out her husband's name, she was overly nervous at the best of times. Susan continued searching with some urgency when there was no reply. 'Gerald, where are you, honey?' she cried out and flung open the glass door of the steam-filled shower cubicle, there was nobody inside. 'Oh my God!' she cried aloud, she was frantic but had no idea why. Why was she like this? She turned and run out of the bathroom in search of her husband. 'Gerald, Gerald—'

'Whoa . . . hold on there, wait a minute!' he said. Her husband cut her off and was nearly knocked over as she slammed into him coming out of the bathroom.

'Oh my God, oh my God!' she said over and over again. 'You're okay, you're okay,' she mumbled and, still shivering from the experience, she squeezed him tight. In those few moments that she sensed he wasn't where she expected him to be—in the shower—her anxiety had gone haywire and now she clutched hold of her precious husband and hugged the life out of him.

'What's the matter, Susan?' he asked, knowingly. He never ceased to be amazed at his wife's reaction to his well-being, or lack of it today more like, or to any other unusual habits he portrayed. 'I'm fine, Honey,' he quickly reassured her. She never said another word and instead continued to shiver and hug him tight. He hugged her back tightly whilst struggling to breathe from her over-zealous grip.

That night was tense, although it did not show. Even the earlier than expected arrival of Jason, accompanied by Gordon and Mary her parents, couldn't stop Susan from worrying about Gerald. He was not himself. Dinner was fabulous; their visitors for the night had said so. Gerald made out that he'd eaten too much earlier, which he hadn't but declined more of the same anyway. Jason, however, merely took his mother's cooking in his stride much to Susan's frustration.

'Why do I bother?' she sighed looking at the untouched food. She casually turned and spoke to her mother to moan about the amount of food that got wasted in their household after seeing their only son, Jason, and her father, Gordon also leave most of the evening meal. They'd joined Gerald in the lounge where all three men were now glued to the weekly football game. Indy Colts were on the road at Denver where the home team, the Bronco's, was kicking butt by twenty points. It seemed a perfect family household.

It was nearly midnight when her parents insisted that it was time for Jason to go to bed. There was no school the following day but, despite all the tantrums, Jason was going to bed and that was final. There wasn't much resistance from the youngster after being told that and he was soon upstairs and soon fast asleep. Grandma and granddad were right behind him, they bade Gerald and their daughter goodnight after thanking her for dinner amongst other things. Mary had discretely asked Susan if Gerald was okay on her way up the stairs since she recognized he was saying little, a trait that was definitely unusual for their son-in-law. Susan just laughed it off and said he felt a little unwell, a cold maybe, she convinced them both.

Soon, all the family was asleep apart from Gerald. He'd been awake for hours and sometime during the night had removed a miniature tape recorder from the inside pocket of his well-worn and beloved leather jacket. It was the one he wore that day. He sat in a chair beside the bedroom window listening to the conversation he was a part of inside Jeremy Isaacs' office a couple of days ago.

It was not the first time Gerald had kept the small, concealed recorder running during these working occasions. It helped him compile the minutes of numerous meetings he was asked to chair and by now, without anybody knowing it, he had it hidden in his jacket, it had became almost a matter of routine. During their last meeting the tape got switched on as soon as he sat down and all conversations with Gerald Sinclair were recorded. But now, in the dark confines of his bedroom it was being played back for all the wrong reasons. What should have been the safe comfort of his home was now likened to being in a dungeon. He felt trapped inside and demons looked from every dark corner and every crevice as he listened to the events that had unfolded earlier in stunning style.

Everything was clear, right down to where Darcy had accused them of gross negligence. He was right of course. They were negligent, grossly negligent. Worse than that perhaps, he thought to himself. Damn! How could he have been so stupid? He felt sick. Gerald turned the tape off at the point where Hammond had assaulted Isaacs. That incident only made him feel worse. He hated violence of any kind. Even when he was marginally bullied at school he would run a mile rather than stickup for himself.

Desperation was creeping up on him, although he did not know it. He looked at his wife, sound asleep in their bed and unaware of the fact that he, unlike Hammond who was sacked on the spot, had tendered his resignation at precisely eleven thirty. At eleven forty five he was escorted out of the building after being allowed to collect only his personnel possessions from his office. God only knew how he felt at that precise moment. How could he tell Susan? What could he tell Susan? He had his reasons for failing in his work. He was a man of course and the trouble with men was . . ., well they were men. Like a lot of men his age they were predators and on this particular conquest a young blonde, blue-eyed girl from the IT department had been his prey. He should have left the sordid romance there after the first time but no chance; the sex was too good and he continued seeing her. Ignoring his work to secretly be with her had cost him dearly.

* * *

It was an all too familiar sight when he was in Manhattan. Music blasted out through over-sized loudspeakers and multi-colored lights dimmed, then brightened, then revolved with no particular pattern in all directions around the darkened room. On the front of a small stage, a scantily clad girl slid up and down and wrestled with a shiny chrome pole, strategically located to allow her to be surrounded by the *clientele*. A line of balding and scruffy men were holding out dollar bills in order to entice the girl closer, if they were lucky they'd get a quick, *feel*; it was pathetic! Hammond sat on a stool at the bar drinking vodka, unaware of his surroundings. It was ironic that, compared to what he'd been a party to in Nigeria and his earlier assault of Jeremy Isaacs earlier, he'd only been charged with possession of drugs. A few tablets were found inside his jacket pocket and taken away to be examined by the narcs—hardly anything to worry about. Isaacs' behavior on the other hand was something to worry about he thought to himself as he scrutinized the small glass of spirits that he slowly turned around in his hand. Sometime after his arrest—and safely secure in the county jail—a burly sergeant with the NYPD had shouted to him through the bars of an overcrowded cell whilst slowly unlocking the metal door to release him. Advanced Strategic Energy—Hammond, took that to mean, Isaacs—had been specific about two things, said the police officer directly to him, but for all to hear—and every criminal in there did. First, they did not want any charges brought against their former employee, at any cost. *The publicity would not be good*, he added aloud and then laughed.

'Do you hear that boys?' he shouted to the other inmates and the cell erupted to instant cheers and whistles. No surprises there, then! The drunk smirked to himself and remembered some of the ruder comments that were made at that time.

'Secondly, he continued. 'They inform me that you've been dismissed for gross negligence and then further dismissed'—it was a double whammy if that was at all possible—'For gross misconduct following the assault on a senior VP.' No surprises there either, he thought as even more cheers went up upon hearing the news! The sergeant was acting like some kind of game show host rather than a public servant.

The officer followed up his earlier statements by confirming he was indeed, *a lucky son-of-a-bitch*, especially in New York where criminal damage lawyers were biting at Isaacs heels at this very moment. The VP could sue him for thousand's, perhaps millions of dollars judging by the horrific injuries that were inflicted, he added. Isaacs had needed twenty stitches to his face from the force of Hammond's punch to the head and more surgery would be required. Even more clapping, screams of delight, and a host of congratulatory slaps to his body rained down on him from his fellow inmates as he left the cell. And so, for those briefest of moments, he was officially recognized as one of them—a hardened criminal—even though he wore an expensive suit. Loud chants of approval continued as he disappeared through the metal doors, but Hammond never acknowledged any of them. Ignoring the loud shouts and distasteful comments from the other inmates, he slowly walked out of the county jail without saying a word.

Now he was free again and swallowed hard to finish off his drink before ordering another vodka; a large one on the rocks. It had been like this since his release. The bar tender silently acknowledged his request by cleaning the bar immediately in front of him before throwing a paper napkin down on the dried surface. His drink would soon follow.

Now what? Yesterday he was bragging to himself about how he had such a wonderful job, but now he was unemployed! Life had a funny way of showing itself! Being out of work was a good leveler he suddenly realized. There was little he could do and whatever options he thought he may have had were slowly becoming pie-in-the-sky as the drink and drugs combo, he had sniffed cocaine in the toilets of another bar earlier, began to take effect. He had tried not to think of Laxrois, but that was becoming almost impossible. He'd have to go into hiding for the next few days. The very thought of the former mercenary scared him shitless. Now he would blank him out, or try to, or watch and wait perhaps, or . . . . what could he do?

'Fuck him,' he muttered. His courage increased with each drink and with each lashing of cocaine. The man he had left for dead just under two years ago had already got to him and, as usual, there was no escape. If Laxrois wanted him, and he obviously did, then Laxrois would have him. Whatever way he wants me, he can fucking have me, he thought somewhat irrationally as once again the narcotics clouded his mind.

But in turn he would get even with the others. His revenge against Isaacs and Darcy would be quick in coming he told himself. That thought boosted his ego, but it was difficult to dismiss the Frenchman from his dulled thoughts. He then turned his imagination once again to Isaacs and Darcy. Perhaps the murders in Nigeria would finally pay off? Blackmail had figured high in his many sordid attributes in the past and he wouldn't have to think twice about it again, he had proved that, but it would still not be enough. His vengeance would have to account for more than a couple of hundred thousand bucks. It would have to go deeper. He wanted blood. His life had been on the line in Nigeria and now their lives would be in jeopardy he told himself. His conviction was made more convincing with every sip of alcohol, but the sad thing was, those ideas would be implanted into his brain and despite the weird thoughts conjured up from the cocaine, the idea of killing the two of them would become reality as soon as he was sober, which would be some time away yet. It was early and the night was young and he was in New York.

* * *

Recent events should be something to forget, if only they could. Pretty soon, the whole of the Advanced Strategic Energy Inc. senior organization wouldn't sleep if things continued in the vein they were going. It was well past one-thirty in the morning and Eamon Darcy was still wide-awake, wondering what the repercussions would be from the previous fracas a couple of days ago, he knew there would be. Hammond still played on his mind. His dismissal had not been thought through. It was not clean enough, but how would they know how events would turn out? Hammond, as usual, hadn't quite played into their hands in the way he was supposed to. Darcy had contacted the CEO, John Arnold, and informed him of what had occurred at the first opportunity, including the smallest of details. JA was not a happy chap. The bad news would spread through the company like a virus. Senior managers fighting with Vice Presidents and Senior Vice Presidents on the fourteenth floor was bad public relations, although he found the fact that his son-in-law was in hospital with a fractured cheek bone quite amusing! But he agreed with Eamon that Hammond was unstable; anything could happen where he was concerned.

So that night, he also struggled to sleep for reasons relating to the mountains of trash Hammond could potentially unleash on the company. He'd have to do something about that, he'd done it in the past and wouldn't hesitate to do it again; he had the contacts and would make the call in the morning. But in the meantime, something else was also bothering him. He'd found a pair of panties in the back of the limousine earlier that morning. It was obvious to him Charlie was using the car for his own personal pleasure, which had John Arnold seething. How dare he compromise his position and use the car in that way?

Arnold thought about sacking him, but Charlie knew too much about what went on between him and Gaynor. He then realized that he'd been careless when it came to being discrete with his secretary, especially with Barbara out of sight. So that he could deal with Hammond and stop him throwing all kinds of shit around the place, he decided to let Charlie off the hook. So what if he'd had a little fun in the car? No big deal, it was nice car with comfortable leather upholstery, probably comfier than Charlie's bed at home. John needed to chill-out. Perhaps he needed to be a little more adventurous in the back seat too. He made a mental note to work something out with Gaynor. It would be nice to buff up the leather with her gyrating under him! Yes, John needed to chill-out. Finding a pair of panties was the last of his problems he eventually reasoned. If he'd known they were Barbara's underwear, he might have looked at the situation rather differently!

Jeremy Isaacs, slightly less traumatized now but still heavily bruised, lay still in his hunting lodge bed, awake but numb from the cocktail of pain killers he was still being administered nearly every other four hours.

All he could think about was revenge, his face would be heavily scarred and now Hammond would pay he decided, in and out of severe bouts of pain.

Gerald Sinclair just stared at the red, illuminated digital clock most of the night. He was worried sick but eventually returned to lie next to his wife who was sound asleep. She'd probably dropped off dreaming of next year's holiday, unaware of what was to come! He loved his wife as much as she loved him. He couched up to her bare flesh and squeezed her, but she would not know that, ever!

His former colleague, Richard Hammond, was wide-awake one minute but totally out of it the next. He was too busy trawling the seedy bars of New York for his next fix, a woman, and somewhere to stay the night. His only solace was that by now the hardened figure of Laxrois was becoming more distant in his thoughts. Spasmodic memories of the Frenchman kept him only momentarily on the same planet as most of the others he now acquainted with and for that, he was grateful.

For these men, the next few days would prove to be the most crucial of their entire lives!

Chapter 26

THE FOLLOWING DAY, IN THE State of New Jersey, the sun was uninhibited from bayous, lakes or other waterways that might have caused a mist to form. Similar to the weather in Port Arthur, the sun shone high in the sky and the temperature quickly rose as Gerald sat on the wooden deck outside the bedroom. He hadn't slept in days. It wasn't too long before Susan joined him and they gave each other a warm and tender kiss, right smack on the lips as was customary in their relationship.

'Hey, big boy,' his other half teased. 'How about I make breakfast and then we go to the racetrack this afternoon? Forget work, take the day off,' she half joked and half-insisted, edging her bets.

'Sounds good to me,' he lied, thankful that he now had an excuse for not going to his false place of work, at least not for that particular day. He didn't have a job but Susan wasn't to know that. The last few days had been spent trying to get work at other oil companies. He had no chance. The reasons for his dismissal were now in the public domain.

'My, you're chilling out. Good for you, honey,' she told him smiling and then leaned back, still a little confused at his reply. She knew something was terribly wrong and had decided to confront him later that evening; she couldn't take much more of the uncertainty surrounding her husband of late. 'You should do it more often,' she added before regaining her closeness and playfully flicking his ear. 'I'll go get breakfast,' she whispered as Gerald tried to grab hold of her. She managed to wrestle free of him. Dragging her body from his clutches she disappeared back into the downstairs bedroom and towards the kitchen before he changed his mind. The newspapers were already thrown onto the lawn. It was Gordon who had retrieved them and within a short time they were unfolded and neatly shared out on the table. Gerald had no stomach for breakfast, nor did he feel like going to the racetrack, or reading, but he would eat and read anyway; he'd lost a lot of weight and it was becoming very noticeable. He'd think of an excuse not to go the track later on, in the meantime, he did his best to appear to read or just merely pretended to look at the pages would be a more precise motion, at least that way he did not have to make conversation. He was becoming extremely depressed and it had occurred all too quickly, rapid even. All the signs were there but nobody, including Gerald, realized it. They soon would though!

'Beautiful day, Gerald,' announced his father-in-law as they sipped coffee from a hot jug Susan had placed on the table not two minutes earlier.

'Yeah, mighty pretty ain't it?' he replied, stretching his arms out, pretending to appear fresh. A light breeze blew a few pages of his newspaper open and he struggled to hold it together. Then, unsolicited, the elder man sat opposite began to read out a small article from the New York Times.

'Advanced Strategic Energy is in the news again, son,' he announced. Gerald's stomach churned on hearing the name of his former employer. He felt sick. That fateful day came flooding back with a vengeance. Darcy, Isaacs, York, Hammond, they were all there, right in front of him, right in his face.

'Oh yeah, stock?' he speculated.

'Nah . . . ! Some Courtroom bust-up it appears . . . in New Orleans. Says here, and I quote—*Today, Judge, Roland Hastings, presiding in the New Orleans County Parish, suspended a trial involving a race discrimination lawsuit after some outrageous in-court behavior by both the plaintiff and defense council's*—Can you believe it?' said Gordon, reading with his spectacles held in one hand. 'Here, take a look for yourself,' he said, and handed him the paper.

'Well, I'll be darned!' replied Gerald louder than he ought to have done. 'I'll be darned!'

'You know the guy in the lawsuit, son?'

'I sure do, Desmond Haynes, pretty bad deal too.'

'Is that so?' replied Gerald, prompting his son-in-law to say more.

'Yeah, pretty bad deal,' he muttered. Gerald would say no more and closed the paper. Gordon seemed uncomfortable all of a sudden. Perhaps he shouldn't have behaved like that. Poking his nose into other people's affairs was not his business, it was unlike him to do so and he felt bad about it.

'Sorry if I've opened up a can of worms there, son.'

'No, no, not at all, Gordon,' he reassured his father-in-law. With that, Gerald got up from the table and left, holding the newspaper under his arm and without saying another word just as Susan arrived with two plates full of scrambled eggs and lean ham. It smelt delicious but now nobody would eat. What was the matter with her father? And what was the matter with her husband and his son-in-law? Both father and daughter just sat there, wondering.

Somewhere amongst the mess there was a tape, he recalled. It had to be there and he started to frantically throw out a host of different artifacts from inside an open drawer of an old desk he kept in the garage, along with other bits and pieces they had collected over the years. For split seconds only, some of these items brought back memories but he was confused. He would not allow anything to disrupt his concentration. It was a simple task but now, in his condition, he needed to be focused on what he was looking for. That's all the intelligence he could muster. People who suffered from severe stress do not think straight and that's what was happening at that precise moment. How he wished he'd recognized it. How others wished they'd recognized it before it was too late. They had of course, but in a casual sort of way and soon they would regret it! To acknowledge that Gerald was suffering from severe depression was not easy for them and to-date they hadn't realized just how bad he was. He acted strange, but that's all they knew. Inside, his mind was in a mess and he was being mentally torn apart. The search became frantic and the mess got worse.

'It's got to be here,' he said to himself aloud, and then the search was made even more frantic by an increased panic that swept over him. It was an easy task but the tension inside his body was rising. His pulse quickened, his blood pressure increased, his anxiety heightened and his patience lowered all because he was becoming obsessed with finding the tape, which may not have even been there in the first place.

Bingo! Several tapes were found tucked inside an empty, plastic lunch box of all places. He relaxed a little when he found what he was looking for. It contained the taped conversation of a meeting held in Eamon Darcy's office to discuss the dismissal of one, Desmond Haynes. It was decided during that meeting that Advanced Strategic Energy would sack the middle-aged black man outright for gross negligence following an explosion in one of the operating plants in California. Instead of using a secretary to scribe the minutes, Gerald was asked to attend the meeting as a scribe and also be an independent witness to the discussions given the serious nature of what had happened in California. He usually scribed the minutes for senior management meetings anyway.

When the discussion got under way, Hammond, Isaacs, and Darcy had all too quickly decided Haynes destiny he realized. Gerald thought this punishment to be extreme at the time and said so, but the others were hell bent on the idea. Haynes had to go with immediate effect, they'd insisted. He now knew how Haynes had felt at the time. Gerald had argued for him citing that it was ludicrous to hold him accountable, he had no involvement in the incident he argued but was overruled. There was no doubt in their minds that Desmond Haynes had been negligent following the poor shutdown procedures the operators used to close down the plant. He was responsible for revising them and making sure they would work. The company had an obligation to the public to make sure their process plants were safe. The shutdown procedures for this particular process were critical, they argued. The strange thing was there was more to it than that. Nobody had even asked Desmond to revise these particular procedures so how could he be responsible? For some strange reason they all agreed that but then went about fabricating his job description to say it did! Gerald was fuming and told them that what they were trying to do wasn't right. They ignored him and instead of justifying their actions, they went off on a tangent talking about events in Nigeria as if this had something to do with California! To add to his discomfort, soon the men started arguing amongst themselves. It was bizarre! Yes, there was definitely some underlying reason for what they wanted to achieve but exactly what he hadn't a clue nor cared at the time.

He was asked to leave the room when Hammond and Isaacs did not see eye to eye over some other incident in Nigeria, whatever that was? Gerald knew it wasn't the chemical plant explosions, but it was related he sensed. A morsel of the facts arose during the conversation by mistake, it was not uncommon for these two to argue during some of their more heated meetings and he was privy to a host of indecipherable innuendos more than once. On this occasion, the Nigerian government did not like Haynes asking stupid questions regarding the unfortunate death of one of their citizens, he eventually gleaned. Strange, thought Gerald but nothing untoward registered with him at the time. He was so naive in those days and merely left the room when asked after the discussions became really hostile. His jacket remained though. It was draped over the back of his chair with the tape still running; all conversations with Gerald Sinclair were taped! Whatever it was that ate them up he would hear about it on tape later in the day. He never did, however. The tape had remained silent to this day. At the specific request from both Isaacs and Darcy there were never any minutes produced. Nobody had wanted them and they'd been very specific about it—*no minutes required.* The tape, therefore, as never been heard and had been discarded, kept in an old plastic lunch box that had, up until now, been tucked safely away in the garage of all places!

Chapter 27

Judge, Roland Hastings was in a very bad mood. He sat quietly in his chambers sipping cold tea whilst leafing through specific pages from section nineteen, eighty-one. Bright yellow *post-it* stickers were already attached to the paragraphs he thought he might need to refer to during the trial such was the simplicity of the man. A feeble, gentle tap on the ornately carved oak door that led from *his* courtroom into *his* personal chambers broke the silence. The Judge refused to respond, especially since he knew who was on the other side. Heycock and Briggs would have to wait until His Honor was ready. Another knock followed, louder this time. The now irate and normally less-than-impatient Judge shouted back towards the closed door.

'Wait, goddamn it!'

Hastings was definitely in a bad mood and they would wait until he was ready, there was no way he was going to be rushed. And wait they did, like two schoolboys waiting outside the headmasters door, neither men dare attempting to look at each other nor enter into small talk in the meantime, such was their dislike of each other. It was a peculiar affair. What seemed like a long time became even longer as the waiting dragged on. Still they dare not move from where they stood, fumbling around impatiently in the small corridor that led from the courtroom to the chambers.

Suddenly the door flung open without so much as a word from the Judge, who had by now made his way back inside the room and was stood behind a highly polished and leather inlayed oak desk. The two men gingerly entered the room. They were anxious and it showed.

'Mr. Briggs, Mr. Heycock,' said the Judge looking directly at both men. Roland Hastings leaned over the desk and would address the men cowering before him with some considerable contempt judging by his body language and tone of voice. They noticed he was struggling to restrain his anger, his face reddening with each passing second. The veins in his neck were pumped up and dark blue as he began to talk with gritted teeth. What had made him angry neither man knew nor cared to know?

'Following the disgraceful scenes in my courtroom two days ago you should be in no doubt as to why I have summoned you here this morning!' he growled solemnly, eyes boring into the two men stood to attention before him. He wasn't really asking a question, making a statement more like. 'You do understand that, right?' he then asked.

'Yes sir,' answered Briggs too quick off the blocks and committing a cardinal sin in the process.

'Sir . . . sir . . . are you tired of practicing law, boy?'

'No sir . . . err . . . Your Honor. Definitely not, Your Honor.'

Judge, Hastings walked from behind his desk towards the two men stood nervously some ten feet away. He detested being called, *sir*, and homed-in on Briggs, face-to-face, nice and close. They could smell each other, Hastings bad breath mingled with Briggs' expensive after-shave. Each man felt nauseated by the other as Hastings began his assault.

'Let's get one thing straight, *boy*. I will be addressed as, *Your Honor*. Got it? And no smart-ass lawyer is going to go messing in my courtroom, do y'hear?'

'Yes, Your Honor, I hear you loud and clear.'

'Yes, Your H-O-N-O-R.' Hastings spelled the words out slowly, the letters resonating right into Briggs face, eyes glaring at each other, their lips almost touching. 'Your HONOR,' he repeated the words again, out loud and Briggs squirmed from all the bad breath being poured over his face. It took all his resolution not to turn away and puke. He just held his breath for as long as he could. 'And for the record, you call me, *sir*, once again and your history, *son*, do you understand that?' continued the Judge, forcefully. 'You'll be practicing anything you damn well care to practice but it sure as hell won't be law. Got it?'

'Yes, Your Honor,' replied Briggs, now hurting from being humiliated in front of his opposite number. Heycock hoped His Honor would keep up his mortifying onslaught and give JB some more lip, he was enjoying it.

'And as for you!' bellowed the Judge quickly catching Lance off guard. The Judge had turned on his heels and swung immediately to face Heycock, it was his turn now and he shuddered. 'Don't think for one minute that I don't know what stupid, dumb-ass game *you* were playing to the jury out there the other day. Trying to be the good fucking Samaritan, get the jury thinking that you're whiter than fucking white. Well I do know. I've been around a long time, Heycock and I ain't fucking putting up with it. Fuck

Peter Nutty

with me and you fuck with the meanest son-of-a-bitch Judge you've ever had the pleasure of fucking with, comprendo?'

'Yes, Your Honor. It will not happen again,' Heycock lied.

'Now, we're all going to go into *my* courtroom and conduct this trial in the manner it should have been conducted two days ago,' he told them. 'Oh . . . and Mr. Briggs,' he added, as if he'd almost forgotten something.

'Yes, Your Honor?' replied the attorney, wondering what else was coming his way.

'You ain't got any racial policies that need explaining. Your client doesn't have any! So, whatever it was you wanted the postponement for, it had better be pretty damn good. Now get the fuck out of my chambers.'

Briggs nearly choked. The two men spun around double quick and left without saying another word. Judge, Hastings returned to sit behind his desk and opened a pillbox, took a look inside to examine the contents before throwing the container back into a drawer without taking anything to lower his blood pressure. Instead, he swigged from a bottle of Scotch whisky he kept on a cabinet to the right-hand side of a large bookcase positioned thoughtfully inside the overly spacious room; the old man preferred natural medicines!

'What the fuck is he on, man?' muttered Briggs, still shocked following the Judge's outburst. 'He's nothing but a fucking bully,' he moaned as he walked down the corridor to the courtroom. It was the first time he'd voluntarily talked to Heycock since they'd met. Lance in turn acknowledged the fact by maintaining his silence. He had seen Judge, Roland Arthur Hastings in much more of a temper than the one he'd just witnessed. Most of it was all show and under better circumstances he would have told Brigg's just that, but not at that moment in time, and not today. In any case, as it stood he had no desire to talk to Brigg's, especially knowing that in a couple of moments the two men would be flogging it out once again in front of the big man himself, the all-swearing Judge, Hastings. JB had received the brunt of the Judge's wrath and that suited Heycock just fine. Let battle commence he thought.

Still feeling a little disheveled at the treatment dished out by the Judge, John Briggs sat back down in the courtroom and started to revise his opening statement only to be interrupted by Pete Masters, his paralegal, who'd quickly edged closer to where Briggs sat quietly reading.

'What's the score?' he asked. Briggs gestured flippantly to a pile of documents he needed passing to him and the paralegal obliged.

'The fucking Judge is crazy, man,' he whispered to Masters when he'd edged a little closer. 'He should be in the dock for harassment.' Masters looked bemused but he knew not to enquire further, JB had been ruffled. He was none too happy about being called, *boy* or *son* either, a term frequently used by Hastings to almost everybody. But what could he do about it?

For the second time in as many days the Judge addressed the jury in the same manner as he'd done so at the start of the previous hearing. He scowled several times at the two groups of lawmen in the room as he endorsed the fact that he was not, *under any circumstances*, going to accept bad conduct in *his* court. The ever-smart courtroom clerk, Wendy Lloyd, once again read out the plaintiffs' charge of racial discrimination and unfair dismissal. It broke the silence that followed the Judge's warning. She went on to inform the occupants that this action was being brought to court under the Forty Second United States Constitution, Section Nineteen, Eighty One and so forth . . .

The jury had sensed that, unlike the start of proceedings two days previous, this particular trial had a sense of being unjust. This was based on very little, just a hunch. There was a kind of apprehension in the air too following on from what the Judge had said earlier and for that reason there appeared to be restraint shown by all concerned, even the jury fidgeted less and that satisfied His Honor no end. Pity, they must have thought, it would have been far more interesting the chaotic way. The Judge then consulted John Andrews, another clerk of the court on a technicality arising from a reference he'd made in his personal notes before instructing Wendy to continue with proceedings. This she did and asked the plaintiff's attorney, Lance, to present his opening statement. He wasted no time in doing so.

'Ladies and gentlemen of the jury, not for the first time in my twenty five year career, I find myself in a strange court, talking to people I hardly know, about the wrong doings of our fellow Americans, all because of their race and the color of their skin,' said Lance Heycock who couldn't wait to deliver his address to the jury. With the preliminaries over and done with, he then continued with an overall summary of what they believed to be the unfair treatment of Desmond Haynes and so forth that could only be described as ordinary. He mentioned the usual stuff; that Desmond was a caring, committed, and extremely bright employee who had been with Advanced Strategic Energy for fifteen years and in that time he'd provided a good service, etc, etc. Heycock slowly walked the jury through Desmond's career, before and during his time with ASEI, pausing to describe in more detail the highlights of his achievements and the many commendations he'd been given from the company. People genuinely believed what he had to say and it showed in their faces, even the swearing Judge, Hastings believed most of it. The lawyer from down south continued with his well-rehearsed opening statement with passion, excitement, and pride, and was hopeful from the fact that there would be justice in Section A of the Orleans Parish, Civil Court. When all the niceties were done and dusted, Lance upped the tempo.

'You will hear from witnesses of how this totally committed, *model* employee has been abused and ill-treated by his employer, Advanced Strategic Energy. Of how some of their highest serving managers have acted with the utmost disrespect against my client and several of his fellow black workers, of how the company have ignored the pleas for help from black and ethnic minority workers who have been so blatantly harassed and prejudiced against. You will be appalled at the extent and depth of racial hatred and discrimination that exists within one of America's largest oil company. They claim to have policies in place to protect people like Desmond Haynes, but the fact is simple, they have none. And, even more extraordinarily, you will hear of how one of the bravest men in their employment was dismissed, disregarded, dumped without compassion, without any formal notice or inclination of their intent, without remorse . . .,' he paused before continuing, his head visibly bowed to the floor. 'Without feeling for either him or his family, and for what?' he asked, looking straight at the jury for the answer. 'For no reason whatsoever other than the color of his skin,' he told them, using a well practiced tone. 'Several more senior employees, so-called *managers*, did not like the color of his skin!' he emphasized for good measure. 'They did not like the fact that here was a man that could be relied upon, whereas they could not.' Lance pondered those last words whilst keeping his eyes fixed on the jury. He put out his left hand, felt for a glass and sipped some water before continuing.

'You will hear clear and convincing evidence to support my clients' allegations. Matters of fact, statements from witnesses that will clearly tell you more than just a preponderance of the evidence,' he went on to add. 'The facts are highly stacked in favor of my client and are beyond a reasonable doubt,' he told the jury members, rather convincingly. That last statement brought a tap of the gavel. *Bang*!

'Mr. Heycock!' the Judge intervened and Lance quickly looked his way, a little bewildered at being interrupted to say the least. 'Are you psychic?' he asked. Lance was taken aback by the question but knew what was coming.

'Err... no, Your Honor,' he replied with some hesitation and becoming embarrassed at such a question.

'Then you do not know the outcome of this trial and it is not for you to predetermine the outcome of events. The jury will decide if there is *reasonable doubt* as you so politely put it.' With that the Judge himself sipped a glass of water, shook his head and told our counsel to continue.

'Shit,' muttered Lance, but only to himself. 'Hastings is really pissed off over something,' he then whispered to his team as he bent over to refill the glass from a bottle of water close by. He had every right to say what he did. He could see Briggs smirking from one corner of his eye but ignored him and continued with his speech instead.

'Here in the United States there are laws that protect a person, or persons, from racial discrimination. You will hear quotes and references to the Forty Second United States Constitution, Section Nineteen, Eighty One, and Title Seven of The Civil Rights Act of nineteen sixty-four. These laws are in place to protect people like you and me, ordinary folk who go about their ordinary business. I don't want to be prejudiced against. Would you want to be prejudiced against?' he pointed a finger at several of the jury members. 'Just think about it,' he told them holding his hands out as if catching a ball. This struck accord with the jury. They knew exactly what Lance was referring to. They knew the legislation more than he did probably. Briggs entourage also noticed the reaction of the jury, nodding of heads was a clear sign and they scribbled madly on legal pads before handing the notes over to Briggs, who took a quick glance before discarding them to one side. They would be used later by the shrinks if needed, but we doubted that requirement. Lance did another round and once again walked slowly in front of the jury as he pondered those last words.

'Just think about?' he repeated the question whilst directing a thoughtful look towards a middle-aged white man, Clinton Mac, who sat in the front row but looked self-consciously to the floor. Then he looked at Molly Price sat next to him who did the same. Again, Phil Middleton, who was seated at the back, Penny Smith and Al Bourne sat next to each other in the middle row. Five of the eight white folks picked to form the jury of twelve had shied away from the question, every one of them. The black jurors shook their heads though, just as Lance had intended. The grey-haired attorney stood close to them, looking at their bowed heads and spoke even more passionately to the remaining white jurors who he'd not picked out.

'Why have they dismissed this hard working man? The same man I have described to you, the same man sat next to me there,' he said, pointing to the plaintiff, Desmond, who sat motionless and expressionless on the chair. 'You do not dismiss good, honest and extremely committed workers for goodness sake!' he despaired and frowned towards the opposing counsel. They frowned back, shaking their heads in mock disgust. The tit-for-tat would not cease.

'We rely on you good, law-abiding people to lift your heads up high, look towards Desmond Haynes and bring justice into this courtroom,' he told them. The jury did as they were instructed and they all looked at Desmond, who in return shied away. 'Look at him closely, a black man who has suffered immensely since Advanced Strategic Energy callously disregarded him. Do you see yourselves there? Do you?' Nodding heads confirmed some of them had placed themselves in Desmond's' predicament. Good move. Home runs to Lance, one to nothing. Our lead counsel sensed the Judge fidgeting in his chair, the old man was getting impatient and so that was the signal for the lawyer to complete his opening statement. Lance began to wind up his speech.

'Your judgment over the next few days should be entirely consistent with society's deep commitment to the eradication of race-based discrimination. To come down hard on companies like Advanced Strategic Energy who abuse their black employees, good working folk who have done no harm to anyone. Yet they continue to abuse them with a vengeance, all because of nothing more than the color of their skin or their race.' Lance held his gaze towards the jury, looking at each one of them in turn. After a while he relaxed his posture and walked over to his chair and uttered the immortal words, 'May God bless you all,' he said, finishing the script and then quickly sat down. Not one of his finest openers but it was good for starters. He had sold himself to the jury and they were on his side for the time being.

John Briggs wasted no time. He stood for a split second before putting on his suit jacket. It had been removed during the opening proceedings to allow some extra comfort and now he composed himself, as good attorneys do from time to time. Standing behind his desk he rubbed his chin and shook his head in false wonder whilst looking at some hand-written notes taken during Lance's opening remarks. He was deep in thought at what had been said and it showed. Another shake of the head followed before he walked slowly over to the jury.

'Ladies and gentlemen, it is good to see you and I sincerely hope you are all well this fine morning?' he asked affectionately, trying to win them over from the very start. He then rested his arm on the rail in front of the wooden pen that housed the small group. Nodding heads confirmed everybody's wellbeing. 'Good,' he told them in a fatherly kind of way. 'My name, as you may already know, is John Briggs. I am a lawyer, a black man from New York who has been asked to defend the good name of Advanced Strategic Energy Incorporated and several good employees of that company.' JB was at ease with himself, too at ease perhaps judging by the way he slouched against the rail. The earlier rollicking from the Judge had, in a strange way, given some purpose to his sense of wellbeing and, contrary to his earlier composure, he now appeared more relaxed.

'In sharp contrast to what my learned friend has just said, most of what will be presented inside this courtroom will be *hearsay*. Yes, *hearsay*. To you and me that amounts to nothing more than gossip. He his right with one vital piece of information though!' Briggs raised his tone of voice at the revelation he was about to tell them. 'The part where there should be, *no reasonable doubt*.' Briggs paused for those words to sink in before repeating himself in exactly the same manner that Lance had done moments earlier. Thousands of practicing US trial lawyers employed the same well-trodden tactic; one that had passed the test of time and for that reason would be used for years to come. It always had maximum affect.

'*No reasonable doubt*, ladies and gentlemen of the jury. It is your duty to determine that whatever is said against my client in this room is said with true conviction and accuracy. Matters supported by only the facts. Isn't that what my learned friend, Mr. Heycock, said not two minutes ago?' he asked them, refreshing their memory in the process. We all thought that was a home run to Briggs but with no real experience of how to measures the jargon. Anyway, all square, he had leveled the score with incredible ease in my opinion. He had our attention and that of the jury.

'So, above all else,' continued Briggs, who had now raised his voice not unlike a priest giving a church sermon before lowering it again to deliver the punch line. 'There must be no *reasonable doubt.*' He prolonged the words before continuing. '*No reasonable doubt* as to what is, and what is not a criminal act as described in this lawsuit,' he told them whilst holding up the outline of the case being filed against them, the document was wafer thin. Briggs had gone for the classic opening. He knew that there would be doubt. Of course there would be, unless it's clear-cut murder, any past juror will testify to that. There always was and always would be. It was just a matter of how many doubters he could convince in his favor. It would be a balanced decision. Nine to one against us, I thought callously!

'Ladies and gentlemen,' he continued. 'As discussed earlier in this courtroom and also by the Right Honorable, Judge, Hastings,' he reminded us all, getting the plug in and looking politely at the Judge who, incidentally, showed no emotion at all, which only served to prompt the black lawyer to quickly continue with his spiel. 'The plaintiff is obliged to obtain, *prima facie*. You are not expected to know this legal jargon but it is a Latin phrase for, *at first view*. Thus, translated it refers to the minimum evidence the plaintiff must have to avoid having a case dismissed.'

Bang, Bang! The sound of the Judges' gavel took everyone by surprise. He sensed where the defense counsel was taking this one.

'Have I got to remind you so early? Counsel will not . . . I repeat . . . will not intimate that this case is to be dismissed. I have seen enough evidence for that not to happen. Have you forgotten our pre-trial conference, counselor? Do you think I would be sat here if there were insufficient evidence brought to my attention? Do you take me or the jury for fools, counselor?' shouted Hastings, only those words would backfire on him he'd find out in due course. Anyway, own goal from Briggs but a pretty smart move nonetheless, perhaps we were back in the lead but who other than us cared this early in the game? The Judge was angry as ever and I'd decided that was good. Something or somebody was bothering him and it was increasingly becoming more obvious that it could even be the man himself, John Briggs!

'No, Your Honor, definitely not, Your Honor.' Briggs was flustered now and backtracked quickly although, like Lance, he found nothing wrong with that type of wording before. He'd used it a number of times during other cases without cause for reprimand. 'I apologize to you and the jury, Your Honor.' Briggs was suck-holing them. 'Let me put it another way,' he continued but in a less relaxed manner, he had noticeably lost his composure. 'You, the jury, will have the comfort of preponderance relating to the evidence given. That level of proof required to prevail in a civil case such as this. You, my friends . . .,' *Bang, Bang, Bang!*

'Briggs!' he shouted out loud. The Judge had dispensed with formalities and beckoned the young lawyer towards the bench and JB obliged by walking quickly towards him as ordered. 'These are not your friends!' he told him sternly the minute he was within whispering distance. 'They are decent folk that would be more at home fighting with alligators than associate with the likes of you!' The Judge spoke in a hushed tone but several jurors, including Lance, heard what he'd said. The court reporter had even started to record it, word-for-word. 'You will not refer to the jury as your friends, do you understand?' he told him once and for all. Briggs nodded. Another own-goal, we led by two clear points.

'Yes, Your Honor, I apologize once again.'

'And furthermore, you will not talk about preponderance of evidence. I will decide the level of proof required, do I make myself clear?'

'Yes, Your Honor, I understand, sir . . . err . . . I mean, Your Honor.' Hastings growled, turned to the jury and instructed them to dismiss the last statement made by the counsel for the defense. Wendy Lloyd was also instructed to erase the remarks from the court records. The Judge had a way of hating young, black, smart-ass lawyers thought Lance and many others inside the court must have thought the same. Briggs returned to the centre of the room and once again apologized to the jury but, nevertheless, continued where he'd left off.

'You need to be satisfied then, ladies and gentlemen,' he continued. Again the bright attorney turned to the Judge when he said this. The Judge in turn frowned and nodded in less than mild approval but recognized that Brigg's was taking the piss out of him once again. 'You must be entirely and convincingly persuaded that the facts presented here are probably more favored one way than another. You must convince yourselves that the evidence is presented in such a way as to fall heavily in favor of the plaintiff, which is most unlikely giving the facts we intend to present to you over the next couple of days. They allege unfair dismissal on the grounds of racial discrimination. My client denies this. They have a multi-billion dollar business to run and safety is of paramount importance. And for the record,' began Briggs, looking towards Hastings for approval. 'Not only are we going to explain fully the extent to which the plaintiff, sat before the bench over there,' he pointed towards Desmond and the jury all nodded in unison as Briggs continued. 'Not only was he grossly negligent, but we're also going to tell you how he was strongly connected to another incident involving a large explosion. Only that incident resulted in multiple deaths!' he said, raising his voice at the seriousness of what he'd just said.

'Point of order, Your Honor, that's pure hearsay and totally unsubstantiated. There is nothing connecting my client to any personal death, anywhere, period,' argued Lance jumping to his feet. The Judge pondered what he'd heard. This was new to him.

'I'm merely pointing out that Mr. Haynes was there,' added Briggs in his defense.

'Overruled, counselor,' said the Judge in Briggs favor and gave a dismissive wave in Lance's direction. It was a sign to sit down, shut up and listen. The jury also agreed. They were like a team of nodding donkeys.

'As I was saying,' continued Briggs, pleased with the Judge for once. 'ASEI will simply not tolerate anything, or anyone, that compromises the high standards they place on their safety record. The evidence presented on behalf of Advanced Strategic Energy will show them not to be the callous employer that my friend makes out but the caring, considerate, and above all else, *safe and responsible* operating company the whole of the US citizenship knows and expects them to be. Desmond Haynes employment with Advanced Strategic Energy was terminated not due to racial discrimination but on the grounds of, *gross negligence*, something the company will not tolerate under any circumstances.'

JB sat down, looked at nobody in particular and quenched his bone-dry throat by sipping a glass of water. The jury was impressed, just as they had been following Lance's opening remarks. I made the scoring to be Heycock two, Cranton one. Any legal-minded punter would have scored heavily in Briggs favor! My score counted for nothing.

Judge Hastings was unimpressed by what he'd heard so far. Both lawyers had trod carefully, although Briggs tried to make a steal on his counterpart but had received two warnings from Old Misery guts. It was quite normal practice for the two opposing counsels' to gain the upper hand from the start. Apart from what anyone present thought, the reality of it all was that the opening statements had not really worked, as usual. There was too much supporting evidence to submit before any of the jurors would decide, apart from those who already had!

Chapter 28

During the lunch break I made some concocted lie about something or other and made good my escape from the group. Lance was concerned at my whereabouts, I was due on the stand and he didn't want me to be late. I convinced him I'd only be a couple of minutes and left them sadly mulling over the mornings events. I phoned the mobile number from inside Wendy Lloyd's office while she was out for lunch. I let a young pimple-faced boy who was *just holding the fort* listen in on my conversation. Cheryl answered the phone without asking who it was.

'Good morning gorgeous,' she said in her softly spoken accent. She was safely inside the airport terminal and ready to check in I was informed without asking her whereabouts. My spirits were instantly raised by the very sound of her bubbly voice. The Continental Airlines flight would arrive in New Orleans just after six-thirty. She would have to connect at Houston, which delayed things by three hours. I detected a fake sigh. You would have thought she was a frequent flyer judging by the sulk! Never mind though, she'd be there and nothing was going to stop her she told me. I reassured her that I'd be at the airport to meet her. I could tell she was extremely nervous but excited at the thought of a transatlantic crossing. It was her first. I briefly told her of the progress inside courtroom number three and she listened intently. She had no idea what I was talking about so just wished us luck. I told her to enjoy the flight and said goodbye. A kiss could be heard coming down the line from her end. That perked me up to say the least.

The idea of Cheryl coming to New Orleans was mine. Once the tears had stopped we'd discussed the business of false accounting and the payment made to JGE many times during the last week following our first introduction. We finished work early on the second day and most other days after that going to a nearby bar along the quay. The drink loosened her up and the truth gets told in drink, or so my father always said. And he was right.

Yes, she finally confessed on day two. She had made a payment under false pretences but had taken her lead from a senior VP with the company. About one week after the explosion in Nigeria, Jeremy Isaacs had turned up one day out of the blue and made it his business to get involved with some of the work she was involved in. It caused a bit of a stir at the time and several questions were asked about his involvement, especially the way he had infiltrated the accounts department. *Who was he*, they asked? But the accountants soon found out it was no good complaining; Isaacs was an extremely high ranking US corporate executive. Who was going to listen to their complaints? The best they gleaned from the management was that he was some HR whiz kid from the corporate headquarters in New York who had volunteered to help in any way he could, and any help was welcome. Anyway, nobody was listening. Nobody had the time to do anything other than keep up with the complicated accounting procedures needed to be in place to complete the multi-million dollar payments required for repairs. The damn chemical plant was on its ass! It had been blasted to hell and back and was reason enough to welcome any help from anywhere. The rebuild had started and people wanted to be paid and Jeremy Isaacs knew that only too well.

Slowly at first, but with increasing speed, coupled with his abuse of authority, Isaacs soon had everyone, including Cheryl, eating out of his hand. A few late night dinners, his trademark *open* expense account, which was supported by the company platinum Amex card—courtesy of Advanced Strategic Energy—made sure of that. A host of guaranteed promotions and false promises of work in the US followed. Those who needed to be convinced that he was, after all, a tidy yank and somebody who could be trusted succumbed to the same treatment and it made his interfering just about bearable they later reasoned.

'He was a pain in the ass and knew little about accounting procedures, but his expense account sure as hell buffered the pain,' said Hillary Wilson, tipsy one night in a champagne bar and doing her very best to top-up Isaacs' credit cards. But for all his entertaining and skullduggery, nobody was treated better than Cheryl, he made sure of that. She was convinced at the time that he fancied her. And he did, eventually. How could any man resist such a beautiful woman? Regardless of his motives, he lusted after her. They made love on numerous occasions in his hotel room over a three-week period, but exactly how many occasions I didn't want to know;

for the first time ever I'd became jealous and when she mentioned that, it was painful for me.

Cheryl was in love with Isaacs at the time she told me and it showed, but there was a price to pay. Somewhere along the way, over five hundred thousand dollars was paid to an engineering firm nobody had any idea existed. Isaacs had insisted the payment be made and with the help of the one person who'd been wined, dined, and deceived the most, Cheryl, the money was transferred to a bank account in the name of JGE. By this time nobody would argue or question his authority. Not long after the transaction, and safely knowing he couldn't be tied to the money transfer in any way, Isaacs returned to the States much to Cheryl's surprise. He had not even bothered to say goodbye. Everyone else, however, was relieved at his timely disappearance. Cheryl cried her heart out. She was left to pick up the pieces and somehow knew that the account belonging to JGE would reappear to haunt her one day in the future. How could she have been so stupid?

When I told Lance about the goings on he said it wasn't just potentially damaging it was dynamite and he would figure a way of getting the information out in the open. *The Orleans Parish Civil Court, and in particular courtroom number three, would provide the perfect platform*, he told me but we'd have to strongly connect Isaacs to the corruption. I then left these matters for Lance to deal with as promised but as of yet, he'd resisted all attempts by me to bring it up. *In due time,'* he assured me. *The element of surprise was paramount*, he said, finally convincing me to drop it for the time being.

After the call, my spirits were lifted and I made my way back to the court. I had agreed to be first up. It made sense, besides it would give our side some practice. Neither I nor Des believed that anyone employed in our team had gone this far in their legal careers before! Wendy Lloyd called my name out loud and I made my way to the stand once the Judge was seated. Lance was sat directly to my left, ready to react at the first sign of trouble. The Blues Brothers were further along to his left and Dil sat at a table near the door. Opposite me were Spooner and Melville, both immaculately dressed, both poised and both gave the impression of being extremely good attorneys—and they were. Pete Masters, the paralegal was sat to the right of the table and within easy whispering distance of the lead attorney, John Briggs. All those present had legal pads and were ready to write.

I took my place and was quickly sworn in with the usual few sentences of honesty, truth, and something about God helping me in any way he could. It felt strange saying that having seen it happen a thousand times on television. Lance was first up and took me through the routine we'd planned a few days previous. It was a simple and honest account of Desmond Haynes employment record with ASEI. The entire episode lasted no more than fifteen minutes and made good listening. I remained seated and waited to be cross-examined by Briggs. Knowing what to expect from the type of questions asked during the deposition, I was relaxed and raring to go, and so were the defense. Unbeknown to me, I was in a false sense of security.

Briggs, looking rather dapper in a Valentino pinstriped suit and recently flown in from Florida having just prepared for another high profile lawsuit, stood and slowly made his way towards me. He wasted no time at all. In fact, he gave the impression that he didn't want to waste any time talking to me whatsoever. But he did, he had to. Questions relating to my name, position with the company, family background and minor personal matters were disposed of in under a minute. He was unconcerned along with everybody else, apart from Masters, his silly looking paralegal who confirmed everything by writing the details down on an oversized legal pad that looked like a child's math book.

'Does your employer, Advanced Strategic Energy Inc, know you're here today, Mr. Archer?' he then went on to ask. This was a little too predictable, we had anticipated that one. My response would be as predictable though. Short, sharp and honest, just as Lance had instructed us.

'Yes.'

'Doesn't that bother you?'

'No.'

'Isn't that a little strange? You are a senior manager with Advanced Strategic Energy, right?' he took a smart-ass look at his notes to make sure I was. 'Or did I misunderstand the situation?' asked Briggs, who'd taken a derisory approach almost immediately. It bothered me not in the slightest. This was nothing like the deposition but I was prepared for it nevertheless.

'No, it's not strange. Yes, I am a senior manager and no, you understood perfectly well.'

'You are a senior manager then, right?'

'Like I said the first time of asking, I am.' I didn't know if I was lying at this point. For all they knew I may not have received the fax from Frank.

The Last Hangman

More scribbling, perhaps it was a joke; perhaps I was still employed in a senior position? It would be checked out. Anyway, I presumed Briggs knew the situation but chose not to pursue it.

'Okay, so you don't think it's strange that you're testifying for a friend of yours against your current employer, and you say it doesn't bother you,' he confirmed for the benefit of nobody. 'So I take it you had the courtesy to inform them of your intentions then, Mr. Archer?' he then asked me.

'They know,' I replied.

'I know that,' he said, fishing for more. 'But did *you* inform them personally?' he added, emphasizing the question.

'Does it matter?' I replied. 'The fact is they know I'm here.'

'Mm . . . yes. Actually, it does matter, Mr. Archer because I can't help but think there's a conflict of interest in all of this! I mean, I can't begin to imagine that whatever it is you intend to say will change anything that's happened. I honestly can't,' he told me sternly. 'So forgive me if I happen to also think that perhaps you're hitting back at the company for some other underlying reason?' he said, posing the loaded question directly at me and the jury. 'It happens quite frequently you know!' added Briggs frowning at me and turning once again to the jury for maximum effect.

'*Conflict of interest . . ., hitting back,*' I repeated, trying to understand what he was getting at. 'In what way?' I asked, not sure where he was going with this.

'I'm simply saying that some people who've worked for a company for the length of time you have may hold a certain grudge of some kind, Mr. Archer,' he explained. 'Especially after say, not getting a promotion or particular job you wanted,' he suggested, leading us nowhere. 'Or it may be that you've been pushed aside to make room for more energetic, younger blood, for example. Who knows?' he said, now being more precise in my particular case. It was obvious Cranton & Associates had collaborated with ASEI to decide my future with the company, the shuffling had already begun and I'd been pushed aside. It all added up and that fitted in nicely with what was going on now. I'd be overly aggrieved at the news following the latest reorganization; a move to a lower position that I hadn't even been privy to yet!

Unbeknown to me at the time, and following Frank's warning, I'd played straight into their hands and felt stupid all of a sudden. I wasn't really prepared for that as Briggs continued along the same theme. 'Or it could derive following a certain trauma of some kind,' he once again hinted, referring to events in Nigeria of course, and who wouldn't be annoyed after that! He was attacking on all fronts and any bystander would be amazed why I wasn't pissed off after such ill-treatment! I was already becoming a very unreliable witness.

'I've got no axe to grind against ASEI,' I told him dishonestly. 'I'm simply here to give a character reference for a friend. I'm not here to pass judgment on my employer,' although I would have liked to, I thought to myself.

'Nobody is asking you to pass judgment, Mr. Archer. The jury will take care of that,' said Briggs with a little smile. The Judge wasn't too pleased at that but the taunting would continue at every opportunity. Briggs then picked up on the previous thread. 'You are here to praise your friend, Mr. Haynes. That is your intention. Nevertheless, I am going to find it hard to understand how you can do that without prejudicing yourself with your employer, Mr. Archer.' Silence from me.

'Well?'

'Well what?' I replied.

'Answer my question.'

'What question?' It was my turn to frown. 'It wasn't a question you asked me, more of a statement, wouldn't you say?' I looked serious enough to be doubtful of his approach and besides, he'd already proved my testimony would count for nothing very soon. I couldn't wait to get off the stand and I'd only been there a few minutes!

'I see. We are not here to play word games, Mr. Archer. You know what I was getting at and you are obliged to co-operate. Do you understand?' he asked looking at the Judge for approval. The Judge nodded towards me. I had to comply. I wasn't a criminal and I'd done nothing wrong. I probably wouldn't have a job when I got back but that was my fault. But this guy was going to treat me with respect or we were going nowhere.

'You're the one playing games. Ask me a question and I'll answer it. Make a statement and I'll listen. You should try it sometime.' The Judge rolled his head back, sighed but said nothing, he was not happy with me.

'Frank Dawes was amazed when we contacted him yesterday,' Briggs continued, totally ignoring my ignorance of the way these things were meant to happen. 'He had no idea that you were here today,' he added, backtracking to his earlier question for some reason. *Lying bastard*, I thought to myself. Frank knew darned well I was here. What's he playing at?

'How is the old goat?' Hands scribbled the reply. Frank would be informed soonest. My employment with Advanced Strategic Energy bored me anyway and so what if JB was aware Frank knew that I was there—I couldn't care less, it was a power thing. He also knew that I could say what I liked, it was no sacking offence. I waited for him to mention the demotion letter I received at the hotel but it never came. JB continued to ignore my sarcasm and carried on. He had made his point, they'd contacted Frank in England and they'd contact him again if need be. They were trying to ruffle me. I didn't give a shit and he knew it. I felt ill-at-ease by the line of questioning though. They never asked me these questions during the deposition! Clever bastards!

'From your body language it looks as if something's bothering you, Mr. Archer,' he speculated.

'I'm fine,' I told him in return, but he'd hit the target, there were a multitude of things bothering me and there was more to come!

'Good,' he replied falsely. 'Now I'd like you to answer either *yes* or *no* to the next question if you would be so kind,' said Briggs, pausing to make sure I understood what he'd asked me to do. I nodded. 'Are you, or are you not an aggrieved employee, Mr. Archer?' he then asked slowly and plainly after the short lead-up to the question.

'Depends,' I replied, wanting to say *yes, most definitely.*

'Let me ask you again, have you got any grievances against the company, Mr. Archer? *Please*, simply answer *yes* or *no*,' he ordered me.

'No.'

'None whatsoever?' he replied in amazement!

'None whatsoever,' I repeated back to him.

'Could you explain to me then why your marriage has failed?' That question came out of the blue, and more to the point, where did he get the information? Only Julie and I knew that. It must be in the public domain I reasoned. Knowing the way Julie talked, I would be made out to be an ogre, a womanizer, drunkard, and gambler, anything that painted me in a bad picture. She on the other hand would have been hard done by! These guys were on my case.

'No, I can't.'

'Why not, it's a simple enough question?'

'Because I don't really know . . . marriages last, marriages fail. You fall in love, you fall out of love, you move on. It's as simple as that.'

'Oh! *It's as simple as that,*' he mused, wondering if it was, *as simple as that*! He let those words linger and then continued firing off the innuendoes. 'I suppose you work long hours in your position, Mr. Archer?' Briggs was taking us down the exact road we had predicted; employee works long hours, employee suffers failed marriage due to work commitments, employee becomes aggrieved, employee gets the company back somehow, anyhow. Briggs highlights these facts and the jury rubbish's whatever I have to say. It wouldn't work. Even though we hadn't discussed the news of my pending job move, simply because nobody other than Yours Truly knew about it just yet, or Nigeria, simply because nobody had even thought about it, we had nevertheless prepared well for this period of questioning.

'No longer than you do, I dare say,' I replied, hitting back.

'Just answer the question, please.'

'Yes I do. It goes with the territory.'

'Does this have an effect on your private life?'

'No.'

'Then let me put it to you another way. Do you love your wife then, Mr. Briggs?' he quickly asked, getting back to the thread. I paused. I didn't expect that one. Lance objected but Briggs argued that he needed the question answered since it was essential part of their determination of whether or not I was an aggrieved employee. Satisfied that he had no real argument against the line of enquiry, Lance backed off and let Briggs roast me further. Why hadn't he asked more about the long hour's stuff, or Nigeria? Briggs upped the tempo and the questions were coming faster. He didn't seem interested in the answers. His posy was recording them. They would be analyzed later by some eggheads from some university for human behavioral studies no doubt.

'What's that got to do with this?' I tried to argue, despite Lance giving in too early.

'Everything, some people blame failed marriages on their workload, others do not. We are keen to know where you fit in,' he said, goading me. 'Now, for the second time of asking, Mr. Archer, do you love your wife?'

'No,' I replied in frustration. My mouth became dry the instant I'd lied. I looked at Desmond. He looked back, expressionless. He must have known anyway. It felt strange actually denying your love for somebody who for such a long time worshipped the ground you walked on. I had obviously stumbled. I hadn't really convinced him of the answer and I swallowed hard to get saliva back into my mouth and throat. I had gone from being a natural to becoming a nervous wreck. Then I thought about Cheryl for a split second.

'You do not sound so sure, Mr. Archer. Could you repeat your answer one more time for the record?' *Bastard*, he had me on the run. I composed myself.

'No, I do not love my wife.' To hear myself saying what I had just said hit home. What was I saying? Was that the end? I looked at Lance and then at Desmond for reassurance. Both men looked towards the floor. Soon I was going to become mincemeat. Again, I thought of Cheryl. John Briggs didn't let up no matter what I was thinking or how I felt.

'On average how many hours do you work, Mr. Archer?' The lawyer had changed tack. He had put me back on course after watching my sails flap around in the wind a little. I would have to put in a couple of reefs if I didn't want to be blown over and sink.

'Oh, I would say ten, eleven, twelve hours a day maybe,' I pondered the idea as I spoke.

'And I suppose six days a week looking at the information I have here.' Briggs then waved a printout of what looked like the standard Advanced Strategic Energy employee time-keeping statistics.

'I don't know. I don't fill in a timecard. Managers don't have to do that,' I corrected him with a feeling of being useless. I felt a little childish too. Lance and the Blues Brothers liked it nevertheless and raised their head momentarily. They acknowledged my response with a slight nod.

'Oh, this isn't a time card, Mr. Archer. This is the security log. It's a record of when you come and go through the security gate,' he told me.

'Jesus!'

'Why act so surprised?' he said, in mock amazement. 'You spend a lot of time at that place,' he added, providing an admirable smile at the same time as if announcing I was employee of the month. It was another matter-of-fact statement and so I didn't bother to reply. I kept silent and just looked at Briggs who was still happy as ever, he was enjoying this. JB's team also smiled with him, they simply marveled at their top man who'd taken me from one place to the next before turning me upside down and inside out almost at will. Yes, they were mightily impressed. My side looked to the floor for the umpteenth time. In this war, it seemed that every bomb hole was a trench! Briggs continued with a torrent of difficult questions starting with the obvious.

'Mr. Archer, could you now tell us please, about your assignment in Nigeria?' he asked me following up on the earlier innuendo. It was quicker coming than I expected and would wrap things up nice and neat and tidy for old JB. It was surely going to be the coup-de-grace.

'I was there from ninety-five through till ninety-eight.' I answered simply, leaving the detail out completely and knowing the next question. JB couldn't wait to ask it.

'It was a five-year assignment, Mr. Archer,' he reminded me. 'So could you explain to us why the assignment came to a premature end?'

'The facilities were badly damaged. Both Desmond and I were badly injured from . . .'

'Thank you, Mr. Archer,' he intervened. 'Just answer the questions we ask, no need for details,' he said to me quickly moving on. *Bastard*, I thought for the umpteenth time. 'There was a large explosion following a leak at the time, was there not?'

'Yes, the place . . .'

Briggs cut me off again. 'And where were you and Mr. Haynes at the time the alarm was raised, Mr. Archer?'

'We were in the camp bar. It's normal to have a couple of beers after work,' I replied. He'd obviously been talking to Frank for longer than he cared to mention.

'*Normal*, I wouldn't call that *normal*, Mr. Archer. I would call it *strange* wouldn't you say?' supposed Briggs emphasizing the important points and looking straight at me as if I'd committed murder.

'No, most expats have a couple of beers after work.'

'After work, mm . . .,' he mused, pacing the room and making his way toward the jury. 'What else was going on at the time?'

'There was a lot going on, what exactly would you like to know?' I replied, knowing that I'd made a big mistake saying that.

'Let me take you back briefly to the time of the leak. What did you do about that?'

'Yes . . ., we had a leak just outside the refinery,' I answered, nonchalantly, fed up with it all. 'It was no big deal. Rob Drew was looking after it.'

'No big deal . . . mm . . . no big deal,' repeated Briggs making a familiar meal of things. 'But according to this report,' he said, again waving a thick document in the air for all to see. '*It was a big deal*, Mr. Archer. In fact *it was a very big deal*,' he told the room. 'There was a *major* chemical spill inside the plant and countless other oil-spills outside the boundary fence of the refinery and you and Mr. Haynes took it on you to have a couple of beers. Incredible!' he claimed, reminding everybody of the facts. 'And you have the audacity to call it *normal* and . . . what was the other expression you used?' he hesitated to ask and then made out as if he were looking at his notes placed in front of him, it was a charade meant to get maximum exposure. He knew the phrase; he'd been repeating it over and over not fifteen seconds earlier! 'Ha, here it is! *No big deal!*' he said finally, laughing at me in the process. On the face of it, he was right of course. Why hadn't we helped Rob?

'I wouldn't like to see your bar bill under *abnormal* circumstances, Mr. Archer,' he smirked. The jury laughed along with him, even the Judge grinned. 'And as far as chemical or oil leaks are concerned, I'd be a bit more wary if I were you. The fact is they are *a big deal*,' he emphasized for good measure. 'And they have a tendency to *kill innocent people*, Mr. Archer,' he added, digging the knife in up to the hilt. 'And that's exactly what happened wasn't it?' he went on to say, and those last few words kind of finished me off. John Briggs walked back to his chair. When he passed by Lance and the team, he paused and looked back at me as if he'd had some kind of afterthought.

'Perhaps my client should look at *your* irresponsible behavior during these *normal* situations, Mr. Archer,' he then told the court. 'Perhaps you should be on the stand for other reasons!' he said viscously, and without waiting for a reply, JB sat down without acknowledging anybody. Those across the table from our team had the widest of grins. I was irresponsible. I felt stupid. The jury thought that, the Judge thought that. I'd just dropped Desmond right in it!

Our remaining witnesses were put on the stand one by one and quickly slaughtered during the afternoon. The questions asked during the depositions completed by Briggs in New York almost two weeks ago were very fair. There were no serious points of contention and His Honor wasn't required to intervene. But here in New Orleans the questioning was ruthless! Briggs had lulled us all into a false sense of security. Now he was undermining everybody's resolve, how could we have been so naive? The overall result was going miserably in their favor. Our sorry-looking bunches of disgruntled former employees were humbled. They were made to feel as though they had done Advanced Strategic Energy Inc a disservice. I was convinced some of them had. Briggs' team had done their homework but at the end of the day, they hadn't really had to try all that hard either. Elmo had miraculously been treated like a Senior Vice-President. Nobody, absolutely nobody had made even the slightest remark about his intelligence. We wanted to but couldn't. It was racist, or not ethical, or disrespectful, or something else. It was shit! He was treated with the utmost of respect—and judging by his remarkable increased intelligence would obviously become a brain surgeon very soon. And no, he had not seen anybody treated badly during his ten-year employment with Advanced Strategic Energy.

Everyone we offered to give evidence that day, Briggs took the opportunity to shaft them and I had led by example. Our only hope was to concentrate on the policies of racial harmony, respect and fair play, which they didn't have. At least that way we could perhaps get enough evidence to suggest that there were no barriers in place that would stop a racially prejudiced decision being made. Briggs would argue that it didn't really matter. Desmond Haynes was dismissed for gross negligence, and that's what we would have to prove wrong—not if policies were, or were not in place. Even if they were, the company would still have dismissed Haynes, he was grossly negligent. For that reason, Lance had solicited our support to waive our rights to question any further witnesses that were to be called by us on the first day. In his opinion, they were unreliable and would take us down. I agreed with him. His Honor wasn't at all happy about that. *Were we taking the piss*, he asked? The fact that there were few policies, if any relating to racial harmony would go in our favor, we were sure of that, but the chances of getting a win on that alone were slim, very slim indeed. Following Lance's orders, we never questioned anybody other than Elmo that day; we had nothing to ask. Our case was becoming a lottery, although our strongest witness, Moira, had yet to take the stand. Isaacs too had to take the stand on the third day since he'd be the one person who could provide the information relating to the non-existent racial policies. For me, that was the key to all of this. We also scored when Lance asked for Hammond to also be present on the third day of the hearing. That had JB slightly rattled for some reason, that much I could tell.

The next day, Lance had asked for his first witness to take the stand immediately the Judge was back in his seat. It was Moira. She was previously sat several seats away in the same aisle as Nick and me. We both stood to allow her to pass and take her seat in the dock where she now sat letting off steam. She wasted little precious time being sworn in. She would tell the truth, the whole truth and nothing but the truth so help her God she promised quickly, eager to get started. For the next hour and a half the court was filled with her accusations of racial hatred and discrimination that had seemingly built up and been embedded in the company for the past ten thousand years judging by the strong outbursts. Yes, she had personally been subjected to the most humiliating discrimination and there were others within the company who'd also suffered the same fate, make no mistake about it. Racism existed within Advanced Strategic Energy; in her mind there was no doubt. She was on fire and the court was becoming ablaze.

Moira was in buoyant mood and could not wait to tell her story. Most of it was true but we noticed a lot of lies had crept into her testimony since she was deposed some two weeks earlier. She continuously looked around the room as she spoke. The ex-secretary was hoping to get a glimpse of her former boss, Richard Hammond, but he was not there. His whereabouts were unknown but it did not matter. He'd *had other business to deal with*, she was told. All credit to Briggs; this fact was the best-kept secret so far. Like Moira sat before us, we had no idea he'd been fired!

Anyway, she imagined that she'd meet him at some point during the trial and that he would try to greet her in haste with a polite, *hello*, as if they were old friends. She had fantasized about it on the plane whilst flying down from New York. Her imagination told her that she would bump into him twice, the first time in a small cafe bar somewhere around the corner from the court and the second time in the corridor outside the courtroom itself. On both occasions, Hammond would say *good morning* to her and make small talk as if they had much to catch up on. At the first chance she would politely tell him to, *shove your 'good morning' up your ass*, and it would be a similar choice of words if they met anytime thereafter. Ultimately, Moira dreamed of having the opportunity to politely tell him to, *fuck off,* on at least one occasion and she would enjoy saying it. She even practiced saying it, she was free of Richard Hammond and free from Advanced Strategic Energy and free to say anything she wanted. She had no job and so she had nothing to lose. She was, *a loose cannon,* as Masters had put it to Briggs when discussing their prospects with possible hostile witnesses during the deposition.

'Miss. Walters, could you describe to the court your position within Advanced Strategic Energy and the periods of your employment?' asked Lance politely, easing her into it.

'I was employed by the company as a secretary for just over seven years,' said Moira quickly.

'Did you enjoy working for the company, Miss. Walters?'

'Nope, and you can call me Moira, less the, Miss. crap!'

'OK . . . Moira . . . so, you did not like your time of employment with Advanced Strategic Energy. Why was that?' Lance expressed his inquisitiveness and gently eased her into the vital answers she needed to provide at the same time. She had to be precise and he took his time leading up to the big one. He knew Moira's feelings and he was definitely not going to stop them from coming out.

'It's simple, cos I worked for the son-of-a-bitch, that's why!'

'The son-of-a-bitch?' enquired Lance. 'Who could that be, Moira?' he asked, looking around the room as if to see the person she labeled, *son-of-a-bitch,* standing up upon hearing his name. A few people did fit the bill, I thought to myself.

'No good looking round, he ain't here. Too chicken, that's why.'

'Then who is it?' enquired Lance for the second time.

'Richard Hammond . . . thinks he's God Almighty, that's who.'

'Point of order!' said Briggs, quickly standing up. 'Your Honor, that's no way to talk about one of my clients' employees. I have to ask you to intervene and readdress that statement.' It wasn't what JB wanted to hear.

'Sit down, counselor,' replied Hastings, nonchalantly dismissing Briggs before turning back to smile at Moira. She blushed and smiled back at him. 'This woman has something to say and you are going to listen.' What on earth had Briggs done to deserve the Judge's ongoing wrath was anybody's guess? 'Carry on Miss., err . . . Moira,' said the Judge, still holding an affectionate smile. Hastings enjoyed the authority to allow the lesser folk to air their views in court however crude they might be. And he thoroughly enjoyed witnesses like Moira, she added to the spice of things.

Moira endorsed the fact that Richard Hammond was definitely a son-of-a-bitch several times more without intervention from the defense counsel. The last thirty minutes or so were spent with Lance supplying the bullets for Moira to fire them off in the direction of Advanced Strategic Energy, but for some reason, more were aimed at Richard Hammond than John Briggs would have liked. Perhaps the fact that they couldn't get Hammond in the witness box may work out after all, he suddenly realized! Moira knew she would get her just revenge and JB had to just sit there and take it. He was being humiliated. Our team in the meantime was gaining hope; perhaps Richard Hammond would drop ASEI right in the cart! That he was racially prejudiced there was no doubt if you listened to Moira, and at that moment in time everybody was, including the jury. They were being treated to some really tasty morsels and even the sound of several giggles could be heard coming from the black jurors. If it kept on going like this it would be a no-contest thought Nick at the time. He'd kept up to speed

The Last Hangman

on his lap-top, which was placed on both knees as he listened and typed away with interest as Moira continued her story. We were astounded at the way she'd been treated. Even I thought we were gaining the upper hand and was amazed at how quick events had turned in our favor.

Richard Hammond was due to take the stand on the third day and that would give Briggs the chance to redress the situation. It would be interesting to hear what he had to say? But it would be well rehearsed, no doubt . . . and well polished. I presumed that's when Lance would ask for the HR Policies, he'd ask the same question to Isaacs too I presumed. Little did we know that Richard Hammond had become invisible!

If I was amazed at just how quick events had turned in our favor then I was even more amazed at how quick events had turned against us. I had been lulled into a false sense of security once again and no sooner had JB started his cross-examination of our best witness, Moira, she had mascara running down her cheeks. She was reduced to a liar and an idiot in a very short time. Her relationship with one of the black guards working for the company bode badly; JB had insinuated that the pair was out to make a buck on the back of Desmond Haynes. They'd been well treated by ASEI and there were no records of any ill-doings. On the contrary, the guard was fired for his part in a small robbery when another employee, James Wright, tried to pinch a computer screen from another office close to his. The monitor he used at home had broken and the thought of buying a new one never entered his head, he'd always gotten his computer hardware from his place of work; ASEI had hundreds of these things, who'd miss this one he reasoned only with himself? James offered the guard fifty bucks to keep his mouth shut. The guard dutifully accepted since it was nearly a full day's pay, but the crime was flawed. They were caught on video by a security camera that showed him holding the trunk of James's car open whilst the computer thief heaved the precious hardware inside. When he had the sack Moira had the hump with ASEI, she thought they were heavy handed in dealing with such things.

'Oh, and by the way, it was obvious she was an aggrieved employee,' JB informed the jury as a matter of fact. 'When she went back to pick up her belongings after she'd resigned (of her own accord, emphasized Briggs) Moira, had thrown a brick through Hammond's office window,' he told them. A few other innuendoes about her being spiteful, holding a grudge and other distasteful traits were spilled until she was made out to be a lunatic and a liar. The Judge and jury alike were also convinced of these facts. Hastings even returned to calling her, Miss. Walters, Moira seemed too friendly a term all of a sudden! Nick too had to almost rewrite his notes regarding Moira's ill treatment. Most of it was true but proving it was an entirely different matter.

Tomorrow we had the advantage of being able to cross-examine two engineers from the California refinery, the one that had been the cause for Desmond's dismissal. They would obviously have been primed to agree with their employer and state that the shutdown procedures were incorrectly written or something to that effect. We had to depend on Lance to turn that around and make them out to be incompetent instead, which on the face of it was hardly likely. Nevertheless, Lance had hired an expert witness in these affairs. He was a professional engineer and experienced in these matters, the only trouble with that was he had agreed wholeheartedly with ASEI; according to him the procedures were badly written. The fact that Desmond didn't actually write them didn't matter, he should have!

Officially, Richard Hammond and Jeremy Isaacs were now our only olive branch. We had no idea what line of questioning Lance had decided upon but we were confident that we'd get some sort of result given the mysterious surroundings relating to the alleged offence, not to mention the *element of surprise* that Lance constantly kept on about. So far we were a laughing stock and, believe it or not, Isaacs still hadn't officially been called as a witness as far as we were aware! Lance was waiting for that *element of surprise*, he told us. Nevertheless, I wondered whether or not, officially or otherwise, to plug the underhanded and corrupt accounting that occurred involving the VP in Dorset but that would inevitably lead to Cheryl having to take the stand too. I decided to broach the suspect and ask her to consider it when we met later that evening. I then spent the next hour wondering how she'd react to such an incriminating request!

Chapter 29

Y**OU CAN ALWAYS TRUST A** storm to ruin the best-laid flight plans and this particular transatlantic crossing was no different. It was to be Cheryl's first and last flight in an airplane, period! They were more than two hours late because the plane was struck three times by lightning and the turbulence had flipped the Boeing over onto its roof and then back onto its belly somewhere across the Atlantic! How some passengers hadn't been killed was a miracle! She wasn't going to fly anymore. Her fellow passengers, however, would tell a different story. It took at least two hours to calm her down. The plane was delayed in Houston due to a technical failure but I wasn't to know. For all her moaning and groaning and childish ways it was good to see, feel, and hold her tight in my arms once again. I had missed this woman immensely. That night we made love with a passion neither knew we possessed, but afterwards the event was tempered by me thinking of her standing in the dock crying nonstop from the onslaught of counter accusations that would inevitably be delivered by Briggs. On top of that the court would get to hear of the criminal part she'd unwittingly played in the proceedings and that would be far worse given the penal system in these parts I reasoned to nobody other than myself. I never mentioned it to Cheryl or anybody else and wondered if I ever would?

* * *

Nick was wide-awake when he received the call from Joe Mayo. It was almost six-thirty in the morning and Joe, as usual, had been working for almost two hours.

'Hello, who is it?' asked Nick straight away, alert.

'Nick,' the caller bellowed. 'It's Joe. You're not going to believe this,' he said quickly.

'What's up, Joe?' replied Nick, all of a sudden yawning. He looked at his watch half expecting Joe to break into one of his renowned, poor journalist jokes at this silly hour.

'We need to talk, straight away,' he said with some urgency. Nick sensed it was serious as Joe continued his spiel. 'I'm coming down to N'Orleans. I have a flight out of Newark at ten with American. You can ring and get the flight arrival details. I haven't got time to go over them right now, but you need to meet me at the Airport, Nick,' said Joe, talking faster now. It was very serious indeed.

'What the hell's going on, Joe?' he asked, irate. 'Just tell me what's bothering you, man,' demanded Nick, sensing the huge concern in Joe's voice.

'We . . . err . . . you,' stuttered Joe correcting himself rather clumsily. '*You* received an audiotape two days ago. You know what it's like, Nick,' said Joe half apologizing and trying to explain the delay at the same time. 'We get a hundred of these a week. Like the rest of em, it was sent anonymously,' he went on, stating the obvious. 'Well, I can't go into detail, Nick, but I had Brenda take a listen as usual. She gave me a ring last night to tell me this was no ordinary stuff, the language was kinda horrible. Brenda thought I should listen to what was on it. So I picked up the tape from her desk early this morning. Do the names, Hammond, Isaacs, or Darcy mean anything to you?' he asked.

'Ugh . . . yeah,' he said, hesitantly. 'Well, I think so?' he replied, again hesitating as he reasoned at such a peculiar question so early in the morning. 'At least they would if they worked for Advanced Strategic Energy,' he managed to say coming awake all of a sudden. 'They're the bastards we think stitched up Desmond. Why, what've they done?'

'I was right,' said Joe punching a fist in the air but Nick would never have known that. 'It is about the Advanced Energy case,' the editor said, emphasizing the point to him proudly. 'I think we got ourselves a story my friend.' Joe briefly outlined what he'd heard on the tape and it was indeed spectacular. Nick filled the telecommunication with a thousand questions, which Joe couldn't answer. They had to listen to the tape together to make any sense of it he said more than once.

* * *

To say the timing was incredible was an understatement and, furthermore, the way it presented itself nearly gave me a heart attack. I thought the door was going to come off its hinges. *Bang, bang, bang*!

'Doug! Doug! Are you in there? Open the door, quick. It's me, Nick. Doug! Can you hear me?'

'Okay, okay. I'm coming,' I answered, drowsily making my way to the door before Nick battered it to the ground. I was being raised from a deep sleep by an express train. Nick burst into the room the minute I edged the door open.

'Doug. Joe's been on the blower,' he said, out of breath and pushing me aside as he entered. I just looked at him, what was there to say at such a mysterious revelation?

'Okay, calm down,' I told him. 'Now, what's all this about?' I asked, still yawning whilst closing the door. Nick had already entered the room in a rush and began to spill what he knew about the tape.

'Looks as if we've got our big break, buddy. Somebody has sent in a taped conversation held with this guy, Hammond, and a couple of others from ASEI,' he told me quickly. Then, as if he'd had some kind of afterthought, or worse, somebody was listening to the conversation, he scanned the room starting and ending with the only other room there, the bathroom. 'Where's Desmond?' he asked as if we slept together. All he saw was Cheryl's naked backside sticking out from under the quilt as she stirred half asleep on the bed; I quickly covered her up before Nick's eyes popped out from their sockets.

'Slow down, Nick, what tape? What's been happening?' I asked, none too happy with the intrusion. Satisfied that Desmond wasn't in my bed or lurking in one of the closets, Nick settled himself down and gave me a blow by blow account of the conversation he'd just had less than ten minutes ago with Joe. He was excited and his enthusiasm was running away with him. Listening to what he said it seemed too good to be true, and for that reason I just couldn't believe what I was hearing.

'Are you sure about this, Nick? I mean, how does Joe know it's for real? The Times must receive thousands of hoax calls and tapes of this kind. What's different about this one?'

'Oh, it's real for sure. Trust me, Joe is no fool. He can tell if there are alligators in the swamp, believe you me.'

'Oh yeah, we'll see,' I said, rather doubtful. But deep inside I must admit, it was spectacular and I prayed he was right, but believing other people amongst all the lies being told around us was getting too much of a habit.

'We gotta tell Des,' he said, quickly getting up to leave.

'No! Wait a while, Nick. Let's not build his hopes up just yet. Suzanne got into town late last night. Leave them rest a while. It'll make no difference,' I pretended. Something wasn't quite right. I didn't want my friend getting churned up more than he already was. Unless Hammond threw up a few surprises later on today or better still, if only we could get Isaacs to crumble on the stand things might turn out a little better. The racial policies were one thing but the misdemeanors in the accounts department were worse. But if that was mentioned Cheryl would be up there as well. We'd practically lost the case so we had to go for broke today. Briggs was chewing us up one by one. The mechanical and operations engineers brought in by Briggs to explain the process malfunction in the California plant was a master piece and would surely wrap things up nicely. Desmond was incompetent and grossly negligent, they'd both agreed. Despite our best efforts to keep his spirits up, Desmond must have sensed defeat was imminent.

'Let's just wait and listen to the tape first, yeah?' I said, taking one step at a time.

'Sorry Doug, you're right.' The young man apologized at the same time his shoulders dropped to the floor. 'I'll pick you up as usual and then we'll figure out how to get out of court without raising suspicion,' he said, slowly walking to the door. 'It's about a five-hour flight from New York. Joe should be here about three, I guess.'

'Getting out from the courtroom will be easy,' I told him. 'Leave it with me. I'll think of something. Meanwhile, let's just act as if nothing's happened.'

'Okay, I get the message. See you later.' Nick turned and made his way out of the room.

'Nick!' I called out to him. 'Not a word. Not even to the Blues Brothers, promise?'

'Yeah, you got my word. Like I said, see you later.'

Nick left quite subdued but he needn't have. His youth and inexperience was on display. He would have to control his emotions if he was going to make it in his profession. If what he'd told me was correct, it would have to be handled in the right manner. The less people knew the more chance we had of revealing its contents to the best effect. But, judging by the contents, not to mention the implications of the conversation Nick had told me about, somebody would have to call the shots and I was convinced there was only one man who could handle it; our *friend* the Judge.

The second surprise to my system was only thirty minutes after the first. It came in the form of a phone call from Lance. Our *friend*, Judge, Hastings had sent a message to Lance requesting his presence. Be in his chambers at eight-o-clock sharp he was told. Lance guessed that Briggs had had the same message. Nobody else was required to attend as far as he knew. This could mean only one thing. His Honor was not going to waste any more of his, or the jury's, time despite what he'd said on the opening day to Briggs! The outcome of our civil lawsuit was inevitable and he wanted it wound up today, one day earlier than planned. Our friend had turned into our enemy.

'What about Hammond?' I asked. 'He's due in court today and we haven't had chance to see what he's been up to yet!' I said to Lance, pissed that we'd not had our fair share of cross-examining anybody from the other side. 'And what's happening about Isaacs?' I added, getting really hot under the collar now after realizing both men were going to get off Scott-Free!

'What can I do about it?' he replied, giving in all too easy.

'Well, you can argue that to close the case too early would be a disaster for one thing. You gotta convince him that it's imperative we cross-examine Hammond. He's a key player in all of this. And what about Isaacs, why haven't we put him up there?' I asked, not sure I'd thought things through, especially now since Cheryl was under the spotlight. I hadn't even discussed this issue with her yet!

'Yeah, yeah, all of those things and a lot more besides,' replied Lance, stating the obvious. 'But then what?' he asked, turning it back on me. He was convinced the Judge wasn't going to listen to anymore of our ill-founded lawsuit, despite the fact that I'd spent the last ten minutes arguing otherwise. As for Isaacs, that was a total disconnect, it had nothing to do with what we were trying to prove, he told me. I naturally disagreed, once again arguing that *the corrupt little shit* should be exposed, but Lance warned me to let it go; that issue was another lawsuit in another court, he said.

'But he needs to prove they have the racial harmony policies in place we've argued so strongly for,' I said, dumbstruck at Lances acceptance of the situation.

'The Judges isn't going to buy it, he's heard enough,' replied Lance hardly bothered by my attitude. The fact that Lance was behaving in this way had me seething. What was going on? I asked him. He said nothing was going on. We didn't have a case, we never had a case in the first place and now it was already proven. Every witness we'd herded into the stand had contributed to our demise, he argued sensibly. It really doesn't matter about the whether or not the policies are in place, he added. Desmond was fired for gross negligence and in Judge, Hastings mind that was already proven. The racial discrimination was another lawsuit in another court!

There was no other alternative I decided after eventually realizing that Lance was in the same corner as the Judge; he'd also thrown in the towel and all too soon in my opinion. Besides, unbeknown to us, neither Hammond nor Isaacs was going to be in that court today, or tomorrow, or the next day . . .

'Lance, there's something you should know,' I then told him praying I'd get the facts right. I was about to break the confidentiality that I'd insisted upon with Nick only thirty minutes earlier. What the hell, things were happening fast and events had taken a different orientation in a matter of minutes. I had to come clean with Lance, for Desmond's sake.

'Are you sure?' It was the only question he could ask after what I'd just told him. I knew Lance would be trying to figure out how to take this information to the Judge as soon as I'd spoke. Thinking about it, it would also be the question Hastings would ask, and of course he didn't have to accept our account of what was said on the tape. *Are you sure? Why should I believe a fucking newspaper man from New York of all things?* I could hear him cuss.

'Yes, as far as I can tell, I'm sure, Lance. Trust me,' I said, sensing his denial of what I was saying, but then I didn't fully trust my own intuition either. I now knew how Nick had felt.

'It'll be difficult to tell the Judge. Hastings just won't believe a word of it, Doug,' he told me, trying to wriggle out of it. I was right, Lance was so predictably negative.

'He *has to*, Lance,' I insisted. 'We've *got* to get to him before the eight-o-clock meet. I'll see you over there in fifteen minutes.'

'Doug, its only seven-o-clock!'

'Spot on, Lance,' I replied. 'See you at seven fifteen, sharp.' I hung up with no further resistance from the attorney, who must have been wondering what the hell he was going to say to the Judge about some pie-in-the-sky tape that supposedly contained new information to support his client's lawsuit; but apparently it was dynamite! I hadn't given Lance all the details, just a few tidbits, which was enough to get his interest. I wanted to be the one to tell the Judge the finer details of what I expected to be

The Last Hangman

contained on the tape and hoped it would be as accurate as Joe and Nick had made out. I was very skeptical though, not whether or not the tape was damning as was made out, but of Lance's approach to matters lately. This was the last throw of the dice as far as we were concerned and I'd long ago decided that I'd be the one throwing it on the table. There was something about Lance that didn't add up. Then, for a split second, my mind raced back to the warning Gloria gave me back in Port Arthur!

* * *

'Well?' he asked the moment he saw us. We hadn't walked through the door properly when Hastings pounced, but at least he was there and willing to listen, at least that's what we thought.

'Your Honor, we have some very interesting news,' I said before Lance had a chance to say anything.

'I'll be the judge of that,' he replied, amazed that it was me who'd opened the conversation. 'And when did you decide that you would represent the plaintiff, Archer?' he asked looking at me as if I was standing in a pile of fresh donkey droppings. 'Are you a qualified attorney now?' The Judge was glaring straight at me. 'And have you diminished your responsibility councilor?' he then asked, quickly turning his head to hone in on Lance. He looked him straight between the eyes and flexed his horrible, trademark frown. Three rapid-fire questions revealed the mood of the Judge. It was serious. We hadn't had a chance to reply to any of his questions, he seemed not to want to listen.

'Please,' I continued whole-heartedly. 'With all due respect, Your Honor please let me speak. I have some very important information that I would like you to hear,' I said all too humbly. 'Mr. Heycock can tell you what little he knows but the bottom line is he doesn't fully know all the facts,' I told him looking towards Lance. The lawyer looked back at me and frowned in pretty much the same fashion as Hastings had done at this latest disclosure. The Judge, meanwhile, probably realized from the start that Lance barely knew anything at all factual about this particular case, not even at the best of times. I now had two enemies.

'Is that right councilor?' he asked turning towards Lance once again.

'Ugh . . . err . . . I guess so,' he stuttered, holding his arms out and dropping his shoulders in mock surprise. Lance squirmed at not being told the details in full but, nevertheless, after his performance in court he was happy to take a side seat.

'Why should I be interested? What's difference will it make? I'm winding this farce up. Why I ever agreed to it in the first place I'll never fucking know?' he said, turning his back on us to hide his disappointment. Instead of wanting to listen to what we had to say, Old Misery slowly edged towards his beloved bookcase. He was uninterested. I ignored those last remarks and give it to him full bore.

'We may be looking at a murder case, Your Honor,' I told him and upon hearing that he quickly turned to face us once again. Those words registered in an instant with the big man. I'd got his attention. Now I prayed once again that what I said would be proved in the tape. Lance bowed his head before slowly shaking it from side to side. He couldn't believe what I'd just said.

'Carry on, and don't bullshit me, Mister cos we still got time for a purgatory trial if need be!' said the Judge, eager for more news. With his point taken I slowly outlined what Nick had told me earlier. When I'd finished with what little I knew you could cut the air with a knife. The adrenaline was flowing and all three of us were in a state of enormous excitement. The initial response was as I expected. I had responded in exactly the same way just over one hour ago.

'Are you sure? Why should I believe a fucking newspaper man from New York?' shouted the Judge, as predicted. I reassured him that what I was saying would be proven by late afternoon and he backed off, more so in hope than in believing in what I'd said!

Both men realized the implications and the Judge tried not to get too carried away. It would be natural for him to do so. It was natural for all of us to do the same. Judge Hastings practically licked his lips at the thought. A murder trial, in *his* courtroom, he couldn't wait. He gave nothing away, holding his composure like a Judge was expected to but underneath the snarling quietly continued, nevertheless. It was his way, I guess. Good or bad news usually meant nothing to him and so all news was treated with the same contempt. But this was different. We were talking about murder.

'Who else knows about this?' he then asked pacing the room with a new found spring in his step.

'Nick, Lance, Joe Mayo, the Editor and you, Your Honor.'

'Haynes?'

'No sir,' I replied quickly. His head jumped up the instant I had said that bad, bad, word and a frown came my way. It was a mistake but fortunately I was spared, protected by what I knew presumably. Lance shook his head in disgust. Much to his annoyance I was not scolded in the same way he'd been treated during earlier conversations.

'Briggs and his entourage of male models, do they know anything?' he continued to ask. Not for the first time the Judge openly displayed his true feelings towards the modern wave of lawmen. In his opinion, they needed to know the law in the first place and once they knew that, only then could they dress in the manner they did. To Hastings it seemed the other way around. There were other arenas to display their designer suits and expensive jewelry; they needed to spend less time in front of the mirror and more time in the courtroom.

'No-one, Your Honor, we are the only ones apart from the newspaper men,' I reassured him.

'Tell Knight and the other guy that they'll be doing twenty years if they tell another soul.'

'I will, Your Honor. They will not disclose the contents of the tape. You have my word,' I said again in order to make things sweet between us; just in case the tape was a load of rubbish. The Judge's mind was in overdrive, we could tell by just watching him. Just then, Hastings thoughts were interrupted by a knock on the door. I looked at my watch. It was eight-o-clock on the button, it had to be Briggs. The young star would be laughing from ear to ear. Notwithstanding the fact that he'd have correctly guessed that the case was being wound up in his favor that morning, he no longer had to find an excuse for Hammond's no-show. Neither he nor Dinger had a clue what to tell the Judge other than to say he was sick! They still hadn't a clue where he was and nobody at ASEI could be bothered to tell him, not that they knew his whereabouts either, but now that didn't matter. Briggs felt a load being taken off his shoulders. To top it all off, it was time to meet the Judge and we were nowhere in sight, it didn't get any better. The delight he felt inside must have been overwhelming. He was there and Lance was not. Oh, how he would tell the Judge. *What was the plaintiffs' attorney playing at?*

'Who is it?'

'It's me, Your Honor, John Briggs. You requested my presence at eight, Your Honor.' We squirmed at the tone of voice used to answer the Judge.

'Creepy bastard,' muttered Lance.

'Stay right where you are,' he told him making his way towards the door but then stopped and looked back to us before reaching it. He looked a bit of a mess stood facing us dressed in a loosely fitting tracksuit that hadn't been ironed. 'I want you in here with that newspaper jerk as soon

Peter Nutty

as his plane lands,' he said to us. 'Sheriff Doylee will come with you to the airport.' We agreed and he opened the door. We could see the feeble figure of Briggs nearly bowing to the man inside, any minute now he would curtsy too.

'You asked to see me, Your Honor. I'm afraid there's no sign of, Mr. Heycock,' he said, overly surprised at the disrespect shown from our side!

'Little shit!' whispered Lance loud enough for me to hear but nobody else. He was still afraid of the Judge, even after all we'd told him.

'Good morning, Mr. Briggs. I just wanted to tell you that I've decided to suspend the trial today. I'll get my officials to formally notify all parties. Good day, Mr. Briggs. Oh and . . . err . . . thanks for coming,' he said, as an afterthought. The Judge proceeded to close the door.

'But . . . Your Honor!' said Briggs trying to stall him before surprise turned to astonishment upon getting a sneak glance at us inside the room, just as the door continued to close in his face. He leaned closer to talk through the ever-narrowing opening. 'Are you sure about this, Your Honor? Is there a possibility that . . .' *Bang*! The Judge slammed the door shut in his face.

'No, Good day,' he said, laughing behind the closed opening. The Judge cut him off and returned to his bookshelf and wondered what to do next. Lance and I waited for him to make the next move whilst we gloated over what had just happened. The look on Briggs' face the moment he saw Lance and me standing smartly in front of His Honors finely polished desk was a picture.

'What the . . . ?' Briggs had never had a door slammed shut in his face before and it silenced him in an instant. He was fuming.

'Fuck that man!' said Briggs out loud and not caring if anybody close by heard. 'And what the fuck were we doing in the chambers of Judge, Hastings?' he mumbled even louder. He scurried off to report to Cranton & Associates. What would Dinger make of all this?

Chapter 30

THE TEARS STREAMED DOWN HER face. There was no make-up to worry about. She hadn't worn any for days. Susan Sinclair had been numbed from the news and now sat comforted by her mother.

'Why? Oh, why? Oh, why?' she asked repeatedly. 'Why Gerald, why not somebody else?' she asked her mother time and time again. Mary simply had no answer to her daughters' plight. They had everything; love, affection, a caring family, *a good job*! What was so wrong that he could take his life instead of discussing it with her? They could have sorted it out, gotten help; there were no end of trained people that could have helped make him better. He had deprived them of a future together, for what? The question was repeated time and time again. Their lives were previously filled with more fun and love than anybody could ever have imagined, but now it was suddenly filled with emptiness; it surrounded them from every angle. The crying continued, sometimes uncontrollably. Along with her mother and father, Susan Sinclair and her son, Jason, were brokenhearted and nothing was going to bring back a dead husband or a dead father or a dead son-in-law; suicide never made sense to anybody left behind?

* * *

'I'm afraid he's busy at the moment, sir. May I take a message?' Jeremy Isaacs' secretary was ultra polite and ultra efficient.

'Yeah, get a message to him straight away,' demanded the caller. 'Tell him it's, Mr. Dinger. I need to talk to him most urgently. I'll wait for as long as it takes,' he told her with the same sense of urgency she'd detected in his voice the moment she answered the phone.

'Mr. Dinger, it's difficult to . . .'

'Please, just do as I ask,' he instructed her coldly. 'He'll want to speak to me, I can assure you.' Dinger was adamant.

'Yes sir, right away.' She understood the language, understood the urgency and quickly proceeded to contact her boss.

'What is it, Dinger?' replied Isaacs sooner than Dinger expected; it was as if he'd been listening to the conversation on another line.

'Briggs has just rung. The Judge has suspended the trial. I don't know the reason why just yet.'

'What are you bugging me for then? Anyway, I thought this was in the bag. You better not screw up on this, Dinger,' Isaacs reminded him. The senior partner with Cranton squirmed as he held the phone.

'Everything will be fine. I just thought I'd let you know in case you heard the news from another source. The Judge has suspended the trial for reasons that are unknown, that's all we know.'

'Are they still keen to talk to either Hammond or me?' he then asked.

'They wanted Hammond up there but it looks as if that's been put to bed now the trials suspended, it'll give us time to make excuses for a no-show thank goodness. And your name as never been mentioned,' he lied, not sure how the lead had gone cold all of a sudden. The last he'd heard there was talk of Isaacs taking the stand but how that never came about he'd no idea!

'Okay, keep me posted.' The line went dead as Isaacs hung up. Dinger's charges were extortionate. Isaacs simply wouldn't pay to say any goodbyes. For his part, Dinger refrained from telling him of his suspicions. What they were he had no real idea, other than he was suspicious. He smelt a rat. Archer and Heycock were in the chambers of the Judge when Briggs was told that the trial was suspended. When he asked Briggs what he thought about it, the answer he got back was simple enough. *What could possibly go wrong*? They had the plaintiff reeling on the back foot; they had em by the balls. They had won. A glitch, that's all. Perhaps the plaintiff wanted to go for an out-of-court settlement. Tough luck, they had their chance and blew it. Briggs had won and now they would be made to pay. He was rather quite chuffed with himself. Dinger respected Briggs version of events and so there wouldn't be a problem. Another day would be another dollar.

* * *

Desmond and Suzanne sat in the glorious sunshine outside the Civil Courtroom talking to Dil and the Blues Brothers, all of whom were mystified as to the reason for the suspension. It was no wonder that our arrival was greeted with a great deal of suspicion. Briggs had told Spooner and Melville of what had just happened and now they were practically spying on us in a feeble attempt to find out what was going on. Our colleagues rounded on us as we approached.

'Not just yet, guys. Let's take a walk,' I said, suspiciously gesturing towards the two spies, who had by now gently edged closer to where we would eventually rendezvous outside the court. Lance pointed a way forward. With eyebrows and suspicions raised even further, we walked in a gang towards the French quarter. After searching for a small bar that held only a few more than just us, we settled comfortably inside *Les Deux Escargots* and ordered coffee. Once inside there wasn't sufficient room or interest for Spooner or Melville to follow us. Why should they anyway? We weren't hiding anything, were we?

'What the fuck's going on, Doug?'

'Dessy!' shouted Suzanne reprimanding her husband whilst Dil laughed out loud.

'Oh, sorry Sissy, what's going down, man?' he corrected himself and looked to his wife for approval. She nodded.

'Listen, we want you to understand something. We . . . that's Lance, Nick and I,' I told them. 'We've received some information that might be of great interest in the lawsuit. Unfortunately, it's a little sensitive. We dare not tell you just yet.' I tried to be as convincing and sincere as I could but it hadn't worked.

'Cut the bull, man. What you up to?' Des wanted to know and judging by the collection of nodding heads all around the table it would be difficult not to at least give them a morsel of what we knew. I told them about the tape, which held a conversation between, Hammond, Isaacs and others. They were discussing Desmond's dismissal and perhaps there might be something that was racist in what might have been said. It was the biggest lie I had ever told. It contained dynamite never alone racist remarks. I further told them that the tape needed to be authenticated and that gave me the opportunity to explain the presence of Joe Mayo, who was on his way down from New York to talk to me and Nick. We had to tell the Judge because, in our opinion, the case was lost and he was calling in his cards. Desmond was ranting and raving at the news, but the facts were the facts, nothing we could do about it I told him. We were sure that today was going to be the last day. We even doubted that the jury was going to be asked to deliberate; Hastings was simply going to wrap it up. They seemed stunned at what I had just said and turned to Lance to confirm what I was

Peter Nutty

saying was true. Lance just nodded, but his gaze never left the table. It was an embarrassing admission as far as he was concerned, especially at this moment because, as I suddenly realized, the others honestly thought we were on top and winning the case! I was amazed by their innocence. They were so gullible, or were Lance and I that convincing? At that moment the door sprung open and a familiar voiced piped up.

'Where the fuck have you lot been? I've looked . . . .'

'Nick!'

'Oh! Sorry Suzanne.' Nicks' young, freckled face reddened with embarrassment. 'I've been looking for you guys,' he said politely, patting Suzanne on the head like a schoolgirl. She just shook her head in mild disgust.

'How'd you find us?' asked Ant, the younger of the Blues Brothers.

'I'm a newspaperman, remember? I'm trained for this kind of stuff,' replied Nick sarcastically.

'We know about the tape,' said Chuck spitefully and the older Blue chuckled in his usual manner. I clenched my teeth and shook my head as Nick looked toward me in disbelief.

'Oh yeah, what tape is that then, Doug?' he emphasized my name in a raised voice which was coupled with an angry look. I told Nick everything, about what happened shortly after we met earlier that morning, about the Judge wanting to end the case, and what we'd said to him in an attempt to stall things. We told him about His Honors reaction and eventually what I had told the team sat around us at that very moment. I winked and he realized that it was the abridged version. He accepted the facts as I had presented them. He ordered coffee and smiled at all of us before holding out his hands in self-defense. I was a little more relaxed at the gesture.

* * *

The blue and white patrol car was parked outside the Hilton hotel and Doylee already had the engine running as we approached. I felt like a criminal as the tourist's turned to see what was going down. Stares turned to small talk and gossip turned to pointed fingers and disgust. We were criminals that had been caught up to no good and now we were going to jail. I half-expected some of them to start spitting at us as we sat in the back of the Sheriff's car waiting our turn to exit the ramp. It was worth it, Doylee gave a quick tweak of the siren and waiting cars parted with unbelievable haste. I found it hard to believe that there'd been a queue there in the first place as we sped down Canal towards the airport. We

The Last Hangman

would experience the sensation four times more as we approached slow moving traffic. It was nice to be somebody. I even felt like giving some of the more disgruntled drivers the bird as Doylee gunned the car along the freeway.

At the airport we met two people. One person we had expected to see, the other we had not. Joe Mayo was greeted by Nick and introduced to Lance and me. Sheriff Doylee's presence was further explained to the newspaperman who tried to object but was soon convinced otherwise by Doylee when told that his objections would be reported to His Honor. The second person we met did not need any introductions, we all knew him well. Not even a warning from Doylee and then supposedly the Judge was going to stop Desmond from coming with us. He'd taken a taxi from the hotel to the airport and now he was signed in as one of the few who would listen to the tape. I couldn't say anything to the contrary. It was all about Desmond, we had somehow forgotten about the lawsuit. The contents of the tape had overridden whatever it was we were trying to prove and we had to remind ourselves that the conversation was about Desmond for goodness sake, how could we stop him from listening to the tape? Lance and the newspapermen travelled in style with Doylee. I travelled back to the court in a taxi with Desmond constantly bitching in my ear. I paid the fare as usual.

* * *

For a whole hour and a quarter we sat stunned. We listened to the taped conversation and began to put together the picture as it unfolded before us. The introductions and small talk took up only ten minutes. Then, according to the conversation, what started out as a friendly enough meeting soon became heated. It then quickly turned into a full-scale argument and pretty soon things began to get ugly. At some stage, at least one person was asked to leave the room following the hostile discussion. Talk of some shady dealings in Nigeria was then added to the agenda and they were definitely not for Desmond's ear. Events in Nigeria were mostly laid bare, included accusations of murder, which had everybody's interest. Desmond's problem was put on the back burner for a while.

The first hearing was in complete silence and it was evident our audience had been treated to something extraordinary. The second sitting was at the request of Judge Hastings. It was continuously interrupted by strong bouts of coughing, which saw Lance being excused to go to the bathroom and get some fresh air on several occasions. Our lawyer seemed to be affected the most by what we'd heard. The third play would require brief notes, which were to be made by all present, including Desmond and me—who had the least experience of doing such things. Who owned the voices on the tape? Who were they referring to? What had happened and to whom? A who's who of Advanced Strategic Energy Inc session was on the cards. The tape was replayed at the same time it was being copied for obvious reasons.

We'd also established without difficulty that the meeting was definitely held to discuss the dismissal of one, Desmond Haynes. For his part, Desmond was soon able to identify all of those present bar one—we referred to him as Mr. X. The juicy part started when Richard Hammond, who'd been named in person on the tape, suggested a charge of gross negligence and Jeremy Isaacs, the human relation's VP who endorsed his dismissal, agreed to it. This was confirmed by the accused man sat next to me. Eamon Darcy, another VP was not so convinced about the whole affair. He argued that Haynes could sue for unfair dismissal. Hammond responded by asking Darcy if he had a better way of getting rid of Haynes? He sounded frustrated. Why were they pussyfooting around anyway, he asked? We should do a, *Jericho*, was one suggestion, but it was difficult to say who had spoke, it sounded a lot like Hammond. It made no sense to us and it seemed to make little sense to them judging by their muted response. Nobody seemed to have anything better to offer and so they continued arguing.

One by one they started to shout louder until in the end a point of order was needed. It came in the form of Eamon Darcy who finally managed to quell them down with his powerful voice. Darcy seemed the brightest. He was aware of the possibilities of civil lawsuits—the CEO would not like it, we heard him say. His Irish accent made him quite distinguishable from the rest. There had to be a better way. Several less convincing ideas were proposed, all were without substance but still Darcy and Mr. X—Desmond could not identify him since he spoke very little, were not satisfied. At this point, the debate once again became hostile. We could hear Hammond raising his voice and half-shouting at Darcy. *There were other ways they could get rid of the interfering nigger*, he mocked. Mr. X spoke against the language being used. He objected to Desmond being called a nigger. Furthermore, why was this man interfering? What had he done? What were we—I took that to mean Advanced Strategic Energy—hiding?

Desmond had an ally in the room. It was obvious that Mr. X did not fully know all the facts. There was a hidden agenda and for that reason, they seemed to talk in code. He knew little if anything of what had happened or what was going to happen. The conspiracy was beginning to unfold as we listened. Isaacs asked Mr. X to leave the room. There were some things they needed to discuss at a senior level. There was a ruffle and the tape went quite. It was as if it was turned off or muted in some way. Soon enough, however, normal sound returned. We didn't know it at the time but Gerald Sinclair had actually made to put on his jacket when asked to leave the room but thought better of it. Unaware that the tape was there and still running, the remaining occupants carried on talking about some pretty bad goings on. The contents were such that it would not only shock us, it would eventually shock the whole of America and beyond!

Chapter 31

THE OTHER SIDE OF THE bed seemed snug and warmer, and that was reason enough to pull the sheets over his naked body and edge to where the girl lay in a similar state of undress. Even in his drugged state, Hammond part-sensed the bedclothes on the prostitute's side were moist. That could mean only one thing!

'Dirty fucking bitch!' he mouthed angrily, quickly backing away from her. *He'd teach her not to piss the bed, fucking whore*! He leaned forward and swiped at the girl with the back of his hand. It crashed into the pillow and even that was wet he noticed. He tried to focus and took another swing, lower down this time, again no contact.

'Don't fuck with me, you bitch!' he shouted at her. Raising his body, and still swaying from the drugs, he readied himself to pull the blankets completely off her body. He needed to get eye contact with his target—her face. The bed was soaking and his left hand made a squelching sound on the sheets and mattress as he raised himself up on one arm. Hammond went berserk at this.

'I'll teach you to piss the bed you little slut!' he shouted at her before pulling the sheets off completely. At first it did not register. Something just didn't add up. His eyes rolled and his head spun. The combination of those sensations sent the room swirling around in his mind. With every revolution he saw her body lying next to him, even if only for a millisecond.

'Shit! What the . . . ?' His head still rocked, but the spinning sensation was slower and then eventually stopped. He focused the best he could and, slowly but surely, stiffened like a poker.

'No, no, it can't be. Please no!' His whole nervous system collapsed. Hammond was hysterical. He could not believe what he was seeing. A figure stood in the far corner of the poorly lit room, the slight movement caught his eye. He still couldn't focus properly. His eyes darted from one thing to the other, to the body on the bed and then to the movement he'd noticed across the room. The headless corpse of the girl lying beside him was too much to handle and he passed out.

* * *

There was a stage in the taped conversation when we all knew that Desmond had indeed won his lawsuit. It would be a mammoth victory judging by the racist remarks made by senior executives of the company; almost every other word was, *nigger,* or *coon,* or some other derogatory name. The tape was dynamite. It was everything Joe Mayo had promised and more. Two of the four speakers were Vice-Presidents of the company. We were sickened by what they were calling Desmond and it was not all because of the color of his skin. There was more to it than that. We could clearly hear Hammond telling those present that they'd be better off hanging Desmond; *they owed it to society,* he said. Our Jamaican friend showed no emotion, but inside he must have been really minced up. To be a fly on the wall when you are the subject of such hatred must have been devastating for him.

The alleged murders in Nigeria were still confusing since all the details had not emerged during the discussion. But the words murder or murders were mentioned several times. Hammond was definitely involved; he was without doubt the craziest of them all. He was blamed for paying, *a fucking crazy murderer?* Isaacs made those allegations pretty soon after Gerald Sinclair had left the room. It was difficult to say anything about the others. They were all involved with the conspiracy that's for sure, but more proof was needed I assumed. Nigeria would be a hard nut to crack. Finally, the conversation ended and the tape was stopped.

The overall picture was shocking. The whole episode had painted quite a gruesome scene. It was obvious that Hammond had travelled to Nigeria to meet somebody—who, we did not know. It was more than probably an oil-related issue. During his visit, *a fucking crazy Frenchman had murdered some people,* as Isaacs had so elegantly put it. Hammond defended these actions and it seemed from the subsequent allegations that he might have been the cause of it? There was a heated debate about somebody double-crossing somebody else, but it made no sense. The word, *murder* and, *mercenary* was mentioned a few more times. Exactly who had been murdered was again not so clear apart from several clues which mentioned the Ijaw Youth Council and a couple of Nigerians, whoever they were?

Then the real reason for wanting to dismiss Desmond rose to the surface. He'd been asking too many questions to the Nigerian government—it did not go into detail. Hammond had informed them all that if he (Desmond) continued they would be in serious trouble. His exact phrase was . . . *we'd all be up shit creek!* Darcy endorsed what Hammond had said. He'd received a telephone call from the Nigerian Embassy in the US asking them to politely, *sort it out*. Politicians from both sides were becoming anxious. We interpreted that to mean the US and Nigerian officials. After a long debate of how they could bribe him (we again took that to mean, Desmond), or pay him off somehow to keep his mouth shut, they eventually agreed upon the original proposal. Haynes would be sacked for gross misconduct. They had their reason when the operation in California went wrong, although nobody in the room knew a damn thing about operating a refinery, or anything else remotely connected to that part of their business. Hammond simply jumped at the chance to be part of Desmond's dismissal; he wanted to be seen to be doing the right thing in the eyes of the others. They'd nail the *nigger* on a technical matter then, simple as that said Darcy reminding them that all other proposals were too risky. They had the best lawyers and the worse that could happen would be an out-of-court-settlement, he argued. Isaacs, for once, supported him. He strongly disagreed to any involvement from Hammond, but that only brought about another round of hostilities from the wild man. Hammond was adamant, he wasn't interested in, *nailing the nigger* on a technicality, he wanted to, *nail him to a cross*, he interjected and again ranted on and on wanting to go *the Jericho route* but we didn't know what *the Jericho route* meant at that precise moment!

Before going into detail about anything else on the tape the Judge was keen to learn what exactly it was that required an answer from the Nigerian government and turned to face our friend. Desmond looked back at him. His face was saddened by what he'd heard. For the next few minutes, Des struggled to give the answers as tears began to well in his eyes. Once again he explained the few details he'd told us the very first day we met in Lances' office. It was no big deal then. He had merely enquired about the tragic death of a friend. It had now become obvious that Brandt Allto had died in a more savage way than first reported. Drowning would have been a luxury compared to what must have happened. His friend had been murdered he said, the tears finally running down his cheeks. That's what they were trying to hide he told us after slowly putting all the pieces into place. It was a conspiracy and Desmond had sensed it from the very beginning. But why had they murdered him? What was he doing there? He wasn't a threat to anyone!

Judge Hastings had listened to Desmond's short story, there was very little to tell. It had the desired effect nonetheless and, ably assisted by several clerks, he swiftly issued warrants for the arrest of Messrs., Hammond, Darcy and Isaacs. The ever-efficient Sgt. Doylee had soon contacted the various precincts in New York and the ball was set rolling. It would take a while to unravel the whole thing. Charges would be brought, of that there was no doubt. Murder would present itself high on the agenda but exactly who the murderers were was still not clear. Conspiracy to murder would be hard to prove if the so-called *crazy Frenchman* was acting alone. Corruption and aiding & abetting murder was seemingly a formality. The Judge would enjoy talking to John Arnold and his attorney Vance Dinger about that little matter, assuming he knew about it that is. The fourth man in the tape, Mr. X—the one who was ordered from the room—would also be identified and brought in for questioning as soon as the others were in custody. The Judge was sure of that; little did they know, he was dead. Gerald Sinclair pulled the plug on his life as soon as the tape was sent.

'Okay, now what do we do?' I broke the ice. The morning had been full of surprises and shocks. Now there was a lull from the preceding chaos.

'Kinda anticlimax, ain't it?' Desmond was full of anger and stood looking out through the window with bloodshot eyes. The opening was small and his body blocked most of the suns attempt to brighten the dimly lit room. There was no reply from any of us. 'Perhaps we should drink Champagne?' he gestured, half-hearted. Again, nobody took him serious so nobody replied. We left him alone, deep in thought. Lance was not himself either. He had consistently left the room several times using one excuse after another. Nobody cared too much; we had other things on our minds. But for now it seemed the grey-haired attorney was busy outlining the finale to the case in his mind. By more luck than judgment he'd just won what would eventually turn out to be a massive lawsuit. I could see dollar signs in the air; we all could. The final announcement too would be extraordinary spectacular when it came. What would he say? When would he say it? And whom would he say it to?

Nick was busy with his laptop. He too had been a winner. He had a scoop when the Judge finally gave permission to publish. It would be an exclusive. Who would have believed it? No doubt his career was made after this, assuming Mayo didn't take all the glory that is.

Judge, Hastings retired to a backroom. He had already contacted the DA and the New Orleans Police Commissioner. They were to attend a meeting that afternoon. They'd both agreed to cancel previous engagements—they had no choice. A full team of detectives would be employed to investigate the alleged murders and corruption and whatever else might turn up. He also wanted to talk to Briggs, immediately. It was all happening at speed.

Nobody present inside the room was to utter even the slightest word of what they'd just heard on the tape, Judges' orders. We were sworn to secrecy. Damn shame, I thought to myself. He had just dampened the excitement. All I wanted to do was phone Cheryl at the hotel and tell her the outcome. She would be as shocked as we had been—and upset; unbeknown to her she'd now conspired with an alleged conspirator to murder. My predicament was growing by the hour. Sooner or later I would have to come clean about Cheryl's' relationship with Isaacs. Fuck that son-of-a-bitch! I put my head in the sand for a while longer. Judges' orders or not, I'd already decided to tell Cheryl. I had to.

* * *

Briggs was found in an expensive restaurant halfway down Bourbon. He had a plateful of oysters in front of him and sipped from a chilled champagne flute when he was asked by two police officers to accompany them to the Judge's chambers.

'Hold on a second, officer,' he replied, playfully holding up two arms in all innocence. 'Here, help yourselves to a few oysters,' he offered relaxing back in his cane chair as he spoke. He smiled as he held his hand out, encouraging the law enforcers to dig in. 'Better put a coupla more bottles of Moet on ice, Rialto, it looks like there's going to be a party tonight,' he shouted over his shoulder. Rialto the waiter smiled and Briggs laughed along with his pose, Spooner and Melville, who'd already prematurely started to congratulate their man. It was obvious to all three lawyers what the old man wanted. He'd had enough of the bullshit from Lance and the rest of us. Not before time too. He'd even sent a car to pick him up! It was judgment day.

They were in a false sense of security. The well wishes were cut short when one of the policemen grabbed Briggs' arm, shoved it up behind his back so that the highly paid lawyer had to forcibly stand, before marching him swiftly out of the door. It wasn't what the trio was expecting at all!

'Straight away,' the Judge had said, the broad shouldered officer reminded him. Spooner started to get up in protest but was shoved back into his seat by officer number two as he followed his colleague through the door. Melville, just coming back into the room after taking a leak and wondering what the hell was going on, jumped in immediately and tried hard to stop JB being marched unceremoniously through the door and into a waiting police car. When Briggs was eventually carted away, another two officers appeared from nowhere and had Melville cuffed too in no time at all. He was also marched unceremoniously towards the back of a blue and white police car to be charged with interfering in an arrest, or some other trumped-up charge to that affect. The officers would radio the desk sergeant to see what technicality they could get him on; it would probably be wasting police time! Briggs arrest went practically unnoticed, but Melville was putting up a struggle, shouting obscenities and threatening legal action all in the same breath. The scene stopped several shoppers dead in their tracks. Other diners sitting outside the many first floor balconies and terraces along Bourbon were also watching intently from close range.

'Seems they're arresting a lot of white, smartly dressed, dudes these days. Why'd police leaving us black folk alone all of a sudden?' shouted a balding black man watching Melville being marched past him. Somewhere further down the road a saxophone stopped playing in mid-tune. The saxophonist had never seen a white man being treated in the same way as his kind! He'd just committed a felony and justice was being done right in front of their very eyes, it was a first! Rialto removed the recently stocked bottles of champagne from the fridge and put them back in the cellar, he could wait a while longer. Besides, *there'd be another case soon*, he supposed to Arthur, the other black waiter. *They'll soon get back to arresting us blacks like they're paid to do*, he told him!

* * *

The only thing that went in his favor was the fact he was naked at the time. His clothes were spared from being stained. The bedclothes were soaked with blood, which had poured from the prostitute's decapitated body and completely covered one side of his pale-looking, baggy skin. He'd only passed out for seconds, but it was enough for the stranger to disappear. It was a small room and there were no hiding places, the stranger was nowhere to be seen. It was like a nightmare. He breathed heavy and his heart pounded. The room seemed to have a pulse of its own too. Traumatized from seeing a mutilated body for the second time—he still hadn't recovered from Nigeria, Hammond swayed heavily but somehow managed to gather his belongings. He also somehow managed to shower, get dressed and in full view of other guests and hotel staff, ran for his life from the hotel room, through the small lobby and into the masses. Manhattan seemed a small place all of a sudden; there was nowhere to hide when you really wanted to! He slowed upon reaching the subway. He was distraught and full of fear and completely out of breath. For the next twenty minutes his mind was tormented by the decision about whether or not he should jump under the train en-route to Queens and end it all there and then? In the end he decided not to, life was too precious, even for a down and out junky like him!

Chapter 32

JB started to protest to the Judge. The way he was manhandled by the law enforcing officers was disgraceful. It was nothing compared to the way His Honor would treat him. To stop all the unnecessary moaning the Judge grabbed him under the chin with a grip that screwed his cheeks almost together and simply told him, *to shut the fuck up.* This he did. Hastings was becoming more miserable by the minute thought Briggs. It was no use arguing any longer, he was used to being abused by Old Misery guts. Then, the minute Briggs was silenced, the old man squeezed his cheeks even harder together so that his face contorted and his eyes nearly bulged out of the sockets. Sure that Briggs was well and truly in pain, the Judge began to speak. He was to summons Dinger, he was told. No matter where he was, what he was doing, who he was with. The *little shit* was to be in his chambers that afternoon. Failure would result in his arrest. Got it? It never dawned on the Judge that they were in New York, over a couple of thousand miles away!

JB had no real way of acknowledging his willingness to comply with the request under the circumstances, but he somehow managed to nod his head ever so slightly. Upon seeing that minute movement, His Honor let go his grip and JB stepped back in some discomfort. His face bore the reddened blemishes of Hastings restraint. Tomorrow he would bruise. Respect was not going to present itself. Black or white, the Judge would have dished out the same treatment. Like ASEI, he hadn't any racial policy's either; he didn't need them since he abused everybody fair and square!

'What do I tell my client, Your Honor?' JB asked politely, still rubbing his bruised face and then wondered if he should have just kept his mouth shut.

'Oh, I shouldn't worry about ASEI,' said the Judge, smiling. 'I believe the CEO is on his way as we speak.'

'He'll need legal representation until Mr. Dinger arrives,' reasoned Briggs. 'I'll hang around in case he needs me,' he told the Judge, loyal to the last.

'I wouldn't hold your breath, *boy*. I ain't in too good a mood with your profession at this moment in time. I might do something silly,' he mocked. 'Come to think of it, that's where Dinger could come in handy! I might just get a little stupid and have some fun with Dinger now. What d'ya say, *son*?' he suggested, just for kicks.

JB nearly, *shit in his pants*, as Desmond would say. He had the sense not to ask why. He would immediately get on the blower to Cranton's senior associate who in turn, *would shit his pants*, before contacting Lorne Cranton in person. He would have to keep him briefed. About what, he couldn't say? He hadn't the slightest idea about the tape. JB left muttering obscenities at the Judge; under his breath. What the fuck had gone wrong? He had the case in the bag, what the fuck's going on? He was lost for words and thumped the walls as he walked down the corridor.

'Fucking Judge should be on trial for professional hatred, abuse and actual bodily harm,' he cussed as he went along his way.

Meanwhile the Judge was on a roll. He picked up the phone and ordered Doylee to get his ass in there. The burly sergeant entered without knocking, it was a first and there was no reprimand . . . for now. The place was a hive of activity. His Honor, Debra, Clint, and a number of lesser-favored clerks were sat in front of a flip chart. It was covered with disorderly notes of some description and the scribbling was in different colors. They were bouncing ideas from all angles and the scribbling got worse. The Judge turned to Doylee the moment he set eyes on him.

'Issue a warrant for John Arnold' he ordered the sergeant after asking Debra to look up the CEO's name and address on the ASEI website. To the Judge, it was inconceivable that the top man didn't know what was going on in all of this 'It'd be nice if we get him on the stand squealing like a pig,' he said, sounding like one of the smart-ass lawyers he constantly loathed. 'I'll sign it as soon as you're ready.'

'Yes sir. What's the warrant for, Your Honor?' asked the policeman who thought he was immune from punishment or reprimand now Old Misery had other things on his mind. His Honor smiled, walked over to the unsuspecting officer, grabbed his earlobe and twisted it, bringing Doylee's face closer so that his ear was merely a few millimeters from the Judge's mouth. He whispered playfully.

The Last Hangman

'Why don't we arrest him for not having a dog license?' he spat out. Doylee winced as the Judge twisted the lobe almost full circle. Once again he was confused as the Judge continued his torture. 'What the fuck do we normally issue a warrant for when somebody has been murdered?' he rasped. The second he let go of his ear Doylee was gone, rubbing his lobe as he scarpered out of the room. The Judge sat down with a huge grin. He had become forty years younger in an instant. Murder did that to some folk.

* * *

Vance Dinger almost played his part to perfection, coming to within a whisker of *shitting his pants*. JB was dismissed over the phone for not being able to give him the details. How could he call Lorne about events that were unfolding without the detail? They're lawyers for goodness sake! They had a right to ask. JB had no balls he decided, which justified the dismissal in his book. Briggs was history. The ex-golden boy simply stood motionless in the hall of the New Orleans Parish, Court, gob smacked and still holding the dead phone. He was stunned into silence at Dingers reaction. He was jobless too!

* * *

Lorne's first response was one of obvious disbelief. They were lawyers, he told Dinger! The best money can buy and they didn't know why they were being summoned to the Judges' chambers? And not with any old client, ASEI were their best client! What could he tell Arnold? Jesus! Why hadn't Dinger handled this personally, he asked his senior associate? Why leave some green-assed kid to handle such a high profile case, what type of stunt was he trying to pull? Lorne went on and on and Dinger had no option but to listen. The whole argument was out of proportion. Lorne Cranton hung up after instructing Dinger to pull his finger out and report back the instant he knew something. Meanwhile, he would phone the Judge personally and see what it was that was eating him up. Then he would phone John Arnold. Maybe he would have an explanation by then. He had no idea Arnold was wanted by the police at that moment in time.

* * *

Jeremy Isaacs took the call from Dinger at one minute to midday. At precisely midday he was covered in sweat and being sick in the toilet. The phone was left hanging for the next few moments whilst Dinger talked to himself.

'Jeremy!' No reply. 'Jeremy! You okay?' Nothing, Dinger shook his head and hung up. His bags were packed by twelve fifteen and Isaacs left the hunting lodge shortly after making an urgent transatlantic phone-call. The person he had tried to contact wasn't there but a young lad with a pucker-sounding Surrey accent informed him of her whereabouts the moment he answered her phone. At least he had a contact address for her and as luck would have it, it was in the US. Dinger had no details of the problem, which infuriated the shit out of him, but Isaacs knew what the undertones were all about. Home was out of bounds, he would take no chances. He drove down the short drive through dense woods that led onto a dirt track that connected to the main highway. He took a left and headed south towards New Jersey and onwards through the night. It was a long drive to New Orleans.

* * *

The hotel air conditioning was cranked up and the chilly climate was welcome. Cheryl appeared from the bathroom with her trademark smile and only a towel stood between her immaculately curved naked body and me. She was irresistible! Sex was scrubbed from her agenda as I told her about the tape. She cringed when I mentioned Isaacs.

'Are you sure it's him?'

'That's what Desmond says. He's pretty sure about it.'

'I can't believe it. Isaacs wouldn't commit murder!' she argued, seemingly convinced of his innocence, well, at least from murder but nothing else I hoped.

'I'm not saying he did. Nobody is suggesting that, but he's obviously part of the conspiracy.'

'What conspiracy? You can't make allegations like that!' she argued with her human relation's head on.

'You know what I'm on about,' I protested, becoming agitated at her reluctance to accept what I was insinuating and even more frustrated at her for defending Isaacs. 'Between them they're responsible for murdering some poor bastard out there. And Isaacs is part of it, I just know he is,' I told her, the jealousy gnawing away my insides, making it sound worse.

'But why the hell would he want to murder somebody in Nigeria? Why would anybody come to think of it?'

The Last Hangman

'He wouldn't,' I replied and then started to explain; Cheryl had tempered my earlier enthusiasm. 'Look it's a complicated story. I only know what I've heard on the tape but even the fringes of it smell rotten. It stinks.'

'Tell me then, go on!'

'I can't. Well . . . I can't fully. It was mostly jargon,' I said, note sure what I'd heard now.

'Jargon, uh!'

'Okay, okay . . . most of it was nonsense,' I said, quietly putting my arms up and immediately set about convincing myself of what I thought I knew.

'But you said Desmond had won his lawsuit?'

'Oh, yeah, for sure, Desmond is home and dry but there's more to it than that. C'mon, get dressed. We'll talk it over at Ruby's. I'm ravished.'

'Doug,' she replied. 'You're avoiding the question.'

'I'm not. I know enough to paint a dimly lit picture, that's all,' I eventually confessed and now entirely unsure of what I knew. 'But suppose I'm wrong?' I added in an attempt for her not to ask too much.

'That wouldn't surprise me!'

'At Ruby's,' I insisted for a second time. I wasn't going to get drawn.

'Okay, you can talk while we're eating,' she suggested.

I agreed. 'But for now, stop gabbing and get ready.' I stopped any further questions by covering her mouth with my right hand. She disappeared into the bedroom. 'Wear anything,' I shouted through the open door. I needed to get the hell out of this room. I had that strange feeling again. The relationship between Isaacs and Cheryl was somehow beginning to hurt.

* * *

Phillip Laxrois watched as the Mercedes drove by. Hammond was pathetic. It was obvious he was in hiding and going back to his residence would prove to be a big mistake; in fact it would prove fatal! He wouldn't have thought about the risk. It was so, so easy for the Frenchman. He would kill him sometime soon, but just as those thoughts were becoming a reality things quickly changed. Hammond never bothered to stop at the house and, from his vantage point, Laxrois suddenly knew why. He'd just seen the police knock down the door! What on earth had Hammond done that required the cops to batter his door down he wondered? He followed, unaware that his prey was actually running from a murder scene!

Peter Nutty

* * *

The door had already been repaired by the time Richard Hammond drove past for the second time later that evening. He would have to keep on driving. The law was on to him and now he was a wanted criminal being hunted from two corners; the cops who wanted him for murder and a mercenary who wanted revenge. Should he give himself up to the cops? It made sense. At least he would stay alive! It would have been small comfort if he knew that the cops actually wanted him for other reasons; those associated with the tape. It was unrelated but, nonetheless, just as serious. They hadn't been alerted about the fate of the prostitute yet!

* * *

'So, what's the big deal in Nigeria?' Cheryl asked, wasting little time. We'd hardly arrived at Ruby's and both she, and all too soon the waitress were on to me in a jiff. It was a two-pronged attack.

'Hi ya'll, my name's Wilma,' she said in a familiar-sounding, Texan drawl. 'And I'll be your host for tonight. Now let me just familiarize you with a few things. By the way, ya'll folks been here before?' a rather short, plump lady asked after a whirlwind intro. 'Would y'all like something to drink?' she continued at lightning speed before we could say anything. It seemed to me her questions didn't necessarily warrant an answer and instead, she threw two menu's down onto the table like Frisbee's. She then spent the next two minutes reciting the menu from memory. 'Tonight, we have . . .'

'Just order starters,' I shouted over to Cheryl after Wilma had almost reached the deserts. The waitress stopped reciting upon being rudely interrupted.

'. . . and cherry pie!' she said slowly, coming to a premature halt and throwing a real bad look in my direction.

'We'll order the main dish later,' I said sheepishly but with a big smile, trying to convince her that I wasn't really the rude imbecile she'd taken me for.

'Chicken wings and a Caesar salad,' said Cheryl without remembering a word she'd recited.

'Is that for ya'll?' asked Wilma rather miffed at the small amount. She was kitted out in Ruby's regulation striped shirt and ill-fitting, blue pants. She played the part.

'Yeah, we'll share thanks,' I said, keeping my smile and Wilma immediately dismissed my gesture with the contempt she thought it deserved; was she related to Old Misery I wondered?

'Any dres . . .'

'Ranch please!' Cheryl chirped up beating the young girl to it.

'Now,' she said slamming down her pad and pencil before looking back and for at us both. She was a pro and wasn't going to be sold short we suddenly realized. She then proceeded to speak slowly. 'Can . . . I get ya'll . . . anything to dri . . .'

'Two bottles of Bud light and a bottle of Chilean,' I replied quickly for fun, and also before Cheryl ordered mineral water. With that latest rebuff, Wilma turned on her heels, slapped her hands on her rounded waist and was off with a grunt when Cheryl called out to her.

'Number thirty-five, the Red, right there,' she hollered toward her holding up the wine list and pointing to the aforementioned number. Wilma gave an overly false smile and then curtsied! We both laughed as our server was gone with our order, which was supposed to be dispensed within less than two minutes according to the commercial.

'Now, c'mon . . . tell me,' she demanded eagerly whilst holding a chicken wing between her teeth.

'Oil . . . politics . . . civil unrest . . . Advanced Strategic Energy . . . other oil companies . . . . Do you want me to go on?'

'Murder!' she added.

'Murder, yes, I'd forgotten that one. Thank you for reminding me.'

'You're welcome, now get on with it! Tell me what you goddamn know,' ordered Cheryl. Spiced sauce ran down her chin as she spoke. I wiped her face clean, much to her annoyance as Wilma brought the beers. I took a sneak look at my watch to see if she'd made it before the allotted time. Wilma noticed what I'd done and quickly pointed to the food.

'The wings were on time, honey!' she told me, spitefully satisfied that Ruby's had once again walked the talk. 'The beers ain't part of the gimmick, cowboy' she then said acting rather smug. 'Unless you ain't happy with the service?' she added sizing me up and itching to slap my face at the thought. I smiled at her, sipped my beer and looked around the room looking for nobody in particular. Wilma got the message and left us to it. We watched her go through the same routine as she approached a small family the moment they'd entered the establishment. *Hi ya'll, my name's . . . .*

'Okay, this is the way I see it, but don't hold me to ransom if it's a little pear-shaped,' I warned her, taking no more notice of Wilma. 'Advanced Strategic Energy has a major interest in Nigeria. They've also just announced another large oil find. I'm not entirely sure where, but you've seen the press bulletins, right?' I asked her but didn't bother holding my breath waiting for a reply; not that there was one coming. She hadn't a clue. 'I reckon we—*we* meaning Advanced Strategic Energy,' I clarified for her benefit. 'Have obviously got caught up in the civil unrest there, I saw that when I was there. The Niger Delta provides a lot of the riches gained from oil exploration. The locals never benefit though. The Nairos' go straight into the coffers of the oil giants after the government has their cut. Greedy bastards the lot of them,' I told her talking from experience.

'Nairos?' questioned Cheryl.

'Money, it's the local currency.'

'Oh! Go on,' she then said leaning over the table to hear what I had to say. I noticed her eyes sparkled from a candle placed between us. It also flickered every time Wilma approached the table!

'The local villagers have had enough over the years. With a government that ignores their pleas for help they are getting their voices heard in other ways.'

'Protests?' she suggested sensibly.

'And a lot more,' I confirmed. 'Chaotic is not the word, but they have become more organized over the years. They have actually formed a political wing.'

'Good for them,' she said with a smile. 'I hope they shove it up em!' she added sounding a lot like Dillwyn.

'You're not on the fence then?' I sneered.

'Nope, I haven't even begun to tell you about the *human rights* side of me yet!' Cheryl kept her smile but I knew she wasn't joking.

'Pretty much the same throughout Africa if you ask me,' I went on to tell her.

'Who can blame them, Doug?'

'I know. Anyway, as I recall a Youth Movement was formed to get their concerns raised on a worldwide level. The young men are really pissed with it all and now they're causing havoc in the region and boy aren't they doing just that, big time!'

'Don't tell me. The oil companies don't like it, naturally! The villagers are triumphing and shit-face Isaacs starts a crusade and murders the fucking lot of em!'

'Close,' I nod again in part agreement and stunned at her choice of wording.

'Their poverty stricken that's for sure,' I tell her. 'The natives will do anything for money. They try desperately to give the oil companies more shit than they can deal with. It just escalates from there. Between the oilers and the government, the locals have been pretty hard done by. Nothing gets put back into the community! They're polluting the land, reaping the riches and getting away with it.'

'Corruption and illegal dealings must be rife, right?'

'Right,' I said, again in agreement. 'But why should we care? They're all losers in the end!' I said, not really meaning what I'd said; I was getting a bit tipsy!

'Who, the government or the oilers?' she asked.

'Both, and the tribesmen,' I added for good measure and without any serious thought. I finished the contents of my Bud. The candle flickered, alerting us to the presence of Wilma and soon another bottle of red Chilean was plonked on the table in front of us without a word being said. Lucky for us our waitress had taken the cork out but we were left to pour our own. Wilma had probably given up on the tip, but she needn't have. She'd get her fifteen percent. As for me, I was going to get drunk.

'They're all at it I bet,' said Cheryl continuing where we left off. We were indeed united in our condemnation of everyone in Nigeria. We had no idea of the pain and suffering that occurred, otherwise we would have sobered in an instant.

The wings and salad disappeared and two portions of Red Snapper, fries and vegetables followed. The red wine was consumed quickly and another ordered; Wilma seemed to cheer up the more I drank. Cheryl had a fair idea of how things were in Nigeria. We had talked for nearly two hours.

'The locals have had enough though!' I exclaimed and we were back to where we started. The conversation had gone full circle. I spoke with a slur that had developed with each glass of wine.

'They should blame the oilers for everything as far I'm concerned,' said Cheryl, spot on with her assessment.

'And the government,' I added. 'What about them?' I pressed, expecting a similar answer.

'They're just as bad.'

Peter Nutty

'They need the revenue, stupid!' I argued, playing with words and quickly turning it around. Just then a hand landed on my shoulder with force and a voice startled us both.

'So they do what the Welsh did in the sixties and seventies. Blow up a television transmitter or two!' The Welsh accent was a give-away. It was Dil. Our petty arguments stopped before I had the chance to talk about Isaacs. It would have to wait. Dil instantly began feeding Cheryl with his barroom banter; we had entertainment for the night.

By midnight we had drunk another two bottles of wine and we had put the world to rights, not to mention solving the mystery that had unfolded itself on the tape without mentioning any of that to Dil, of course. Isaacs had seen an opportunity to embezzle money from the company so that he could finance something or other in Nigeria and we all knew what that was! Desmond's inquisitiveness about Brandt Allto had cost him his job. The stress took nearly ten years off his life. It was as simple as that. We would have to go through the same jigsaw tomorrow, when we were sober. Being a drunk was becoming a habit. No sooner had I got rid of one drunk in Des, I had another ally in Cheryl. She was as drunk as Dil and me.

* * *

There had been a lot to do. The earlier message from Dinger was vague. Arrest warrants had been issued he eventually told him after talking to the Judge earlier, and that was enough of a concern. Like Isaacs, Arnold knew the score. He'd received several more updates throughout the morning; he'd suspected all along that this particular trial could unravel some of their clandestine habits in Nigeria. Arrangements were hastily made by the CEO for others to seek out Isaacs and Hammond and take the corrective action before the police found them; the order was to kill them in other words. He had no time for them, not even his son-in-law. If he vanished he'd consider it a good thing! He'd rather have a grieving daughter than spend time in the slammer! Eamon was less of a threat. He would keep quite when questioned by the police, and for that reason John spared his life. He had an inkling of how bad things were becoming. Along with the others, why else would a warrant be issued for his arrest? But he had no idea about the tape! But when Hastings finally got around to revealing the contents to him he would quickly learn that it *was* incriminating and, whilst he wasn't directly involved or privy to what was being said, he *was* an accomplice in the overall scheme of things. He knew damn well they'd sacked an innocent man, Desmond Haynes, on some trumped up charge of gross negligence.

In the meantime, he felt sorry for Eamon whom he respected for a number of reasons. He was a good man. He didn't deserve to go to jail. Not in his wildest dreams did the CEO expect events in Nigeria to turn out like they did. But they had and along with the other two, they had to sweep things under the carpet the best they could. Hammond was a liability. They knew that from the start, but he knew certain things; things that they'd rather forget. It would be unwise for anyone to disclose the detail, for everyone's sake. That was the deciding factor in his decision. Hammond could not be trusted with the police. He would crack under the pressure and rope them all in. Isaacs wouldn't be any more loyal.

And so the calls had been made. Difficult calls from private phone booths. The arrangements had already been put in place some months ago—Hammond's increasing instability and the fact Haynes' had been granted a hearing had prompted that. That little problem would be sorted and then forgotten. Afterwards, he double-checked the nigger story. Desmond Haynes was a good employee but a mistake had been made, which had caused the company to dispense with his services. They had a very high safety record and would not tolerate low standards, negligence, or gross misconduct. Safety was paramount!

Then he would need some time alone with the Judge and later some time alone with the nigger and then both of them together. If he was smart and settled out-of-court then their original offer would be trebled. Dinger would sort the detail. He was meticulous in his approach in order to ensure that he played no part. The chief exec' even looked in his personal diary where he recorded most of the events that had developed in Nigeria, decided they were incriminating and burnt the entire book on a log burning stove. There was no more to do; he'd covered his own tracks reasonably well. He couldn't afford any mistakes. He wasn't at all sure about the agenda Hastings had on the table for him, but he would be well prepared nevertheless. He knew this day would come!

As they drove to the airport, the information he was given following events in Nigeria was once again read out to him in some detail from diaries held only by his PA. Like Charlie, he was another *trusted* employee! The script related pretty much to what went on—with a few minor elements missing of course. It wouldn't take long to piece together the crime and then put names in the frame. They couldn't trace anything that happened in Nigeria to him, he was sure. He would deny everything. The last couple of hours had been busy and on top of it all he had an oil company to run. The latter made sure he was in big demand—he was a keynote after-dinner speaker at affluent political occasions on at least two evenings that week. John Arnold was dropped off at JFK by Charlie, who'd then spun the car around and made his way back to Barbara, who had a bottle of Bollinger's on ice beside the bed ready.

When he landed in New Orleans, Arnold was once again driven from the airport to the Orleans Parish District Court using a local limousine company. He had arrived with a clear conscience and was determined nobody was going to pop his cork. Barbara, in the meantime, had no clear conscience whatsoever. She'd already popped her cork, celebrating another night with Charlie whilst her husband played the big oilman!

Chapter 33

ILEFT THE HOTEL EARLIER THAN I previously wanted to after Des practically knocked the bedroom door down; he was in a serious mood. Where was I last night? Why didn't we have dinner with him and Suzanne? How come Dil got asked out and not him? How come I'm drinking too much all of a sudden? Was it him? Was it Suzanne? Why this? Why that? I ignored him. Desmond was living dangerously and I was hung over. I left Cheryl snug in bed with her bare backside once again on display after I'd thrown off the quilt earlier. The sight of her naked flesh eventually got Desmond's attention and with his eyes poking out of their sockets like trumpets, he quickly faltered into complete silence as he stared at Cheryl's assets.

'Mm, mm, mighty pretty,' he muttered to himself. I pulled the sheets over her and flicked a *V* sign towards him!

* * *

Apart from a federal agent, nobody else bothered to turn up for yesterday's meeting. The District Attorney had phoned to say he was out of town, a lame excuse according to Hastings. Despite false promises, it would take time to get back to New Orleans he argued. As for John Arnold, it didn't matter if he chartered an F15, he still wouldn't get there in time from New York, said Lorne Cranton after phoning around to get to the bottom of things. As for the Police Commissioner, he simply failed to turn up, there were no apologies or excuses given; besides, it was New Orleans and everybody had enough murder cases to solve without Hastings adding to the tally!

Apart from informing Cranton about the arrest warrants, the Judge ignored his request for more information and insisted they get their feeble asses inside *his* chambers, preferably under their own steam. Hastings preferred the modern day criminals to be more obliging when they'd been caught out. *They should do the right thing and turn themselves in*, he'd said on more than one occasion. Using State Troopers to run around arresting people wasn't cheap. *It would save the State a lot of tax dollars in the long run*, he argued. He was pissed off when there was a no-show.

'Was John Arnold really in New York?' he asked his secretary later in the day.

'Good morning Judge,' we said in unison as we entered the room. We were greeted with a huff-and-a-puff from Old Misery guts, which was no more than we expected.

'Is it?' snarled the most miserable man in the world—he even looked more miserable than usual. 'Sit down,' he ordered. 'Mary, get some coffee going here,' he snapped in her direction. What a difference in two days! The old man had not yet dressed and so we waited a little longer than we cared to sipping coffee served from a chrome plated jug and laying bets on the reasons for his ill temper. I had a double helping of very black coffee in no time at all.

Sheriff Doylee then knocked the door and entered all of a sudden without waiting for an answer. His actions had been par for the course yesterday, especially after the Judge gave him a rollicking every time he waited for an affirmative to enter. '*Didn't he know better than to keep pestering him with requests to enter the goddamn room?*' he snarled. '*They had work to get on with,*' he reminded Doylee. '*Just enter for goodness sake!*' he told him. That was yesterday, today was another day.

'Since when do you just fucking walk in to *my* chambers acting as if you're a fucking resident here, Doylee?' The Judge was donning his loose fitting tracksuit top as he came out of a room towards the back and caught the Sheriff doing the unthinkable.

'Ugh? Err . . . sorry Judge.' Doylee about turned and left, flabbergasted. Two seconds later there was a knock on the door. The Judge shook his head in amazement. He couldn't believe the Sheriff was partly responsible for law and order!

'Yes, who is it?' asked the Judge, grinning.

'It's Doylee, Your Honor.' The Judge burst into laughter.

The agenda was checked off from the previous day's list, which was poorly scribbled on the white flip chart near the table. The ever embarrassed Doylee had taken care of most tasks and it pleased Old Misery. He was, therefore, partly restored to his former status and continued to brief us with regard to overnight events. They had no idea where Hammond or Isaacs were? The FBI had agents keeping a watch at the last named address in New York. They were also on their way to other known addresses that were kept by the fugitives. Eamon Darcy had been arrested overnight in New York. They'd flown him down overnight and now he was in custody. He felt obliged to help in any way he could, they were told.

'Oh, he wants to help us, does he? That's nice of him!' said the Judge sarcastically. We just looked at each other and frowned. 'Have the Feds talked to him yet?' he asked.

'Not yet, waiting for his attorney to turn up. Then he'll cooperate,' explained Doylee.

'He'll cooperate, he hasn't any choice!' confirmed Misery. 'What about the others, any leads?'

'No Judge. We're working on it though,' added Doylee quickly before another reawakening came his way.

'Okay, what else you got?'

'We managed to get into Hammond's apartment,' Doylee told us—which meant they'd broken down the door. 'He's got some really shitty stuff in there,' he said, giving us a taster. 'Forensics is taking a look at it downtown as we speak.'

'What do they expect to find, jungle shit on the bottom of his shoes?' mocked Hastings. Another funny but nobody was willing to laugh. The Judge was unpredictable. Laugh and you're in the shit. Don't laugh and you're in the shit.

'We did find this though' Doylee then said, seriously ignoring the funny and handed him an old Polaroid photo taken from inside the house. The Judge took one look, shook his head and turned the photo face down on the table without giving anything away. It would serve no purpose to debate the image at that precise moment. We were kept in suspense. The Judge was not happy by what he saw. The picture would remain face down on the table for the time being he'd decided.

'Get Arnold in here. Now!' he ordered Mary Lloyd, who just happened to walk by holding some neatly bound briefs that required filing. She disappeared almost straight away.

'Doylee!'

'Yes, Your Honor.'

'Get me all you've got on the Klan!' Desmond and I suddenly began to take notice. Doylee didn't question what he was asked to do. Soon he was gone, gunning the black and white downtown with sirens wailing.

* * *

'Hold on!' she shouted happily upon hearing the knock on the door. Cheryl came quickly from the bathroom covered in a thick, white bathrobe and hummed along with MTV. She dried her hair with a large towel that practically drowned her as she sang along badly with the music. She was in love and in good spirits. When she finally answered the door a familiar face appeared. It had caught here unawares and she struggled to catch her breath.

'Hi Cheryl, how are you?'

'Jeremy!' she shrieked, her face twisted and to one side. 'What on earth are you doing here?' she asked nervously.

'I was going to ask you the same thing, Cheryl?' Isaacs was demeaning. Cheryl had to react quickly; it wasn't a social call. She panicked and tried to slam the door in his face but it was too late. There was no way she could stop the intruder and within seconds he was inside the room and holding her tight by one arm.

'Hey . . . steady now my little, English Rose.'

'Leave me alone, you bastard!' Cheryl struggled and flailed her arms in a vain bid to escape his clutches.

'My, you've changed, girl. You're friskier than I remember!'

'How did you know I was here? What do you want?' He let go of her and she withdrew further into the room rubbing her arm. She was petrified.

'Your friends in England, very obliging,' he said. 'Young man named, Scott. He'll go far,' he mocked. Cheryl remained quite. It wasn't Scott's fault he'd told him of her whereabouts. He wasn't to know; anyway it was hardly a secret. Most people knew she had come to New Orleans to meet Doug. You just couldn't keep a secret where they worked. 'I was just passing on my way through to Pensacola, I have a condo there,' said Isaacs still acting smug. 'And I couldn't drive by without saying hello. You'd never have forgiven me now, would you?' he smirked, menacingly. Cheryl kept staring at him, staying silent. Isaacs was wide-eyed and she knew he was dangerous.

'Now, Cheryl. Tell me why you're here?' he asked, scheming.

'Bullshit! Get the fuck out of her. Now!' she ordered. Jeremy laughed. He'd planned to have some fun. She was alone for the time being. Nobody would disturb them. He could do want he wanted to the young girl.

'Where's that dumb-fuck boyfriend of yours?' He looked nonchalantly in the mirror as he made the request. Cheryl remained silent. 'Where is he,

The Last Hangman

with Heycock? In the courtroom maybe, is that it? C'mon, Cheryl, tell me. Where is the nigger-lover?' Isaacs was agitated. He turned his face to one side. More light reflected off the mirror and he rubbed his fingers over the scab that partly covered the deep wounds just below his right eye. Surgery had taken just over three hours and was painful. The stitches would come out soon, but there would be a scar. Oh what he could do to Richard Hammond right now! She maintained her silence, carefully watching as he groomed himself, trying to think of a way out.

'Very well, have it your way,' said the intruder. He walked slowly towards her. Cheryl trembled and just stood still, her head bowed. Isaacs grabbed her by the chin, forcefully, and picked her head up. He tried to kiss her. She kept her lips shut as he smothered her with his mouth; it was wide open and he slobbered all over her. His breath smelled and he had not shaved for a couple of days and it hurt. For Cheryl it was a feeling of being raped, which was most likely to happen. She stood her ground. She was emotionally struck dumb and sobbed as Isaacs continued with his *fun*.

* * *

It was just too uncomfortable and a very humbling experience for John Arnold. He was not used to being talked to like this, by anyone. They were inside the Judge's chambers now. There were four of them in all. Federal agents, Daniel and Saunders paced the room, sometimes sitting on the edge of a small conference table used by the Judge for private debates. At other times they placed themselves on the side-arms of the comfortable leather chairs. The Judge sat behind his desk, quietly scowling at their abuse of his furniture. It was going to be a rough ride. The Polaroid had changed the feelings of those who asked the questions. The niceties had been dispensed with extremely quickly.

'What are your interests in Nigeria?' asked FBI agent Daniel. Arnold frowned as if he was trying to remember the detail before answering.

'We have interests in three large offshore fields,' he informed his interrogators. 'The Ambunda, Argonaut and Balaki. It's a forty-sixty split. The Nigerian government, in partnership with others, has the larger part and operates two of the fields, Ambunda and Balaki. We operate the third. We've also invested heavily in a medium-sized oil refinery and chemicals plant further inland, only that little venture has bitten us in the ass in the past, as you probably already know!'

'Go on,' urged Saunders. It was not the answer he was looking for. Both agents knew more about Advanced Strategic Energy than the CEO did. They knew about the business in Nigeria, the US, Far East, stock prices, trends, reserves, number of employees, you name it, they knew. The FBI had done their homework. Pity Hammond and Sinclair hadn't done the same.

'It's a troubled region, gentlemen. What would you like to know?' He held his arms out as if preparing to give a sermon and then quickly dropped them on his lap in submission when there were no takers. Arnold had turned the clocks on them.

'You're getting warmer,' said Saunders after a short wait. He kept looking to the floor waiting in anticipation for Arnold to provide more information. If it dried up, he would simply continue asking more difficult questions.

'Over the years, the Nigerian government has not played ball,' said Arnold finally, now playing by the rules. 'The economic climate and recent changes at the top have made it difficult for us to support some of the infrastructure needed to maintain the business strategy we agreed on when we first went in there,' he told them. The concern of being the CEO under such circumstances showed on his face. 'Oh, it's not all their fault though,' he conceded. 'We're just as bad. You've read the papers. Oil is a dirty word in Nigeria. We've learnt our lesson the hard way. Millions of dollars have been lost in one way or another, billions even.' His admission was met without surprise and he continued looking around the room, watching his audience for signs of forgiveness as he spoke, there was none. 'Exploration blocks that were earmarked for licensing have been held back, part of the government's tit-for-tat against us for not coming up with the goods,' he admitted.

'Get to the point,' ordered Daniel. The oilman ignored him, he wasn't going to be bullied by him or anybody else and carried on with what he was about to tell them before he was rudely interrupted.

'You cannot build a business on promises and false hopes gentlemen. The Nigerian government wants us there, they want the revenue we give them for their oil, and they want the spin off that we bring from working there. In a nutshell they need our dollars. The bottom line is this; they're not spending the revenue where it's needed most. Their people are being taken for a ride while government officials cream off whatever they can.'

'What do you mean?'

'It's not unlike the US. Some of the proceeds go missing in some way or another, so to speak. Most of the legitimate money gets ploughed back into Lagos. But that's not where the problem is. There's no oil in Lagos and they don't have to deal with the stench, pollution or the massive poverty and starvation!'

'So, what's the big deal?'

'The Niger Delta,' said Arnold. 'That's the big deal, as you call it. That's where most of the oil comes ashore, either being refined or turned into chemicals feedstock and that's where we come in. The villagers have been poorly treated though and over the years they've sort of revolted . . . and in a big way too. The Ijaw Youth Movement was formed, amongst others, and for some years now there's been chaos. It's been a headache, a lot of trouble as come our way.' The FBI knew about the Ijaw and the troubles caused by other factions. The Judge was on a learning curve and knew better than to butt in. Arnold talked for a further thirty minutes before the conversation took a turn.

'Okay, time to relax, Mr. Arnold,' said Daniel, who'd listened to enough spiel. There was nothing new coming their way and he had more pressing things to do other than take a boring geography lesson or oil seminar, or whatever else it was they'd been listening to. 'Get comfortable, I want you to listen to this,' he said, walking to the tape recorder. 'With your permission, Judge,' he asked. Old Misery nodded and the agent pressed *play*.

Chapter 34

I ARRIVED BACK AT THE HOTEL at around eleven-o-clock. There was little we could do at the court, the Judge would be busy—he had a host of planned meetings. He now had a murder inquiry to help conduct too. The sun was out and we had arranged a walk along the river. Later on that afternoon I wanted to drive across the other side of the water, might as well see what was about. Des and Suzanne got sidetracked with Dil, who wanted to show them this weird bar down Bourbon St. Suzanne had protested. It was too early in the morning she argued, but she lost the vote two to one. The Judge would call him on his mobile if needed. Lance too had disappeared with the Blues Brothers. I was on my own. The room was empty when I eventually got there. Nobody around . . . no note . . . nothing in fact; which was not that surprising, Cheryl was hanging around the hotel I told myself and then went walk-about trying to find her.

* * *

An hour and a quarter later John Arnold tried to act surprised. He hadn't a clue how all that clandestine shit was on a tape of all things, but he did know about most of its contents. The people in the room wouldn't know that though and that fact went in his favor he'd quickly decided. He was devastated, he told them, and quickly proceeded with the partly improvised charade he'd devised for this very occasion. When the guilt-ridden boss had finished claiming his profound regret at the disrespect shown to one of his employees, he held his head in his hands. He'd convinced them of that, and then went on to explain the real reason for Desmond's dismissal. It was actually for gross negligence, being held accountable and a whole list of nonsense, which on the face of it seemed too severe he now admitted. Desmond Haynes would of course get proper compensation and Hammond, Isaacs, and Darcy would be history he reassured all those in the room.

'Who was it?' asked the Judge not interested in his regret or about Desmond's dismissal. 'Who was in Nigeria and what happened?' he repeated the question. Arnold would have to think fast on his feet. He could in fact say anything. By the time he finished, Hammond wouldn't be around to say anything different. The CEO composed himself and spoke with a deep passion. It was a calculated risk but was plausible if he put a twist to one or two minor detail.

'June, ninety-eight was the start of a major turning point in the history of the Niger Delta,' he began. 'The locals had become extremely organized, especially the Ijaw Youth Movement. They seemed to know a lot more about what was going on than we, the oil companies believed. Yes, they were extremely well organized,' he repeated. 'The Nigerians thought there was infiltration from Gadaffi given the Libyan link or even worse, Iraq—they seemed to be that well briefed with all sorts of issues. Then, out of the blue we get to learn of, *Operation Climate Change*. Ever heard of it?' he asked. Nobody spoke. 'Then there was *Operation Acid Rain*,' he added knowing that he'd shouldered the brunt of that particular escapade. Again nobody spoke.

'It was extremely well organized and bloody and caught us by surprise. The Ijaw brought the oil industry to its knees practically overnight. The increased violence even took the unsuspecting government by surprise. We, along with several of the other majors even thought about pulling out! Anyway, we didn't—we had too much investment to lose. It wouldn't have looked good to the shareholders.' Arnold asked for a drink and Daniel handed him a less than warm, black coffee. The CEO took one sip and put the cup to one side.

'Following this latest outrage by the Ijaw Youth the government hit back by deploying tanks, warships and hundreds of troops in Beyelsa State. Soldiers scoured villages, searched cars at roadblocks, and tortured individuals in search of the organizers of the bloodied protests. They drew a blank, which further raised their suspicions about Gadaffi et al.' His audience listened intently. They were learning something new. 'Advanced Strategic Energy wasn't going to hang around and do nothing so we sought out the services of a senior member of the Environmental Activist Group. His brief was to meet the Ijaw and discuss dialogue towards their fight for fairness. It would help break the deadlock,' he said.

'Name?' asked Saunders taking notes.

'You'd need to talk to Richard Hammond, he organized it,' said Arnold remaining extremely calm. After all, he was partly telling the truth. It was

Hammond who'd come up with the original idea to infiltrate the Ijaw, but that lunatic had organized everything but what he was told to do, including hiring a mercenary to finalize matters once and for all.

'Where's Hammond now?' Saunders persisted.

'How should I know? We sacked him a couple of days ago. The guy's a junky. We don't employ junkies!'

'Is that the reason he was fired?' Saunders appeared suspicious and he wanted Arnold to know it. It was basic FBI training. Daniel his partner raised his brow and looked to the ceiling at such a feeble question.

'Yes, Advanced Strategic Energy has a drink and drugs policy, but you boys know that too,' he quipped.

'That's a little harsh isn't it? The program states that rehab would be needed rather than dismissing them,' speculated Saunders using is training technique to the full.

'That's for drink-related problems. We don't tolerate drugs,' he insisted. Saunders let it go.

'It seems you got a habit of sacking people, Mr. Arnold!' claimed Daniel, not knowing any real statistics.

'Only those who are *grossly negligent* or have *drug problems*,' emphasized the CEO smartly. He despised the FBI, especially the two agents that were now in the room with him.

The Judge stood, stretched his arms and slowly walked to the window. He rubbed his chin, which was becoming pretty much a trademark of his. He was deep in thought.

'What else happened in Nigeria?' he asked, keen to learn the detail.

'I don't know the final outcome, it's sketchy. I can only tell you what we wanted to do.'

'Go on,' he was instructed.

'Other companies were invited to help solve the situation but declined, apart from a well service supplies company based in Nigeria. They were hurting from the drop in sales. Two of their employees would meet Hammond and the guy from the Human Rights Activist group in Lagos. From there they would attempt to meet with the Ijaw—there were a number of known contacts who could arrange that. Hammond by then would have briefed the Human Rights twerp on what was required.'

'Twerp?' asked the Judge, seemingly offended by the remark.

'He wanted fifty grand for helping!'

'Oh, twerp, right.' Satisfied that the Judge agreed with his derogatory remark, Arnold continued with the story.

'The Nigerian businessmen would also fund the most important aspect of all, an agreed bribe of five hundred thousand dollars. It would be the main reason to stop the bloodied violence against, Advanced Strategic Energy,' he said, without the slightest bit of guilt. Everyone looked at him.

'Isn't that a bit self incriminating?' asked the Judge, which was most welcome in his book of course. Owning up to these types of crimes is what he'd been preaching about all these years, and now it had happened!

'Oh, c'mon, it happens all the time in these regions!' he said, shaking his head at the others in frustration. 'Don't tell me you're that naive?' Nobody said a word. 'It's the only way in these third world countries,' said the CEO. 'Why the fuck do you think the American economy is so strong in these parts of the world, technology?' he speculated. He was right of course and they knew it and so maintained their silence, self incriminating or not.

'What about the rest? All that stuff on the tape?' the Judge asked, interrupting once again—he was irritated. John Arnold was taking too long to get to the point.

'The Ijaw had been previously told a meeting with the government was out of the question until all violence and demonstrations against the oil companies ceased. So, such was the way of world politics, a meeting was hastily arranged through *the grapevine* with so-called *sympathizers* from within the Nigerian government. The twerp from The Human Rights group would be able to discuss their concerns and mediate between them and the government.' John Arnold could tell them what he wanted and up until now they believed him.

'So, what went wrong?' It was Daniel's turn to ask the questions.

'As far as I can gather, the twerp did exactly the opposite and helped them plan further protests against strategic oil stations within the region— those that would have the most economic impact. The protests should have been non-violent, but known factions of *The Movement* were encouraged to go that little bit further and the violence and bloodshed that inevitably followed provoked the military into retaliation. The Ijaw used this to get maximum media coverage whilst increasing their worldwide support for official negotiations with the government authorities. We'd shot ourselves in the foot, gentlemen,' he said, humbly. It was a fantastic performance. Who would disagree? It mirrored some parts of the tape, if you took in into another context! He finished with a flourish.

'The Nigerian government could not hold out much longer against the mounting world criticism, which was by now becoming increasingly louder through the voices of world-leading Human and Environmental Rights Activists!' he emphasized once again. 'Already there were many reports being released by the New York-based, Human Rights Watch appearing in International newspapers telling the world of, amongst a host of other things, the repressive response by the Nigerian military has only embittered the struggle. And they were right. For that reason the oil companies had decided on another way of dealing with the crisis and Advanced Strategic Energy were ostracized because of their actions. It would have cost us dearly but for the continued support we have shown towards the government and the tribe's people alike. We've stuffed a bunch of money in there. Now, I'm proud to say that ASEI has been very successful there ever since,' he said, finally sounding like the CEO of a major oil company.

'Stay in town, we'll be in touch,' gestured Daniel in his FBI way. The interview had finished. Misery got up.

'Tell Doylee where you're staying. Oh! And by the way,' said the Judge pausing for a second. 'You're not talking to the press on this one, Arnold!' he warned. Saunders then picked up the CEO's jacket, noticed the designer label on the inside—Geives & Hawks, Saville Row, London, and shrugged his shoulders before handing it to him. John Arnold put on his jacket and left the room. He knew little that would add to the contents of the tape—he'd convinced them of that. They had little to gain from him but they still had an ace up their sleeve though. Tonight John Arnold would sleep like a baby unaware that he was *in a sense of false security* as the Feds liked to call it. Tomorrow they would show him the picture taken from Richard Hammond's apartment.

Chapter 35

BARDSTOW ROAD WAS BUSY AND traffic was slow. The long drive through the Blue Ridge Mountains had brought him to the Blue Grass State. He liked Kentucky and it was far enough away. He would hold up in Louisville for a while. Another couple of blocks and he would take the next two left turns. Twenty-forty-two, Bill Hurst Drive would be more comfortable than he deserved. There had been plenty of time to think during the trip west. He had many bad memories—too many ill doings and the list had become incredibly long. Things were bad, but not all that bad. He planned to make amends. Most of his misdemeanors, however, he could do nothing about and that was tough, but there were others he could fix. Little things, like making it up with Moira, he could do that. He could do something for her, couldn't he? Why did he treat her so bad in the first place? She had carried him for years. Black wasn't too bad was it? He'd put it right. Hammond would get a job. Not in oil, something that involved working outdoors. Once he had some other form of income he'd work hard to put his past behind him. He would be a new man, putting right those things that needed to be put right. There were a few plus's too he reckoned. The first was his willingness to stay clean and he was determined to start straight away. No booze or drugs. He also promised he would get fitter. That would improve his health and sharpen his mental state of mind. He couldn't do a damn thing in his current state.

He eventually pulled into the drive of a pretty detached house. The place needed a lot of maintenance, which was why he'd chosen this particular house in the first place. The chores would keep him focused; keep him from feeding the drink and drugs frenzy he craved on a daily basis. The trunk was stacked with food of all sorts, mostly health foods of some kind or other. He had bought a whole fruit basket and three cases of spring water and struggled to carry the many plastic bags.

Whilst he unloaded the groceries he noticed a blue Cadillac slow down as it past the house before speeding up again. It frightened Hammond for a second or two, but he quickly composed himself and dismissed it. Nosy neighbors, which was fine by him. He wanted nosey neighbors but nobody else nosing around! Laxrois would soon become a distant memory. He'd never track him down to here. He completed his task, showered and then sat in the kitchen, shaking. The rehab wasn't going to be easy. He opened a tin of tuna and mixed in some mayonnaise. A jacket potato was already in the oven. He would eat and then retire to bed early. Tomorrow, the house would be cleaned and a list made of all repairs. *Marlen*, would be his home for the next few weeks, months, or years, who knows? That night, the same Cadillac slowed nearly to a halt as it passed. The driver had taken his time to look at the house, the detail was important.

* * *

The phone rang and my heart was in my mouth. I was back in the hotel room and hoped it was Cheryl phoning to say, *all's well*. She would apologize and tell me she'd been shopping in the French Quarter. I picked up the receiver.

'Doug, I need to talk to you straight away.' My heart sunk. It was Des and he was wound up.

'Can it wait?' I asked, tired of all the hassle.

'Ugh, ugh,' it was a negative. 'We need to talk. I'll come down,' said Des, hastily.

'Okay, I'll . . .' He hung up as I was in mid-sentence. Perhaps he's got some news of Cheryl's disappearance, I thought, trying somehow to be upbeat about the situation. Something was wrong. Terribly wrong, I could tell. Cheryl wouldn't just get up and go like that. She loved me, well I think she did? I'm sure she did. Something was definitely wrong and I hadn't got a clue what? Meanwhile, Desmond had broken all records getting between rooms three floors apart. The door was banged rather than knocked.

'Okay, okay. I'm coming,' I yelled at him and quickly opened the door before it ended up on the floor. Des marched in.

'You're not going to believe this, Doug!'

'Not more bad news!' I said, deflated, bracing myself.

'Yep, there sure is,' he told me quickly, still out of breath. Des wasn't going to beat about the bush telling me either.

'Remember the photo Doylee gave to Misery?'

The Last Hangman

'I do if it's the same one taken from Hammond's apartment,' I said in response.

'That's the one. Well I took a sneak look at it this afternoon.'

'How'd you manage to do that?' I asked in amazement. Des must have read the words, IDIOT, written across my face.

'It was in Doylee's office. The Judge left it there. They want the Feds to ID the people in it.'

'Oh, so you took a look! Nice one. Did Doylee mind you doing that?' I enquired whilst shaking my head. I knew what the Sheriffs' answer would be.

'He was next door filling out some transfer of evidence stuff. He didn't see me,' replied Desmond sharply, as if that was reason enough to go snooping. 'It's disgusting, Doug,' he said, too seriously to ignore him.

'Oh yeah, don't tell me. It's a picture of you!' I said sarcastically and not remotely wanting to get involved. I was annoyed at Desmond's stupidity. He'd won his lawsuit. Just leave the murder stuff to the others, I told him.

'It's not that easy, Doug,' he replied, ignoring my earlier remark. 'The thing is. The picture seems to be some kinda trophy.'

'Don't tell me, Hammond's dressed as the Fairy Godmother coming out of a cake at the Super Bowl,' I said, showing a deliberate lack of respect to what was being said.

'It's a group photograph with some friends,' he replied, again ignoring my sarcastic comments.

'Group photograph, that's hardly a fucking trophy—stupid!' My frustration at not knowing Cheryl's whereabouts was being taken out on one of my best friends and the minute I'd said it, I apologized. I felt like shit!

'You know what I mean. It was taken in black and white, a Polaroid, about twenty five, thirty years ago maybe,' he told me and not in the least bothered that I'd retaliated in the way I did. 'There's a gang of guys laughing and posing in front of two dead bodies. One woman, one man for what I could make out,' he continued, saddened at what he was saying.

'Jesus! Carry on,' I urged him and all of a sudden feeling like the dick I'd made myself out to be.

'Two black folk, they're hanging from a bridge,' muttered Desmond simply. With that said, he went quite, he was stunned into silence.

'They'd been hanged?' I asked, not sure I'd heard him correctly. 'Are you sure? Why did Hammond have it?' I asked rapidly without waiting for an answer. 'Don't tell me,' I then said, ready to take stab at it for some strange reason. 'He was in the photo?' I suggested as a long shot and not really meaning it. 'Jesus! He was wasn't he?' I shouted when I saw the look on Desmond's face the minute I thought I'd guessed right.

'How would I know, I've never seen the guy. Anyway, it's worse than that!' said Des looking back at me in shear disbelief.

'It can't be,' I doubted but in the back of my mind I knew otherwise. I probed a little further. 'What can be worse than that?' I asked with my anxiety increasing as I waited for the bad news, which was soon to come.

'We both know one of the people in the picture!' said Desmond startling us both.

* * *

Lance had been waiting in the cemetery for fifteen minutes. He drove there as soon as the man had contacted him on his mobile from a payphone located just off Canal and Bourbon. He was nervous and it showed; he constantly dabbed at his brow and wiped the moisture from his neck. It was overcast but still very humid. The sweat continued to run down his back and soon covered his entire upper body. His shirt smelled of the stuff. Soon it would rain and clear the air for a while. The respite wouldn't last, sooner rather than later the humidity would once again close in.

Not before time a black Lincoln came to a halt in the opposite parking lot. The hired chauffeur kept the engine idling. The passenger got out of the car, looked briefly around for a suitable place to talk in private and proceeded to walk towards a large statue of the Virgin Mary, which was located towards the top of the cemetery. It was nestled amongst many white, raised, tombstones that littered the graveyard. Lance walked a different route but rendezvoused with him almost immediately.

'It's gone a little wayward, John,' said Lance not bothering with any formal greetings.

'Why'd you fucking represent him, Lance?' asked the other man straight off the bat, angry. Lance remained silent, preferring instead to study the array of tombstones that jutted from the ground in all directions around them.

'I've no idea, John,' he eventually replied. 'I have no fucking idea,' he repeated, shrugging his shoulders, deflated. 'Stupid of me I know,' he said, all too humble. 'I never thought it would come to this, I suppose,' he conceded as if that would be sufficient an answer and good enough explanation for his ill judgment.

'Tell me you know who taped the conversation,' replied John Arnold quickly changing the subject. He'd completely ignored the feeble and stupid non-explanation Lance had given for representing Desmond. The CEO wasn't really expecting an answer from Lance regarding the owner of the tape, but nevertheless, he asked, he needed to know.

'I haven't a clue. Thought you could tell me,' he replied, lackluster.

'Haynes said anything?' he then asked bluntly.

'If he has, he hasn't told me,' replied Lance, genuinely wondering if Desmond had in fact known the recording artist but had refrained from telling him.

'You gotta put the lid on all of this shit, Lance. I want each and every tentacle cut off at the roots before it gets out of control. It's our worst nightmare,' he conceded knowing full well the implications that would soon engulf them.

'Tell me about it. Your boys were pretty fucking dumb too, ugh!' snapped Lance out of frustration whilst shaking his head slightly. Arnold acknowledged him with a nod; he knew who Lance was referring to.

'Can't argue with that but how the hell did Haynes manage to get a tape like that anyway?'

'Some newspaper guy from the New York Times . . . its dynamite!' the lawyer reminded him, which jolted the CEO. The fact that the NYT had supplied the details was the last thing he wanted. 'Simple enough to do of course, tape recorders are getting smaller all the time. Whoever it was simply hid the thing whilst they were talking. The guys around the table must have been pretty fucking stupid to let it happen though,' repeated Lance, again taking a swipe at the others.

'Okay, Lance. Leave it. I got the message,' replied Arnold sternly. He hadn't come here to take any nonsense from Lance, or anybody else for that matter!

'How'd it go with the Feds? They got anything on you?' asked the lawyer merely trying to make amends.

'Their pretty smart, won't take them long to put all this shit together,' he replied without waiting for Lance to agree. 'We've got to act fast.' He removed his sunglasses and squinted. There was no sun but even the overcast sky was still too bright to someone who spent most of his time in an office. He looked around a few times whilst he cleaned the lenses before continuing the discussion.

'I gave them the low down on Nigeria,' he said. 'The Ijaw, the riots, the loss of sales, they know the lot, Lance. They also know the blame lies fairly and squarely with Hammond and Isaacs,' he added; *his boys* as Lance referred to them. 'I knew nothing about it, of course,' he quickly conceded just in case Lance was about to run off and summons Doylee. 'It all ties up nice and neat and tidy. They don't suspect a fucking thing other than a couple of crooked oilmen making an illegal buck under the nose of their CEO,' he smirked confidently. 'The other matter is a little trickier though,' admitted Arnold. 'The racist comments made against the nigger will stick like shit to a blanket. But you already know that, don't you?' he said, quickly turning his head and again looking angrily towards Lance. Arnold was livid with his friend for representing Haynes, and a black man at that, how could he? The lawman merely confirmed the obvious. Lance nodded silently and that gave Arnold his cue to continue. 'It'll cost us. We'll go for treble the previous out-of-court offer. If he's got half a brain he'll take it,' he scoffed. 'Dinger will contact you with the arrangements. Just make sure the dumb fuck takes it,' he said, not wanting anymore fuck ups.

'Dinger!' replied Lance looking surprised. 'What's happened to Briggs?' he asked. Arnold smiled and said nothing. Lance tightened his lips as if to say, *don't bother telling me. I should have known anyway.*

'Don't screw up on it, Lance,' warned the CEO. He was conducting affairs as if the formalities were over and done with. Lance would have to say something to the contrary for the benefit of John. He knew his friend was being far too sure of himself.

'You know we wanted to talk with Jeremy and Richard, I guess?' he informed him before the CEO started another unrelated conversation.

'Too late, Lance' he replied quickly and solemnly.

'Too late, what do you mean, too late?' queried Lance, his suspicion raised.

'I've made the calls, Lance. Like I said . . . it's too late!' he confirmed and looked away. Lance breathed heavy, his chest expanded to drag in more air; he seemed to grow in stature. He didn't need John Arnold to explain his actions. He knew exactly what the so-called, *calls*, were all about.

'You fucking shit!' he snapped. 'We're supposed to be friends, John,' he argued, slightly gasping for breath now. He was struggling to hold back his temper. 'The five of us, fucking friends forever, we made a promise, remember?'

'C'mon, Lance, wise up. They've screwed us. Look at the fucking mess we're in? And it's all down to them.' He wouldn't hesitate to challenge

Lance further. He had every reason to do what he'd done and Lance knew it. It would serve no purpose for the remaining two to argue. *They needed each other*, he'd said several times.

'Forever, John. Forever,' repeated Lance getting louder, more irate. 'And forever, means forever. How can you break that promise, John? How? Tell me, c'mon, tell me?' Lance was becoming hysterical. Tears began to well in his bloodshot and baggy eyes. He was enraged at what was going on.

'Fucking cool it, Lance,' said Arnold hitting back at him forcefully, the anger was obvious. 'They deserve what's coming. Like you keep telling me, they're fucking stupid and we aren't going down with them. Do you think for one minute they'll keep their fucking mouths shut?' The CEO closed in on his friend. 'The Feds will bust their ass in minutes,' he said, second guessing the outcome. 'They'll have the dopey bastards singing in no time at all.' Arnold was on the attack. 'I've put a lot of time and effort in, Lance. We both have. I am not gonna stand by and support a couple of jerks all because of the past,' he tried to reason. 'No way, Lance. They're history, man,' he insisted and turned his back. He needed to cool down.

'And Eamon?' asked Lance pathetically. 'What's his fate, John?' Lance could hardly speak. Perhaps he didn't really want to know?

'He's inside, they arrested him this morning,' he replied still speaking with his back to him. It was his turn to look aimlessly at the rows of uneven tombstones precariously placed high off the ground. 'Eamon can be relied upon, Lance. He won't let us down. He'll be done for minor misdemeanors, but that's about it. Couple of months, he'll do his time and that will be that.' Arnold was being sincere. He knew Lance and Eamon were extremely good friends, they all were once upon a time, ever since high school. Lance just stood there, nervously. He wanted to say something on behalf of Richard and Jeremy, argue for them maybe but he couldn't. The tears began to run down his cheeks. John Arnold turned around. He noticed his friend was crying and that hurt him too. He edged close, put his arms around his shoulders and hugged him affectionately before whispering in his ear.

'Forget them, Lance. Please,' he pleaded with him quietly. 'They're gone for good, they won't cause us any trouble, believe me.' He squeezed his friend tight before letting go, then turned and walked back to the car without another word. Lance sat a while on a nearby tombstone and thought about his former friends; two friends who'd either been killed or were about to be and a third who would end up in jail. He would do nothing to stop it and so he cried instead. John Arnold was right and it was painful.

Chapter 36

THERE WAS NOTHING ELSE FOR it. He had to be told. Old Misery guts had steam coming out of his ears when we entered his chambers without knocking. He was deep in conversation with Saunders, Daniel, and Hank Dickson the District Attorney. There would be no prizes for guessing the agenda, which had just been rudely interrupted.

'Sorry, Judge,' I said, ignoring the over-reactive threats of jail coming from the DA. 'We need to talk, straight away,' I told him, then put my arm around his shoulders and gently persuaded him to follow us into the back room we knew he frequently retreated to when not in our presence. It was a complex operation, the Judge didn't like it one bit and, along with the others who protested in unison, he went ape-shit. But despite all the griping, we eventually got him there.

Desmond was quick to tell him what he knew. Misery listened to what we had to say and then amazed us by calling us, *fucking liars*. It was both a humbling experience and a shock but, nonetheless, followed the protocol we'd become accustomed to. It was also obvious to us that he'd not calmed down sufficient for us to *have a chat*. *We were insane*, he went on to say. I turned and paced the room while Old Misery kept up a barrage of four-letter insults towards us.

'Do you fucking numbskulls know what you're saying? Have you heard yourselves?' he ranted. I looked at Desmond, who in turn looked back towards me. The Judge was right. It was absurd. How could we be so stupid? Correction! How could I be so stupid? Desmond was wrong. It wasn't who he thought it was in the picture. He had it wrong and I foolishly believed him! Why didn't I check for myself? At that moment I wanted no more from Des than I wanted eye contact with the old bastard who stood shouting at us and instead, looked around the room trying to act as if nothing had ever been said. Besides another bookshelf, I noticed it contained no more than a few filing cabinets, some wooden shelving,

The Last Hangman

and a couch. It was obvious the old man came in here for some therapy or something else perhaps. I imagined Mary Lloyd pleasing him while we waited outside. I dismissed the thought as Desmond continued to argue his corner. It would be hard to get Old Misery to listen from here on in. He was preoccupied with deciding our fate at the hands of Doylee, et al.

'This fucking numbskull knows exactly what he's saying,' replied Des with a sudden outburst. He'd had enough of Hastings. The Judge momentarily stopped thinking about the nastiness that he would insist come our way and raised an eyebrow at what had just been said. It was war! I couldn't believe what I'd just heard. Desmond was dead meat in my books, which was confirmed when he continued with his self-assassination. 'Why don't you just go and fucking ask Doylee to see the photo for yourself, Judge?' Desmond blurted, going on the offensive. I stood wide-eyed and still. The Judge would retaliate any time now.

'Why don't I just lock your sorry fucking black ass in jail for a couple of days?' replied Hastings. Not pleased at all with Desmond's onslaught, Misery then rounded on him and gave him a good poke in the chest to make sure he understood what was at stake should Desmond continue with any more *verbal bullshit*, as the Judge liked to call it. I looked at my friend. It was his turn to fire another round into his already bullet-riddled foot by my feeble reckoning.

'Cos the first thing you'll do when we leave here is go take a goddamn peep at the photo in Doylee's office. Am I right Doug?' said Desmond right on cue and looking in my direction for support. I cringed and wished he hadn't sought a second opinion—we were supposed to be friends! I tried hard not to *shit my pants* and attempted to respond.

'Ugh, yeah, too right,' I replied nervously. I was now caught in the crossfire. Misery looked on and now scowled at both of us. He would have something to say pretty soon and so I had to act quickly.

'Okay, Des,' I said, turning to face my pal and looking at my watch at the same time. 'We've gotta go r-i-g-h-t now,' I added, slowly emphasizing the fact so that the words would register. 'Remember? It's Suzanne's birthday today,' I lied. 'Can't be late for her party, can we,' I joked and then held my watch in front of his face. My eyes were wide open in amazement at what he'd just done and now we needed to get the hell from there. He looked back in utter disappointment, which would not be a problem for me. I could handle Desmond's wrath but the other one, no way!

'Judge,' I began to say speaking in an overly shameful tone. 'Sorry to upset you like this. We'll just go and leave you to your meeting. It's been a long few days, the trial, the tape, talk of murder and all that. Forget that we ever came to see you,' I groveled. Desmond ignored my feebleness. Instead, he held his ground and looked towards the Judge. It was his call. Both men stared each other out for what seemed an eternity.

'Let's go see, Doylee,' said Hastings amazingly, reluctantly breaking the deadlock. His Honor quickly walked out of the room leaving us in his wake. Desmond exhaled. I dropped my shoulders. It was a big relief. We followed the Judge.

'Excuse me, gentlemen. I have to go see Doylee, won't be a moment,' he said to the others stood wandering what the hell was going on as they watched us traipse quickly down the corridor to a small office towards the end.

Doylee was stunned when Old Misery barged in. He cleared away the mess from on top of his cluttered desk with one well-timed swipe, turned down the radio, and emptied the left-over's from lunch into a small bin stuffed between two, large, metal filing cabinets. It was the first time His Honor had been in the Sheriff's office and true to form, it was a mess. The original photo was not there, it was downtown with the Feds he explained in rapid defense—but a photocopy could be retrieved within seconds he quickly told the Judge. Six minutes later we were still waiting, which gave Hastings time to rifle through the Sheriff's unlocked drawers and personal belongings. Several, hard-core, pornographic magazines were retrieved in no time and left open on the desk. When Doylee returned with the Xerox he noticed the naked flesh straight away and went red. The Sheriff struggled for something to say.

'Confiscated them this morning, Judge,' he muttered in the way of an apology. Misery picked up a magazine and rested the open pages on top of the Sheriff's head. He looked both embarrassed and ridiculous. Two other deputies looked on through the glass partitioning and laughed at the humiliation being shown to their superior.

'Go take a cold shower,' suggested the Judge, then snatched the Xerox from him and made his way out, laughing as he went.

'There, right there. Look!' Desmond pointed at the person stood smiling in the front row. We purposely ignored the background. The Judge frowned. He wasn't sure, but I was convinced the second I laid eyes on him. I immediately took back all my blasphemies made against Des in the last thirty minutes.

'It's him alright,' said Desmond, again with conviction. 'It's similar to the group photo I saw in his office. He's wearing the same clothes too,' he'd noticed.

'Probably taken the same day,' chipped in Misery who had also been converted by now thank goodness—he was a believer. I had to agree with both men. I had little to add. We were saddened. The positive ID and confirmation that our trusted and well respected attorney, Lance Heycock, was stood proud as punch, laughing along with five others waiting for his photo to be taken whilst two people hung from a rope behind them was indeed a blow. It was sickening. Worse, it was highly likely that these men, the ones proudly posing in the photo, were responsible for the wrongdoings, which were plain to see if you took notice of the background.

'Doylee?' barked Hastings.

'Yes, Your Honor.'

'Bring Lance Heycock here. Quickly as you can,' he ordered.

'Yes, Judge,' came the reply. Doylee wondered what all the fuss was about. He knew the Judge wasn't happy.

'Arrest the son-of-a-bitch if you have to,' he added making sure he was being fair and square; equality had been one of his main pillars of fairness for some time now. 'And Doylee,' shouted the Judge watching him leg it towards the door. 'Not a word,' he told him.

'No sir,' he said by mistake and went from the room in haste before the Judge could reprimand him.

Back in Misery's chambers, the FBI men, along with the DA, Hank Dickson who was so far a bystander—he wasn't invited to the interview with John Arnold—had started to piece together the chain of events. They'd tackled it from two directions. What they *definitely knew*, which was mostly from the tape and the personal interview held with Arnold earlier that day, and what they thought *might have happened*. The Judge's favorite communications method was used—bullet points on his beloved flip chart. The three men stopped momentarily as we followed the Judge and once again entered the room. Saunders, the senior Fed, immediately took one step forward.

'This is how we think it's all working out, Your Honor,' he said proudly and for some reason accepting our presence. The Fed man pointed to the neatly penned bullet points. 'We know about the racism of course,' he said without surprise and tapped bullet point number one with a pen—they worked the *definitely know* chart first.

'That's a cert and one for Heycock to sort out,' interrupted Daniel casually. He was quick to be dismissive and looked to Dickson for signs of resistance. There was none.

'Second point,' said Saunders regaining control. He tapped another bullet further down the chart. 'Advanced Strategic Energy has a great deal of interest in Nigeria. They work closely with the government in order to secure licenses for oil exploration, drilling or whatever it is these people do? This process has been greatly disrupted by the locals. Their violent protests have caused a lot of lost production, which equates to lots of dollars so I'm told?' he said, again being sarcastic before continuing. 'And so, Advanced Strategic Energy decides to go it alone and try to resolve matters themselves.'

'Go it alone?' quizzed the DA who was coming in cold.

'Yeah, they managed to get one of their business analyst managers, ugh . . .,' he struggled to read from a notepad on the table. 'A guy called, Richard Hammond,' he finally managed to inform them. 'He was to meet with someone from one of the Human Rights Movements and two others from a local supplies company we think? It was to be a double whammy.'

'What the fucks a double whammy, some kind of burger?' bellowed the Judge.

'It's just a saying, Judge.' Daniel butted in again and Saunders shook his head. Daniel looked back apologetic.

'The Human Rights connection is used as the bait to get their interest,' he told us. 'After all, they want the world to know what's going on down there.'

'The Nigerians, the ones hired by the supplies company. Are they used as guinea pigs to make the bribe then?' The Judge was trying to keep one step ahead of the Fed boys.

'You got it,' said the senior man. 'They probably put their necks on the line judging by what we think may have happened. Together with this guy, Hammond, they were to meet with some local tribesmen somewhere in the Delta.'

'The Ijaw,' said his partner, Daniel, reminding us of what Arnold had said earlier.

'The Ijaw,' repeated Saunders bluntly. 'Shall I continue?' he asked his mentor, frustrated from the ongoing interventions. He carried on regardless. 'We don't know exactly where this was going down, the landscape is massive and they could have met anywhere? The get together was arranged to offload a bribe of half a million bucks. By the way, that's chicken feed in the world of oil and politics gentlemen,' he reminded them. 'We don't know who the Human Rights guy is but we think we've got a lead on the other Nigerians.' He looked across the room towards Des. My friend showed no emotions.

'The other oil majors were far too smart to be caught up with what ASEI had planned,' said Daniel, who'd once again taken over—Saunders looked at him in amazement and simply bit his lip. 'Shell, Chevron, BP, and a host of others I can't remember have all voiced their concerns at the deteriorating situation but have stayed neutral. In fact, they've done pretty darn well, plugging more money into rural community programs than ever before, and at the same time . . .,'

'Okay, okay, just get on with it,' interrupted the Judge. Old Misery didn't want the detail; he'd already heard most of what had been said so far from John Arnold earlier on. Desmond and I sat patiently, listening to what was being said. It didn't take a genius to get to where we were in the case to-date and besides, like the Judge had hinted, we'd heard it all before somewhere. Saunders acknowledged the Judge's impatience and carried on, skipping over most of the boring detail.

'If the tape is anything to go by, we're talking of murder, gentlemen,' he said, surprising nobody. Desmond cringed and thought about Allto as Fed agent one continued with the list of actions that needed to be resolved. He then again skipped along the narrative and it was plain to everybody there that the Judge was not amused; they'd told him nothing he hadn't already known. Why the fuck the State wastes money on the FBI he never knew, but he continued listening. With a miracle something might come from it, but *it would take a miracle* he thought!

'We need to ID this mysterious so-called Human Rights guy pretty damn quickly,' said Saunders nearly towards the bottom of a long list, unaware there was never such a person in the first place.

'The twerp?' posed the Judge light-heartedly.

'That's him,' said Saunders looking up from his notes in a likewise manner. 'We've got resources working on it,' he said before anyone had a chance to butt in. The Judge refrained from posing the inevitable. 'We know Richard Hammond was out there,' he repeated again what we already knew and Daniel put a tick alongside his name on the flip chart. 'So, that leaves us with two more. Where do Jeremy Isaacs and Eamon Darcy fit into all of this? He then tapped the *probable chart* where the two VP's names were penned and a question mark scribbled immediately after them. 'They're definite players, no doubt about that. What're they up to?' Saunders threw the question open to the floor. Again there were no takers, something that followed a pattern of late. 'As soon as we get Isaacs in custody we'll know a little more,' Saunders assured us.

'Anything else?' asked the DA who'd come alive all of a sudden.

'Darcy's locked up in the downtown precinct. We're talking to him as soon as we've finished here. He'll fill in some gaps on the chart no doubt,' said Saunders reassuringly. 'As for the other two . . . they've vanished into thin air!'

'Okay, who sent the tape?' asked the DA.

'Mr. X we presume, whoever he is? We just haven't a clue on that one,' confessed Daniel.

'What's Arnold told us?' the senior lawyer asked with a little more conviction than before.

'Nothing more than we're telling you now . . . but he's lying. We know that much. He's just protecting his ass!' Saunders paced the room before continuing. 'We're going to show him the photograph we snatched from Hammond's apartment yesterday,' he continued, hastily trying to make amends for not yet getting a positive ID on Mr. X. 'That'll loosen him up. That's some bad stuff going on with some of his employee's. He'll tuck them up to protect the company. Or protect himself! We're pretty sure about that.'

Both Daniel and Saunders then looked at the Judge. They hadn't mentioned the photo at all to the rest of us during the briefing and now the DA looked inquisitively at them. We weren't sure if they'd slipped up. At least they showed no signs of having made a mistake and seemed to accept the fact that Des and I hadn't seen the photo. But they may have mentioned it to the DA, we didn't know at that moment in time. The old man was obviously well aware of that and was now busy mulling over what had just been said. He had a predicament. Besides the Judge and Doylee, only the Feds had access to the photo, but in the last half hour or so both Des and I had seen the contents, but they didn't know that. The DA would also need to see the photo if he hadn't already. Besides, regardless of who'd seen the picture, things had changed; we'd identified one of the hangmen! His Honor decided to be honorable for once and come clean.

'Things have taken a twist, gentlemen,' he said, in a less argumentative tone. 'We have ID'd one of the people in the photo, which makes things a little different.' He looked around the room at each one of us in turn. The Feds looked at Des and me for the umpteenth time—the *'we'* in the Judge's last comment. Nobody spoke. Misery walked up to the flip chart and stuck up the photograph using some *blue tack* conveniently placed in a tray underneath. The DA grimaced; it was his first time to see the atrocity we noticed. Everyone else just stared.

'There,' he said, just as Desmond had done a few moments earlier. 'Right there,' he pointed enthusiastically to one of the four men smiling in the front row, there were two others clumsily hanging on to them with draped arms towards the back. 'Do you know who that is?' he asked turning around to face us. 'You're not going to believe this,' added the Judge quickly since he doubted if there was ever going to be an answer. 'It's Lance fucking Heycock, that's who!' There was silence for a few moments while it registered with the DA, and then finally with agents Saunders and Daniel. The youngest agent spoke.

'How'd you know, Judge?' asked Daniel not yet fully realizing the similarity, he'd hardly had contact with the accused so was a little cold making a connection. The Judge turned to Desmond, who felt obliged to tell them of how he'd seen a similar photo in Lance's office and how he'd taken an underhanded sneak preview at the photo in Sheriff Doylee's cubbyhole earlier. He'd simply put two and two together. Lance was surely incriminated in the murder of two black folk. The Judge returned behind his desk and sat down. The room was quite. The revelations were spectacular to say the least.

'That's two murder cases we have to solve, gentlemen,' said His Honor.

'I need another lawyer,' said Desmond without joking.

Again promising not to disclose our conversation we disbanded. Soon the FBI would have ID'd all the men on the photo—they were pretty sure about it they kept telling us! We could then put a large piece of the jigsaw together. It was already gelling in parts but rather too slowly for our liking. On the way out, I diverted quickly into the gents and took out my cell phone. I tried phoning the room for the third time. After letting it ring for over five minutes—I remained the eternal pessimist—there was still no answer. I put the phone back into my jacket pocket and instead of doing nothing, half-thought about telling the Feds of Cheryl's disappearance. Now we were friends with Saunders and Daniel perhaps they would initiate a search? I dismissed the idea and went back to Desmond who was waiting in the lobby.

'When did she go?' he asked as we walked alongside a vacant and quite courtroom.

'This morning sometime, kinda strange though,' I conceded. 'I thought all was well between the two of us, Des.'

'She's a young girl, Doug. Perhaps she's had second thoughts. It sometimes happens. Cheryl wouldn't have wanted to hang around and tell you,' he said genuinely, trying to temper the blow.

'Yeah, I suppose you're right.' That was the obvious reason and I reluctantly accepted it. His words had hit home, it was like a sledgehammer blow and my stomach churned. I liked Cheryl. I liked her a lot. 'Just didn't expect a no show like that, that's all,' I said in a sulk and lowered my head. I quickly followed Des and walked out of the building and towards Suzanne who was waiting by the entrance. She smiled when she saw the two of us. We dared not tell her about Lance, not just yet. It would be too much of a shock.

Chapter 37

'**A**RE YOU OUT OF YOUR mind?' screamed Suzanne. Desmond scurried away like a shit-house rat. His advice was bad and I should have known better. I was left on my own to reason with Suzanne outside the hotel lobby.

'That girl's in luv with you, Douglas! In L-U-V . . . d'yer me? Somins' wrong, honey? You gotta go get yer girl!' she insisted and then hollered after her husband who'd taken refuge in the lobby bar nearby. I knew it, but it took a bloody woman to tell me! If I could have, I would have kicked myself and then kicked Desmond even harder. By the time we'd brainstormed her whereabouts we were still in position A. back at the start. It was no use pretending she had gone somewhere on her own free will. She'd been abducted, or kidnapped, or whatever else it is that happens to somebody who goes missing? We decided that our best bet was to seek out Dil; perhaps his scattered brain could help, they usually kept each other company. The Blues Brothers were of no use, they were getting ready to go back to Texas. Their work was done. Lance was a no-no, but if he was around he would have normally been tidying up the finer detail of Desmond's lawsuit. It was supposed to be payday soon, but the FBI was pursuing him and probably had him arrested by now. Then Suzanne looked at us in amazement! We accidentally let it slip and Suzanne, who always insisted there was something about lawyers that she disliked, was proved right—she was as stunned as we had been.

* * *

It was most peculiar for John Arnold to receive a call on his cell phone of this particular nature. The caller, a Nigerian, apologized but had phoned only to give him a brief update, but he also needed to clarify the situation. Jeremy Isaacs had been followed from New Jersey to New Orleans. The caller presumed he was staying at the Riverside Hilton. He'd entered the building and had remained on the fourth floor for some time. But, oddly enough he had no booking and if he had, he certainly hadn't checked in yet. The target was now en-route to the French Quarter on foot said the caller breathing heavily, keeping pace. Would he still want the original instructions carried out or would there be a change of plan, especially since the goal posts had moved somewhat considerably from the original request. The CEO, who was absolutely furious at first, calmed down and gave other instructions. Isaacs was to be followed but left alone. He needed to work things out and besides, he was also in New Orleans! It would be too much of a coincidence. The caller repeated the change of orders and hung up.

Arnold smelled a rat, what the fuck was Isaacs doing in New Orleans? He wasn't sightseeing that's for sure. Isaacs was the last person he wanted hanging around the place. He couldn't tell the police of his whereabouts, he'd be arrested and the silly fuck would spill the beans. The man was becoming a bloody nuisance. Arnold would have to rethink the situation through. He didn't want Isaacs loud-mouthing to anybody. It would be bad for business not to mention his fragile wellbeing. He considered his son-in-laws' motive. The only conclusion he could come to was the connection with Lance Heycock. Isaacs knew what was happening, perhaps he knew that he was a marked man with but a few hours to live—unbeknown to him, he'd gained a longer stay of execution by being in New Orleans. But how would he know? Where was he getting his information? John Arnold needed to find out.

* * *

Dil hadn't seen Cheryl he told us in no time at all and then for some reason best known only to him, he laughed when we told him about Lance's stupidity. We didn't tell him the full hanging story, just that he was being taken into custody for some criminal technicality related to Desmond's lawsuit.

'*I knew that photo would get him into trouble,*' he then said, rather amazingly.

When he mentioned this we were stunned! We thought we were the only ones to have seen the photo. Now we sensed there was a lot we didn't know about Dillwyn, something strange, something we'd never noticed before. The fact that he'd practically ignored what we'd just told him, coupled with what he already knew about Lance troubled us. Desmond grunted a few obscenities at the mysteriously odd way in which Dil greeted the news. What was particularly disturbing to us was the fact that he knew all along about the photo! The way in which he casually mentioned having seen it was even more troublesome! Desmond wasn't happy and made a feeble excuse to leave, but not before venting his anger about the smell of the Welshman's bare feet, of all things. Dillwyn ignored him and turned to look at me instead.

'Need a hand looking for Cheryl?' he asked getting up from sitting on the bed. He seemed genuinely concerned.

'Nope,' replied Des still angry and now looking at the mess strewn around the hotel room. He shook his head and started walking towards the open door.

'Yes please, Dil,' I overruled. 'We need all the help we can get, thanks.' Dil made a grab for his shoes and socks and sniffed them before putting them on. They smelt of rotten fish. Desmond screwed his face in disgust when he saw this.

'Where do we start?' he said, tugging at his shoes.

'I dunno! Who's she likely to be with?' I asked still reeling at Dil's strange attitude.

'The only ones I can think of are Ant and Chuck,' he suggested, seemingly comfortable with the situation.

'That's a no brainer. She wouldn't be with them,' I said confidently. Cheryl secretly despised both of them.

'Let's start with Lance then,' he suggested instead.

'Lance? Didn't you listen to a word of what we just told you?' I asked him out loud. 'Lance is probably banged up by now,' I said, utterly amazed by Dil's lack of understanding.

'Doubt it. The Fed's got no chance! They'll never find him.'

'Oh yeah, how's that then?' I asked delving deeper into the odd way he was managing all of this.

'Cos he's *scarpered*, that's why,' replied Dil, smirking. I shook my head and again wondered why Dil wasn't all that surprised at the news of Lance's misgivings given the gravity and serious nature of the crime he'd supposedly committed!

'*Scarpered*? What do you mean, *scarpered*?' I asked becoming more and more bewildered by the second. By now Des had returned back into the room. He couldn't wait to get Dillwyn out of his sight, and since that wasn't happening quickly enough he was in a really bad mood.

'C'mon, Doug, what's keeping you, man? Say goodbye to that fucking smelly-assed gook and let's get outa here,' he said spitefully and again made his way out of the room.

'Fucking gook, ugh, we'll see about that!' replied Dil seriously offended.

'Take no notice Dil, let him go,' I snapped looking back towards Desmond. Upon hearing my reproach, Desmond stopped and turned on the balls of his toes and grunted another barrage of obscenities towards me but I completely ignored him. I had other things to think about.

'Where's Lance *scarpered* to?' I asked again in earnest.

'I think I've got a fair idea,' he said, still looking at Desmond suspiciously. 'But I can't be sure of it . . .' he said, pausing. Our frustration was overly evident, which fortunately prompted him to carry on. 'All I can remember is a little pad he'd use just inside the French Quarter. Somewhere along Bourbon,' he went on to say. 'It's in a Hotel. What's that fucking place called now?' Dil's head dropped into his hands as he tried to recall the name of the joint. Des, meanwhile, resumed throwing obscenities into the room.

'Okay, take your time, Dil. Just give it to us in your own time. We'll go take a walk around if you want, it might jog your memory,' I offered trying to coax him in some way, anyway.

'It's no good. I'll have to show you,' he said, finally agreeing with my first suggestion. We wasted no time and set off straight away. Soon we were dodging the hundreds of tourists along Bourbon as we followed Dillwyn with pace. It was pointless phoning the Fed's or Doylee to tell them of our attorney's whereabouts—they'd only get too ate up. If Lance was there, then we'd talk to him first and then convince him to go see the Judge. It would be better that way, but God knows what we were going to say if we did manage to find him?

'When did you first see the photo, Dil?' I asked trying to resurrect the conversation as we walked from the hotel towards the French Quarter at pace. I was intrigued to know more.

'What photo?' he replied looking back vacantly at me. Another blunt shake of the head from Des followed.

'Dil, are you on the same fucking planet as the rest of us?' I asked, and then stopped in mid-stride. The next moment two Chinese men bumped into the back of me but I hadn't even noticed, inside I was fuming.

'You know he's not,' said Desmond blatantly blurting it out loud. 'He's in cuckoo land,' he added with some considered accuracy.

'You're the one who's cuckoo,' replied Dil. He'd had enough of Desmond. 'You should enter a, *I'm an ugly bloke*, competition!' he snapped back and screwed his face up to emphasize the point. I held Des back and, realizing I was about to thump somebody soon if this carried on, he eased off a little. Des was boiling over following Dillwyn's childish response.

'Cut it out will you. You're like a coupla kids!' I said, wanting to slap the both of them in order to bring them back to their senses. 'Dil, tell me,' I demanded to know. 'When did you first set eyes on the photo?' I asked forcefully for the second time and getting really mad with the worsening situation.

'A long time ago,' he then told us remembering it well all of a sudden. 'When I first started to work there, but it's not there now though. Lance took it down soon after *he* came along,' he added looking disdainfully in Desmond's direction. 'I told Lance at the time that he shouldn't have handled this case,' he went on to say. Something quickly stirred inside me. My first reaction was to naturally think we'd had our wires crossed, but then I had a gut feeling there was more to it than that. Then Moira's warning crept into my mind again.

'Is there any particular reason for saying that Dil?' I asked following my hunch. He hadn't a clue we knew just about everything by now, but he'd just gone and stirred up a hornet's nest, all three of us realized that.

'You're having a laugh, aren't you?' he declared turning it around on us. He seemed amazed at the question I'd just thrown at him.

'Ugh . . . I'm not with you, Dil,' I said, and not for the first time feeling utterly confused. The Welshman had us in a complete spin now. 'What are you on about?' I asked angrily. Something was going to snap soon and by my reckoning it was going to be my patience!

'The photo of them fishing,' he said finally, wondering why we were pestering him for the detail. 'He took it down.' Both Des and I looked at each other, confused from getting nowhere. We were thinking of the hanging photo, the same one we thought he'd mentioned earlier on. Why all of a sudden was he referring to the fishing photo? This guy was a lunatic.

'What the hell as the fishing photo got to do with all this?' It was Desmond's turn to ask the question, I was numb from talking to such a brainless, dumb-ass, smelly geek!

'Cos most of the fucking ASEI board is in it!' he declared as if we should have known. 'They're all there. Isaacs, Hammond, Darcy, and I know the others,' he went on to say like a little kid. 'I know the lot of em. They're all his mates,' confessed Dillwyn. 'That's why Lance should never have taken this stupid case on in the first place,' he told us wondering why we hadn't come to that conclusion earlier, especially after we'd mentioned the photo to him. 'I thought you found that out this morning. What else would they bang Lance up for?' he asked looking back at us in astonishment. Those few words stopped us dead. What had he just said? The penny dropped. We'd simply told Dil about Lance being in trouble because it was the right thing to do under the circumstances, something related to the lawsuit we were involved in we said—we never went into detail so when he mentioned the photo we'd simply put two and two together, wrongly thinking he was referring to the hanging photo.

What Dil had just said now seemed to connect everything together all of a sudden. We hadn't the faintest idea who the others were in the hanging photo, or anything else about it other than the fact that Richard Hammond had a copy in his apartment—and even he hadn't been positively identified. Apart from knowing Lance was in the photo, we knew very little else about the others up until now. At that precise moment both Des and I knew the implications of what had just been mentioned. A web of deceit had been spun over the years according to what Dil had just said. The people in the fishing photo were the same people in the hanging photo. They had to be, Dillwyn had just named them! We, meaning everybody in the Judge's chambers earlier on, couldn't possibly have identified them. Apart from Lance, we'd never set eyes on the others. But Dil had. And now it all seemed to fit to together. Even Desmond now recalled how they looked familiar all of a sudden. No wonder Lance was having kittens the whole time! And that's what Gloria was trying to tell me!

The fallout was enormous! Desmond grabbed Dil by the scruff of the neck and half-dragged him into a nearby doorway—away from the hordes of tourists now mulling around us.

'Is that why he wasn't too keen to get anybody from Advanced Strategic Energy to testify?' Desmond asked him, forcefully squeezing his cheeks together, he was tamping. It was understandable I guess.

'We were told not to say anything,' he said nervously. He was ruffled by Desmond's aggression but kept quickly speaking. 'It was fair enough by us,' he went on to say.

'*Us*, who the fuck is *us*, tell me? Desmond demanded to know who was who? He was also ready to dish out his own justice at the same time.

'Lance told us . . . Chuck, Ant, and me,' he said. 'The men in the photo were his buddies from a long while ago. They all worked for the oil company soon afterwards. They're respectable, law-abiding people. There was no problem with these people, Lance assured us of that.' Dil was sincere when he said this, and why not? He had no notion that these men were murderers. As far as he was concerned, they were just friends; ever since school. He knew there was a connection with the Haynes case and Advanced Strategic Energy but nothing else. Dil continued to give us Lance's version of the many excuses he'd used when we weren't around. Several people squeezed past to get into the shop.

'Shouldn't even have to get them on the stand, he'd said several times . . . in your absence of course,' he then hesitated to say. That was nice to know we both thought and continued to find out more.

'And the Klan?' I asked boldly, but hardly wanting to know the answer. The owner of the shop came to take a look at who was being roughed up in his doorway. We saw him pick up the phone and dial; it was probably a 911.

'Yep, they were fucking Klucker's!' Dillwyn's voice faded and he turned his head in shame, he'd finally realized what a prat he'd been. Des and I looked at each other. We didn't have to say another word. It fell into place all too quickly. The fishing trip photo, the contents of the tape, Darcy, Isaacs, Hammond, Nigeria, Allto's murder, Desmond's dismissal, Mr. X whoever he was. The guy was asked to leave the room because he wasn't in the Klan, and then finally the hanging photo, which was taken on the same day as the fishing photo. They were covering for each other; they were Klucker's every one of them. Whatever Hammond had done in Nigeria they would cover for him. Klucker's stuck together, or was it that they knew too much about each other? Either way there'd been a massive bond between these men. A bond probably brought about by a hanging? It was frightening and sent shivers down my spine.

'Why did Lance make a run for it? Does he know that we know about his involvement with the Klan?' It was Desmond's turn to once again interrogate Dil.

'Not about the Klan,' he told us. 'But he was smart enough to realize that you'd eventually find out about his involvement with the top brass in the oil company.' Dil was giving his boss a little too much credit for our liking. 'I doubt if he knows you know about the photo though, not yet anyway,' he said.

'What photo are we talking about, Dil?' I butted in, making sure we were talking about the same photo and also that the pieces fitted together as previously thought.

'How many fucking photo's are there?' he asked, confused and getting more frustrated at all the strange questions coming his way. His reaction told me he knew nothing about the hanging photo. Satisfied with his response, I told him there was just the one and we left it at that. It was a relief to know Dil wasn't covering up for anybody connected to that horrible crime. It was a mistake to have thought that earlier.

'But why did Lance run, then?' asked Desmond again, much calmer now that he'd realized Dillwyn had played no part in what was going on; he'd simply been deceived and then innocently manipulated by his employer.

'He didn't run,' replied Dil noticing the change in Desmond's demeanor. 'He had a call from Isaacs. He wanted to meet with him!'

'Isaacs!' I shouted out. It was spiraling now—we were shocked for the umpteenth time. 'Where for Christ's sake?' I asked again putting two and two together. Cheryl came flooding back to me; I was ashamed to admit it but we'd forgotten about her during the mayhem caused by Dillwyn's incredible revelations.

'To wherever it is I'm trying to take you!' Dil shouted back at me.

'Let's go,' I demanded and with that we ran, searching frantically for our destination in every direction possible.

Chapter 38

THE LOBBY WAS SMALL, THE furniture looked very expensive and the atmosphere seemed warm and friendly. A middle-aged woman came from behind a genuine, English antique writing desk that doubled as the reception, introduced herself and asked if she could assist him. Her southern drawl would have had an effect on Jeremy under other circumstances. He wouldn't let her distract him though and just politely asked for room twenty-eight. She pointed to a narrow but well-lit stairway, which led to the comfortably furnished rooms on the second floor. Isaacs zipped up two flights of stairs and quickly found the room. Lance was already inside waiting; the door was ajar in anticipation of his friend's arrival. Isaacs gave a light tap and the door yielded.

'Jeremy!' Lance looked towards the opening and was both relieved and pleased to see his old friend. Isaacs entered the room without saying a word. Ignoring Jeremy's odd behavior, Lance got up from his seat and quickly walked over to greet him. 'Hey, man, look at you. You're finally here . . . safe,' he hesitated to add sincerely, and then hugged him tight. Isaacs stood motionless. He'd noticed what Lance had just said. The word, *safe*, confirmed his worst suspicions.

'Wanna drink my friend?' asked Lance quickly freeing himself and now making his way towards a well-stocked mini bar to one side of the room.

'Bourbon, on the rocks,' Isaacs replied, poker faced.

'You betcha, what's going down, man?' he then asked, smiling and wanting to know the reason for the meet.

'Thought you could tell me? You're the fucking lawyer.' This was the second time that the phrase had been said to him in the last two days. Must be something about lawyers he told himself as he poured the drinks.

'Me? What do I know that you don't?' he lied still smiling before adding. 'You know Haynes has turned us upside down, right?' Lance felt uncomfortable from telling him the bad news but Isaacs probably knew he reasoned.

'Yeah,' he replied, deflated. 'Dinger filled me in with the details about the tape. But what other shit is flying around, Lance. I need to know?'

'Hasn't Dinger told you?'

'Only about the crap we piled on the nigger.'

'Some fucking tape, ugh!'

'Yeah, some fucking tape!' he replied, repeating the sarcastic remark but he hadn't come to listen to all that, there were more pressing matters to discuss.

'It's not good, Jeremy. They know about Nigeria. Not all of it, but enough,' he told him. 'And on top of all that shit we piled on Haynes, there's more. It's all out in the open now,' he went on to say.

'How come?'

'The tape, it's all there, the fucking lot.'

'They put you in the frame yet?'

'Ugh, ugh,' replied Lance shaking his head, unaware of events of late. 'But they will,' he said, as if feeling left out. 'Search warrants are already out for you, Eamon, and Richard. They've already had John in.'

'And?'

'Don't know what he said but they've let him go for now. Dinger should have gone in with him but there was a no show. John probably smoothed it over, clever bastard!'

'Have you talked to him?'

'Yeah, we met in the cemetery yesterday,' he told him before hesitating to tell him more. 'Jeremy, there's something you should know,' Lance said cautiously. Should he tell him?

'There's something I should know?' replied Isaacs with a false sense of humor. 'That's a fucking understatement if I ever heard one,' he added, nervously playing with a glass tumbler that was by now almost half-empty of Bourbon, it was the same one Lance had given him full to the top moments earlier. He was feeling the pressure of events that lay ahead.

'You gotta get out of here, disappear,' Lance then warned him with some urgency. Isaacs stopped fumbling with the glass and paid attention to what was being said. 'They know what you did to Haynes and it's only a matter of time till they put you and Richard in the frame for Nigeria. Take my advice. Get the hell outa here. I'll even lend you some money.' Lance liked all his friends. He wanted no harm to come to any of them, ever. But after meeting with Arnold he knew otherwise, a bullet was loaded and ready to fire in Isaacs' direction, no mistakes about it.

'What's the point? They'll get us in the end,' replied Jeremy playing it out.

'No they won't. Not if you go now. Just get the hell outa here,' said Lance repeating the warning.

'Relax, Lance. What's up, man? You're acting kinda strange, something bothering you my trusted friend?' he asked knowing the answer.

'Ah . . . c'mon, you know what I'm getting at,' he replied, frustrated. 'We both know it's getting too messy. It's getting out of hand,' he told him. 'Get out now while you can,' he begged. Tears were welling in his eyes.

'C'mon Lance. Give it to me. What's really troubling you for fuck sake?' Lance paced the room, he was nervous and it showed. He had to come clean.

'Okay . . . you're right, that's not all . . . It's John,' continued Lance, now sweating. He did that when he was overly nervous. 'He's taken a contract out on you,' he said quickly, relieved that it was out.

'Oh, really?' said Isaacs, who wasn't surprised at all considering what he'd just been told. He expected it.

'Hammond? Darcy?' he asked.

'No . . . no, not Eamon, just you and Richard, he says he can rely on Eamon,' he confessed. Then he turned away before continuing to add more. 'I begged him not to but he wouldn't listen.'

'He broke the promise, ugh! It doesn't surprise me. The little shit always thought he was better than we were.'

'What'll you do?'

'I've a little something stashed away to protect me and I'm not scared of John. I don't know about you though, Lance. What'll you do?'

'Me? Nothing, I've got nothing to hide. What have I got to do with all this?'

'You've obviously got a short memory, my friend.'

'Not the hanging! No way. Don't even think about going down that road. That stays where it is, Jeremy. We made a vow. No fucking way. Nobody gets to know.'

'What do you think got us into this fucking mess in the first place, Lance? Ugh? How can we forget it? Tell me, Lance? How the fuck can we forget what we did, tell me that?' he demanded. The ghastly reality of what had happened all those years ago was plainly rising to the surface as they knew it would, eventually. Like the rest of them, the crime they'd

Peter Nutty

committed had tormented them their entire lives. There were nightmares upon nightmares. The lawyer remained silent. Jeremy was right. If they hadn't hung the two blacks none of this would have happened. They would probably never have seen each other again. But it had happened. And instead of just leaving it there, they not only kept in touch but also helped each other to be where they were. Each of them in positions of high authority and well paid. They even made a vow; it was a pact not to reveal their secret. Ever!

'You gotta get close to John,' he ordered. 'You gotta do it, Lance. For all our sakes goddamn it. Can't you see what he's doing? Nobody knows about what went on in Texas. Let's keep it that way. We gotta stop him once and for all,' he urged, slowly becoming hysterical from what lay ahead.

'What are you saying, Jeremy?' asked Lance screwing his face. His blood pressure was going through the roof. He kinda knew what was being hinted at but he couldn't imagine it would ever come to this.

'Don't play, *Mr. Innocent*, with me, Lance. You know what I'm asking. You're the only one who can get close to the son-of-a-bitch. Here, take this,' he said, and handed him a small revolver. Lance flinched. He was traumatized and instead of turning away simply did what he was told and took the gun from him. Suddenly, there was a tap on the door and both men froze.

* * *

'Lance! Lance! Are you in there, Lance?' I asked. Not getting an answer I rapped hard once again on the locked door. We waited impatiently for a reply. There was no response and by my reckoning there was no other way for it. I pushed the others aside and barged down the door.

* * *

Sheriff Doylee was having lunch when a report came in of a strange-looking black man loitering outside the Hotel Paris. The caller was sure he'd seen a gun protruding from inside his jacket. That morsel of information narrowed the suspect down to any one of half the population of New Orleans, there was a thousand black men hanging around with a gun hanging out of their pants! The policeman hung up and then grunted before finishing off a meat Poboy in two mouthfuls. In another bout of grunting his coffee went the same way before he made tracks towards the French quarter to investigate; the chewed remains of the Poboy covered the front of his shirt.

Chapter 39

There were few surprises when we eventually tumbled into the room—we half knew what to expect, but that changed when Isaacs pulled another revolver from inside the waistband of his trousers. Now, we were in trouble. We just froze and looked at the two hangmen. The attorney was taken aback at our intrusion and also from the fact that Isaacs had pulled a gun on us. He looked genuinely confused at what had just happened.

'Doug, what on earth are you doing here?' Lance demanded to know. He looked worn out.

'It's kind of a long story but I'm sure you know already, Lance,' I replied.

'So, these are the people that are causing all the problems, hey?' spouted Isaacs navigating the room and keeping the gun pointed in our direction as he spoke. I immediately hated the little bastard and wondered if he knew of Cheryl's whereabouts? Of course he did! The gunman rounded on Desmond.

'Hello nigger-boy,' he teased. 'How's your friend, Brandt?'

'Shut the fuck up or I'll shut you the fuck up,' replied Desmond.

'Leave it, Des. It's not worth it,' I shouted towards him. My friend eased himself back following my efforts to restrain him from confronting Isaacs full on. Instead, Desmond fixed an angry stare towards the assailant. Dil just froze as I slowly inched forward towards Isaacs.

'And you're the infamous Jeremy Isaacs no doubt!' I said, knowing there wasn't any doubt. There was no reply from our captor. 'It's no use, you know that. We know about the photo, the hangings, just put the gun down,' I told him. Lance looked at us bewildered. He'd literally shuddered at what had just been said. We returned a distrustful look.

'It's true, Lance,' confirmed Desmond scathing inside. Dil looked on, trying to work out what was being said.

'Why Lance? Why?' I asked. The attorney remained still, embarrassed by what we now knew. He just stood there in silence, sweating heavily and shaking his head before slowly speaking, he wanted to explain.

'I . . . I . . . don't know. It was Hammond's idea I guess.'

'Quite, Lance. You don't have to answer to these people,' said Isaacs.

'Go on, Lance, don't be afraid of him,' I said, and urged him to continue. The shame and embarrassment was piling up.

'Stop it, Lance, stop it now!' Isaacs turned the gun towards him. 'Don't say another word, I'm warning you.'

Lance looked at his friend, he was confused. He couldn't comprehend what Isaacs was saying or doing. He then changed his composure and looked somewhat accusingly at him. It was as if he'd come out of a trance.

'It was you, wasn't it? It was you and Richard,' he said, his anger rising. 'You couldn't wait to get the rope out and put it around their fucking necks quick enough, could you? They'd done nothing wrong but between the both of you, you had them tried, convicted and sentenced to hang.' Lance turned towards us. 'It was them, it was Isaacs and Hammond. They did it. The blacks had done nothing wrong. They'd done nothing wrong,' he cried pathetically, breathing hard. His nervous system was falling apart.

'Shut up, Lance. Shut the fuck up!' ordered Isaacs, who'd now appeared to become deranged all of a sudden. Then, Lance quickly raised the gun he was given moments earlier. Taken by surprise, we braced ourselves, not sure what was about to happen.

'Lance, don't be stupid. Give me the gun.' demanded Isaacs nearing closer to his life-long friend. He quickly pointed his gun away from Lance and back towards us in an attempt to keep us at bay. It seemed like an idle threat but we didn't know that and so we did nothing, we didn't want to take any chances—the situation was too delicate. We just stood and watched.

'Give me the gun, Lance. Just give it to me,' he said, forcing the issue. Lance just stood there, traumatized. The gun was held loosely in his right hand. Isaacs neared, slowly edging closer. Lance looked at him for a brief second with tears in his eyes and then, in a flash, put the gun into his mouth and pulled the trigger. A dull shot rang out and Lance collapsed in a heap. Blood and brain tissue scattered the wall and curtains behind him. We were stunned and tried to make a move to help him. Isaacs immediately trained the gun our way, stopping us in our tracks, we'd hardly moved.

'Stay there,' he screamed at us.

'You're a fucking crazy son-of-a-bitch,' hissed Desmond, distraught at the sight of the carnage in front of us.

'You won't get away with this for Christ sake,' I also yelled at him, frightened that we could be the next victims. 'Just give it up before it's too late,' I begged. Lance fidgeted on the floor as blood poured from the wound in the back of his head. His shirt collar turned crimson in an instant. Then his body seemed to twitch and spasm. He was in the last throes of death as the blood drained from him. A pool of red appeared on the carpet under his head, he was dead. Dil was incensed.

'Too late for what?' asked Isaacs, menacingly now that Lance was dead.

* * *

The Nigerian was stood alone across from the hotel when he heard the shot fired. He had watched us enter the hotel moments earlier and suspected that our presence involved something to do with Isaacs, but in what way he had no idea. He brought out the cell phone and dialed his paymaster. He would need to be told.

* * *

The radio crackled into life and he took the message on the hoof. It prompted Doylee to engage the red and blues, which also deployed the siren. He put his foot down. The brief update was bad news. He had received reports of gunfire coming from the vicinity of the Paris Hotel.

* * *

It was stalemate for the next few seconds. Isaacs had to do something quick though. The police would surely have been called. He looked out of the window, cautiously, whilst keeping one eye on us. With that small maneuver distracting his concentration for a millisecond, Dil saw his chance and lunged at our captor. Another shot rang out and a loud, *thud* filled the room. Dil had been hit and fell limply towards Isaacs in mid charge. Both men were knocked to the ground. Now, it was my turn. I quickly pounced and grabbed Isaacs' arm—the one that held the gun. We grappled for control, both of us sprawling around the room. Desmond, meanwhile, had gone to the aid of Lance but it was futile. He then turned to help Dil who was bleeding badly from the abdomen. I couldn't believe he'd left me to struggle with the assailant alone. Soon though, I had Isaacs well trussed up but his trigger finger was still on the gun, which was somewhere between us.

'Where's Cheryl,' I asked fiercely. We were face to face, flesh touching and nervous sweat poured from both of us. My enemy tried to shrug me off but I continued the struggle. Isaacs fought back and we settled for holding each other as tightly as we could. The first to give up was dead as far as I was concerned. The gun was still between us.

'She's fine, just fine,' he purred, and then sucked the blood from a cut on his lips before spitting it in my face. If I had control of the gun at that moment I'd have pulled the trigger. Instead, my heart sunk to new depths. He had her.

'I don't want any harm to come to her, I'm warning you, Isaacs,' I told him tightening my grip.

'Well . . . that kinda depends on you now, doesn't it,' he replied, his mouth filling with blood from the cut. 'Just leave me go and I'll make sure you'll see her again,' he offered.

'Fuck you.'

'Have it your way then,' he replied upping the tempo and the struggle intensified. I could feel the gun being turned towards me. There was no way my life was going to end in this way. With all my strength I managed to resist the movement and, after a huge struggle, turned the situation around. The gun was buried right into his abdomen. Isaacs grinned and then spat at me again. I was covered in blood and saliva but it made no difference; I was intent on squeezing the life out of him just to keep the gun from pointing in my direction. Then his mood changed, he was already deranged, but now he took on another form of life. He continued to ridicule me as we fought. Then his face started to twitch, something inside was changing. I could tell by the way his face contorted. I could feel his muscles spasm.

'Say goodbye to Cheryl, Archer,' he said spitefully, and then I realized what was happening.

'No . . .! No . . . ! Don't do it,' I screamed ready to let go of him. It was too late. He pulled the trigger. Another shot and a dull, *thud*, echoed around the room. Isaacs menacing grin slowly vanished, his eyes opened wide, the look of death appeared as the blood drained from him. I released my grip and watched as his miserable body went limp. His face was still mocking me. It was too much. I got up and started to kick the little bastard. He had hidden Cheryl and now we'd never find her. I continued kicking until Desmond threw me back onto the floor in an effort to restrain me.

* * *

At the time of the shooting, the house maintenance of *Marlen* was proving difficult for a man with the shakes, but it needed attention and so sanding and painting the deteriorated, wooden sash windows was something he was determined to finish and get right. The first couple of days had been hard, not physically but mentally, but it would get better and easier with each passing day he constantly told himself. The start of Richard Hammond's new life had begun in earnest.

Chapter 40

The room was photographed, names of witnesses were taken, film crews working the afternoon news bulletins poked cameras and microphones into every crook and cranny. While all this was going on, men and women wearing white paper suits combed the room to get the required forensics before the two dead bodies were removed in black body bags. The film crews rolled their video tapes to catch the lifeless images. They would be edited and be ready for the evening *News Headlines*; tomorrow it would be somebody else's turn in a body bag! Dil was whipped away quickly by a couple of hard-handed paramedics. He seemed in good-spirits despite the enormous amount of bleeding that came from the gunshot wound to his stomach. He was still conscious as he was wheeled out of the hotel singing one of his favorite Welsh hymns!

Our explanation of events was not satisfactory judging by the way the police, ably led by Doylee, manhandled us all the way to the downtown precinct—they were our friends not a couple of hours earlier. When the FBI men arrived, alerted to the connection between Lance and Isaacs, the questioning was relentless and lasted for three hours; *were these two idiots the same men we befriended earlier?* Desmond asked. We left cell four only when the time came for them to roast Darcy some more. The senior Vice-President was our savior for the time being. They needed answers quickly.

The fact that we'd identified at least three of those present in the hanging photo—ahead of the FBI, went in our favor, although we didn't precisely know who was who? Lance and Isaacs who we'd labeled hangmen one and two on our list following the order we'd identified them, were now a good match. Eamon Darcy, hangman number three could point himself out since he was in the next room being grilled. That left Richard Hammond, the fourth hangman who still had to be identified to us. He could have been any one of the remaining three out of the six in the picture since nobody present knew what he looked like. Eamon would be forced to ID him of course, along with the others for good measure. Hammond's ugly mug would be screened around the US and be posted on *Wanted for Murder* posters throughout every law precinct.

For a newspaper reporter, Nick still had a lot to learn—he'd arrived far too late. When he finally reached the hotel it was swarming with cops. They eventually let him view the crime scene but when he saw all the blood he left quickly to be sick in the street outside. It was now our turn to fill in the detail of his missed opportunistic journalism. He would have to wait his turn, but we assured him another scoop would come his way. He gave a distrusting look at us as we were led away by Doylee, who'd came to collect us after being released. Two of the three amigos, Des and me—the third, Dil was in hospital, were whisked away to the Orleans Parish Courtroom to be further interviewed by an *old friend*.

* * *

Following our grilling from Saunders and Daniel we were once again back, free from harm or so we thought, in His Honors chambers in the company of Old Misery guts, who was surrounded by an entourage of different law people. We had missed his sour humor!

'We got ourselves a coupla' loose cannons here, gentlemen,' he grunted towards me and Desmond and everyone sat across from us agreed. 'Why'd you go barging into the room like that? We got trained people to do that kinda stuff. Now, because of your dumb Starsky and fucking Hutch antics we've got a couple of dead bodies lying in the morgue,' he swore at us and not caring a hoot about the language being used. A collection of nodding heads and facial expressions that amounted to total bewilderment further condemned us to the gallows. The room was full of all those we'd upset—there were too many to list. The Judge rose quickly from his chair and paced the room. He would be contemplating our punishment no doubt.

We sat quite. Desmond had his eyes focused on the pattern on the carpet but I looked around the room. Doylee had the largest of smirks. He enjoyed the fashion with which Misery had made us feel inadequate, particularly the comment about trained people, although the last person on the Judge's mind was Doylee! The law enforcement officer was a Jekyll and Hide. One minute we're his friends, the next we're arrested just so that he could please Old Misery. It was no surprise when the Sheriff practically fell over himself to get into the hotel room following the shooting and arrested everyone present, including several of the hotel staff taking refuge in the lobby. We were all suspects—much to Misery's dismay.

* * *

Eamon Darcy was singing like a choirboy. Whatever they needed to know he told them, but only up to a point. He knew nothing of the recent shootings but sensed something big had happened since his arrest nearly twenty hours earlier. Downtown was a hive of activity. His story was repeated time and time again and was identical with each recital. Richard Hammond was instructed by Advanced Strategic Energy to accompany a Human Rights Activist to Nigeria; he never really understood why Hammond pretended to be that person and, under the circumstances, he never told anybody the Activist never existed! Or at least that's what he believed. Hammond could have had him murdered too, who knows? In any case, they were to meet with leaders from the Ijaw Youth Council or Movement or whatever name they chose to use. Along with two other prominent businessmen from a local oil supplies company they would try to bribe the tribal leaders into stopping their organized and violent crimes against their oil company—Advanced Strategic Energy. Yes, it was a lot of money, yes he knew it was illegal, yes, it was immoral, and yes not ethical, but that's what they had done. So far he was looking at a very short jail-term.

Somewhere along the way it had gone pear-shaped, Richard Hammond had taken it on himself to employ the services of a mercenary. He did not know this at the time and so, therefore, Eamon could hardly be held responsible he argued. They would have to talk to Hammond about the detail since Eamon knew no more about the ordeal; their business analyst manager had told them little, if anything about it he told them truthfully. The lie detector confirmed what he'd said was true. The FBI men constantly interrupted him with questions. Several petty arguments followed.

Jeremy Isaacs knew only what Darcy knew, nothing more he confirmed not knowing that he did not have to lie to protect Jeremy anymore; Isaacs was dead. Hammond was working alone at the time it seemed. He was a rogue, he added to emphasize the point. During the events that followed, which have never been made clear to him or anybody else as far as he was concerned, Hammond was seriously hurt and the two Nigerian businessmen were killed. Their throats had been cut. Also, the Ijaw leaders and many of the natives were killed in a bloody gun battle. Nobody knows what happened to the mercenary or the whereabouts of the money.

No, John Arnold knew nothing about what had been arranged. It was the most embarrassing aspect of the whole affair. Had he known he would have stopped it and fired those responsible suggested Eamon! This was contrary to what Arnold had told them the previous day, but the FBI ignored the lie for the time being and continued with the cross-examination before this part of the interview was complete. They would then start on other matters of more importance.

Desmond Haynes was dismissed because of gross negligence, not because of the color of his skin he had said. Now, in the plain light of day he admitted it all seemed pretty academic following the revelations on the tape; they had played that to him earlier. Eamon then went on to identify Mr. X. It was Gerald Sinclair he told them. He was the second business management analyst who had since committed suicide following his dismissal. He found his affair with a pretty blonde thing working on the fifth floor far more tempting than anything his job had to offer, said Darcy. The serious relationship eventually resulted in him losing his job, again for negligence and gross misconduct. It was too much of an embarrassment to confess to his wife, whom he adored. Could they keep it that way pleaded Eamon, feeling a little remorse for his colleague's death and feeling even more sorrow for Sinclair's family! Gerald had paid the ultimate penalty for his mistake, no use in telling his wife the truth.

When Saunders and Daniel had heard enough the timing seemed right for them to do a neat double act. The first Fed produced a copy of the black and white Polaroid from inside his pocket and the hanging picture was thrown onto the table directly in front of Eamon Darcy. He turned an instant shade of white; his pale face was crumbling before them as he stared vacantly at the image. That fateful day more than thirty years ago was relived in an instant. The memories never left him and, at that precise moment, it seemed like only yesterday—it had come back to haunt him like it had haunted the rest of those present that day. He couldn't believe what had just happened! Then, the second Fed, Daniel, told him of the shooting incident involving the deaths of both Lance Heycock and Jeremy Isaacs. Eamon crumpled up in a heap on the floor, weeping.

Cell five held another potential bag of worms. Doylee's deputies had arrested the loiterer immediately they arrived at the scene. The Nigerian never suspected anything and his arrest was straightforward and simple, which infuriated the hell out of him. Their reports were accurate; Oron Ogaji had a gun part-hidden in his coat. The quick-thinking deputies also removed his cell phone and pressed the redial button. A number was displayed but there was no answer. The number was being traced as they spoke and within minutes, Saunders was handed a note by a young uniformed girl who went by the name of Jennifer. He gave a very, *I told you so*, grin to Daniel that was bigger than any Cheshire cat could have done before walking over to him and covertly showing him the name neatly scribbled on the pad. They had their first incriminating evidence against John Arnold, but what he was guilty of they didn't know just yet? Ogaji remained tight-lipped throughout his embarrassing ordeal; he should never have come, he realized sitting in the cell wondering if they were going to put him in the electric chair like he was told back in Warri before accepting the assignment!

* * *

It was now nearly nine-thirty in the evening and only a handful of people remained. The Judge was not as miserable as we were led to believe. He'd ordered Doylee to get several mixed, Chinese, Thai, and Mexican take-away meals for those of us left behind. Doylee handed the order down the line and it was eventually dispatched to a cab driver to get the food. Desmond and Suzanne, the soon-to-be millionaires, ate like there was no tomorrow. Lance and Isaacs meant nothing to them; in fact it pleased them more than winning the lawsuit, which had been practically forgotten for the time being. The food smelt delicious but I declined, I just couldn't eat knowing Cheryl was out there somewhere, probably dead or dying. For me, there was no tomorrow. Not before too long, *his* favorite flip chart was positioned in front of the table and we talked as we ate. Led by Saunders, the Fed man, we were all brought up to speed once again.

'Darcy has produced the goods. All six men in the hanging photo have been ID'd. Two are dead, as you know from this afternoon's little squabble,' he added not bothering to look at either of us; the two culprits. But Old Misery did, just to let us know one more time he was pissed with our efforts. 'Bit of a shock about Lance!' he felt obliged to say before continuing. 'Anyway, the others are being *roped* in as we speak,' he informed us then realized what he'd said and paused. 'Err . . . perhaps I shouldn't have used that phrase,' he said, embarrassed. Hastings looked at him daggers. He carried on. 'Shouldn't be a problem, they don't suspect anything,' he went on to say feeling silly from his earlier blunder.

'What's he said about the photo?' asked Hastings, still scathing.

'Nothing more than we already know, Your Honor. Darcy is with the doctors right now, he collapsed under the strain.'

'The photo,' confirmed Daniel sympathetically. 'It was the cause of his seizure,' he told us.

'Good,' replied Des, who attracted looks from everybody present.

'Darcy is probably looking at a twenty-stretch. But that's his problem, he deserves it,' confirmed Saunders, mostly for Desmond's sake. 'Carlene Bourne and her son, Eddie, will soon be off the *unsolved*,' he then confirmed as if talking about a lunch menu.

'Who?' asked Misery, who seemed the only one prepared to challenge what was being said.

'The two hangers, Judge. The murders will be officially solved,' he confirmed. Daniel never missed the chance to fill in the gaps.

'Hangers?' Hastings spat out, not quite sure he'd heard correctly.

'The two swingers,' confirmed Daniel using everyday FBI slang. The Judge was raving and Saunders quickly intervened as any good partner should.

'The two black folk. The two that were hung, Your Honor,' he said, quickly diffusing the situation. The Judge, along with Desmond and Suzanne who'd never trusted the cops anyway, took an even more dislike to Daniel after what he'd said. Saunders nodded to Daniel, who then took up where he'd left off without missing a beat.

'There's still no sign of Hammond but we'll get there, I promise. The guy *hanging* around the hotel has been hauled in,' he then told us, again not realizing his bad choice of words and again Hastings picked up on it. 'He's Nigerian but won't say a damn word. I feel like kicking the shit out of him,' admitted Saunders.

'Then do it,' reasoned the Judge forgetting about Saunders earlier bad choice of language for the time being.

'Not just yet, Judge. We pressed the redial on the cell phone he was carrying and, *hey presto!* Guess what?' he asked not expecting an answer. 'John Arnold's number pops up. Now why is a Nigerian trying to get hold of John Arnold? And why would he be holding a gun?' he asked inquisitively, strongly trying to implicate the CEO in all of this. 'He's guilty of something and we'll find out soon enough,' he told us confidently. 'Don't worry.' Getting there without worrying was becoming a bit of a trademark with Saunders. Nobody believed he'd get there and we all worried.

'What's the SP on him?' it was the Judge again.

'The Nigerian? Nothing we can think of apart from the connection between Arnold or ASEI and his native country,' said Saunders. 'He won't say a dickybird. He has no passport, no wallet, no credit cards, no nothing.'

'But you'll get there, right?' Old Misery said, taking the piss; perhaps he *was* in a humorous mood inside and things were going *his* way for a change. He liked the way John Arnold was being implicated in affairs for one thing. What was he up to? He decided that he would ask the CEO personally and made a mental note to ask Doylee to *rope* him in later on. He then cursed himself inside for thinking the word *rope*, it was becoming contagious!

'Yeah, we'll get there,' replied Saunders, eventually realizing the Judge was pissing down his trouser leg. I continued to sit in a trance and missed most of what was being said. I was thinking about, *you know who* and wondering if she'd actually been, *you know what?*

'Okay, so where's this whole thing going?' asked the DA trying to act intellectual all of a sudden.

'You tell us,' replied the Judge quietly emphasizing the DA's lack of intellect; he was beginning to put the DA in the same bracket as the other law enforcers, he was pathetic!

'Too many loose ends, Your Honor,' replied the DA trying to raise his IQ for the benefit of Old Misery. 'We gotta tighten things up. Isaacs and Heycock are out of the frame now, obviously. Darcy is admitting to everything and anything, but who knows for sure what he's saying. Could be a fucking big cover up for all we know? We need Hammond's version of events . . . if we ever see him again?' He gave a doubtful look towards Saunders, who for once remained tightlipped. 'And Arnold, we gotta nail that son-of-a-bitch somehow? You gotta lean harder on the Nigerian,' he ordered Saunders, who reluctantly nodded an affirmative. 'And there's something else that's bothering me. It's Cheryl, where the hell is she?' he asked out of the blue. I jumped out of my sub-consciousness. Somebody had mentioned her name.

'What . . . . err . . . what was that?'

'Where in the hell is Cheryl, Doug?' asked the Judge, taking over all of a sudden after being awakened to my predicament.

'I wish I knew,' I replied, like a dope.

'Doylee, get Arnold back in here. Now!' he ordered him. 'And get your boys to take a look inside the trunk of every parked car in New Orleans with a New Jersey plate on it.' The Judge didn't have to give a reason why he'd asked for that to be done, or where to look; it was New Orleans and dead bodies turned up in trunks all the time!

'You got it, Your Honor.'

'And Doylee, make sure to check every car in the Hilton basement,' added the Judge, obviously giving it some thought; he was concerned.

'Yes, Judge, you got it,' he replied again, and then Doylee did his quick disappearing act.

'Mr. Haynes?'

'Ugh . . . err . . . yeah . . . Your Honor,' spluttered Desmond behind a face full of sweet and sour chicken.

'You're right, you do need another lawyer,' he said, and then disappeared out of sight giggling as he went.

Chapter 41

THE SHOWER WAS HOT AND soothed his aching body. It felt good. When the remaining three of the eight windows were finally rubbed down and painted the house would look brand new, he told himself, pleased with his efforts. His body was getting into shape. There was nothing he could do about his state of mind, but he was working on it. It would definitely get better. He had already felt the benefits of a no drugs or booze campaign. Grilled chicken and mineral water had replaced the poisons. He stepped out of the shower and wrapped a towel around his lower body; it was time to trim his days-old beard. Hammond removed the cover from a new blade and wiped the condensation from the wall-mounted mirror and froze. There, in the partly obscured reflection stood Philip Laxrois, larger than life.

* * *

Nick's journalistic instincts were bettered when he pestered John Arnold for a few words on his way into the personal chambers of, His Honor, located on the east wing of the New Orleans, Parish Court. A squabble broke out on the steps and the reporter was pushed aside by Arnold, which obviously meant he wasn't going to say a word.

Judge, Hastings was alone when the CEO entered the room, ably led in there by Doylee.

'Take a seat, John,' offered the Judge kindly, showing respect. Arnold accepted and made himself comfortable whilst Doylee, in the meantime, about turned and left them to it.

'Do you know, John,' said the lawman rather affectionately. 'It's kinda strange. You know . . . us . . . me and you. Look at us! Me, the Judge handling all sorts of complicated life and death situations, rather like a surgeon,' he smiled. 'And you, the leader of an almighty company that deals in billions of dollars. Both of us in similar situations, both successful, both powerful men,' he emphasized. 'But for what? Money? Prestige?' he suggested. 'What is it that gets us to where we are, or where we want to be for that matter?' he asked. The CEO remained silent.

'Oh, I know what you're thinking, *what's the old bastard on about now, ugh*? Well . . . like I said, it's kinda strange. Mm . . . strange, what's our motive, John?' The Judge slowly maneuvered around the room acting as if he was a predator and Arnold was his prey, which was most likely to be the case. Hastings spoke slowly, pondering his every word. 'Me? I do this because that's all I ever wanted to do. It's a power thing. To be powerful in a courtroom that commands my respect, to be in front of men far cleverer than I could ever dream of and yet I could do and tell them whatever I wanted without the slightest cause of redress or remorse. They would listen and do whatever I told them, John,' he gloated. 'They don't like it,' he added quickly and rather dismissive. 'I can tell by the look on their faces, but they'll do what I say or be damned. These most brilliant of lawyers haven't got what I have, John. Power . . . power, the stuff that makes me almighty and them smaller than me, clever . . . but small men. But you know what it's like to have power, don't you? Tell me, what's *your* motive, John?' teased Hastings.

'What are you getting at, Judge?'

'Oh, come now. What am I getting at? The truth, John, it's as simple as that. The truth, that's all. I don't give a shit for the law, just as you don't give a shit for the oil company you're in charge of. The law just happens to give *me* the power,' he told him, raising his voice. The Judge rounded a table and advanced towards the CEO, he wanted Arnold squirming. Of the two men, he was the most powerful and he would prove it. No matter that his adversary held the keys to a billion-dollar industry, he was nothing compared to the Judge; two different men in two different industries and in two different forms of power, but one more powerful than the other. Hastings knew Arnold was being belittled. In the last ten years nobody had been in a position to talk down to this man, it would be hurting his pride; the Judge sensed Arnold's pain and it showed on his sweat-ridden face.

'I've nothing to hide. I've told you all I know. What more do you want?'

'Lance Heycock and Jeremy Isaacs are dead.'

'Tell me something I don't know!'

'You're not sorry? You don't feel any remorse?'

'Why should I. I'd have shot Isaacs myself after his comments about Desmond,' he scathed. It wasn't a bad strike. The Judge had played right onto the CEO's bat but then the Judge fielded a blinder.

'That's kinda harsh isn't it? After all, he is your son-in-law. What'll Beth be thinking?' he replied. Arnold cringed. The bastard even knew her nickname! He thought quickly.

'We never saw eye-to-eye,' he argued, sweating hard now, thinking things through. He couldn't afford to fuck up now, not after everything that's happened.

'Well, that's interesting,' said the Judge delving deeper into Arnold's way of thinking.

'What do you mean?'

'Motive, John. The fact that you don't see eye-to-eye with your son-in-law, as you say, is a good motive to have him murdered, wouldn't you say?' Arnold nearly crumbled. He wiped his brow, his mind was spinning. He was struggling to keep calm. Hastings knew a murderer when he saw one, he'd seen hundreds, and John Arnold was no exception. He kept up the pressure.

'And Lance, what about him, what about the death of Desmond Hayne's attorney, any regrets? Don't you think that's just a little strange, John?'

'Didn't know him so why should that bother me?' he replied, nervously.

'Oh? It seems that Isaacs, Hammond, and Darcy were big friends with him. What do you think that was all about?'

'Search me?'

'We will.'

'Ugh?'

'Search you, everywhere, everything, and everyone, John. Oh, we'll search you all right, until we've found what we're looking for,' he reminded him, and then bent over closer so that Arnold was within a whisker of him. 'Trust me,' he whispered towards his right ear.

'What is all this? Give me a break. You've got nothing on me.'

'Who's the black fella in town, John?'

'Dunno what you're on about, there's plenty of blacks in town. This *is* New Orleans, you know!' he said shakily, and then dabbed some more at his sweating brow. His blood pressure was rising and his face reddened. He would keep his composure, concentrate, he tried to constantly reassure himself.

'Not from Nigeria there isn't . . . and why would a Nigerian with a loaded gun require the phone number of the top man in Advanced Strategic Energy, John? I wonder what's going on there. Unfinished business, perhaps, like getting even with a son-in-law you don't see eye-to-eye with! Is that it?' suggested the Judge as he rubbed his chin in mock amusement. John Arnold broke out in more of a sweat, there were rivers pouring from his entire body. The moisture was leaping out of his skin in gallons now.

'Perhaps he wanted to buy some oil from us! Is that a crime?' he replied quickly, not helping his predicament. John Arnold was seething. It was the second time Ogaji had fucked up. Why had he persevered with the stupid idiot? And now they'd try to connect him to the death of his son-in-law, Jeremy Isaacs. He always knew Isaacs was going to be trouble, why'd the fuck Beth married him he never knew. He's been nothing but a pain in the ass! And even now, lying dead in the local morgue, he causing trouble! There was a knock on the door.

'Come in,' ordered the Judge without asking who it was. Saunders and Daniel timed their entry to perfection after listening in on the conversation. Now it was show time. Saunders once again took the lead. He flung the hanging photo on the table, just within striking distance for Arnold to see the image. The CEO took one glance and visibly shook. His reaction had given a guilt-ridden affirmative to the FBI and the Judge too. Although he wasn't part of the image, Arnold knew about the photo, they'd guessed right. Why was he being protective? What had he done? John Arnold's body language gave the best signal yet; everyone in the room knew he'd been involved in the murders!

* * *

'Bonjour Richard'—*'Hello Richard.'*

Hammond turned and held his chest. The pain was instant and almost unbearable. His heart was beating like a racehorse.

'How . . . ?' he muttered, speaking towards the reflection in the mirror.

'Oh, it was easy. You're not that much of a challenge. It was so easy to find you.' Hammond had no choice but to accept the situation and tried to calm himself. Now that he was in a self-imposed rehab, life meant a lot more to him. He didn't want to die.

'What do you want?' he asked the Frenchman.

'Oh, I think we both know what I want. To complete our little agreement in Nigeria . . . that little matter you wanted sorting out . . . remember?'

'But it's sorted. What more do you want?'

'Sorted?' he smirked. 'Sorted? Please, don't play games with me. Where's the money?'

'I . . . I . . . haven't got it . . . I thought . . . I thought you had it?' replied Hammond, confused.

'Mm . . . Yes . . . wishful thinking. Now, for the last time, where is the money?' The Frenchman would not listen to lies. 'Or do I have to kill you instead!' he warned him. Laxrois took out a long-handled pistol that already had a silencer fitted on the barrel. The lies would be stopped one way or another.

'Wait a minute!' Hammond raised his arms in a petty show of self-defense. 'I haven't got the money. I presumed you took it when you escaped from inside the tent,' he offered. The excuse was more of a plea to spare his life.

'Escaped ugh? You shoot me in the back and then make out, I escaped! What are you, a dreamer? Are you mad or something?'

'But how did you get away?' The situation always did confuse him. Whenever he was asked what happened he couldn't say. He just didn't know. He had woken two days later in a makeshift army hospital. A military patrol team had taken him there after they found him lying unconscious amongst the carnage following the gun battle. The government was eager to cover up the events and Hammond was quickly shipped back to the US with no questions asked. Other than that he knew nothing, but always assumed the money had been taken by Laxrois since the army didn't mention it—not that they would have, anyway.

'My escape was by chance, but I will not bore you with the detail, some other time maybe?'

'And the girl, why did you do that to her? She hadn't done anything to harm you.'

'The girl . . . what girl?' he replied. It was Laxrois' turn to be confused.

'Oh c'mon,' he said, annoyed. He then turned to face him. He didn't want to be shot in the back like he'd shot Laxrois. 'The headless corpse beside me in the bed, it was you, wasn't it?' Hammond despised the Frenchman even more as he thought about the images of the decapitated girl. Her blood was still warm when he'd reached out to touch her.

'I have no recollection of any girl,' he said, truthfully. 'Stop trying to cloud the issue. Now! For the very last time, where is the money?' Laxrois was becoming irate and that familiar feeling began to surge through his body. The sensation was well known and Richard Hammond, still frightened for his life, sensed the change in his mood. From now on, Laxrois would be practically unpredictable. The situation was hopeless. But instead of panicking, Hammond kept the vacant gaze he'd held throughout his short ordeal. He didn't believe Laxrois for one minute. He'd murdered the girl, no doubt about it. Laxrois came closer, raised the gun and pointed straight between his eyes.

'The money, where is it?' he demanded to know.

* * *

So far, the fact that an unidentified Nigerian had his cell phone number was no reason to charge the CEO of any wrongdoings. Despite the FBI and the Judge knowing he was somehow guilty along with the others related to the hangings, they let him go; they had no proof. He wasn't in the picture but the ploy taken by the Feds was that he would be followed in an attempt to *rope in* the remaining suspects, as Saunders had so crudely put it. John Arnold walked out from the protection of the courtroom lobby straight into a melee of reporters. Word was out that the CEO might be connected to the recent deaths in New Orleans and the exposure might get him to trip up in what he'd said, or was about to say. It would make a sensational story if it were true. Nick Night led the scrum of press and once again was the first to be shoved aside. Arnold escaped without comment.

* * *

He couldn't believe that the hanging photo was shown to him. Where the hell did they get it? Six of his previously trusted friends had been identified, every one of them! It was a curdling experience. He wasn't implicated of course; he had nothing to do with it, he wasn't in the photo. But now he also knew that Eamon Darcy, along with Lance who was the two most visible and easiest of the hangmen in the photo to be ID'd, would be doing a lot more time than previously thought. There was about ten years' difference between the charges of racial abuse and being an accomplice to murder, and then a further ten more for first degree murder.

Lance and Jeremy, on the other hand, had resolved part of the problem for Arnold, which he found pleasing, although he had to distance himself from his now deceased son-in-law. Now, there was only one more person that could relate *him* to the hanging photo! Richard Hammond would have to be disposed of in any way possible; then he was in the clear from that little episode in his life. The other little episode, Nigeria, was also coming to a dead-end. Oron Ogaji just had to stay tight-lipped, although he would easily be discredited if the need arose. He made his way back to the hotel. He would work from the business centre; he had a billion-dollar company to run. And he had to phone Beth, she'd be distraught at the sad news. Unbeknown to her though, her father was glad with the way things had worked out for her, but he couldn't tell her that!

* * *

The afternoon was spent muddling in whatever reports Doylee had fed back to us. Practically every car in every New Orleans parking lot seemed to be from New Jersey. What is it with these guys from up north! The costs for busting open the many trunks were mounting. It would have to stop sooner rather than later said Roolenski, one of Doylee's trusted deputies.

'Let's try the hotel register again,' I pleaded in vain, desperate. 'We can then double-check the basement car park,' I suggested for the third time. The others gave me a disdainful look but respected my position.

'We already did that, Doug,' said Doylee, sympathetically.

'Okay, what about guest houses, deserted houses, brick houses, shit houses, whore houses, any fucking houses?' I shouted at him. I was desperate to hold her safe in my arms once again.

'Okay, Doug. Calm down, we'll do our best,' replied Doylee, sensing my frustration. 'Roolenski!' he shouted.

'Yeah, what is it?'

'The Feds' turned up anything yet?'

'Nope, but they're working on it though, don't worry.' There it was again; even the deputies had taken the lines from our entrusted FBI men. I poured a drink and sat next to Suzanne. *No*, they probably weren't working on it and *yes* I worried. She put one of her large arms around my shoulder. I felt completely useless. Desmond stood up from behind a pile of police reports.

'Let's go see Dil,' he suggested. With that the pair left Doylee and me to it after I politely refused the offer. I had other things on my mind and waited until they had gone before pouncing on Doylee one more time.

'The hotel parking lot,' I said, again for the benefit of the deaf. 'That's an ideal place to hide somebody, isn't it?'

'Doug, leave it. There are a million *ideal places* to hide somebody in New Orleans. We've looked everywhere,' he said, shuffling uneasily across the room as if looking for something non-existent.

'But it's only a short hike from the hotel room,' I cried. Doylee stopped what he was doing and rounded on me.

'*If* Isaacs actually managed to get in to the hotel room?' he argued. 'Jesus, Doug. Look at it from our point of view. We can't go smashing in cars all over town. We've done enough damage already. Do you think the hotel manager is going to write a *thank you, please come again* note to us after we've bust up half their clients' cars?' Doylee was on the defensive but he was right.

'We know the car, it's a red Sudan. Should be a piece of cake?' I argued, still pushing it, pathetically.

'No, Doug. We're not sure if it's a red Sudan or a green one-eyed monster. We've bust open four red Sudan's already. No more, Doug.'

* * *

Richard Hammond was forced to lie down on his back on the shower room floor, he was completely rigid, eyes bulging and mouth agape as the barrel was pressed against his sweating temple.

'Last chance, tell me where the money is or say goodbye!' Laxrois straddled him; Hammond couldn't move an inch.

'I . . . don't know . . . honest,' he managed to say under the stress.

'Very well . . .' Laxrois squeezed the trigger. That second a dull, *thud*, rang out and Hammond flinched, naturally bracing himself for the impact from the bullet. Oddly, he felt nothing, no pain, nothing at all and instead, Laxrois twitched vigorously before his weighted body collapsed on top of him. He struggled to comprehend the situation. Hammond's face was clenched with fear, but for some strange reason there was no pain, no blood coming from him, he'd frantically checked the moment he'd come to his senses, but he was still shrieking with terror. But the strangest thing of all, Phillip Laxrois was lying on top of him with blood pouring from a head wound? The red moisture started to cover Hammond's face.

Christ! How many more times did he have to suffer this? Still delirious, he pushed the dead body aside and rolled over to see a familiar face staring at him behind the smoking and silenced barrel of a gun. He looked again to double-check the situation. Laxrois was dead. A young black boy stood defiantly in the doorway, still pointing the gun at him. He thought he knew him but couldn't think straight, who was he? He was still alive thank God and his mind worked overtime to understand the reasons why?

'Wa you lookin at, man? You shood be kind an all!' He'd heard the phrase used before, the Pidgin English was a give-away. Hammond's mind raced back to Nigeria. There was no mistaking the identity. It was the young helmsman from the *Mista*! The same one that Laxrois maimed on that dark, rain swept night near Warri. It was Binman! What on earth was going on?

Chapter 42

THE NEXT FEW DAYS WERE a blur. Desmond hadn't needed another lawyer; Old Misery lifted the reporting restrictions made previously regarding the many racial comments contained in the tape. The *NYT* serialized most of the conversation—the Nigeria bits were still restricted, however, but still the whole of the US was up in arms of the racial abuse dished out to Desmond. Nick Night would obviously win every journalist award going for the entire year. There was nearly a revolution at the sensational news and the civil guard had been deployed to break up the unrest and rioting that was sweeping America. Every one of Advanced Strategic Energy fuel stations was boycotted, picketed or in some instances set alight such was the damning evidence against them. In true *damage control* measures, John Arnold had instructed Advanced Strategic Energy Inc to pay an unprecedented, out-of-court settlement of nearly one hundred million dollars solely to Desmond. In addition, every black or ethnic minority employee was given a twenty percent pay rise with immediate effect. The company also employed no more than three, State Circuit Judges to oversee the most stringent of diversity programs the world had ever seen.

With all that was happening, it was easy to imagine the CEO being hoisted from his position. On the contrary, John Arnold had handled the most damning period of his entire life, and that of Advanced Strategic Energy Inc, with such skill and manipulation of the truth in denying any involvement that he became a national hero. The swiftness in which he executed the employee pay rise, the Desmond Haynes payment, and the diversity programs that were put in place ensured that he slowly became recognized as doing more for the black people of America than Martin Luther King had ever done! Within a short time he could be seen at many of the racial equality meetings and affairs throughout the world. *How had Advanced Strategic Energy done it,* they asked? And boy was he proud to tell them. Books would be written about this affair, said many leading rights activists.

* * *

Oron Ogaji was released and deported back to Nigeria after remaining silent throughout his ordeal. The FBI had even sat him next to Eamon for a couple of hours to analyze the reaction, nothing occurred. He had finally managed to get something right.

He was hired by John Arnold through an intermediary located in Lagos, which was far enough away not for Arnold to get involved in matters. Had Arnold realized that Ogaji had been the same person who'd screwed up in Nigeria, when he'd paid to have Hammond splattered all over the Delta in a bid to stop him making a mess of other plans he'd put in place, he'd have asked for somebody else to come to the USA and do his dirty work.

Back then, he'd decided to take an alternative route to resolve the troubles in Nigeria; unbeknown to anyone in ASEI a dialogue was already set up with other tribesmen in the Delta, including the Ijaw, and it would have worked if Hammond hadn't interfered the way he did. If only Darcy and Isaacs had told John Arnold sooner!

Coming back to events in New Orleans, again Arnold hadn't banked on the ineptness of Ogaji. Had he known it was him, or read his credentials more closely, he wouldn't have employed him. And if he'd taken that decision, he certainly wouldn't have been connected to any of the murders in New Orleans! Anyway, at least the end result was close to being what he wanted; Isaacs was dead! It was a pity about Lance; the CEO never wanted any harm to come to him, although when he took his own life it was probably for the best, he decided on reflection!

Soon enough, somebody in the Whitehouse ensured that Ogaji was deported and they contacted the Nigerian Government to make sure that he would be charged with something, just what nobody knew or cared—he would have been much wiser to spill the beans to the FBI when he had the chance. He would only realize this upon his return to Nigeria, however.

* * *

I was pleased for Desmond but found it hard to show my true elation—even after my friend had given a huge share of the windfall to me. Cheryl was still missing and slowly but surely I began to convince myself that it was just as Desmond had said some time back. Perhaps she did just get

The Last Hangman

up and go of her own accord. But even that fact was hard to take in at the time. I was hurting bad.

We said our farewells to the Judge and Doylee. They would be busy in the coming weeks and months. Eamon Darcy was awaiting trial for being an accessory to murder in Nigeria, first degree murder in Texas and a multitude of other charges—mostly racial that seemed to pop up with each passing day. Everybody had been glad to see the back of everybody else it seemed. We'd had enough and were all in. A quick stop at the hospital to ensure Dillwyn was recovering and well-cared-for took up another bit of the day. Desmond discretely handed him a rolled up bundle of cash for the future. Dil cried and then Desmond cried and then Suzanne cried.

In a short space of time I had become a rich man and returned to England rather sad. My homecoming was met with a barrage of questions about Cheryl. I couldn't answer any of them. After a couple of weeks, Julie and I had split up for good. After paying her off from the proceeds of Desmond's windfall, I bought a cottage in Cornwall and settled down a lonely man. Time was slow living alone and it was made slower as I retraced our every step. The memories lingered if nothing else.

* * *

It would be Judge, Roland Hastings, last trial; retirement beckoned and not before time, either. There was so much evidence stacked up against Eamon Darcy that the defense council, Dinger et al, would plead guilty in a desperate attempt to gain a shorter sentence. It was most likely to happen.

Not long after all the euphoria had died down in *his* chambers, a senior clerk opened the everyday mail and the contents now lay exposed on the well-polished desk ready for *his* attention. The correspondence was disregarded with vigorous contempt as each letter was quickly read, then binned. All apart from one shabby piece of paper, that is. A note the size of a playing card, which had been torn from a larger piece of paper, had been sent in a plain white envelope that carried a Colorado postmark dated the previous day on the upper right hand corner. It took the Judge by complete surprise. Scribbled in somebody's worst, almost childish handwriting were the words,

> How is the murder trial going?
> How is the CEO?
> Who took the photo?

What was this all about? The Judge looked around the room as if a conspiracy was breaking amongst some members of his staff. It was a wind up.

'Where'd this come from?' he asked, panning the room, scathingly. He held the scruffy, folded note up in the air for them all to see. It didn't gather any votes—there were too many shaking heads. What did it mean? The Judge picked up the phone as if to call somebody. He'd get Doylee to issue arrest warrants against somebody for wasting his time but thought better of it. Someone had tried to register a thought inside his dulled brain.

How is the murder trial going, he thought to himself later that morning after thinking some more about the crunched up note?

'Good,' he replied out loud, pleased with progress so far. Contrary to what the FBI promised, they still hadn't *roped in* the three remaining hangmen and never would. The two in the back row, Hughes and Cuthbert, were of no concern now; they'd died in a tragic car accident. Eamon had told them that and it checked out. Hammond on the other hand, the fourth of the hangmen to be identified, was still at large but he'd disappeared off the face of the earth! On a more positive note, Darcy, the third hangman, was looking at twenty years and that pleased Old Misery no end. On balance, it couldn't get any better.

How is the CEO?

'Mm . . .' he mused, studying the words carefully. 'Too fucking good judging by the accolades that seemed to be bestowed on him every other week!' he said sarcastically to nobody in particular. 'The clever bastard is guilty of something, though,' he muttered out loud, still seething they hadn't got anything solid to charge him with. Heads began to turn in his direction as he held his own conversation in the room; his small team wondered what tablets he was taking?

Who took the photo? Hastings read the line over and over in his mind and then started talking to himself again for inspiration.

'Who took the photo? Who took the photo?' he recited aloud several times for all to hear. The room went quite as those present stopped working and watched as the Judge raised himself off his chair and scurried around the room constantly repeating the words louder and louder as he went along. Then he had an idea!

'Yes, yes, of course! Who took the fucking photo?' he again repeated, time and time again shouting it out loud. The whole room thought the Judge had lost it. Wendy phoned for Doylee, he may be needed to restrain His Honor who was clearly having some sort of moment.

'Somebody had to take the goddamn photo for Christ sake!' he said openly to the whole room. 'How had they missed that simple fact?' he said, pointing an accusing finger at Doylee who'd slowly sneaked up close to him to check things out! Doylee took a few paces back, stunned at the accusation! His Sheriff's startled response would normally unhinge the Judge but His Honor looked straight through him, it was as if he wasn't there!

* * *

Dinger, on one of his uneventful weekly visits to Eamon, was ordered sharply out of the cell and Judge Hastings quickly filled the void. Dinger cursed and couldn't wait to phone Cranton who would then phone John Arnold. He now found himself in the same predicament as John Briggs. What could he tell them? A call of this nature had cost Briggs' his job. Perhaps he wouldn't phone after all.

It was the first time the Judge had been in such a confined, grubby hole and he felt a tinge of embarrassment at some of the longer-term sentences he'd handed down over the years. With Dinger well out of sight, most likely licking his wounded pride somewhere close by, the Judge closed in and met Eamon eye-to-eye. The prisoner thought the Judge had come to fight him judging by the proximity. The Judge spoke softly.

'Eamon, let's be straight with each other. We both know you're covering a lot of this shit up and prepared to do the time to protect others. Okay, so you're a fucking hero. But the hanging thing was bad and you're gonna pay, but I need to ask you something? I don't want any lies. Just tell me the truth and I'll make sure you'll do a five stretch, probably paroled before then,' he offered, genuinely sincere and enthusiastic about getting a result.

'What's the deal?' asked Darcy quickly, keen to listen to any offers after spending so much time locked up.

'Who took the photo, Eamon?'

'I want Dinger in here.'

'Ugh, ugh, no way, leave Dinger out of it.'

Peter Nutty

'Why? What's Dinger done that's so bad?'

'Nothing . . . yet! But he's not coming in here while we're talking. This is between you and me, Eamon. Now, c'mon, we both know who was standing behind the camera. Who took the photo? Tell me, Eamon, please,' he asked, desperate for the right answer.

Eamon got up from his steel-framed bed and walked the short length of the small cell until he reached the locked door. Prison officers close by neared as they saw his hands grip the bars. He was deep in thought. The Judge held up a hand and the officers backed off.

'I need Dinger here,' he said again, unsure.

'Dinger! What do you think Dinger's doing right now, Eamon?' he asked, shaking him a little. 'I bet he's on the phone to him as we speak. He's got Dinger in his pocket, son. That's why you're here and he's not,' he said, not daring to mention the name on both men's lips for fear of incriminating himself. 'He's quite a celebrity now, you know that?' The prisoner didn't answer so the Judge continued pressing, trying to break him. 'You know the way he's dealt with you and the others . . . there's no love lost between any of you, Eamon. And he's singing like a jaybird,' he lied to him, the way old cranky Judges were allowed to after thirty years on the bench. Eamon turned around in surprise. The Judge had hit a nerve.

'Oh yes, he's heaped enough scorn on you to last more than twenty years, Eamon,' confirmed the Judge. 'You'll be hated for the rest of your living life, son. I dread to think what they'll do to you in the state penitentiary? After all, most of those guys in there *are* black, and *you did* hang one of their brothers!' Fear gripped Eamon and he turned to face the bars once again.

'Why'd you keep calling me, *son?*' he asked. 'I'm probably only a coupla years behind you!' he managed to say.

'Ah . . . Just a habit I guess.'

'What do you want me to say?' he asked, ready to give in.

'The cameraman, Eamon,' said the Judge quietly in anticipation. 'Who was the goddamn cameraman?' Hastings wanted to say the name himself but couldn't. Darcy had to say it; he needed to confirm the Judges suspicions. Eamon turned and looked at the Judge.

'How'd you know?' he asked, looking pale all of a sudden. Hastings hoped he wouldn't have another seizure!

'Got a screwed up note this morning, it was post-marked in Colorado.'

'Tsh . . .' Eamon shook his head in slight disgust. 'He's not in Colorado, I can tell you that much for sure.'

'Hammond?'

'Yeah, Hammond, the sneaky, dull bastard probably took a ride out there and posted it proud as hell. Lucky, lying, free son-of-a-bitch. I shoulda done the same.'

'Five years, Eamon. Five years, I promise . . . and a guarantee of parole.' The Judge was desperate to know the identity of *the last hangman*.

'John Arnold!' he suddenly told him, softly. The Judge looked at him without surprise. A huge weight had been lifted off both men's shoulders. 'Richard Hammond caused the fracas, Jeremy and John couldn't get the rope out quick enough,' he said, disdainfully. 'Along with Lance, I tried to stop them but the beer kicked in and the others soon convinced us it was the right thing to do, not that we needed that much convincing. They would be taught a lesson. The rest is history. I think of those poor bastards every single night, do you know that?' Eamon tuned to the Judge as if to ask forgiveness, his eyes were bloodshot and tears welled, they were close to running down his cheeks.

'I've had over thirty years to think about it, Judge . . . the two of em hanging there. They haunt me every single night. I try to switch off . . . but can't. I constantly think of John's part in the whole affair. Clever guy,' he said, with meaning and feeling cheated. 'Ugh,' the prisoner shrugged. 'Not clever for what he took part in, just clever in other ways.'

'Like staying out of the photo,' suggested the Judge, urging him on.

'Yeah,' he half-laughed. 'He insisted on taking the photo, we . . . the rest of us never thought anything of it. The last thing we expected was a showing—especially not fucking framed and hanging in a public gallery somewhere! That's Richard for you! Yeah, we were fools, but not John. Oh no, far too clever even then. That's how we got to the top in Advanced Strategic Energy. John took us up the ladder with him. Jeremy and me, Richard wasn't so lucky. He had a big mouth and upset John on too many occasions. If he could have kept his mouth shut he'd have been there with us. VP's, can you imagine it?' Eamon wiped the tears from his eyes. He looked pathetic.

'And the Klan?' asked the Judge. Darcy gave a sigh. He might as well go for broke.

'Yeah, we were in the Klan, we were in it up to our necks alright. We were Klucker's from that day on. Imagine how they feel now with John's one-man crusade on human equality and racial rights?' he said quickly, suddenly realizing the implications! His face contorted and he seemed not to comprehend what he'd just implied. 'Spouting his mouth off like that is likely to attract a bullet. The Klan won't take too kindly to that. He was an imperial wizard, you know,' he confirmed, as a matter of fact.

'Go on,' encouraged the Judge, keen to learn more.

'And then there was Jim Anderson!' The Judged edged closer; this was new to him. 'We'd scarpered from the hanging as fast as we could, drunk, laughing. It was a game to us and the adrenaline was flowing. John was egging us on. He wanted more. With that, we stumbled across Jim. He was a disabled Negro just going about his business as folk do. He was walking along an isolated dirt track; God knows where he'd been or where he was going? John drove up behind him and tried to tap him lightly with the bumper. Only lightly mind you . . . to wake him a little. We laughed. It was hilarious at the time. But it wasn't good enough for John. He wanted more, especially when he realized the guy couldn't run. He had something wrong with his legs. That's when John grabbed him and tied his ankles to the bumper. Jim squealed like a pig. We thought John had gone crazy, his eyes were on fire. We couldn't talk to him. Richard was just as daft. Anyway, John put the Chevy in gear and just drove. He just drove, man! Straight through the fucking town, can you believe it? That poor bastard was being dragged by his ankles and screaming for dear life. It was horrendous. I was sick when I read about it the next day, sober. What had we done?' Eamon began to cry once more. 'That's when we made the bond, it was the very next day,' he sobbed. 'We made a vow never to tell anyone what we'd done.' Eamon gave a low and sarcastic laugh. 'I'm so fucking dull.'

'Why's that?' asked the Judge, waiting for an explanation for the laugh.

'Cos, the fucking Klan turn up out of the blue and suddenly we're all fucking Klucker's. I wonder where they'd got our names?' he cried out loud, looking the fool the Judge knew he was. Eamon sat down and curled up on the hard wooden bed. 'Yeah, Your Honor,' he emphasized, slightly lifting his shameful head in a mock show of pride. 'It was John Arnold who took the photo. I swear to God, it was John Arnold.'

* * *

Nick stood alone, ready with his camera poised and pointed towards the front of the stage. The lights dimmed and John Arnold was introduced. A loud burst of applause followed the guest speaker onto the rostrum. It was billed as the *Oscars* of the Oil world. The National Petroleum and

Refiners Association couldn't have wished for a better speaker. ASEI were about to announce a mind-blowing production sharing agreement with Dubai National oil Company that would propel them into the number one spot and shares had increased by over twenty percent upon the news being leaked earlier that day. They were the envy of the oil world in more ways than one.

It was an expensive occasion—tickets for the event retailed at over one thousand dollars. No sooner had he begun to speak he was quickly joined on stage by Doylee and two fellow officers. The reporter's camera flashed and clicked with speed and the audience gasped in amazement as the guest speaker was arrested for murder right in front of one thousand fellow oilmen, not to mention a large gathering from prominent members of congress. The arrest of *the last hangman* would go down in history. All those present agreed that a thousand bucks was well worth the spectacle—for the first time ever at such an event they'd had their monies worth!

An army of cell phones came to life as the news was quickly wired to the analysts, who would in turn start to dump ASEI stock at warp speed the very next morning following the incredible series of events. At the same time, Sheik, Ahmed Bin Kalid Al-Rashid sat motionless on the podium. His speech, prepared days in advance, hung limply in his hands, he was stunned! Instead of all the euphoria he'd known would follow the brilliant announcement he'd planned so meticulous, he'd been humiliated. Grabbing his Energy Minister strongly by the arm, he ordered him to issue a statement denying any agreements with ASEI. Yes, John Arnold had approached him but in his Excellency's opinion, they were simply not up to the job neither did he trust him. He was personally seeking out discussions with the other, more experienced majors. He then quickly left the arena, a volley of cameras catching the angry look on his face as he left.

Epilogue

He walked slowly into the florist and, after looking at the many varieties of blooms, paid for another bouquet of flowers in the same manner he'd done on numerous occasions before. They would be sent to Moira that morning. Next week, it would be flowers for the grave of Jeremy Isaacs and Lance Heycock. Then he would place flowers on the grave of Carlene Bourne and her son, Eddie, the two unfortunate black folk that were hung from the bridge. He cried when he did this. In between other good deeds, he would help young disabled black children to overcome some difficulty or other. Then he would assist in some other local charity. The police never caught him and he became a model citizen. Richard Hammond stayed clean and indeed made amends for the misery he had imposed throughout his underhanded career with Advanced Strategic Energy. He had managed to cheat death several times. The first was in Nigeria, inside the tent following the murders. A nearby patrol boat quickly raced to the scene after hearing the gunfire and hoards of Nigerian military men got involved in the gun battle. Richard Hammond was taken away unconscious by the soldiers having been mistaken for another US citizen who had been previously taken hostage by the Ijaw. By some means, he was released very quickly without anything being said.

The final escape from death was in his rented home and come about entirely by accident; he owed his life to the young Nigerian—Binman, the boy helmsman aboard the *Mista* all that time ago. It was pure coincidence. Just before the tent murders, Oron Ogaji had managed to board the *Mista* when the crew trekked inland following his failed attack on the patched up boat—it was a non-event. He slipped the moorings and made his escape quietly. It was the break he needed. Soon though, he stumbled upon the wounded boy below decks. Ogaji cared for the youngster as if he was his own and soon they'd become companions. The elder man trained the willing youngster to become a mercenary just like him. Their latest job, another commissioned by no other than John Arnold, brought them to the US. They were instructed to kill both Richard Hammond and Jeremy Isaacs. The job was to be completed at the earliest opportunity and so the two men split up. Ogaji tracked Isaacs to a hunting lodge in New Jersey and was making plans to kill him when Isaacs suddenly made tracks to New Orleans. Ogaji followed his target south where events finally led to his arrest but with the co-operation of the US and Nigerian governments, he was later deported after remaining silent throughout his ordeal.

Binman, meanwhile, was extremely cautious. He remained covert and tracked down Hammond within a couple of days of arriving in the US. It was all too easy for him. The young boy was about to take him out when, from nowhere, he saw the Frenchman. It was Laxrois, the very same man who had thrown him across the wheelhouse that fateful night. Binman changed his plans. Laxrois became his first target, for obvious reasons. He watched and waited—much better than he was ever trained to do as events went from one situation to another. It was almost instinctive. He shadowed Laxrois up to a point where he realized his enemy was indeed following Hammond. It was a marvelous piece of luck. He now tracked both men at the same time. He could have taken out Hammond at any time but at the cost of losing Laxrois. He had to get Hammond out of New York, somewhere quiet. It would give him an edge over the more experienced French mercenary. That's where the prostitute came in. Binman decapitated her whilst she slept with Hammond; it was over the top but he knew it would make the American react. He went into hiding just as he predicted with Laxrois in tow. When he finally shot the Frenchman it was all too sudden. He wanted to torture him as well but it had not worked out, he had only one shot and he took it and at the same time had saved Hammonds life in the process! Up to that point, he'd done what he set out to do, but then events had taken a turn. In the time it took to finally dispose of the Frenchman's body he hadn't quite worked out what to do with Hammond.

The two men remained in the house for ages after the shooting. Laxrois' blood filled the floor. All the time the American was pleading for his life. He cried like a baby. Binman knew then that he couldn't do it. Not in cold blood and certainly not looking at him in the face. Finally, he left. It was no big deal, especially so after killing Laxrois. That gave him immense pleasure.

Richard got a grip of himself, eventually—he cried for three days. Some sort of normality finally returned and again it was without the help of drink or drugs. Richard would rather have been killed by Binman such was his resolve to kick the habit. Some weeks later, he read about the trial in the Louisville post, and he read about the massive payoff made to Desmond and others at ASEI, and he read about the swift measures taken by the CEO. John Arnold was well on his way to becoming an icon in the world of human rights and racial equality. Unbeknown to Richard, it had made world headlines a couple of weeks previous. The huge sums of money awarded to Desmond pleased him a little. But all the while the very man responsible for all of their misgivings was getting away with murder—literally. That's when he decided to send the note to the Judge. *Ask the question?* The Judge would act upon it. He had to. And all the while he knew that if he didn't mention John Arnold in person, then he hadn't broken their promise. He never told anybody, ever. They were Klucker's and men of their word. The hanging in Texas was to be kept a secret between them, the Jim Anderson ordeal also. They had made a vow. Richard Hammond would be the only person to keep that promise, forever.

* * *

Sometime later I received a letter from Old Misery. A badly decomposed body had been found inside the trunk of a red Sudan, which gathered dust on the lower floor of the Hilton, Riverside Hotel parking lot. It had been there ever since Jeremy Isaacs had dumped the very much alive, but drugged and naked body of Cheryl Davies inside over three months ago. If only we'd gone that extra couple of yards? That's all it would have taken. Sheriff Doylee was on sick leave when the press tried to talk to him. I'd become an alcoholic in a very short time so the pain of finding out what had happened to the woman I loved come and went with each bottle!

* * *

The third time Richard Hammond placed flowers on the graves of Carlene Bourne and her son, Eddie, it was going to be his last. He'd noticed he was getting a lot of attention during the previous two visits and this time was no different. It would be his final visit, no need to put himself in danger from the local community. As he left the cemetery a Ford pick-up screeched to a halt and five black men jumped out and ran quickly towards him. It happened so fast that Hammond had no time to react, he

Peter Nutty

had no escape. He tried to put up a fight but it was useless, within seconds he was tied by his ankles to the rear bumper of the pick-up and they sped off at speed. Thirty minutes later his disheveled corpse, what was left of it, was trussed to the same bridge Carlene and Eddie were hung from thirty years earlier.

Eddie's brother, Michael, shouted for the others to smile as he took the photo. *Click*. It was a somber moment and the big black man cried; he'd finally got revenge for his little brother and mama. His papa would have been proud had he still been alive. The whole story had ended where it had all started, with a *Click*!

Lightning Source UK Ltd.
Milton Keynes UK
UKOW052113170212

187489UK00002B/2/P